To You, Iyla

KATE LAUREN

This book contains coarse language, dark themes, erotic scenes and mature subject matter. It is intended for those who are 18+. TW: death, grief, gun violence, addiction, domestic violence and drug-use.

First paperback edition July 2023

Book Design by Ashley Santoro

ISBN 979-8-3757-9049-7

To You, Iyla

Coastline	Hollow Coves
Fade Into You	Mazzy Star
Older Than I Am	Lennon Stella
The Night Is Still Young	Nicki Minaj
Everywhere	Fleetwood Mac
You Are In Love	Taylor Swift
I'm With You	Vance Joy
State Lines	Novo Amor
Little Did I Know	Julia Michaels
Bigger Than The Whole Sky	Taylor Swift
Matilda	Harry Styles
Repeat Until Death	Novo Amor
What They'll Say About Us	FINNEAS
Opaline	Novo Amor
I Almost Do (Taylor's Version)	Taylor Swift
Ready To Fall	Boundary Run
The Night We Met	Lord Huron

This book is dedicated to those who escape through fiction—life exists from cover to cover.

To You, Jyla

Prologue

CELESTE

19 YEARS AGO

AUGUST 31

From the moment we take our first breath, we begin to die.

I mean, it's the truth, right? Think about it right now. Every passing second becomes another moment you'll never get back— another moment that brings you closer to the end.

And I know that's a morbid thought. Trust me, I do.

But the thought of death never scared me. It never scared me to know that when my time came, there would be one second when I'm here and the next I'm not. I guess there's a lot of simplicity in death, unlike life's complications.

He once told me that my destiny lay within the stars. That amongst trillions of small lights in the sky, my fate had been sealed. Frankly, I never knew much about the stars before him, nor did I believe these tiny specks of light could hold a deeper meaning. The thought itself seemed all too consuming.

Yet, here I am on the cold ground, looking up at the night sky— feeling inches away from death, wondering if this is what fate had suggested.

Is my destiny coming to a close?

Is this what the world had in store for me all along?

I don't know. Instead, I'm gazing up at the stars, not because they're the only thing I can focus on, but because they remind me of the night we first met. The night we first laid eyes on one another and the moment I knew my life would never be the same.

CHAPTER ONE

IYLA

PRESENT DAY

"What do you think of these?" I held a few of my favorite t-shirts against myself, turning to face my best friend, who was sprawled across my bed. Like most of my closet, they were bright, colorful, full of prints, and floral.

"Definitely not. You should have donated those ages ago," Hallie muttered under her breath, just loud enough for me to hear.

"Gee, thanks," I responded with a roll of my eyes. Hallie's opinion was nothing if not extraordinarily blunt or honest. In this case, her comment was both.

I tucked the shirts underneath my arm and reached back into my closet to find some alternative options. Ideally, something worthy of my best friend's approval.

"Listen, all you need is the basics," Hallie explained, placing her hands on her hips matter-of-factly. "You know, a *good* couple pairs of t-shirts."

I noticed her emphasis on a particular keyword in that statement.

"Some tanks, shorts and comfortable clothes. We're going to California, for crying out loud! We'll hardly have to wear any clothes with that heat." A wink escaped her hazel eyes as she danced her way over to my dresser.

"Yeah, that sounds like a *great* idea," I scoffed. "Let's show up on the first day of class in a bikini top and shorts. That'll leave a memorable first impression."

"Now, *that*, Iyla." She pointed in my direction proudly. "Might be the best idea you've had all day."

I shook my head in frustration, shooting her a glare as she grinned playfully. "Haven't you ever heard of the saying 'modest is hottest'?"

"Haven't you heard of the saying 'modest is'... wait, what was it again?" She paused, furrowing her brows in feigned thought. "Oh, I remember. *Boring*."

"Why did I not see that one coming?" I groaned, kissing my teeth as I removed the t-shirts from underneath my arm and reluctantly tossed them into the donation pile, much to Hallie's approval.

"In all seriousness," she carried on. "This year will be all about you and me. The California sun, the endless memories, and let's not forget about all the guys we'll meet." She reached into my drawers, a devilish grin coming across her lips. "Especially if you show up on move-in day in this little number." She revealed my red bikini top, holding it oh-so-theatrically held up to her very full chest.

Unlike Hallie, I'd never been exceptionally blessed in the upstairs department. In fact, my bikini top resembled a nipple pastie I'd once seen lying on the inside of her dresser.

"You seem to forget that we're going to school to get a degree." I mentally steered my minor chest problems to the side and snatched my bikini top out of her hands. "This isn't a four-year vacation."

Compared to my overly optimistic best friend, I'd always considered myself much more of a realist.

Believe me, I knew more than anyone that going to UCLA was a dream come true—a miracle, for that matter. But that didn't change the fact that this experience would also present its challenges.

"All I am saying is that you've worked so hard. Harder than

anyone else I've ever met," Hallie responded. "All I want is for you to have fun and for college to be one of the best times of our lives. Especially considering six months ago, packing for UCLA seemed like a figment of our imagination."

This was true.

Throughout high school, I'd started to think about the next stage in my life, attributing that proactive nature to my parents' successes in their own respective careers. But still, when it came time to make a decision, I felt lost. I had no real sense of direction, leading me to apply to five general arts programs across the country.

Three in-state: the University of Cincinnati, Toledo, and Ohio State, along with two out-of-state: the University of Louisville and Indiana. Two schools within a reasonable driving distance from Columbus should I ever "need anything."

"We should be close by. It'll be better that way! You never know when you might need us." My parents' voices floated through my mind.

My parents had always been highly protective of me—which was just a nicer way to say they were hover parents.

Something still didn't feel right, though. I was excited about going to college and taking the next leap into my future, but frankly, I wasn't at all excited about what I'd signed myself up to study.

The guidance counselors at school tried to remind me that sometimes you just need to test the waters, but all I wanted was smooth sailing—and to not disappoint my parents. After all, I knew how much my parents had given me my whole life. My life with Lance and Amanda Larson had been beyond compare. Although I knew I wasn't biologically theirs, they loved me as if I was. They'd had that conversation with me from an early age. I think they both understood the importance of a truth like that.

"Mommy and Daddy adopted you when you were a tiny baby."

I recalled my dad's words.

"So, I didn't grow in mommy's tummy?" I'd surveyed them both, slowly realizing I'd never seen a photo of my mom pregnant. "No, you didn't. You grew in someone else's tummy," my mom clarified with a gentle smile. "But you were always meant to be ours."

A six-year-old Iyla had smiled back, feeling a sense of peace accompany those words. It was a sense of peace that had withered as the years went by, and I'd slowly begun to uncover three details of my past, despite my parent's secretive nature.

One: I was born in Los Angeles, California, prematurely.

Two: my biological mother's name was Celeste Kinney.

And three: Celeste Kinney passed away shortly after she gave birth to me.

That's it.

That's all I knew.

And you could say I was okay with that for a good period of time. Content, if you will. However, as my peace withered, my contentment soon followed suit. I started to form questions about my father, whose name I'd never been told.

In an attempt to answer those questions, I learned one more thing—the most crucial detail of all.

The fact that whenever I'd ask a question about him, it would be quickly dismissed.

"He wasn't around," my mom would respond hastily.

"You wouldn't want to know him anyway. He was a deadbeat," my dad had once mumbled under his breath before quietly being shushed by my mom.

Eventually, I realized that was just how things were in my family. A lot of empty words and dead ends. Somewhere along the way, I stopped asking altogether.

But as the saying goes, old habits die hard. In the final weeks before college applications closed, I fell back into my curious ways—only now, with even more deep-rooted questions.

I'd managed to squeeze out of my parents that my birth mother was only a few months shy of 23 when she'd given birth to me. It was an age that suddenly felt within reach—feasible.

With that realization came another, more morbid thought. The thought that I was going to outlive her, replace her, without ever knowing a single thing about her.

"Can you please tell me more about Celeste?" I'd asked my mom one day after finally building up enough courage. "Please, Mom."

She'd placed a hand behind her neck, rubbing it in a soothing motion as an eerie silence fell over the room. I immediately regretted the words that had taken the liberty to fall out of my mouth.

I had never once thought Amanda and Lance weren't enough to be my parents. As a little girl, I'd always believed what they said to me was true—I was always meant to be theirs.

But that didn't mean I wasn't someone else's first.

I'd always known they'd withheld some information about my past. What I didn't know was why they kept it from me.

"Well," my mom finally spoke, hesitation seeping through her voice. "What do you want to know?"

I let out a relieved breath, taken aback by her willingness to entertain the conversation.

"Um," I stuttered, realizing I was completely unprepared. I didn't think I'd get this far. "Do you know what Celeste did? You know, before she gave birth to me? Did she work or...go to school?" I asked nervously, playing with my hands as I attempted to coherently express my questions.

Mom leaned back in her chair, "Celeste was a very smart girl, Iyla. She studied pre-law at the University of California. Graduated with one of the highest grades in her cohort."

She then told me that Celeste had written the LSAT shortly after graduation, scoring high enough to guarantee her a Stanford spot. "The school of her dreams."

"Did she get accepted?" I probed, eager to grasp at anything I could learn about her.

My mom paused at that, leaving the conversation hanging with an aura of hesitation. I couldn't ignore how heavy that made me feel.

"I don't know, sweetie. She passed away before finding out."

And just like that, I now carried the burden that was never mine to begin with. Had I been the reason her life was cut short? The reason she never got to fulfill her dreams?

"I'm sure she got in, though," my mom added in an attempt to reassure me. Her words stung like a double-edged sword.

On one end, she'd finally answered some of my long-awaited questions. On the other, her response carved a new wound that felt much worse.

It was a wound that longed and desired to know more.

And that's when it hit me. The clarity.

Maybe the only way not to replace her was to retrace her. Get a chance to learn who she really was and what her life was like. Walk in her shoes.

But how?

The answer was simple.

I needed to go to UCLA.

I needed to take the pre-law program.

And I needed to make it to Stanford.

That night, I secretly submitted my final college application. For once, a tiny light was at the end of the tunnel.

"California?" My mom debated as I broke the news at the dinner table with not five, but six letters of admission on the counter. "What do you mean you applied to UCLA? We thought you were going to the University of Indiana."

I'd initially shied away from their disapproval, but in the following weeks, all my time and energy was spent convincing my parents that UCLA was the right choice.

As terrible as it sounded, I backed my parents against a wall. They had one of two options. One, let me go to UCLA; or two, share their real reservations about why they were holding me back. I knew it had more to do with being "too far away." The choice became abundantly obvious to them as the deadline to accept my offer approached, and they "realized that UCLA was the best option for me after all."

Unwilling to let them backtrack on their decision, I promptly accepted the offer, inciting a weird state of being in our household. One that until I announced that my best friend, Hallie Jennings, would join me at UCLA in the fall wouldn't come to pass.

Hallie Jennings.

How do you describe someone like Hallie?

Hallie's the type of girl everyone knows. The girl that, despite having a million things on her plate, still manages to do a million and one. She's the friend you see in the movies. The supportive one. The funny one. The one who gives out all the boy advice you could ever imagine, solicited or not. And a total hopeless romantic at heart.

But Hallie had always been more to me than that. It's as if the universe knew that we had to be best friends if we couldn't be sisters.

So, by some miracle, everything had managed to work out. And now, I was in my childhood bedroom, packing my entire 18 years into boxes with my best friend.

"So, you agree, right?" Hallie's voice pulled me out of my deep thoughts and back into the rant she was still so clearly in the midst of. "This is going to be the best time of our life?"

I smiled, placing a reassuring hand on her shoulder. "I can promise you this, Hallie. This is the start of the first chapter of many."

CELESTE

19 YEARS AGO

JUNE 21

I've never proclaimed to be a writer, nor did I ever think I could be a good storyteller. But in law, the whole goal is for the truth to prevail, right? The facts need to be accurate, consistent, and well-executed. The defendants' story deserves justice.

So, I guess becoming a lawyer was a lot like becoming a story-teller. The ability to take on the narrator's role to support your client, all in an effort to convince a jury that their story is correct and worth telling.

You see, before *him*, I never thought I would have a story that I wanted to share. At least, not one that was worthy of telling.

Don't get me wrong—I've gone through my fair share of ups and downs. Stories filled with drama and heartache, stories that are entertaining and chaotic in nature. But those stories are about a girl that doesn't exist anymore. A girl that, over time, has done her best to grow into a new and better version of herself. A version where her scars didn't define her but allowed her to be brave.

Brave.

A simple word that always reminds me of something my favorite professor at UCLA, Dr. Sanders, would say:

"Bravery is a virtue possessed by all but only used by some."
And that's what I wanted to be when I was with him.
Braver.
Who's *him*, you may ask?
Good question.
Where do I even start?

When I was given this journal many years ago, I was told that sometimes, to move forward, we need to re-discover the past. And to do that, I suppose I need to start right from the beginning, on one day in particular.

The Friday before spring break and the night before it all began.

☆ ☆ ☆

"Look, I'm staying in-state this year." My roommate and best friend, Claire, prolonged her antagonizing lecture as I sunk my head deeper into my textbook. "I'm only going to Long Beach. Just an hour away."

"I don't know," I sighed, dismissing her comment. "Going away for spring break doesn't sound like the best idea. You know I really need to ace these finals," I added, throwing out a lie that even I had a hard time believing.

I knew that going on a spring break trip wouldn't jeopardize my chances of acing my exams. In fact, I'd practically memorized each of my textbooks, considering that's what you do when your whole life revolves around school.

She shot me a glare as I fell silent again, turning my attention back to my textbook. It was no secret that Claire wanted me to come with her. We'd had the same conversation year after year. Except this would be the last time, with graduation looming around the corner.

"C'mon, Celeste. This is our last spring break," she groaned,

17

seemingly reading my mind as she pushed my textbook down and planted herself firmly on the bed in front of me. "Besides, it'll only be a couple of days."

"Claire, I really don't think this is a good—"

"You want me to beg? I'll beg." She leapt off the bed, dropping to the floor and onto her knees as she interlocked her hands to form a fist in front of her chest. "Please," she pleaded. "I promise Celeste, if you come with me, I will never ask anything of you again. *Please*."

I exhaled, genuinely considering her offer. Claire and I had always spent our spring breaks apart despite her relentless efforts to convince me otherwise each year. She would opt to travel out of state, adding Miami, South Carolina, and even Hawaii to her list of destinations over the years. Yet, in spite of a location change, each year would end up the same. Claire would drink and party the week away, fall in and out of love with a new guy every night, only to join me back on campus at the end of it all to enlighten me on her adventures.

To Claire's knowledge, I spent each year flying back to Oregon and spending time with my foster mom, but that's always been a lie.

A part of this story that we'll soon get to.

Sure, the intention to go home was there, but as every spring break rolled around, I found myself doing the exact same thing— rationalizing the fact that there was nothing more important than staying on campus and using the week off as an additional study break.

Thrilling, I know.

But truthfully, the idea of partying non-stop for an entire week has never appealed to me. The most important thing had always been doing well at UCLA and getting into Stanford's law program. From the moment I first stepped foot onto the campus, that was what I'd set out to accomplish.

Now, you might be wondering why.

Why was it so important that I got into Stanford? Why did I want to become a lawyer so badly?

Remember that lingering part of the story I promised?

Well, here it comes.

It all started when I was nine years old. Young enough to live freely but old enough to understand entirely. It was late November, and the trees swayed heavily through the gusts of wind as faint layers of snow cascaded over our front lawn.

I'd always loved winter and the cold. It was the time of year when, even though beauty may not exist inside your home, it certainly would on the outside.

My father was always coming home late from work, but as I lay in bed that night, I remembered asking my mother when he'd be back and why he wasn't the one tucking me in.

"He'll be home soon, Celeste," she reassured me as she kissed my cheek tenderly. "Now, get some rest."

As she pulled away, the infamous scent of her "perfume" lingered. It was the kind of scent that came from an unsuspecting bottle, from an item you'd always find glued to her side.

Whiskey.

That night, I managed to fall asleep despite the gnawing questions. When the early hours of morning fell, I was awoken by a series of loud noises.

"Where the hell have you been?!" I first heard my mother scream. "Been with that skank again, huh?"

"It's better than being around your drunk ass all the time," my father yelled back.

I pulled my covers over my head in a pitiful attempt to drown out the noise, but it was no use.

As I heard the argument escalating, an idea came to mind. Maybe if they knew that I was listening, they'd stop fighting.

That naive thought guided my conscience as I slowly climbed

out of bed and made my way down the stairs.

The drunken shouts of my parents masked the creak of each step. My neighbors were no longer surprised that my parents were loud. Sure, we'd occasionally have the police show up at our front door for a noise complaint. But after years of warnings, the neighbors seemed to stop calling the police altogether. I suppose they realized that the fights were inevitable.

After taking a few steps further, I peered over the handrail, catching a clear glimpse of my mother slapping my father across the face.

A silence fell over the room until the breadth of my father's hand wrapped around my mother's throat, pinning her against the fridge.

I could hear her gasping for air as my father inched closer to her face. "You really want to try this again? You're a drunk waste of space and piece of shit mother," he spat before releasing his firm grasp from her throat, causing her to heave in the now-tainted air.

I remained frozen on the staircase, feeling nothing in my petite frame but an overwhelming emptiness. Truthfully, what was unfolding in front of my eyes wasn't something I hadn't seen many times before. Their anger and aggression over the years had become my norm, so much so that I'd grown desensitized to feelings of panic. Chaos became a comfort, normalcy became a danger, and periods of solitude became a rarity.

"Sure, I'm a drunk. Blame me. I'm a drunk because of you!" my mom pushed back as I reached the bottom of the stairs.

"Because of me?" he challenged as a laugh escaped his mouth, and he clutched onto his stomach. It wasn't the same laugh I'd hear when I made a joke, and he'd tell me, "you're going to be a comedian someday, kiddo." This laugh was sly, wicked, and possessed a sense of malicious intent.

For a split second, I regretted my decision to leave my room. Still, I brushed off the feeling, for that's all I ever knew how to do as I steadily inched my way down the hallway and into the kitchen.

"You're sick," my father retaliated as he furiously shoved my mother, forcing her body to the ground and causing her head to connect with the kitchen tiles.

"Mommy?" I couldn't hold in my concern any longer. "Are you okay?"

My father rapidly spun toward me, his agitated eyes turning weary as the faint beams of sunlight made their way through the windows. "Cel? What are you doing up?" He secured me in his grasp and guided me back down the hallway.

"You guys were yelling," I stammered as I looked over my shoulder to see my mother rubbing her forehead as she attempted to sit up. "I...I just wanted it to stop."

"It's over now." His less than reassuring hand fell onto my back. "Now, let's get you back upstairs and into—"

A loud shriek from the kitchen forced the two of us to halt in place.

"I hate you," my mother growled as she shakily stood up from the ground, reaching for her empty whiskey bottle and flinging it down the hallway.

The glass soared through the air in slow motion, grazing past my father's body and racing toward me. Within seconds, shards of glass shattered throughout the hallway, making direct contact with my skin, scratching alongside my arms and the side of my face and finding securement right into my collarbone.

It didn't take long for my body to fall onto the ground, just like my mother had moments earlier. Only this time, my father reached out to catch me rather than being the reason for the decline.

"Celeste!" my mother shrieked, her anger being overruled by fear as she ran over to me, reality finally seeming to hit her. "Call an ambulance!" she fell to my side, looking up at my startled father. "Now!"

"You're going to be okay, baby. I'm so sorry," she whispered once

21

he'd run off, visibly panicked as the warmth of my blood pooled down my chest and soaked through the front of my pajamas.

But it wasn't the blood that I was focused on. It was the ceiling, where the peel-and-stick stars that I'd begged my parents to put up years earlier remained.

Even after all that time, some still glowed bright, while others had lost their power—a metaphor for life, as I'd come to learn. The brightest stars will always find a way to shine, even amidst the darkness.

You see, I was a burnt-out star in my parent's galaxy. And it was only when the ambulance took me away that night that I started to find that glow again.

My whole world began to change when I arrived at the hospital. I was greeted by a social worker who came into my room and asked me some questions about my parents. It turned out that this wasn't the first time that social services had been concerned about our family. My school, our neighbors, and even the parents of some of my classmates had contacted them several times. They'd claimed that there were signs of neglect and abuse in our household—but until that night, there had been no actual proof.

As I explained to the social worker how I came to get the 12 stitches in my chest, a case against my parents was finally feasible.

Foster care became the first viable option while the court began its legal proceedings.

"Can't I go live with Auntie Joyce?" I'd pleaded with the social worker. "I really like Auntie Joyce. She's kind and sweet. She never yells."

She remained silent, but the look on her face said it all. It turned out Auntie Joyce could barely afford to take care of herself. The love of the bottle was apparently a hereditary trait on my mother's side.

"What about Grandpa Kinney?" I'd wondered. "He's so fun. He has a motorcycle and everything."

She shot me another pained smile. A diagnosis of dementia meant that my only other option was out the window.

"Celeste, we will find you a special home." She squeezed my hand reassuringly. "I promise."

Over the next two years, that "special home" became a series of four different homes. Homes where I spent most of my time reminiscing on the happier times of my childhood, grieving the people I once thought my parents were.

All hope felt lost until the universe introduced me to Sharlene Wright. The owner of my fifth, final, and forever childhood home.

Sharlene was a retired nurse with no children of her own. She'd chosen to devote the remainder of her life to creating a supportive, safe environment for children who needed it.

In other words, children like me.

With the love and support of Sharlene, I decided that one day I wanted to work with kids who were just like me—making sure that they, too, went on to live the lives they deserved.

And so, amidst all the drama, the chaos, and the spiraling that was my life, there it was. My calling.

Family law.

Once I turned 18, life changed again. I was no longer an eligible candidate for foster care. Sharlene insisted that I didn't have to go, but I knew I had to move on to the next chapter in my life. One that I'd been busy building all throughout high school.

Work, study, work, repeat became the motto that ultimately granted me a full-ride scholarship to UCLA's pre-law program.

For the first time in my life, I was excited about what lay ahead. Going to UCLA would be the first step in taking control of my life. Giving myself a new start. Making a vow that I'd leave the past behind me and never look back.

This started by cutting off the sparse communication I'd had with my parents for good. A decision that meant I would have no family in my life—a term that, at the time, I only defined as blood.

Until I met Claire O'Donnell.

Remember her?

Yes, we've finally circled back to that.

On move-in day, Claire walked into our dorm room and tripped over her two left feet. "Shit," she muttered, her boxes falling out of her arms and spreading across the floor.

"Need a hand?" I asked, kneeling down to help her gather her things before she could respond.

"Thanks." The embarrassment flooded her cheeks a shade of bright pink. "Great first impression, huh?"

"The best." I helped her to pick up the last of her scattered items. "I'm Celeste, by the way. And you must be Clumsy Dwarf?"

"Claire," she snorted. "But 'clumsy dwarf' is also pretty accurate."

We'd burst into laughter together, and since that moment, it felt like we never really stopped. That day, I learned something incredibly special. That family was much more than a spartan bloodline. Claire has proved that to be true all these years.

This leads us back to where this first entry all began. Claire and I have done everything together for the last four years except for spring break.

"Please." Claire pouted with the biggest puppy-dog eyes known to man.

"Why Long Beach?" I finally decided to entertain the conversation, feeling somewhat intrigued that Long Beach was less than an hour south—meaning if I wanted to come back to campus, it was hardly a hop and a skip away.

"Well, there are amazing parties the entire time," she justified hopefully, only forcing me to make a face in return. "Wait," she added, picking up on my disinterest. "I also found this incredible deal at a nearby hotel. It's newly renovated."

"Why do I feel like there's a catch?" I crossed my arms skeptically. "How have you gone from wanting to travel out of state to only an hour away?"

"Well..." her eyes refused to meet mine. "I might be slightly low in the finance department."

"Meaning?" I pried further.

"Meaning," she paused, biting down on her lower lip nervously. "I can only afford to go if you come with me. You know, split the costs," she finally sought approval in my firm face.

"So, is this about spending time together or splitting costs?" I pursed my lips.

"Listen, I'll be honest with you." She got up from the floor. "It's both."

I shook my head and placed my textbook neatly back onto the shelf. "You know you're terrible at convincing, right?"

"I'm trying, CeCe." She reached for both of my hands, now opting to use the nickname she'd come up with for me. "I need this. Hell, *you* need this. What's life if you're not going to live it?"

I paused momentarily, allowing her words to sink in before reluctantly agreeing, to Claire's surprise as much as my own. "Fine." I pulled away and reached for another textbook off of my shelf. "But this better not be some party galore trip, okay?"

"Oh my gosh! I am *so* happy you said yes!" she squealed, ignoring my stipulation as she grabbed her phone. "I'm calling the hotel now."

"Claire, wait. Maybe we should—"

She slammed the door shut behind her and disappeared into the hallway before I could finish my sentence.

"Ugh." I fell onto my bed, trying to re-organize my study notes and thoughts.

Had I lost my mind?

Possibly.

No, I definitely had.

"Oh, forgot to mention." Claire re-opened the door not a second later as she peeked her head through. "We're leaving tomorrow."

CHAPTER TWO

IYLA

PRESENT DAY

"Iyla!" my mom shouted up the stairs. "Hallie's here."

I looked down at my phone, noticing it was exactly nine a.m. I wasn't surprised— Hallie was nothing if not notoriously on time.

"I'm coming, I'm coming." I called back down, hastily applying another layer of mascara.

"Iyla?" She did that parent thing where she continued to call my name even though I'd already answered.

"I said I'm coming!" I reached for a clip to tuck a stray piece of my hair out of my face, taking a final glance at myself in the mirror. *Here we go. Life's about to change.*

I glided down the steps as my parents stood in the doorway with my suitcases lined up beside them.

"Have you got everything you need?" my dad asked.

I nodded, anxiously reaching for the front door as I spotted Hallie standing in front of her car, donning a massive pair of sunglasses and a ridiculously oversized beach hat. "The day has finally arrived!" she cheered as I made my way over to her.

I shook my head in laughter. By now, our whole family was unphased by the theatrics of Hallie Jennings.

"Why hello, Larson family." Hallie pulled both of my parents in for a gigantic hug.

After my adoption, my parents were adamant that we would be a one-and-done family. Then, they gained a second daughter in Hallie somewhere along the way.

"Now, you take care of yourself, young lady," my dad teased Hallie as I pushed my suitcases into the trunk. "But I know you're tough as nails, and we don't need to worry about you."

"Have a safe trip, my lovely." My mom kissed her cheek, the waterworks filling her eyes.

"Aw, I'll miss you guys." She pulled them back in for a second hug. "I'll see you soon. How's Thanksgiving sound?"

My parents smiled as they released her. "Perfect."

Hallie gave them one final nod before she made her way back over to the car. "LA, here we come!" she sang with a grin, obnoxiously shaking her car keys in the air.

I half-smiled, tucking my hair—which I'd apparently done a terrible job clipping up—behind my ear.

"I'll give you a few minutes." Hallie placed her hand on my arm before she hopped into the driver's seat.

I hadn't prepared myself for this moment: the dreaded goodbye. I'd known it was coming, but any time I thought about leaving my parents behind, tears would well up in my eyes. I'd always try to suppress the thought, telling myself I had time. But now, the time had come—and just as I had imagined, I was a blubbery mess.

I'd like to believe that history has a funny way of repeating itself. Almost 19 years ago, one phone call changed my parent's entire life, and since that day, I hadn't left their side. Now, there I was, heading right back to the place where I was last alone. Ready to start a new beginning. Ready to begin a new chapter.

"Oh, Iyla." My mom embraced me in her arms, soothingly running a hand through my hair. "Where has the time gone?"

"Our baby isn't a baby anymore, Amanda," my dad chimed in as I locked my tear-filled eyes with his. "Don't cry, Iy." He brushed a single tear off my cheek. "We're excited for you. We are." He gestured between himself and my mom. "This is a happy time."

Mom warmly smiled in agreement, wiping away some of her own tears. "We'll always be a phone call away. If you need us, we'll get on the first flight out. Now, go." They released me, not just physically from their embrace but from what felt like the only safe place I'd known my entire life.

With a shaky breath, I reached for the car handle, only stopping at the sound of my dad's voice as he called out my name once more.

"Iyla." He leaned in to whisper in my ear. "I just want you to remember something, okay?"

I nodded, curiously tilting my head forward.

He was brief with his words. "A chapter left untold will become a book well-written."

I pulled back in confusion. "Where did you hear that from?"

In place of a response, he placed a final kiss on my cheek and walked back over to my mom. I brushed off the unanswered question as I stepped into Hallie's car and closed the door behind me.

"We love you, Iyla," they called out as I rolled down the window.

"I love you too." I watched them hug each other in comfort as Hallie ignited the engine and pulled away.

"Ready?" she asked as the image of my parents faded into the distance.

Brushing the now black mascara smudges away from my eyes, I smiled. "Always."

The ☆ Second Entry ☆

CELESTE

19 YEARS AGO

JUNE 24

Bright and early the next day, Claire and I set off for Long Beach.

"I can't tell you how excited I am!" Claire squealed as we loaded our bags into her car. "I love Long Beach. My family visited so many times when I was a kid. The beaches are gorgeous, and there's so much to do, but this will be my first time experiencing it all *adult style*." She pretended to down a shot as she opened the door on the driver's side.

I remained silent, regretting my decision to get myself roped into this trip.

"Oh, c'mon, CeCe." She turned the keys to the ignition as I climbed into the passenger seat. "Aren't you the least bit excited?"

"Not really." I shot her an unamused look.

"Well, too bad." She reached over to turn on the radio. "Your job for the next week is to relax, enjoy yourself and have *fun*." A grin spread across her face as we heard the beginning notes of Fleetwood Mac's "Everywhere" start playing, prompting her to immediately max out the speaker volume.

"Oh my gosh, yes!" She accelerated out of the campus lot and onto the main road. "We *love* this song." She started to sing, completely off-tune as she reached one hand out to hold mine.

I burst into laughter, joining in with my equally unimpressive singing voice.

"See, CeCe?" Claire teased as she noticed the shift in my demeanor, seeing it as a perfect opportunity to do that *I told you so* thing that she always did. "It's a sign. The universe is on your side."

"The universe?" I questioned my disposition on the matter, pressing my head back into the seat.

"Yes, this trip is going to be special!" she winked. "I can just feel it."

As the music continued to blast throughout the car, I couldn't shake the endless spiral of thoughts that passed through my mind—ones that reminded me that maybe, just maybe, the week ahead would be a chance to resettle and relax.

Perhaps that's what I'd been missing out on all those years I hadn't joined Claire for spring break. All the parties. All the trips. All the guys I could've potentially met had I actually given it a chance. The list went on.

But more than anyone, I knew that changing the past wasn't possible, nor would I take away the choices I'd made throughout the years.

I mean, I must have done something right. I'd upheld one of the top marks in my program, completed three internships with reputable law firms in and around Los Angeles, and had job offers lined up the minute I got out of Stanford. It was those achievements that brought excitement to my life. Those were the moments that I held on to.

But Claire did have a point, as much as I hated to admit it. Was the universe finally "on my side"? And maybe this trip would be a chance to try something different. Become a new version of Celeste Kinney.

A version that was more focused on making memories that

might not seem like a lot at the time but would become everything in time. A version of myself that was careful, but *maybe* took some risks, broke some rules, and lived a bit on the edge. Okay, maybe a safe yet risky-enough distance from the edge but someone that actually acted like a college senior, and not a senior citizen.

Those thoughts stuck in my mind for a solid ten minutes before we finally stepped foot out of the car, through the hotel lobby and into our room. I had to practically drag my jaw in behind me the entire time.

"You've got to be kidding me." All that carefree and reckless energy dissipated from my body as I looked over at Claire once we'd closed the door behind us. "We can't stay here."

The hotel reminded me of that old saying, it's not what's on the outside, it's what's on the inside that counts. But *this* was the opposite. The hotel's exterior was immaculate, while the inside looked like it belonged in the 70s.

"I did say they'd just undergone renovations," she protested.

"Yeah, they have. On the outside." I huffed out in frustration.

She made her way over to the two queen-sized beds along the wall. "Well, you know what?" She pulled back the bedding to inspect. "We're just going to have to make it work."

Surprisingly (if things could get any more surprising), the beds looked brand new. Soon enough, we learned that the room was stylistically inspired by the 70s rather than actually stuck in it.

Thank goodness.

"You're lucky, O'Donnell!" I let out a sigh of relief. "I was about to turn my butt around and head back to campus."

"Luck of the Irish." She grinned, nodding off to her Irish heritage as she unzipped her suitcase.

I propped mine up beside hers, taking in the self-sabotaging I'd done the night prior. You know, when I decided that packing four outfits for a one-week trip was a good idea.

My plan had been simple. If I only packed enough for a few

nights, I'd conveniently have to return to campus to grab more clothes. Once I went back, I'd come up with some excuse as to why I had to stay and couldn't carry out the rest of the trip. Truthfully, the plan had sounded much better in my head than it did now as I looked down at my pathetically empty suitcase.

"There's a party tonight down at Junipero Beach," Claire announced, dumping out the entirety of her suitcase onto the bed she had evidently claimed as her own. "Now, get changed." She dismissed me like a schoolgirl. "We're leaving in an hour."

I let out a sigh and quickly grabbed the first items in my suitcase before making my way over to the bathroom.

By the time I stepped out of the bathroom, Claire had also taken the liberty to get changed. She'd thrown on a show-stopping fluorescent purple halter top paired with low-rise shorts, her curly brown hair effortlessly cascading down her back.

I was in awe.

Claire was the epitome of fashion, class, and the ability to look perfect no matter what she wore.

"Ready to go?" I re-emerged in her line of view.

"*That's* what you're wearing?" She looked me up and down, her naturally cheerful expression faltering.

I shrugged. "What do you mean? This is nice."

"Oh, CeCe." She shook her head in disapproval, stomping her way over to me. "You're so lucky I know how to fix this."

She untied my cardigan, hiked my skirt up so much that I was sure my butt was on show, and snatched the clip out of my hair, letting my blonde locks fall on either side of my shoulders.

"Is all of this really necessary?" I frowned as a proud smile fell onto her face.

"Very," she snapped. "Now, let's get going. I'd hate for us to be late."

CHAPTER THREE

I Y L A

PRESENT DAY

Three long, tiring days and seven states later, Hallie and I finally made it to California.

It was my turn behind the wheel as we crossed the Arizona border. And with only 15 minutes remaining in what felt like our never-ending journey to get to the UCLA campus, my pedal was to the metal.

"Make sure you pull off at the next exit, okay?" Hallie re-configured the GPS on the dashboard.

"What? No," I challenged. "The campus is exit 55B-C, not exit 4. We're nearly there."

Hallie glared over at me, clearly unamused. "Have you not been listening to what I've been saying this whole time?"

How could I not? The girl hadn't stopped going on for hours about stopping at a local coffee shop that she'd heard raving reviews about online.

"Take the next exit. You will arrive at your destination in five minutes," the GPS' robotic voice instructed me.

"See?" Hallie turned to face me with a smug smile. "We're close by."

I tightened my grip on the steering wheel as the GPS guided me off the interstate and onto the side roads.

"This is it!" Hallie excitedly tapped her long nails against the glass.

"Tim and Sally's?" I read the sign on the coffee shop as I pulled up alongside the road.

"Yup." She unbuckled her seat belt and swung open the door. "Do you want an iced coffee?"

"I guess." I removed the keys from the ignition. "But Hallie." I caught her attention before she turned to walk inside. "Please don't take too long. We have the next four years to visit this shop. And you know how badly I want to get to the campus."

"I promise I'll be quick, Iyla," she responded before stepping out of the car and disappearing inside the shop.

Hallie was right. Tim and Sally's was a local hit, especially among the college crowd. I'd already seen four students walk by wearing UCLA merch. They all seemed to fit in perfectly with the "California" vibe. The tans, the endless sun, the beach, the effortless waves—

"You can't park here." A harsh voice suddenly interrupted my thoughts.

I jumped back in my seat, muttering the first few syllables of *I'm sorry* before suddenly locking eyes with whom I believed to be the most beautiful man I'd ever seen.

He had short curly black hair and deep brown eyes. I couldn't help but notice his biceps flex as he casually placed one hand on the car's hood and the other inside of my window. From the way he had to bend down to meet my eye level, he must've easily pushed six-foot-two.

A light brown t-shirt embedded with a coffee cup clung to his body, prompting my immediate assumption that he was an employee of Tim and Sally's. That, or he really liked coffee.

Damn, I couldn't help but think. *What I would give to see him without that shirt on. Or without anything on, for that matter.*

"Hey, are you listening to me?" he snapped me out of my trance, irritation defining his features.

"I'm so sorry," I finally managed to speak as blood rushed to my cheeks. "I'm new here," I added in an effort to explain and start a conversation despite his evident disapproval toward me. "My best friend and I just arrived from—"

"Yeah, I don't care, princess," he cut me off. "This is a no-parking zone. So get out."

Ouch.

"My friend will only be a second, and then we will be on our way."

"As I said, I don't care." He moved his arm from outside the window, resting it beside the other on the hood, both ridiculously flexing without him even trying. "Now, get moving or—"

"She's with me, Vic." I heard a voice echo in the distance. "It's all good."

A look of surprise fell over Vic's face. "She's with you?" he questioned, turning his head to face whoever had spoken up.

"Yeah, man, we're just about to leave," the charming yet unfamiliar voice continued, getting closer with each word.

"Well, alright then." He smacked both hands on top of the car. "You have a good day now."

A nervous smile formed on my lips as he headed back inside the shop. And damn, did the rear end look just as good as the front.

Why are the hot ones always such assholes?

"Sorry about him." A fresh frame now appeared in my window, staring off at Vic. "He's a bit of an asshole."

"My thoughts exactly," I mumbled under my breath.

Where was Hallie? Why was she taking so long?

"Hey, you're welcome, by the way."

Remorse washed over me as I realized I'd completely neglected to thank the person who'd just saved my ass. "I'm so sorry, thank you. I really appreciate it." I finally built up enough courage to peer up into a soft pair of blue eyes.

"Don't sweat it." He smiled.

What the hell was going on? With his daring smile and a face like heaven, his guy was equally, if not hotter, than Vic. Even through the hoodie loosely covering his body, I could see his chest was broad. Not as comprehensive as Vic's, but enough that I knew I could seamlessly disappear in his embrace.

His dark blonde hair was long enough that he'd had to messily push a section out of his face. Despite the fact that I felt like a total mess after that strange encounter, as I looked up at this unfamiliar face, I was overcome with the sudden urge to ask him a million questions:

Who are you?

Why did you help me?

Where have you been my entire life?

Instead, I only managed to spit out another "thank you."

A smile grew on his face as he looked down at me. Only this time, he *really* looked at me. It was the type of look where someone sees you, not for what's on the surface, but for what's within. Of course, he was seeing Iyla Larson, but it felt like perhaps he was seeing a version of myself that I didn't even quite know yet. The person that I could see myself being with him.

Jesus, I'd only just met the guy two minutes ago, and there I was, fantasizing about a whole new version of myself.

It was pathetic, really.

When Hallie had told me to think about all the guys we'd meet out here, I didn't think I'd literally meet two within the first few minutes of arriving in Los Angeles.

"Ambert." He reached his arm out towards me. "My name's Ambert."

Ambert.

I choked down the lump in my throat and reached my hand out to shake his.

"Iyla," my voice was just a whisper as I slightly shook his hand.

His touch was warm, and his hands were soft.

Hold me in your hands forever.

"Well, Iyla." He slowly disconnected his touch from mine. "It's nice to meet you. I'd love to stay and chat." He glanced behind him as he spoke. "But if you don't move this car, Vic will quite literally snap my head off." He chuckled after speaking, and hearing his laugh for the first time made me want to melt.

What an amazing sound.

"The car?" I repeated, wholly dazed in the presence of him.

He looked sideways in confusion as realization hit me. "Oh, right, the car," I played it off, acting as if I wasn't coming across as a total love-struck fool.

Get it together, Iyla.

"Sorry." I shook my head as I pushed the keys back into the ignition. "I'll move it now."

He nodded as I turned the key, only to be met with a sharp squeaking noise rather than the engine roaring.

Shit.

I turned the keys once more, hopeful for a different outcome. Yet, the same thing happened.

"It sounds like your battery's dead," Ambert's calm voice cut through the sirens going off in my mind.

"Battery?" I looked back up at him.

Cars have batteries?

"Yeah, it's no big deal. Let me pull up and give you a boost. My car is over there." He gestured across the parking lot. "I'll be right back."

"Boost?" I mumbled dumbfoundedly as he walked away in the direction he'd pointed, leaving me to lean against the steering wheel and scream internally. After a few moments, I finally mustered up enough courage to unbuckle my seat belt and make my way out of the car.

As I did, I caught a glimpse of Hallie inside the coffee shop, our drinks in her hands as she chatted with an oh-so-familiar face that minutes earlier had told me to "get moving."

Of course, she was talking to Vic. But could I blame her? What Hallie didn't realize was that, for once, her flirty nature was coming in handy. She was buying me time to leave this prohibited parking spot.

Lights illuminated the space ahead of me and pulled up a few inches away. A second later, Ambert hopped out of the driver's seat and pulled a series of cables out of his trunk.

"This should only take a couple of minutes," he said, lifting the hood of Hallie's car and propping it up on its stand.

The warmth of the sun had been long engulfed by the night sky, leaving me to hug myself as the cool California breeze washed over me. I shivered as I stood in my tank top and shorts. Thankfully, the shifting of the cables drowned out the sound of my chattering teeth.

"It's pretty simple, really," Ambert explained. "All you've got to do is make sure you connect the cables to the right terminals." He pointed to the engine. "But be warned. You have to make sure you do it correctly, otherwise..." He gestured an explosion with his hands. "Boom."

My eyes grew wide, panic kicking back in as I inadvertently took a step backwards. Did Ambert know what he was doing?

"Should I be worried?" I vocalized my concerned thoughts.

"Not at all." He shook his head. "I've watched a video."

His words didn't ease my anxiety any less. I was now desperately hugging myself for comfort and not warmth.

"I'm kidding again." He laughed, reassuringly touching my arm. "My dad owns an auto shop and would kick my ass if I didn't know how to boost a car. It's one of the simplest things in mechanics."

The wind picked up another cold breeze as my body shuddered beneath his touch, goosebumps forming all over.

"You're cold." He pulled his hand away. "Let me grab you a

sweater. I have one in my car.

Before I could protest, he'd jogged back over to his car, pulled a sweater out of his backseat, and walked back over to me. "It might be a little big on you."

I looked down, questioning if I was really going to put on this stranger's sweater. But before I could further debate that thought, another cold breeze hit my skin, prompting me to slip the sweater over my head.

Ambert wasn't wrong. The length of the fabric fell inches past my jean shorts, creating the illusion that I wasn't wearing anything underneath.

Great.

"A *little* big?" I joked as I peered up at him.

"It looks good on you." He smirked. "Blue is your color."

I paused yet again, unsure how to process the compliment, until eventually deciding that letting the conversation fall flat was the easiest choice.

"I overheard you telling Vic that you're new here." He continued the conversation for me. "Are you going to UCLA this fall?"

"I am, actually. My best friend and I just drove from Ohio to get to campus early. I mean, we haven't *just* driven down all day. We stopped along the way. It took us almost three days to get here," I rambled, cursing myself internally as I awkwardly toyed with the cuffs of his sweater.

"I get it." He leaned against his car, folding his arms across his chest as he studied me.

The blood rushed to my cheeks under his gaze as I asked him a question in return. "So, are you a UCLA student?"

He pointed to the sweater on my chest, where a massive UCLA logo was embroidered. I had to fight not to place my head in my hands.

This was getting worse and worse.

"Soon to be," he added, sparing me from my embarrassment.

"But hey, almost everyone around here is rocking that sweater. Even people that don't go to UCLA. So, it's a valid question." I tried to find some humor in my awkwardness as I picked some imaginary lint off my sleeve. "What will you be studying?"

"History." He surprised me with his response. "But who knows? I'm still undecided on what I want to do in life, if I'm being honest. You?"

"Pre-law." I found some confidence as I spoke. "My goal is to go to Stanford afterwards."

"Stanford, eh?" His voice sounded skeptical, and instantly, I felt offended.

"What's wrong with Stanford?" I questioned defensively.

"Nothing, nothing." He raised both of his hands up with a chuckle. "I'm just not the type that likes planning too far ahead. It's hard to know what the future holds for us. So, I kind of let life come as it will. I mean, I didn't think that I would be boosting a stranger's car tonight. Nor did I imagine giving my sweater to one of the most beautiful girls I've ever seen."

If my cheeks were pink the whole time, they were now, without a doubt, the darkest possible shade of red.

"But here we are." He lifted his hands to the sky lightheartedly. "Sometimes life has a funny way of making things happen."

I shied away with a smile, brushing a strand of hair out of my face as I felt his momentary stare.

"That should've been enough time." He broke the silence and looked down at the watch on his wrist. "Let's see if it worked." He walked back over to his car and ignited the engine. "Give yours a try."

I followed his instructions. As I twisted the keys into the ignition this time, the car's engine roared like it usually did. Well, as much as a hatchback could roar. "Oh my God, you're a lifesaver!" I sighed in relief, a grin spreading across my face. "I really—"

The jingles of a door stopped me mid-sentence as I turned my head to the entrance of the shop, seeing Hallie making her way over to the car. Her brown eyes were fixated on Ambert's unfamiliar face before she shot me a suggestive smirk and pursed her lips in excitement as if to say *who is that?*

Uh oh.

I drew my eyes away from Hallie and back over to Ambert, who had already disconnected the cables from our car, wrapped them up neatly, and tossed them into his backseat. "Well, I'll see you around," he told me, closing the hood and opening his driver's door.

"Wait!" I stopped him. "Don't forget your sweater." I lifted the soft material over my head, taking in the scent of the cologne one last time.

"It's all good. You can keep it. Besides..." Ambert stepped into his car and rolled down his window. "It'll give me an excuse to find you on campus. Good night, Iyla."

As his taillights disappeared into the distance, I couldn't help but feel like I'd just met someone who would do much more in my life than boost my car.

"Two questions..." Hallie finally reached me. "What the hell just happened to my car? But more importantly, who the hell was that?"

"Ambert," I shyly answered the only significant part of her question.

"Hmm..." Her eyes dropped down onto the sweater I was wearing. "What did I tell you?" she handed me my drink. "We've only just arrived, and I've already got a date for tomorrow night, and you've got a guy to catch."

I grabbed the iced coffee from her hand. "Just get in the car. You said you'd be five minutes."

"And it looks like you didn't mind the delay."

The Third Entry

CELESTE

19 YEARS AGO

JUNE 28

Here's a question: if you learned that something significant would happen to you, would you want to know what it was?

If you had asked me before spring break, the answer would've been yes. 100% yes.

Why wouldn't I have wanted to know? If something was going to end badly, I would've gotten myself out of there immediately.

But that's the point, isn't it? I would've left, and this story would've never taken place.

If you were to ask me that same question as I'm writing this entry now, knowing what I know, the answer would be no. Because sometimes the best things in life come unexpectedly.

☆ ☆ ☆

By the time we arrived at Junipero Beach, the sun had started to set. Claire had sought golden hour as the perfect opportunity to snap a million pictures of anything and everything.

"Excuse me?" She stopped a group of men that were walking in the opposite direction of us. "Would you mind taking a picture of us?"

"Claire!" I elbowed her as the group enthusiastically agreed.

"What?" she propped her hands on her hips.

"You couldn't have picked a sketchier group of people?" I subtly cocked my head in the direction of the four boys, all of whom wore ridiculously baggy jeans, white tanks, and some oversized jackets.

"Sorry!" she snickered as she handed them her camera and guided us toward the rails that led up to the beach.

"Alright, let's see a big smile, ladies!" the guys hooted and hollered, holding the camera out in front of them.

As Claire gave them a series of poses to work from, I stood there as if it was picture day—forcing a smile so fake that I knew she would scold me the second she got the photos developed.

"Okay, okay, that's enough!" she said after a moment as she ran back over to the group to retrieve her camera. "You're going to use up all my space."

As a collective, the guys ranged in size and height and weren't unattractive by any means. In fact, it wasn't their appearance that turned me off of them at all. It was the protruding stench of cigarettes and booze.

Claire had always described my taste in men as quite "vanilla." I'll admit, every guy I'd ever liked or dated had been unexciting, dull, and predictable.

But what was wrong with that?

"Why isn't a conventional, average guy enough?" I'd asked her.

Claire had stopped in her tracks and looked me dead in the eyes. "CeCe, let me ask you a question. What was your favorite ice cream flavor when you were a kid?"

Confused yet curious as to where she was going with this, I answered honestly. "Strawberry."

"Okay, gross." Disgust washed over her face. "But I'll continue. What's your favorite flavor now?"

"Strawberry," I repeated the same answer.

43

She smacked her hand against her forehead. "You seriously make it so difficult to be philosophical at times."

"What's your point?" I dared to ask.

"The point is, yeah, when you're a kid, you like stuff that's, you know, simple. But once you taste another flavor, the strawberry becomes boring. You've got to sample different things and see what you like. How will you ever know if you always stick to the same thing?"

"So, what you're saying is that men are like ice cream?" I mocked her with a teasing grin.

"What I'm saying is that you need to switch it up, try something new for once. These goodie-two-shoe guys you go after are clearly not working out."

The term "guys" referred to a small but modest share of men I'd dated or been seeing, where things hadn't worked out. This was partly because in high school, I never did have time to spend with anyone outside of class—nor did I want to invite anyone back to Sharlene's. At that time, the fortitudes of my past had remained unspoken, and I intended to keep it that way. Once I began college, my only love interest was UCLA and my career. An "apathetic love connection," as Claire described it.

In everything I've written so far, it may come across that I'm a dull soul and that Claire is an untameable, wild one at UCLA. One of the two is true. I've always been quite plain, simplistic, and kind of an old woman at heart.

But Claire has always been the relationship type. She's always valued having someone emotionally and intimately available. However, she's also very selective about the guys she dates. One mistake, and they're out of there. She'd always told me that second chances are for boys. Men get it right the first time.

Claire had broken up with her last boyfriend a few months before we'd left for spring break. I was never entirely sure why, but I knew she was pretty upset about it. She'd informed me that the next guy she'd be with would be "Mr. Right."

In other words, every guy was now a potential candidate, including the ones Claire had now opted to break into conversation with. God, I hoped that none of them would pass the test. Not just for my sake but for hers, too.

My prayers were answered a minute later once the group finally headed down the boardwalk and Claire walked back over to me.

"Satisfied now?" I asked.

With her camera in hand and a smile on her face, she scanned through some of the pictures. "Very," she responded smugly.

"Any of them *Mr. Right*?" I pried teasingly, more interested in her recent interactions than the photos.

"Nope." She sighed in defeat. "But they told me about this club they're headed to, and it sounds fun. What do you think? Should we go?"

"A club?" I repeated back to her with a frown. "I don't think so. We only just got here."

She tucked her camera back into her bag. "Good point," she agreed, and for a moment, I was foolish enough to think that she really meant it. "We'll just go tomorrow instead." She guided me down the staircase and towards the party on the beach. "When we look hotter."

☆ ☆ ☆

"Claire!" I tried to shout over the blaring music and astronomically large frat boys that stood in my way. "I need to go take a breather. I'll be right back."

"You're going down, pretty boy!" Claire smirked over to the shirtless guy on her right with rock-hard abs and a backwards baseball cap.

"Oh yeah?" he heckled her back as the countdown to what appeared to be a shotgun competition kicked off. "We'll see about

That."

"Three...two...one...go!"

It took Claire a few seconds to down the contents of the liquid before she lifted the empty can into the air, forcing the crowd to erupt in cheers and applause. "Ha-ha!" She threw the can into the sand and twirled around as the crowd continued to egg her on.

"Claire!" I attempted once more. "Claire? Can you hear me?"

Her eyes finally found mine in the crowd despite her drunken state. "Yeah...okay." She nodded. "Go, be free!" She caught the attention of onlookers as she casually pulled off her shirt, revealing the bikini top she'd so conveniently worn underneath.

"Claire! Claire! Claire!" I heard everyone chant as I made my way back up the steps. A few hours of partying, loud music and drunken adults was all it took for me to become desperate enough to break away from it all.

A yawn escaped my mouth, reminding me it was far beyond my bedtime.

Bedtime?

Gosh, I'm embarrassed even writing that down.

After a few minutes of solitude, I stood up and brushed off some sand that clung to my skirt. By now, the boardwalk was quiet. Everyone had either found refuge inside one of the bars or joined the party below.

The cool ocean breeze washed over my body, reminding me of the sense of peace that California had always offered me. It was a peace that I'd never known before.

"Shut up. You're the idiot that got us kicked out," an aggravated voice called out, pulling me out of my thoughts.

"Me?! It wasn't my fault! It was *his* fault," another voice called out combatively, causing me to turn my head towards a group of men, all of whom were pointing fingers at one another.

"It was Jerry."

"No, it was Stevie!"

"It was all of us, idiots!" one of them finally shouted. As I got a closer look, the group's familiarity suddenly struck me. This was the same group of guys from earlier—the ones who had snapped the pictures of Claire and me. Now, they were extraordinarily drunk and causing a great deal of chaos.

The words "Club Affinity" illuminated the space above their heads. I guessed this was the club they'd mentioned to Claire earlier.

"You know what?" one of them snapped. "Fuck that guy. We're going back inside." He gestured towards the entrance.

From afar, their interactions with one another looked like a sad attempt at a high school pep rally— if the crowd was a bunch of sweaty middle-aged men and not a group of underclassmen.

"I told you all to get the fuck moving. Don't make me tell you again." A tall frame dressed in all black suddenly blocked the group from taking another step inside.

"Ah, c'mon, Z man." One of them drunkenly smacked his chest as I winced in response. "We were only just having some fun. We won't cause you any more trouble."

Before I knew it, the mysterious frame had pushed the man's hand off his chest and pinned him to the floor. I couldn't help but gasp as their bodies made contact with the concrete below. I knew the man, seemingly the club's security guard, would retaliate. Still, I didn't think he'd be able to displace the guy so quickly. So swiftly. So effortlessly.

My hand stayed glued over my mouth as "Z-man" momentarily peered his head up and spotted my frame along the boardwalk.

I promptly turned the other way and pretended I hadn't seen everything that had just transpired.

At this point, a normal person might've walked away or, better yet, re-joined the party. But I, a not-so-normal person, allowed compulsion to take over and turned back around just a moment later, intrigued by what would happen next.

47

"Now, get the fuck out of here," Z-man snarled as he brought the man back up and onto his feet. "And don't ever think about coming back." He pushed him into his group of friends.

Fearful, the group caught their buddy and scurried down the opposite end of the boardwalk. As they disappeared out of range, I finally caught a proper look at "Z man." I assumed that nickname insinuated that his name started with a Z.

His piercing green eyes were full of curiosity as he peered over at me for a second time—unlike the rest of his face, which possessed a deep-rooted sense of anger. His brows furrowed as he tilted his head to get what I assumed was a better look at me. His dark locks cascaded down his forehead and over his ear, casting a shadow over his face that sent a shiver down my spine.

His all- black ensemble made him difficult to make out, yet his biceps and tan skin were incredibly hard to miss. I stared at them for a brief second, taking in how he'd effortlessly slammed an easily 250-pound guy to the floor. That alone should've scared me and caused me to turn back towards the party, but instead, I found myself returning his intent gaze and yearning to be closer to him.

Who was this man?

And why was he making me feel this way?

The questions raced through my mind as someone shouted my name from behind me.

"CeCe!" I forced myself to look away as Claire's drunken frame dragged its way over. "Oh, CeCe." She pulled me into an adoring hug, the smell of booze filling my senses. "Do you know how much I love you?"

Despite my frustration at her less-than-impeccable timing, I accepted her into my arms.

"Woah." She stumbled, making my grip tighten on either side of her shoulders as I helped her to regain her balance.

"Easy now," I spoke softly. "Let's get you back to the hotel and into bed."

To You, Jyla

"But I don't want to go to the hotel," she whined in objection. "I want to get another drink."

I securely wrapped one arm around her waist and another over her shoulder. "I think you've had more than enough tonight."

I peeked over my shoulder towards Club Affinity one last time, noticing that the mystery man had disappeared inside.

"This has been a night to remember, don't you think?" Claire asked, slurring her words as she spoke.

"That it has," I told her as we continued walking, unaware of how true those words would soon come to be. "That it has."

CHAPTER FOUR

I Y L A

PRESENT DAY

As a little girl, I was confident I'd never get sick of fruity cereal. I mean, how could I? I craved it day and night, night and day. I loved it so much that for four months straight, I ate fruity cereal with my breakfast, lunch and dinner.

Waffles and bacon? Add a bowl of cereal.

Peanut butter and jelly sandwich? You bet I'll have cereal.

I liked to call myself dedicated, but that meant "stubborn" in my parent's world.

It wasn't until I woke up one day and suddenly became repulsed by the smell and the taste of fruity cereal overnight that the high finally burnt out.

The same feeling now transpired when I thought about coffee. I never thought I'd get sick of it, but thanks to Hallie, I was on the verge of quitting. In the week since we'd arrived in California, Hallie and I had been to Tim and Sally's every morning.

Hallie insisted it was because they had the best caramel macchiato she'd ever tasted. But I think we both knew the real reason was that it was a perfect excuse to see Vic, whom she'd gone out with almost every night that week. The two had immediately become inseparable.

Hallie encouraged me to join them each night, but truthfully, I didn't mind being alone. I had a list of items I wanted to check off my to-do list, and being the third wheel was definitely not one of them.

It was nice to have some quiet time to read, relax, write, and *think* for once. Most definitely think. My thoughts were consumed with the realization that after 19 years, I was in the exact same place as my mother, writing a new chapter in my life.

But there was another recurring thought that I couldn't seem to shake.

Ambert.

Our brief interaction still lingered in my mind during everything I did. His voice. His body. His smile.

Holy shit, his smile.

As embarrassing as it was, each night after Hallie would leave, I'd somehow manage to find myself back in Ambert's sweater. I sought the comfort that such a simple piece of clothing brought to my heart.

To my surprise, Hallie hadn't addressed my interaction with Ambert that first night. I attributed that to her already all-consuming schedule with Vic—not to mention that I'd remained virtually silent about it.

All it took was for Hallie to catch me sound asleep on my bed with Ambert's sweater on for me to realize I wasn't nearly as sleek as I thought.

"So, are you going to tell me what happened?" She shook me awake.

Confused and still half-asleep, I furrowed my brows and rubbed my eyes tiredly. "What happened?' What do you mean 'what happened'?"

"You know..." She bounced onto my bed and propped up on her elbows, her hands pressed on either side of her face eagerly. "The night we arrived. Who was that guy talking to you outside the car?"

I sighed, accepting the fact that there was no way I would get out of this situation easily. Lying wasn't an option, considering she'd instantly know. I'd always been a terrible liar and apparently an even worse secret keeper, because all it took for me to divulge everything to Hallie was one more raised eyebrow.

"Oh, Iy..." She sat up on my bed after I'd told her everything. "You've got it bad."

"I do not," I objected, pushing aside her comment and sheepishly tucking my hands deeper into the sleeve of Ambert's sweater.

"Oh, yes, you do. And you know what? I know just the thing to do!"

"No, please," I pleaded with her, terrified of what "just the thing" meant in Hallie's world.

"A double date!" She stood up and worked her way toward our drawers. "You said Vic knows Ambert, right? So, let's ask him if he's down for a double date. It'll be perfect." She beamed from ear to ear.

Perfect was not the exact word that came to my mind as she explained the plan. *Stressful* was. I threw my pillow over my face—suffocation sounded much more appealing than continuing with this conversation.

"Better yet," she continued, leaping back onto the bed. "Let's invite them out for your birthday tomorrow night."

I whipped the pillow off my face. "No way!" I exclaimed hysterically. "A double date is awkward enough, not to mention it being on my birthday. I will not allow it," I shook my head, desperate to stand my ground.

"Don't be a party pooper!" She ignored my objections, holding up a black dress that she carefully rested on her lap. "This dress would look amazing on you. And you know how much you *love* dresses."

"Nope." I pulled the dress out of her hands and tossed it across the room. "There's no chance."

"Well, too bad you're not planning the party." She shrugged, picking the dress up from the floor.

"Please, Hallie," I begged. "I don't know if I'm ready to get back into the dating world." The sentence prompted unpleasant memories of my last relationship to come rushing back.

Dalton Abrams.

The guy who decided that starting a new relationship with someone else behind my back was more manageable than ending things between the two of us.

We broke up more than six months ago, but the thought of giving my heart to someone else already felt far too daunting. With Dalton, I'd finally trusted to take things all the way, only for it to have all fallen apart.

"Don't you remind me of that dumbass." Hallie's brows creased in unison, playing on the fact that Dalton Abrams stood for 'dumb ass' in the book of Hallie.

"I'll never speak of his name again." I sealed my lips. "But that's beside the point. I don't even know if I like Ambert that much. I hardly know him."

"The fact that you haven't taken that sweater off in over a week tells me otherwise," Hallie remarked as the heat immediately soared to my cheeks.

Did she know the entire time?

"Really, you should be thanking me. This will give you a chance to get to know him better." She dug through one of her suitcases—the one she'd continually put off unpacking.

"Hallie, I really don't think this is a good idea."

"Please, Iy?" She looked over at me, pleading with that doe-eyed look she'd perfected. "Please let your best friend plan your birthday party. You know it's the least I can do, considering you gave me the most epic party ever. Plus, it's the last day of August. The summer is coming to an end," she added. "Consider this a birthday-slash-end-of-the-summer-solstice."

"Isn't a solstice in the middle of s—"

"Can you just trust me, please?" she persisted, pulling items out of her suitcase one by one.

"What are you even looking for anyway?" I asked, avoiding her request.

"I have this light blue dress, it's strapless, and it would be perfect for tomorrow night, but I can't seem to find it... aha!" she exclaimed as she finally pulled out the dress she'd been describing.

"Here it is. Isn't it perfect?" she waved it in front of me excitedly.

I stubbornly agreed and took the blue dress from her hand. "Fine, but this is only because I've always wanted to wear this."

"Blue is your color."

"Yeah..." Hallie tightened her upper lip to hide a smile. "I'm sure that's the only reason."

✩ ✰ ✫

"Happy birthday, Iyla!"

I squinted my eyes open and was met with a phone screen in front of my face displaying both of my parents on a video call. "Huh?"

"Sorry!" Hallie appeared as the culprit. "They wanted to talk before they left for work."

"Happy birthday, Iyla!" my mom cheered. "August thirty-first was the best day of our lives. The day that the world brought us you." She leaned against my dad, who nodded in agreement.

It felt bittersweet to see their faces on the screen, knowing that this would be the first birthday in my lifetime that I wouldn't spend with them.

My parents hadn't known of my existence until the weeks that led up to my hospital discharge in late December. Yet, despite their initial absence, they'd always managed to make up for it with two special celebrations each year.

One on August 31, my actual birthday, and another on December 22—the day I was discharged from the hospital. My 'gotcha day', as my dad would say.

"I'm going to grab us some breakfast. I'll be back." Hallie handed me her phone before skipping out of the room as I conversed with my parents, taking the time to enlighten them on everything Hallie and I had managed to do over the past week, minus the Ambert and Vic part.

Our conversation lasted about half an hour before my dad finally spoke up. "Shoot, look at the time. Listen, sweetie, we both have got to get to work, but have a great day, okay?"

"We miss you, Iyla bear," my mom followed up with a smile, her use of my childhood nickname bringing a smile to my face too.

"I miss you both, too." I waved goodbye as Hallie re-entered the room and tossed me a muffin.

"It's not quite the best birthday breakfast." She sat across from me. "But it's the best they had."

"Goodie," I joked as I peeled back the wrapper and sunk my teeth into the still-warm blueberry muffin.

"So," Hallie spoke back up. "How would you feel if Vic joined in on our birthday festivities? He mentioned a fair about thirty minutes away. What do you think?"

"Sure, I don't see why not," I responded. Despite my not-so-impressive first impression of Vic, I'd begun to warm up to him, given how happy he made Hallie. "A fair sounds like fun," I pondered, bringing the orange juice to my lips.

"Well, I'm happy to hear you say that. I'd already told Vic we'd be good to go. And that you're excited to see Ambert again."

I choked on my orange juice. "What?"

Did she just say Ambert was coming?

"That's right. *Loverboy* will be there."

"Are you serious?!" I spat out. "I didn't think he would actually

55

want to go."

"Well, let's just say it didn't take much convincing on Vic's end. Someone really wanted to see you." She gleamed. "So, finish up that muffin and start getting ready."

"I'm certain you're trying to kill me." I chaotically grabbed items around the room so I could run to the communal shower.

"You'll think otherwise tonight!" Hallie called out as I slammed the door shut behind me.

The Fourth Entry

CELESTE

19 YEARS AGO

JULY 1

As a result of the theatrics the night before, Claire and I didn't wake up till mid-afternoon the next day.

When I eventually got out of bed, my throat felt hoarse, prompting me to go to the mini fridge and grab a drink. As the fridge door closed shut, Claire rustled awake.

"Morning." She stretched her arms into the air.

"Morning," I mumbled in response. "Ibuprofen?" I gestured, reaching for the walking pharmacy I had in my bag.

"No, thanks." She hopped out of bed, completely refreshed and wide awake. "I feel good. Wasn't last night great? Wait, don't answer that." She beat me to a response I wasn't going to give anyway. "Because tonight will be even better."

"Tonight?" I questioned, acting utterly oblivious to her plan to go to Club Affinity. It amazed me how, only a few hours earlier, Claire was on the beach partying the night away—and now here she was, already in planning mode for night two.

"Club Affinity will be a blast." She walked over to the mini fridge, reaching for water herself. "Don't you think?"

Had it not been for my curiosity outweighing the sensibility in my mind, I immediately would've against going to the club. Club Affinity clearly wasn't the place that attracted the most respectable men, let alone the safest crowd. What I'd seen the night before confirmed that. Yet, desire conquered decision as I blurted out, "I'm sure it will be fun."

"Well, I'm glad you feel that way." She didn't seem to question my sudden shift as she smiled through a sip of her water. "Because tonight, I'm going to do your hair and makeup and choose your outfit. I want everything to go just right. It's your first time going to a club, after all."

I would've disregarded her demand if Claire wasn't so highly talented in beauty and fashion. But I knew I could trust that she'd make me look perfect—something that I wanted to be for the first time in my life.

"Now then..." She marched over to my suitcase. "Let's start with your outfit. What did you bring?"

"Um," I stuttered, "you might not want to go through that."

"Celeste." Her face sunk in defeat as she pushed my few articles of clothing to the side. "*Where* is all of your stuff?"

I cringed at the fact that the sabotaging I'd done was now finally coming back to bite me in the butt, the opposite of what I intended for it to do.

"You know what?" She closed my suitcase as she walked over to her own. "Forget about it. You can wear one of my many options instead." She held a white satin dress with a small side slit and cowl neck in front of my body. "It might be a bit big on you, but we'll make it work. Now..." She carefully placed the dress to the side before bringing her entire supply of hair appliances and makeup products onto the bed. "Let's get started."

✮ ✰ ✩

Claire added some final touches to my face as the afternoon turned into the evening, swiping a makeup brush along my cheek. "And you...are...done. Oh, my goodness!" she pulled back, an interesting look falling over her face.

"What?" I questioned, worried if her look meant she was genuinely excited or trying to convince me that I didn't look like a hot mess.

"Celeste, I mean this in the nicest way possible," she paused. "You've never looked better."

I felt relief wash over me as she excitedly collected her makeup items from the bed and placed them back into her bag.

"Well, I've never had a stylist before. So, I'm honored. But go." I nudged her towards the bathroom. "You've spent hours helping me get ready. Now it's your turn."

"Fine, fine." She gathered her outfit. "I'll be in here if you need anything," she called out before disappearing inside the bathroom.

Once she closed the door, I finally built up enough courage to make my way over to the mirror. As I looked up, I hardly recognized the person staring back at me in the reflection.

Claire had given my freshly washed hair a blowout, leaving me with more volume than I'd ever had in my life. With her master bag of makeup, she'd given my "au natural" makeup look a total run for its money.

Who was this girl? I couldn't help but wonder, all the while questioning if a certain *someone* at the club that night would be asking the same thing.

Claire re-emerged from the bathroom an hour later, strutting like a supermodel on her way out. "So, what do you think?" she grinned, holding her arms out as she showed me her look. "And be nice. I'm sensitive."

Her outfit was the perfect mixture of sleek and sexy. A matching black top and skirt set exposed her toned abdomen and part of her collarbone. Her dark blue eyes popped with her bold blue eyeshadow as her now pin-straight hair cascaded down her back.

"You look incredible," I responded with a smile, placing my hands on my own non-existent hips. "Seriously, you look like a model."

"Oh, stop!" she giggled and shook her head. "But no, keep going, please," she added playfully before pulling me in to stand beside her so we both fit in front of the mirror's width. "We look like Charlie's Angels." She interlaced her fingers into a gun-like shape in front of me.

"Not quite." I shook my head with a laugh as I pushed her hand away.

"Fine...Long Beach angels." She tried as she reached for her bag on top of the dresser. "Are you ready?"

"As I'll ever be."

✧ ☆ ✩

"Thank you, sir!" Claire handed a five-dollar bill to the taxi driver and slammed the door shut behind her.

"Was that ride really necessary?" I asked. We easily could've walked to the Club Affinity rather than taking a five-minute taxi ride up the street.

"I didn't want my hair to frizz up." She shrugged as she clutched onto my arm and we joined the long line toget inside. "Besides, we need to preserve our energy. We have a long night ahead of us."

I smiled timidly as the pounding bass of the music from inside the club intensified with each step toward the door. If this was how loud it was on the outside, what would it be like once we finally made it in?

"Make sure you have your ID out and ready to go," Claire informed me once there were only a few people in line ahead of us.

I reached for my side for my purse and was met with reality

instead. "Shoot," I muttered. "I don't...I don't have it. I must've left it at the hotel."

Claire looked over at me, her expression surprisingly calm. "Let's just try without it, then."

I shook my head, immediately apprehensive of the plan. "I don't want to get in trouble," I whispered as we approached the front.

"It'll be fine, CeCe," she reassured me. "I'll handle it. Just act cool and...hi there! How are you tonight?" Her tone shifted as we reached the front of the line and were met with the bouncer, to whom Claire handed her ID card.

My heart rate quickened by the second when no response followed, which prompted me to sheepishly lift my head to the bouncer's face.

It was *him*.

I didn't need a second glance to recognize those familiar green eyes.

What was he doing here?

God, what a stupid question. The guy worked at the club, for Christ's sake. What did I expect?

He ignored Claire's greeting and reached for her card as I dissected his height.

He must've easily been six foot three, maybe even four. He made Claire, a five-foot-nine girl, appear petite. That left my measly five-foot-four stature to feel like I was looking up at a skyscraper.

His eyes carefully scanned over the card as he glanced up at Claire every so often to match her face to the picture. While he did so, Claire began rhyming off about my lack of ID. She promised him we were both 22—already a year past the legal drinking age.

He remained stern as he peered around her frame, which had been blocking me from his line of vision. Without any doubt, immediately, I knew he recognized me. Even through his pissed-off facial expression, I could see him recap our momentary encounter in his eyes—something I'd been doing on repeat all day.

For a second, I was confident that he would tell us both to get lost. And that I was being ridiculous by reading so much into a momentary encounter that probably had no deeper meaning, despite how badly I wanted it to.

"You can go through." He handed Claire her card back, surprising me with his words. His voice.

"Thank you so much." She quickly secured my arm as his eyes made their way to mine.

Life seemed to slow down for a split second, allowing me to intricately assess each diminutive body movement. His stern yet complex gaze. His refined jawline that cut me to my core, and a look that said, *"uncover me. I've been waiting to be uncovered."*

"C'mon." Claire pulled me in, forcing me to break my stare away from his. "Let's go and find somewhere to sit."

I clung to her side as we walked through the crowded entrance and eventually reached a booth on the opposite side—just high enough for us to have a complete view of the club.

"This will do!" she announced cheerily as she sat down and adjusted her purse in her lap.

I rested my head against the leather, already feeling exhausted from the adrenaline pumping through my veins during that brief interaction with...

"Since you forgot your purse, it looks like drinks are on me tonight," Claire teased with a snicker. "What do you want? I'm getting a strawberry daiquiri and a shot."

"Make it two," I shouted as she got up and started to head toward the bar.

"What did you say?" she screamed back over the terrible—no deafeningly loud—music that only seemed to intensify by the second.

"I'll. Have. The. Same," I responded as loudly and enunciated as I possibly could.

"Okay!" she seemed to understand this time, turning to dance her way over to the bar.

Once she was out of sight, I was forced to finally observe my surroundings. The club itself was much nicer on the inside than it appeared on the outside. The total opposite of our hotel. The lighting was minimal, meaning the only way you could see anyone was through the flashing strobe and red laser lights hanging over the top of the dance floor.

Inside the club was a broad mixture of people like Claire and me, most in their mid-twenties. But others appeared to be middle-aged regulars. Those who seemed familiar with the club and their general surroundings.

Still, despite my slight comfortability with what I'd seen so far, I couldn't help but mentally map out all the escape routes that the club had to offer. As I scanned the ground floor below me, I caught sight of a large group of men stalking through the back door, each of whom possessed a sense of arrogance and rage that I could sense from my seat. The *I don't give a fuck*, and *you better not look at me the wrong way or else* kind of attitude.

Three core members were left observing the space around them as the group dispersed throughout the club. They each wore a black leather jacket, dark wash jeans, and a considerable scowl.

One member, in particular, stood out, sporting icy white-blonde hair and a thick gold chain that hung around his neck. He clenched his fists, took off his jacket, and tossed it to the guy on his left.

Visibly, he was shorter than the average man, but that didn't seem to phase him as he pushed his way through the crowd, making it abundantly clear that he didn't give two shits about anyone else.

Napoleon syndrome, I couldn't help but think.

A feeling of nervousness formed in my chest, one that I desperately tried to push toward the back of my mind. Claire and I had gone to the club to have fun, not stress about some random guy.

I broke my gaze away from him, seeking comfort in the fact that the club's bouncers were clearly well-trained. What I'd seen last night with the now not-so-mystery man made that evident.

Where was he, anyway? I wondered, attempting to seek out his whereabouts as a way to calm my escalating thoughts. I didn't spot him by the entrance anymore. As I looked through what must've been hundreds upon hundreds of people inside that club, I became doubtful that I'd find him—until all of a sudden, the strobing lights illuminated his frame as he hovered above the dance floor.

"Here you go." My attention fell back onto Claire as she came back to our seats, balancing two mixed drinks and two shots of what I assumed was tequila in her hands.

"Thanks." I smiled gratefully as she placed the items on the table and handed me a slice of lime, confirming my assumption.

"Let's start with the shot." She grabbed the saltshaker off the table and sprinkled it onto her hand before doing the same for me. "Should I make a toast?"

I nodded my head with some reluctance. You never know what to expect from a Claire O'Donnell toast.

"Here's to a night full of fun with my best friend in the entire world." She raised her shot glass into the air and prompted me to do the same. "Plus," she paused. "Please, Lord, send me my husband tonight."

"What?" I couldn't hold back my laughter. "How did this turn into a prayer?"

"Amen." She ignored my question, licked the salt off her hand, and downed the shot.

I followed suit, the burning sensation from the alcohol cascading down my throat as I, too, reached for the lime for some relief.

"Here." Claire slid the cocktail in front of me. "Try this."

I pulled the lime out of my mouth and reluctantly took a sip. "Holy smokes." I contemplated spitting out whatever this dreadful concoction was. "This is strong. Aren't cocktails only supposed to have like...I don't know...two ounces?"

She smirked, sipping on it as if it was just a glass of water. "The bartender liked me. He said he'd give our drinks an extra kick."

"More like a stomp down the throat," I winced.

"Oh, don't be a baby." She slid the drink closer to me. "The party has only just begun."

CHAPTER FIVE

I Y L A

PRESENT DAY

"Hallie! You said we were going to 'some fair.' Not the Santa Monica Pier!" I squealed in excitement as I realized where Vic had been driving us this entire time.

I couldn't believe it. Visiting the Santa Monica Pier had always been one of the top things I'd wanted to do in California—not to mention one of the top ten 'musts' on my bucket list.

"Happy birthday!" Hallie cheered ecstatically, pulling me in for a hug.

"Hallie, you're the best. Did you know that?" I grinned, quickly unbuckling my seatbelt and peeling myself out of the car before fluffing out my baby blue dress.

"Oh, I know," she said proudly. "I know."

I looked around at our surroundings excitedly, playing with the hair tie on my wrist that I'd brought just in case I was forced on any rides.

Now, I know what you might be thinking.

How was the Santa Monica Pier one of my bucket list items if I didn't enjoy rides? Well, here's the thing: it wasn't the rides I was opposed to. It was the horrible motion sickness I'd developed after turning 13. But I didn't want that to be what stopped me from having fun. I'd made sure to load up on my anti-nausea pills and brace myself for the occasional ride, especially if it was something Ambert wanted to do.

As Hallie and Vic stepped out of the car, we began our trek toward the entrance. The sun had now just started to set, and the light that reflected over the ocean was to die for.

Even amidst the breathtaking scenery, I grew increasingly anxious as I remembered that Ambert was waiting for us at the front.

Why did I feel so nervous?

Just be calm and be yourself. I kept repeating internally as Hallie looked back over her shoulder and noticed me trailing behind, the gap between us growing by the second.

"I'll be right back," she said to Vic before she jogged her way back to me. "Hey, are you okay?"

I hugged myself in comfort, attempting to downplay how stressed beyond belief I felt. "Just nervous, that's all."

She immediately stopped walking, forcing me to halt and look over at her. "Don't be nervous, Iyla. You're amazing. You look incredible, and you've got that birthday glow. So please, don't doubt yourself for another moment. If Ambert can't see how incredible you are, then screw him. Although..." I noticed a smile playing on her lips as she peered back over her shoulder, nodding at Vic, who had finally reached Ambert. The two of them were glancing in our direction as they spoke to one another. "I don't think you need to worry about him not liking you."

I gave her a smile and, as convincing of a nod as I could muster, linking my arm in hers as we continued to walk toward the two of them. "If you want to leave at all, just let me know," Hallie reminded me. "Okay?"

"Okay." I nodded as we grew closer.

"Ugh, how good do they look?!" Hallie groaned, throwing her head back in disbelief.

I anxiously agreed, my eyes finding their way solely to Ambert, who looked even better than the last time I'd seen him. How was that even possible?

Unlike our first encounter at Tim and Sally's, I could now tell that Ambert had styled the dark blonde waves that fell against his forehead. A form-fitting baseball tee contrasted with his loose black joggers. Clearly, that was an element of his signature style.

"Ambert..." Vic gestured toward me as we finally reached the two of them. "You remember Iyla, right? And this is her best friend and my girlfriend, Hallie." He planted a kiss on her cheek.

"Girlfriend?" She glanced up at him, eyebrows raised. "I don't remember you asking me."

The smile on his face dropped, almost as if he feared he'd said the wrong thing. "I...uh..." he stammered, his cheeks turning bright pink before Hallie broke into a playful grin.

"Oh, you're fun to mess with," she said through her laughter before leaning up to kiss him on the cheek. "Good thing I *want* you to be my boyfriend."

Vic's face broke into a relieved smirk as he pulled her into a full-on kiss, leaving Ambert and me to exchange an awkward glance.

"Okay, you two, get a room," Ambert finally shouted out with a laugh, his voice prompting them to pull away as he found his way to my side. "Shall we?" he asked, gesturing to the entrance.

I nodded, allowing him to lead the way as Vic and Hallie trailed behind.

"Happy birthday, by the way." He leaned down to speak in my ear, his breath against my skin sending goosebumps down my arms. "How has it been so far?"

"Thanks," I bluntly responded. "It's been good."

Gosh, why can't I speak to his guy?

"Good," he replied with a smile while I silently cursed myself for my impeccable ability to forget my entire vocabulary whenever he was around. "By the way, is your car still working okay?"

"Oh, yeah!" I fired back a bit too enthusiastically. "Thank you again for that. You really did save my butt that day."

"It's the least I could do." His blue eyes did that thing again. The thing where he stared at me, and suddenly, everything else wholly disappeared. "I heard this is your first time at the Pier. What do you think so far?"

I let out a breath of air. "Honestly, it's a dream. Let's just say the annual fairs in Columbus are no match for even a quarter of what this pier offers. I'm assuming this isn't your first time here."

He chuckled. "That would be correct. This might be my, oh, I don't know, hundredth time here, maybe even more."

"Hundredth?" My eyes widened.

He nodded. "My parents brought my sister and me here every weekend. Perks of growing up in California, I guess."

"I can't imagine what it would've been like growing up here. You do know you were living my dream, right?" I laughed, my shoulders relaxing as the conversation started to flow more naturally.

"I mean, California definitely has its perks, I'll admit it. Lots of sunshine, beautiful scenery, and endless things to do. But there are cons everywhere."

"I guess." I tried to agree—although I couldn't deny the fact that winter in California beat Ohio any day in my eyes.

"So, Columbus, Ohio, eh? What's a buckeye like you doing all the way out here?"

"Buckeye?" I immediately felt a massive smile forming on my face, causing me to place a hand over my mouth in an attempt to hide it.

"Hey!" He pulled my hand back in laughter. "I did my research. Does Ohioan sound better instead?"

"I'm guessing you've never been to Ohio?" I poked fun at him.

"Nope. I've never been out of the West coast in my life."

"Hey, guys!" Vic called out from behind us as he pointed to a rollercoaster just ahead. "Let's go on that."

"I'm in!" Ambert stopped mid-response and made his way towards the line while I stopped dead in my tracks at the sight of the coaster's height.

"Hey, you coming?" Ambert glanced over his shoulder at me and reached out his hand, seemingly noticing the hesitation all over my face.

I swallowed and nodded, finally accepting his hand as I followed him into the line. "The Super Coaster..." I read the sign that hung above us, more fixated on the terrified shrieks sounding off of the ride than the fact that our fingers were intertwined.

"Yeah, it's a blast." Ambert beamed. "Don't worry. You'll love it." A gentle squeeze of his hand sent a rush of reassurance through me.

Hallie's gaze traveled down to our hands as she shot me a look. "Stop," I mouthed to her, causing her to look away, her signature smirk still tugging at her lips.

"Next," the ride operator called out, gesturing to the four of us as we climbed onto the coaster platform and secured our seats.

"Are you ready?" Ambert smiled over at me as he clicked his seatbelt on.

I gave him a weak smile back as I did the same. As we waited for the ride to start, I couldn't help but debate what the real rollercoaster was—the one I was sitting on, or the journey I was about to begin with the boy next to me.

The Fifth Entry

C E L E S T E

19 YEARS AGO

JULY 5

Here's the thing about my relationship with alcohol. After learning of my mother's struggles with the substance, I made a vow at 13 that I would never drink. I soon realized it wasn't the most rational or reasonable decision for a teenager to make.

Blaming alcohol for my family breaking apart was wrong. It wasn't the alcohol at all. It was my mom's dependency on the substance, in combination with my dad's abuse. The two together were why I'd ended up in the situation that I was in. Alcohol didn't equal the downfall of what had occurred in my life—in moderation, alcohol can actually be a part of life's greatest pleasures.

After I came to that profound conclusion, I knew I needed to develop my own ideation of the substance—one that wasn't based on someone else's harmful and detrimental usage. An opinion that would be solely based on me and only me.

When I turned 21, I allowed myself a chance to see what drinking was all about. Yes, I waited until I was legal. There's that sense of conventionalism I'd grown to equally love and hate about myself over time.

On the night of my twenty-first birthday, Claire and I went to the local bar off-campus, where we tried a mixture of cocktails, and I made my first mistake of mixing too many spirits at once. Let's just say the unique combination led to an exciting night by the toilet and a mega hangover the next day. Since then, I could easily list off all of the times that I'd drank on one hand alone.

My twenty-first birthday.

The end of my third year at UCLA.

Claire's birthday.

The party on the beach.

And tonight, at Club Affinity.

Not only were my exposure and tolerance levels to alcohol still in their early stages, but so was my comfort with being drunk.

It had only been an hour since we'd arrived at Club Affinity, and I'd already downed two more shots and another cocktail. By now, the alcohol had more than kicked into my system. The music had started to sound better, my mind started to feel less cluttered, and my mood lifted with each second that passed.

Claire, who noticed that the alcohol had started working its wonders on me, grabbed my hands and pulled me towards the dance floor. "Let's party!" she cheered as the two of us moved to the music.

For the first time in a while, I felt free. Young. Happy.

Yet, even through my drunken haze, I noticed him peering across the club, quickly pulling me out of my carefree mood.

How long had he been watching me?

Why was he watching me?

Had he been looking for me the same way I had been looking for him?

I forced myself to pull away from his enticing gaze, turning to face Claire and instead being met by a sea of unfamiliar bodies. To my surprise, she was no longer on the dance floor. She was off to the side, conversing with a man I could immediately tell she liked. Claire had her tells—one of which was twirling her hair with her fingers, something she did when a potential bachelor passed her first few screening phases.

As I made my way across the dance floor towards her, a pair of unsuspecting hands found their way to my waist, catching me by surprise.

"Holy shit." I caught the first few slurred words of a sticky jock that mimicked every other drunken frat boy at the club. "You're hot, little lady."

I awkwardly smiled at him, a big mistake that only invited him further as he leaned down to whisper into my ear. "Are you having a good time tonight?" he murmured, the smell of booze radiating from his breath. "If not, I'd be happy to show you one."

Even in my drunken state, his words left me less interested than I already had been. If anything, they made me realize I was not nearly drunk enough for some stranger to dance up on me—let alone have him foreplay my ears.

"I'm going to get a drink." I ignored his invitation.

"Let me get you one," he quickly retaliated, placing a hand on my wrist.

"I'm not interested," I responded curtly, brushing him off and marching my way over to the bar before Claire stopped me in my tracks.

I sneaked a quick glance over my shoulder to make sure the man wasn't following, and much to my relief, the swarm of people dancing in the club seemed to have swallowed him again. I breathed out a sigh before looking back over at Claire.

"CeCe, meet Korey," she chattered excitedly as she grabbed my hand and pulled me over to the side of the bar. "We've been talking for a bit. He works just outside of Westwood."

"Nice to meet you, Korey. I'm Celeste." I automatically reached out to shake his hand, immediately regretting my formality. We were in a club, not a law office.

"Nice to meet you, Celeste." His smile was warm as he shook my hand in return. "Claire tells me you guys are out here for spring break."

Not against my will, I wanted to say, but opted for a simple "that we are" instead.

"We're trying to have some fun before we finish out the rest of our final semester," Claire chimed in giddily.

"Do you go to school here, Korey?" I probed, curious to know more about whom exactly my best friend was talking to.

He shook his head before bringing his beer bottle to his lips. "I'm apprenticing under this auto repair shop. The guy who owns the shop is almost at retirement. I'm hoping he can train me so I can scoop right in and take over when he leaves."

"That's impressive," Claire gushed, placing a flirty hand on his bicep. He clearly seemed to embrace her touch.

"Hey, Celeste?" Korey caught my attention after finally ripping his gaze from Claire. "Do you happen to know Zeke?"

"Zeke?" I questioned, my brows furrowing in confusion as I tried to put a face to the name.

Korey lifted his arm and tilted his beer bottle to gesture to the top of the stairs. I followed his bottle top as my eyes reconnected with the only man it could possibly be.

Him.

Now, I could finally stop calling him that mystery guy. Z-man. All the other things I'd diverted to besides his actual name.

Zeke.

Korey waved his arm erratically, prompting Zeke to nod in his direction before another bouncer walked toward him.

"I don't know who he is," I responded, so bluntly and apprehensively that it almost came off as suspicious. "Why? Did he say something to you?"

"No, no." He shook his head, calming my strangely anxious mind. "He's just been looking over at you the entire time we've been talking. I thought he might've known who you were or something."

I bit down on my lower lip subconsciously. "How do you know him?"

"Zeke? He's worked here for years. I always come here on the weekends. We've just gotten to know one another over time."

Claire seemed thrilled that Zeke had taken a potential interest in me. "You should go over and talk to him!" she urged me enthusiastically in a blatant attempt to continue her quest to break up my love affair with UCLA.

"I don't know." Korey took another sip of his beer as he glanced back over at where Zeke had been standing. "Zeke's not the talkative type."

Claire shot me a look as if to say, *who cares? Go talk to him.*

"You know what?" I cleared my throat awkwardly, desperate to move on with the night before Claire marched me over to Zeke herself. "I think I'm going to get myself another drink. But it was nice meeting you, Korey. Claire, I'll find you in a bit." I was already moving away before I had to see the disappointment grow any more on her face.

I pushed myself through the crowd until I eventually reached the bar. "A fireball, please," I shouted to the bartender above the noise.

He analyzed my face almost as if he'd recognized me. "Sorry, babe," he paused and pretended to clean a spotless countertop. "You've been cut off."

"Cut off?" my mouth fell open in shock. "What do you mean, 'cut off'?"

"Special orders, hon. I can't give you anything else tonight," he responded, his eyes shifting to land on someone behind me. I followed his glance, my eyes landing on Zeke, who was preoccupied with a conversation.

"You," I whispered under my breath, a rush of energy carrying me over to confront him. "Hey, who do you think you are?!" I called out as I finally reached him.

He reacted by glancing over at me, seemingly unphased by my outburst as he shooed away the guy on his side. "Excuse me?" he finally responded, speaking carefully and drawing out each syllable as he looked down at me.

"You heard me. Why are you telling the bartender what I can and can't drink? Are you the owner of this club or something?" My temper grew by the second.

He held his ground, not granting me as much as one ounce of sympathy. "I'm not the owner, but I do make the rules around here."

"Is that so?" I tapped my foot impatiently. "And what gives you the right to make those decisions for me, huh?"

He looked at me from top to bottom, his intense stare lighting my core ablaze.

God, what was I doing? I wasn't acting like myself at all. Celeste Kinney doesn't start confrontations, let alone storm across a club and start an argument with a bouncer who is double her size. His damn biceps were bigger than my thighs, for crying out loud.

"You know, this isn't a place for a girl like you," he finally responded, his demeanor unbothered.

"A girl like me?" I repeated, my frown deepening in annoyance. I was used to the stigma of being miss perfect, but I couldn't help but feel it finally start to get to me right now. "And what does that mean, exactly?"

He observed my expression. "It means you don't look like the type that wants trouble."

"Is that right?" I pretended to laugh. "You know what?" I snatched a shot off of someone's table to my right.

"Hey!" they snapped at me, reaching out to grab it back, but they were too late—I'd already downed it faster than anything I'd ever drank.

"You really think you 'know' me?" I hissed, locking eyes with

Zeke again as I pushed the now empty shot glass into his chest. "I guess we'll see about that."

I swayed from side to side as I stomped back over to the crowded dance floor—this time, with much different intentions than before. Truthfully, I had absolutely no idea what I had just drunk and what was washing over me. The alcohol and adrenaline pumping through my veins were as intense as the music pulsating through the club.

I grabbed the first guy I could find by his collar, turned around and interlocked my hands behind his neck, my rear grinding against his belt buckle. At least, I hoped it was their belt buckle.

Where was all this confidence coming from? Was it that I'd never been quite so challenged by anyone before? Was I just trying to prove to myself that I didn't always have to be perfect? I wasn't sure.

All I knew was that my body was moving in ways I hadn't even known it was capable of. I sought out Zeke's eyes as I continued to dance—but this time, instead of a look of desire, his eyes grew comprehensive. A sense of angst festering.

Before I could read into his shifted state any further, I was flipped around, and came face to face with the man in front of me.

This man commanded control, and without needing to take a second glance, I realized that I knew the face that stood in front of me. He was the man I'd seen earlier. The one with the white-blond hair and the *I don't give a fuck* attitude. From afar, he'd looked short, but as I craned my head to look up at him, I realized that my frail body stood no chance.

If he was Napoleon, I was a Christmas elf.

The reality of whose arms I had wrapped around me now began to sink in, as did a sudden sense of dread.

"Well, aren't you something?" he spoke cunningly as the club's music faded into a slow murmur in the background. "Not many girls have the guts to pull me in." His grasp anchored around my waist. "Especially not ones that look like you."

Almost immediately, I felt myself begin to sober up as I entered into what I could only best describe as fight or flight mode. Before I had a chance to decide which was the more viable option of the two, it was too late. The man yanked me in even closer as he squeezed my backside.

"Let me show you exactly what you've signed up for," he whispered, his lips connected with my neck.

Frozen.

I was frozen in fear for a moment as I disassociated myself from my own body.

Powerless.

I was utterly and completely powerless.

But I knew I had to fight. I had to get away.

I attempted to shove my elbow back into his ribcage, which seemed to have no effect on him as he effortlessly grabbed my arm and tightened his grip, locking me into his grasp. Each desperate attempt of mine was countered with his controlled reaction as he welded me back in each time, tighter, firmer, and without any hint of letting me go.

"Stop resisting," he growled in my ear, holding me back as one of his hands crawled its way up to the front of my dress.

"Stop!" I tried to shout as I squirmed against him, gasping for breath while my heart pounded against my chest. "Please...let me go!"

"What don't you understand, baby doll?" his menacing tone forced the hairs on the back of my neck to stand up in fear. "You're mine tonight."

Tears brimmed my eyes. I wanted to run and get as far away from what was happening as possible, yet my legs buckled beneath me.

"You're not going anywhere." His calloused hand loitered along the edge of my panties.

Every possible alarm now sounded off in my mind.

You're in danger, Celeste.

He's a danger.

Get out. Get out while you've still got the chance.

"Help me! Someone, please!" I called once more, but my hoarse voice was drowned out by the music and the excited shouts that carried throughout the club. It was too crowded. Too loud. And now, as the man's free hand was slapped over my mouth, I could no longer speak.

I'd lost all hope. I just closed my eyes, tried to even my breathing, and braced myself for the worst. All I could do was pray that this would be over soon so that I could go home and—

Before I could finish my thought, I had the wind knocked out of me as an unfamiliar hand pulled me out of the man's grasp and into his.

Zeke.

"Get behind me," he instructed, fury written all over his face as he placed himself between the man and me.

"What the fuck, Zeke?" the man snarled, forcibly attempting to break the space that separated us, which only resulted in Zeke holding me tighter.

"Not tonight, Chaz," Zeke snapped in retaliation. "She's off-limits."

"Oh, yeah?" Chaz shouted. "Says who?"

Zeke stepped closer to him as he maintained a solid grip on my waist. "Says me," he spoke firmly. "Do you have a problem with that?"

Chaz paused as he matched Zeke's foul expression.

This was bad. This was so bad.

I could tell neither party was about to back down without a fight—and here I was, the root cause of it all.

"You know what?" Chaz took me by surprise as he placed a single finger on Zeke's chest. "Remember all that I've done for you. You're on thin ice now, pal. I'd hate to see you fall through."

With that, he nudged past him as he worked his way off the dance floor, shooting me a glare that made my blood turn cold.

As Chaz fell out of sight, so did Zeke's grasp on me. I took the opportunity to break away, rushing towards one of the emergency exits I'd been so determined to discover earlier.

As I raced down one of the back hallways of the club, I pulled on the first door I could. It led me not outside but into a single-occupancy bathroom.

At this point, I didn't care. This was enough. As long as I was alone, I was safe.

I slammed the door shut behind me as the desensitization that I'd mastered as a child, low and behold, finally wore off.

To You, Iyla

CHAPTER SIX

I Y L A

PRESENT DAY

"Iyla, are you alright?"

"Uh...yeah," I mumbled, doing my best to ignore the fact that my nausea was taking a turn for the worse as we stepped off of the Pacific Plummet. "I think I just need to take a break from rides for a bit."

"We should do that again!" Hallie shouted, oblivious to what was happening as she eagerly pulled on Vic's arm. "What do you say, guys?"

Even through my disorientated state, I could see Vic nod in agreement. I wanted to curse his name into existence.

"I think we'll pass." Ambert secured his arm around my wobbling body. "We're going to go on a walk. Catch up with you guys in a bit?" he called over to Hallie and Vic, his hand now resting on my waist.

I wanted to bask in the waves of emotion that Ambert's touch sent throughout my body. Instead, the only thing I could feel was the contents of my lunch churning inside me.

"Cool," Vic responded with a shrug as Hallie started to drag him back into the line. "We'll text you guys in a bit."

As they disappeared from sight, Ambert turned towards me. "Can I grab you a drink?"

I faintly nodded in response, finding a seat alongside the pier as I rested my head and took in the cool air.

A few minutes later, Ambert reappeared with a freshly cracked can. "Hope this helps," he said, handing it to me.

"Thanks." I smiled in appreciation of his caring nature, making space for him to sit beside me as I held the drink in one hand and took another anti-nausea pill with the other.

"I guess I should've mentioned I have pretty bad motion sickness. I'm usually fine after I take my medication, but after the infamous Pacific Plummet, it was game over." I shook my head in defeat and took a sip of my drink, slowly starting to feel my stomach settle down again.

"Well, if it helps at all. I had a lot of fun with you tonight." He smiled.

His words made my eyes absolutely light up. "I couldn't agree more," I responded softly as I gazed up at the fairground lights illuminating the space around us.

"How does it feel to finally be eighteen?" he asked.

"You're about three-hundred and sixty-five days late with that question. I'm nineteen today," I clarified with a laugh.

"Nineteen?" His brows furrowed in slight confusion. "Oh, I'm sorry. I thought we were the same age."

"My parents held me back a year since I was born prematurely," I explained. "I technically wasn't supposed to be born until late December, early January. But low and behold, I popped out in August."

"Better early than late, huh?" he offered in reassurance, prompting me to raise an eyebrow.

"Isn't it better late than never?"

A smirk passed across his lips. "Touché."

"So, tell me." I laughed. "When's your birthday?"

"April first." I sensed the sarcasm in his voice as I realized the date he'd mentioned was April Fool's Day.

"Is that true, or is that just another one of your jokes?"

"Um, excuse me..." He placed a hand on his chest, feigning hurt. "I'm offended. But yes, detective, that was a joke. Good catch. My birthday is actually August first. Only a few short weeks ago."

"Well then." I stood up, my stomach finally settling. "Happy belated. How about that walk to celebrate?" I extended my hand out to him.

"How about it." He took my hand as we began to walk down the pier.

So far, the night had already gone much better than I'd anticipated. At first, I could barely process a single sentence to Ambert, and now it was as if I needed to know everything about him.

"Tell me more about you." My internal thoughts came outwards.

"Ask me anything you want," Ambert countered in delight. "In fact, let's speed round it."

"Well, Ambert," I started. "I've never heard your name before. Any story there?"

"No meaning." He shrugged. "I think my parents just wanted to torture me by giving me a name that I'd never find on a keychain. But it does mean intelligent, so I guess that's nice." He smiled. "Joke's on them, though. I'm far from it."

I nudged his shoulder in response. "Hey, that's not true. If it weren't for you, I'd probably still be stuck in front of Tim and Sally's. Doomed to only drink coffee and donuts for the rest of my existence."

"Would that really be so bad?" he mocked.

"I guess not..." I laughed as we continued to walk.

"What about you?" He tossed the question back over to me. "The name Iyla. Any meaning there?

I sighed. Truthfully, I had no idea why my parents chose the name Iyla. Did they even pick it? Or had it already been chosen for me?

I brushed the uncertainty aside and opted for the easy answer instead. "No meaning," I repeated his earlier words. "I just think my parents liked the way it sounded."

"Do you know what it means?" he finally asked a question I knew the answer to.

"A shining or bright light."

"Well then..." He squeezed onto my hand. "That's more accurate than mine."

I couldn't help but display an outward look of adoration. Ambert felt like home. A feeling that I'd been searching for, for what felt like my whole life. There was something uniquely attractive about him. Something that sent shivers up my spine and goosebumps down my arm.

"I hope you don't mind..." Ambert broke the silence. A serious tone washed over this voice. "But I do have an important question for you."

"An important question?" I asked. "Well, I guess you'd better make it good."

He did just that as he asked me the most resounding question he could've. "Out of all the places to go to school, why did you choose to come to California?"

I paused. How could I even answer that? Was now really the time to dump all my dirty laundry onto him? We'd only just met. There was no way I could possibly explain to him my unspoken rite of passage to retrace my birth mother's footsteps. It would be too much, and he probably wouldn't understand. I could hardly make sense of it myself.

He revoked the question as if he could see the racing thoughts rush through my mind. "You don't have to tell me if you don't want to."

"No, sorry." I snapped myself out of it. "I'm just trying to think of the best way to answer that. I guess California has always been my dream. I've always envisioned a life here for myself. So, when it came time to apply for school, I knew this was where I wanted to end up. And now that I'm actually here, there's no other place I'd rather be. This feels like home."

He seemed satisfied with my answer, as his thumb gently caressed my cheek as we stopped in place. "Well then...welcome home."

I was confident that he was about to lean in to kiss me for a moment, but his phone killed the mood as it buzzed in his pocket.

I noticed the word "Mom" appear on his lock screen as he pulled it out of his pocket. "I'm sorry, mind if I grab this?"

"Go ahead." I nodded despite my internal defeat.

"I'll be right back." He grazed my shoulder with his fingertips and walked out of earshot, prompting me to pull out my phone and find a seat along the pier again.

As expected, Hallie's messages were the first thing on my screen.

Iyla and Ambert sitting in a tree. K-I-S-S – wait? Have you kissed him yet? Plz, tell me you've kissed!

UGH, you guys literally look so cute together. Which couple name do you prefer? Ayla or Imbert? I'm team Ayla.

I ignored her earlier messages and focused on the last one sent eight minutes ago.

Vic and I will meet you at the front soon.

"Soon" in Hallie's world meant that any second now, a familiar brunette would—

"So..." Hallie planted herself beside me, scaring me half to death. "How did it go?"

I clutched my chest as Vic stopped beside Ambert. "You know, you really need a bell."

"Sorry..." She snickered. "But I did warn you. So," she repeated again. "How were things with Ambert?"

"Good." I smiled. "Although, I think I've now been on enough rides to last me a lifetime. Thanks for forcing me on them, by the way."

Hallie narrowed her stare. "Hey, don't you think I knew what I was doing this whole time? I knew the only way you'd spend some alone time with Ambert was if you were completely worn out on the rides. Plus, it was a test to see if he'd comfort you in your time of need." She placed her hand on my back. "Aw, it's okay, Iyla. I'll take care of you," she mocked.

I pursed my lips and pushed her arm away lightheartedly. "Why am I not surprised that you planned all this out?"

"Because you know me too well." She winked. "So, did anything happen that I should be aware of? Did you guys kiss? Fall in love? When should I start planning the wedding?"

"Hallie, stop," I hissed, prompting her to lower her voice. "Nothing happened, okay? We just held hands and stuff."

"Just held hands?" She gave off a disgusted look, obviously expecting more.

"What were you expecting? We're just getting to know each other. Besides, there are thousands of people here. What would we have even been able to do?"

"You'd be surprised what can be accomplished on top of a Ferris wheel. Did you know you're up there for, like, a solid five minutes?"

"What are you two gossiping about over here?" Vic interrupted our conversation.

Thank goodness.

"Oh, you don't want to know," I told him. "Or maybe you do, who knows with you two." I rubbed my forehead as Ambert walked back over to us.

"Sorry about that, Iyla. It was my mom. My dad needs some help back at the shop. Apparently there's some late-night emergency happening. I've got to get going."

I stood up as Hallie and Vic did the same.

"We're going to head back to the car, Iy," Hallie said. "Meet us there?"

I nodded, thankful that Ambert and I would be able to have some time alone.

"It was nice to finally meet you, Ambert!" Hallie jumped onto Vic's back in a fit of laughter. "See you later," I heard her say as they shot off into the distance.

"I'm sorry about having to go." Ambert inched closer to me, reaching a hand out to brush my arm. "This wasn't how I was hoping for tonight to end."

"Don't apologize," I reassured him, meeting his gentle gaze. "I had an amazing time tonight. I promise."

"I did, too." He reached into his pocket and grabbed his phone. "Do you mind if I get your number?"

I started to rhyme off my number as Ambert typed out a message.

A moment later, my phone vibrated inside my bag, and as I looked down at it, Ambert placed a delicate kiss on my cheek. "Good night, Iyla," he whispered before pulling away. "And happy birthday."

His touch froze me in place as he slowly stepped away, leaving me to replay the moment in my mind. It wasn't until my phone vibrated yet again that I broke free of my trance and looked down.

Beautiful in blue. I'd love to see you again.

Ambert's message read as Vic pulled up the car. "Hey, slowpoke!" he honked. "Quit dreaming about Ambert and get in."

"Iyla's in love, Iyla's in love." Hallie taunted me as I stepped into the car and sunk my head back. "Don't you think?" She looked over at Vic.

"Definitely." He nodded in agreement.

"You two are dangerous together." I shot them a disapproving glare.

"Good," Vic responded with a smirk in Hallie's direction. "Just the way I like it."

He pulled out of the lot, ending the day just like it had begun, at a million miles per hour.

The Sixth Entry

CELESTE

19 YEARS AGO

JULY 7

With a slam of the door, my body collapsed onto the floor as the tears escaped my eyes and rolled down my cheeks. My chest rose and fell as my breathing became rapid and untamed, a full-on panic attack now blooming.

As a child, before the numbness kicked in, panic attacks were something that I'd experienced quite frequently. Usually, when things were spiraling out of my control. In other words, every time my parents fought. Typically, the closet or the bathroom would end up being the place I'd seek comfort in, allowing my tears to flow until I could calm myself down.

How did I calm myself down?

I started to count. I counted in ways that didn't make sense. A way to distract my mind.

"Six."

"Eleven."

"Forty-eight."

"Two."

"Sixteen."

I continued to rhyme off scattered numbers as I laid my head into my hands. As a child, it often took me over an hour to bring my body back down to a moderate pace. But now, it only took me a few minutes to resettle my erratic breathing and calm my thoughts.

"You're okay," I reminded myself, taking a deep breath in and out before a knock fell on the bathroom door, causing me to startle.

I hurriedly rushed to my feet and placed my hands under the faucet as if I had just finished washing them. "I'll just be a second." I sniffled as the door cracked open, and I realized that the intruder was none other than Zeke.

"Can I come in?" He paused between the sliver, a somberness in his eyes.

I froze in place for a moment, staring at him through the mirror before finally nodding with some reluctance as he stepped inside.

"You didn't have to come after me." I brushed back some tears.

"Yes, I did," he softly spoke, the stress on my face equally reflected back in his. "I needed to make sure you were okay."

"Well, I'm okay," I lied, considering nothing about what had just happened was even remotely okay. "But thank you for checking on me. I appreciate it."

"Of course," he began, but before he could continue further, I started to ramble.

"I also wanted to say that I'm sorry. I shouldn't have spoken to you like that earlier. I was drunk and clearly not thinking straight." My voice broke as my lip quivered, threatening to allow all of the emotions to spill out. "You were right about what you said. I don't belong in a place like this, and I can agree with that after tonight. "I...I won't ever come back here again."

"Hey, hey..." He tried to soothe me. "You're okay. You hear me? You're okay now." He reached over to the paper towel holder on the wall, ripped off a piece and gently dabbed some of the tears rolling down my flushed cheeks. "I wouldn't have let anything happen to you," he whispered. "I promise."

I took the tissue out of his hand as I tried to calm my voice. "Thank you," I breathed. "And...thank you for what you did down there. I really don't know what would've happened had you not stepped–"

"Let's not talk about that anymore." He cut me off, visibly frustrated by the subject matter.

I decided not to question him. I wanted to forget about what had just happened as much as I could tell he did. Right about now, the only real thing I wanted to do was change the topic of conversation.

"I'm Celeste." I did just that as I scrunched up the now-damp tissue and tossed it in the garbage. "And you're Zeke, right?"

A dreary silence washed over the room, one I hoped would falter but only strengthened as Zeke diverted his eyes away from mine and rested his gaze on the floor. I guessed Korey was right. Zeke didn't talk much.

Korey.

Claire.

I'd told Claire I was going to find her.

How long ago was that?

Time no longer made sense.

Zeke peeled his eyes back up as if he could see the panic wash through mine. "I need to make sure my friend Claire is okay. But thank you again...for everything." I gulped down the massive lump in my throat. "I'm going to head out."

"Claire is fine," he finally spoke back up, his green eyes piercing through me. "Korey's a good friend of mine. He'll take care of her. Trust me."

Trust me.

Those two simple words seemed to wash away my anxieties for reasons I couldn't explain. Somehow, I did trust him, but that didn't mean I wanted to stay in this club for another second. I needed to leave.

"Well, that's good to hear." I sighed quietly in relief. "But I should probably start heading back to my hotel. As you can imagine, it's been a long night."

"You were right. People do call me Zeke. Sometimes Z," he finally answered my question. "But my real name is Ezekiel. Ezekiel Reeves."

I shifted in place, strangely desperate to act on any conversation he was willing to pursue. "Which do you prefer?" I perused. "Ezekiel, Zeke or Z?"

He shrugged. "It really doesn't matter."

"Well, what if it did?" I challenged. "Maybe it matters to me what I call you."

He let out a smirk, ignoring my question as he stood up from against the doorway. God, he was tall. I'd never felt smaller than I did as I stood in front of him.

"You know." He took a step towards me. "I saw you last night on the boardwalk. What were you doing standing over there?"

My throat turned dry.

I knew he recognized me.

"It doesn't matter..." I mimicked his exact empty words in response.

"Well, what if it did?" he took another step closer as he caught onto the game we were playing. "Maybe it matters to me."

My tongue danced along my lower lip. "I'm not quite sure what you mean." I could hardly find enough air to muster that sentence. The tension between the two of us was so thick that you could cut it with a knife.

"Is that so?" He toyed with his fingers. "Then maybe I just need to be a bit more specific." He took a final step forward, his face now only a mere few inches away from mine. "You saw what happened last night, knowing damn well that this isn't a place for you. Yet twenty-four hours later, here you are."

To You, Jyla

The body I could hardly make out in the dark was now more apparent than ever. His chest was firm. His posture was tall, and his expression was straight as I strained my neck to look up at him.

"So, tell me." He ran one hand across my cheek as the other tucked a loose strand of hair behind my ear. "Why did you decide to come back?"

I looked away, taken back by the difference between his fragile touch and heavy question. "I don't know," I whispered. "I don't know."

He gently tilted my chin back up. "You seem like a smart girl. So let me ask you once more, and this time, you're going to tell me the truth." Zeke's warm breath hovered millimeters away from my ear. "Why did you come back, *Celeste*?"

Butterflies unleashed in my stomach as my name fell out of his perfectly shaped lips. It was as if no one had ever said it before.

Which they hadn't. Not in the way Zeke did.

Like clockwork, my body started to revert back to its earlier state.

Heart racing, mind flustered, hands shaking.

Except now, the feelings weren't driven by fear. They were driven by three things.

A desire to know him.

A desire to be near him.

And a desire to be loved by him.

But rather than acting on the heat that grew between my thighs, I remained completely still. I had to hold onto control, yet he continued to make it that much harder.

"Tell me, Celeste," he murmured, his thumb cascading alongside my lower lip as he pulled down on it ever so slightly before his touch ultimately found its way to rest atop my chin.

"I..." I could barely speak, unknowing of what to even say.

"Tell me." I felt him repeat as his lips softly grazed mine, mindlessly taunting me without a care.

"I..." I attempted once more as the version of myself that was

93

KATE LAUREN

unleashed on the dance floor escaped from my body. Not only was I losing control, but now my decision-making skills were being completely tossed out of the window. It was as if all of a sudden, Zeke became the only obvious choice. And for the first time in my life, I wanted to choose my body over my mind.

"Hmm?" He prompted me a final time before the next two words that fell out of my mouth changed everything.

"Fuck it." I firmly planted my lips against his as my fingers intertwined within his dark hair.

He didn't waste a second in embracing the kiss as he picked me up in one quick motion and gently placed me on top of the sink across the bathroom.

My hands effortlessly explored his body, starting with his chest, then his arms and finally his waist, where I tugged away at the front of his shirt, hopelessly trying to reveal what was underneath.

"So, this is why you came," he purred into my ear. "Just to fucking tease me on the dance floor, hmm?" his lips connected with my neck, forcing a moan to escape from my mouth. "You know, angel, if you wanted me, you should've just said. That way, I didn't have to see how that creep had his hands all over you."

"Why do you care?" The ability to formulate a sentence became harder by the second.

"Because..." He used such a poorly descriptive word to answer my loaded question. "I want you..." He inched his hand beneath my dress. "All to..." His fingers brushed up my thighs. "Myself." His voice was raspy, taunting as his touch cascaded over top of my heat.

I grew more intoxicated by his touch than by any alcohol I'd consumed throughout the night. I was drunk off of him.

"You don't even know me." A gasp of air escaped my lungs.

"That's going to change real fast," he murmured. "I intend to know everything about you, angel."

A sense of resistance kicked in as I questioned how far I was really about to go here, especially with someone who didn't know anything past my name.

"Is this okay?" Zeke sought confirmation in my eyes and paused his touch.

I hesitated, playing that endless mind game against my brain and body until I finally gave in. "Yes." I breathed. "I want you...I want you to touch me."

Zeke's eyes darkened as he followed my request and circulated his fingers over the top of my panties. He stayed there for a moment, teasing me as I tried to inch my body closer to him, desperate for more. A soft moan escaped my lips, pleading without saying a word. My chest rose and fell with each breath before he finally pushed the lacy material of my panties to the side and connected his hand directly with my heat.

"Do you like one or two, baby?" he hummed into my ear as his fingers hovered over my entrance.

I was dazed and flustered with emotion as I responded. "One or two what?"

Immediately he slowed down his touch, forcing my body to practically scream and beg for more. "Fingers," he clarified, his voice now slightly tainted with confusion.

I felt my body go numb with embarrassment. "I wouldn't know." I shook my head. "I...I don't know."

He pulled away. "Have you never done this before?"

I refused to look back at him, knowing his question's truth but lacking the confidence to just say it. Instead, I shook my head, giving him the answer I knew he didn't want to hear.

He didn't say another word as he picked me up off the sink and placed me in front of him. "This isn't going to happen here." He planted a kiss on top of my forehead. "And this isn't going to happen now."

"What?" My heart sank in disappointment as I adjusted the hem of my dress. "Why not?"

"Because," he reached toward the bathroom door. "You deserve better than that." He firmly interlaced his fingers with mine as he guided me back into the club.

"Wait." My short legs could hardly keep up with his long strides, causing me to jog behind him. "Where are we going?"

"Wait here," he paused, glancing at someone up ahead as he spoke.

I nodded and stood back as he walked over to another bouncer in the distance. His eyes hardly broke contact with mine as he whispered something into the man's ear and took something from his hand.

"Is everything okay?" I questioned as he made his way back over to me and placed his large hand on my lower back.

"Everything's fine. Ready to go?"

"But what about Claire?" I protested. "I told her I'd find her."

"She left with Korey ago." He stopped me mid-sentence. "Korey gave this to Mitch. He said it was from Claire." He handed me a messy handwritten note that had been inscribed on a napkin.

Desperate times call for desperate measures. I'll see you tomorrow morning back at the hotel.
Love you! Claire

I sighed and folded the note in my hands as Zeke extended his daunting yet enticing touch. "So, what do you say, Celeste? Do you want to get out of here with me?"

I interlaced my hand with his, processing the only possible answer.

"*Yes.*"

CHAPTER SEVEN

I Y L A

PRESENT DAY

My fingers hovered over the keypad and paused in the same position they'd been in for the past hour.

Beautiful in blue. I'd love to see you again.

"Think, Iyla, think," I muttered under my breath, dancing my thumbs over the keyword before I started to type out some plausible responses.

I had a fun night with you.

Too cliché.

It was great seeing you!

Way too friendly.

"What the hell do I say?" I groaned, rolling onto my stomach and staring at the ceiling, pathetically wishing that Hallie had stayed with me back in the dorm instead of attending to her "unfinished Ferris wheel business" with Vic.

I didn't know if I wanted to throw up or pretend like those

words didn't come out of her mouth. I opted for the latter and insisted that she go ahead, which led to her hastily gathering items around the room and throwing them into her bag—including a few condoms that she had safely tucked into her bedside table.

"Let's try this again," I mumbled, sitting up straight and typing out a final message.

Sunday, pick me up at Hedrick Hall. 1PM.

I watched the text cursor flick on and off at the end of the message before I impulsively hit send.

Oh, God. Was that too forward? What if he didn't actually want to see me again? What if he was just being nice?

My phone dinged not a second later.

Can't wait. I'll see you then.

✧ ☆ ✩

"Good morning, sunshine!" Hallie rushed into our dorm room like a bull in a China shop as she yanked back the curtains and allowed the rays of sunlight to burst through the window.

"Hallie," I grumbled, squeezing my eyes shut as I pulled the covers over my head.

"I heard through the grapevine that you have another date with Ambert tomorrow," she sang, throwing herself onto my bed.

"How did you hear that?" I tossed my covers away.

"A little birdie told me."

"Damn, Vic." I threw a pillow over my face. "How did he even know?"

"Ambert told him!" she giggled, pulling the pillow away and forcing me to face the bright light that flooded the room.

"Ambert?" I let out a sigh. "Why in the world would he do that?"

Maybe...and this is just a maybe..." She lifted her hands into the air innocently. "Ambert wanted to know where to take you."

I sat up. "Hallie, what did you say to him?"

"Hey, it's only a theory, remember? I didn't confirm or deny anything."

"Hallie, tell me or else I'm going to freak out," I responded, doing my best to keep my voice level calm.

"Fine." She sighed dramatically. "Only on one condition."

"Which is?" I dared to ask.

"That we go shopping."

"That's it? That's the condition?" I raised my eyebrows in suspicion as I stood up from the bed.

"Yeah!" she shrugged and nodded nonchalantly. "I'm a simple woman with simple needs."

"Fine," I agreed, only because the one thing I hated more than shopping was not knowing what was happening. "So, are you going to tell me or what? Where does Ambert want to take me?"

She smiled. "Well, at first, I thought to myself, what would Iyla like to do? Obviously, she wants to get to know the guy, right? But you know, nothing too awkward where you're totally alone. At least at first..." She winked. "But anyway, I found this super cute botanical garden he could take you to since you love to play in the dirt."

"You mean plant flowers?" I scoffed.

"That's what I said, didn't I?" she joked. "But that's not all. Once you're done that, there's this really nice patio by the waterfront. It's the perfect spot to watch the sunset by the ocean and fall madly in love. What do you think?"

For once, a Hallie Jennings plan sounded perfect. Plus, there was a much smaller chance of being ridden by nausea this time around. "You've outdone yourself, Jennings." I nodded, impressed. "But how did you manage to plan all that since last night?"

"I'm good at multitasking." She smirked suggestively, prompting me to roll my eyes.

"I don't even want to know."

"Fine by me." She grinned. "But you'd better put on the most award-winning performance tomorrow. Otherwise Ambert will never trust me again."

"Oh, don't worry. I will."

"Good." She huffed, evidently pleased with herself, as she threw a tank top and shorts in my direction. "Now, get dressed. We've got a mall to go to."

✫ ☆ ✩

"He just texted me that he's downstairs," I called out as Hallie, and I rushed around our dorm room like headless chickens.

"Do you have everything?" she asked.

I grabbed my purse and made my way toward the door. "I think so." I checked a final time.

"Okay, just call me if you need anything. And don't worry about rushing back early. I'm going to Vic's. Hell, stay out all night for all I care."

I let out a laugh. "How did you go from a mom into a cool aunt in a split second?"

"Maybe because I'm a woman of many talents," she bragged. "Now go. And don't forget to have fun," she added as she pushed me out the door.

I couldn't hold back the kiddish grin as I made my way down the elevator and toward the entrance. "Just be cool, Iyla," I whispered to myself as Ambert came into view with a few white carnations in his hand.

"Are these for me?" I skipped the formalities of a 'hello.'

"No, they're for the other pretty girl I'm supposed to meet today," he remarked, prompting a playful glare on my end.

100

Kidding. They're for you, of course. In fact, they're a slight hint as to where we are going today."

"Is that right?" I played dumb, tilting my head in curiosity.

"Mm-hm." He opened the passenger door. "Hop in."

I stepped into his car as he closed the door behind me, and I placed the flowers on my lap.

"How are you doing?" I asked as he climbed into the driver's seat and pulled out of the campus lot. "How did things go the other night when your dad needed your help?"

"Oh, same shit, different day." He pouted. "A family friend and my dad's co-worker decided that it would be a smart idea to go out on his old motorcycle. The thing is over twenty years old. Needless to say, it didn't end well, and my dad insisted that I go in to learn how to fix it."

"Have you always worked with your dad?" I questioned, glancing out the window as we passed the campus.

"Since I was twelve," he responded. "I think he's hoping that one day I'll take over the shop, but honestly, I don't think it's cut out for me."

Not cut out for him? Ambert was practically a natural when fixing Hallie's car last week. But I supposed that if you've been doing the same thing since you were 12, the thought of a life sentence would feel daunting.

"Is he excited you're going to UCLA?" I wondered.

"Yeah. But you know how parents can be. He's got this whole legacy talk about keeping things in the family. But my mom went to UCLA ages ago, so if we're talking about legacy, that'll be the family legacy I honor."

I immediately thought back to my birth mother and how legacy had played such a huge role in my decision to go to UCLA. I wanted to share that similarity with Ambert at that moment, but instead, I did what I do best and changed the subject.

"So, your dad owns the shop..." I nodded, turning the thought over in my mind. "What does your mom do?"

"She works at a popular school not too far from us. Maybe you've heard of it. It's called UCLA," he joked, glancing over at me to see my reaction.

"You're kidding!" I exclaimed in surprise. "What does she do?"

"She works in the registrar's office. She was probably the one that processed your application...mine, too."

"Woah. That's kind of like a full-circle moment, isn't it? To study at UCLA and then end up working there."

"Definitely." He agreed with a nod. "But it does mean that I can't do poorly in class. I mean, there's no way of hiding it."

"A blessing and a curse," I concluded with a laugh.

"A double-edged sword. What about your parents? What do they do?"

"Total workaholics," I replied with a scoff. "My dad more than my mom. But since my mom is self-employed, she's always working...even when she's not."

"Either of them lawyers?" he guessed.

"Nope. My dad works for a tech company, and my mom owns a boutique in downtown Columbus. I suppose that means I'll be the first lawyer in the family."

"I'll hold you to that," he said with a fond smile as he pulled into a parking lot and took his keys out of the ignition before getting out of the car and walking over to my side.

"Such a gentleman," I teased as he opened my door and I took his hand.

"Well, I have to be." He chuckled as he helped me down. "It's not every day I get a chance to take out a girl like you."

"A girl like me?" I couldn't help but laugh. "What does that mean?"

"There's something special about you, Iyla Larson." He squeezed my hand. "And I intend to find out what it is."

CELESTE

19 YEARS AGO

JULY 12

"Is there a reason you were just...allowed to leave? Don't you have to finish your shift?" I asked with concern as Zeke led me outside of the club.

"Mitch has got me covered," he responded, his tone completely carefree. "Don't worry."

"But won't you get in trouble?" I questioned as I quickened my pace to keep up with his; my mind recalled Chaz's words from earlier.

"You're on thin ice now, pal. I'd hate to see you fall through."

"It's too late for that," he muttered under his breath as he pushed open the back doors of the club, the cool breeze connecting with my hot skin and the fresh air embracing me like a childhood winter in Oregon.

"So..." I spoke up after a moment, "are we going back to your place?"

I could feel the heat rising to my cheeks as soon as the words left my mouth, and I noticed the corner of his lips lift up in amusement. I'd tried to change the subject, but curiosity and anticipation had got the best of me.

"I guess that depends." He smirked. "Is that where you want to go?"

I played with the neckline of my dress nervously. "Well, do you live far?" I asked stupidly. It was a force of habit: questioning every finite detail while weighing what exactly I was about to get myself into.

"Fifteen minutes," he responded bluntly.

I shifted from one leg to the other. "My hotel's five minutes up the road. Maybe we can go there instead."

"Eager?" He took my words as a challenge.

"No, I just thought—"

His body suddenly stopped, causing me to nearly walk right into him and back into his arms—for a moment, I wish I had.

"Wait." I forced myself out of my daydream as I processed what I was seeing in front of me. "This is your car?"

"My bike," he corrected me as he reached for a helmet that hung on the handlebars. "I'm guessing you've never been on one before."

"Actually, I have," I responded matter-of-factly, placing my hands on both hips.

"Oh, yeah?" he seemed impressed as he placed the helmet on my head, a cold shiver passing through my skin—one I couldn't tell was a result of the metal or his fingers gently brushing against my face. "When?"

"When I was five," I faintly answered, forcing my thoughts to redirect back to the one time I sat on my grandpa's motorcycle. It wasn't much of a ride, but it counted. Right?

A grin formed on his lips as he brushed a stray strand of hair out of my face and clicked the strap into place. "I bet it wasn't even on."

My glare confirmed his statement to be true as he let out a stifled laugh. "Yeah, that's what I thought." He extended his hand with a playful smirk. "Let me take you for your first ride."

"What are the odds that I'll come back alive?" I challenged him, trying to hide my nerves as I took his hand and swung my legs over either side of the seat.

"That depends," he replied as he got on in front of me and started up the bike. "Are you living right now?"

The way my heart threatened to beat out of my chest confirmed that I was alive, but *living*?

Maybe I had only just begun.

He must've taken my silence as confirmation as he knocked over the kickstand, prompting me to instinctively wrap my arms securely around his waist. "Wait, you don't have a spare helmet?" I feverishly asked, my anxiety heightened as I realized he'd given me his.

"I do." He revved his engine one last time. "But it's at home."

✫ ☆ ✫

The only thing I could compare to the speed of Zeke's bike was the feeling of riding a rollercoaster. The glaring difference? Unlike a rollercoaster, the bike had no handlebars, no seatbelts, nothing. Just trust. Trust that Zeke would keep me safe as our bodies dipped and curved with the bumps of the road.

It was on that short ride to Zeke's place that I realized things were about to change. It was a feeling I'd always held back from. Change, to me, had always meant a never-ending stream of instability and fear.

But this time, it was a thrill. A rush, a way of letting go.

It was a feeling that Zeke incited in me.

"Holy shit!" I couldn't help but blurt out, adrenaline coursing through me as Zeke parked the bike. "That was crazy! Do you always ride like that?"

He found my question amusing as he kicked out the stand and helped ease my body off the bike, my heartbeat finally returning to normal pace as my feet were firmly planted back onto the ground. "The simple answer is yes," he responded as he unbuckled and removed my helmet. "But usually, I go way faster."

"Faster?" I repeated in disbelief. "Zeke, do you not realize how fast you were already going? Not to mention with no helmet on?" I couldn't help but frown at him as we approached the elevator. "Do you know what would've happened if the police had seen us? You would have gotten a speeding ticket, not to mention a fine of up to two hundred and fifty dollars for not wearing a helmet." I rhymed off facts I'd learned in my municipal law class. "Also..." I carried on as we stepped inside the elevator. "I wasn't even wearing the proper attire for motorcycling. If we had crashed, I could've—"

My lecture was cut short as Zeke turned to me and crashed his lips into mine, pinning my body up against the elevator wall.

I'd never been so relieved to be interrupted in my life.

Like before, his kiss was complex, but there was a sense of passion, essence, and longing this time. As his lips moved in sync with mine, I was certain that somehow, I'd soon come to learn a piece of Zeke that no one else would. A piece that would belong to me and only me.

Ding.

The elevator doors re-opened, forcing our lips to break contact. "Couldn't you have lived on a higher floor?" I asked breathlessly.

"My thoughts exactly," he murmured softly, resting his forehead against mine for a moment before gently taking my hand and guiding me down the hallway toward his suite.

Suite 831.

All I'd ever known was to find logic and reason in everything that existed. Yet, with Zeke, I couldn't seem to find either. His touch sent me into a total whirlwind, and frankly, the only way to recover from the whiplash was to revert the conversation back to where it had been, despite how antagonizing it may have seemed.

"By the way, you cut me off," I spoke up suddenly, acting as if I was truly offended. "I'm just saying you really should try and be a bit more careful, especially when you're riding at night."

Zeke pulled his keys out of his pocket, unlocking the door as he peered back at me. "Are you always this worried about everything?"

"I'm not always worried about everything," I snapped in response, crossing my arms defensively as I followed him inside his apartment.

Or more like *a massive suite.*

"Woah," I whispered under my breath as I looked around, Zeke placing his keys down on his kitchen counter. How many times could my dorm room fit into his living room alone? *Five? Ten times maybe?*

Despite the size of the space, his furniture was minimal, basic, and not at all what I expected from a person I'd already deduced to be extraordinarily complex.

"Wait, you're not a cop, right?" Zeke asked suspiciously, removing his jacket and throwing it onto an armchair.

"No," I answered with a laugh. "Why would I be a cop?"

He hesitated, causing my smile to fade slightly. "You seem to know a lot about the law."

"That's because I'm a fourth-year pre-law student at UCLA." I rolled my eyes, ignoring the raging questions in my mind—the most burning one being, *how and why did he have such a nice place?*

"A law student?" He seemed surprised.

Another new facial expression unlocked.

"That's right," I confirmed proudly. "I'll be writing the LSAT in the next few months. It's my dream to go to Stanford afterwards. Then, I'll join their law program and start the process of becoming a qualified lawyer in the state."

He pursed his lips in thought. "Wow. I mean, I knew you were smart, angel, but I didn't realize you were *that* smart."

"And how exactly did you know I was 'smart'?" I crossed my arms and cocked a brow at him.

He made his way over to me and planted a soft kiss on my forehead. "Sometimes, you can just tell. Let me get you something. Would you like a drink?"

I smirked, remembering the bartender's words from earlier. "I thought I was cut off."

"Oh, you are..." He laughed as he walked towards his fridge and pulled out a water jug. "From alcohol, that is." He reached for a glass in his cupboard and handed me a now-filled cup. "And after what I saw tonight, you need this more than ever."

"Fine by me." I shrugged, bringing the cup to my lips and taking a sip. "After tonight, I don't think I ever want to drink again."

"Now, that..." He leaned against the counter. "Is something I can get behind."

I stifled a laugh until it was replaced with a yawn. "What time is it? I'm exhausted."

He looked down at his watch. "It's just after two."

"After two?!" I nearly spat out my drink. "Zeke, it's late!"

"Late?" he questioned. "What are you talking about? The night's young."

I rubbed my hands over my eyes in frustration, completely unaware of the fact that I was probably smudging the makeup Claire had spent hours putting on me. "Then I must be old," I sarcastically remarked. "These past few nights have been the latest I've stayed up in years."

He smiled as if I was joking.

"I'm serious," I told him. "I never stay awake this late. I live on a strict routine."

He nodded thoughtfully as he moved away from the kitchen and invited me towards his couch. "Care to enlighten me?"

"Well, it's straightforward." I planted myself beside him. "To live like Celeste Kinney, there are three essential rules to follow. Rule number one: no drinking or partying."

A faint sparkle fell over his devilishly handsome face. "I'm sorry to tell you this, angel, but that's not what I saw tonight on the dance floor."

"Don't even continue with that sentence." I placed my finger against his lips. "Tonight was a minor exception. Claire practically begged me to come to Long Beach for spring break. I am *not* here of my own free will, trust me. Before this weekend, I hadn't drunk alcohol in months—let alone been to a club. I could count on one hand how many times I've drunk in my life."

I could tell he wanted to ask some follow-up questions, yet he prompted me to go on instead. "What's rule number two?"

"Work, work, and more work."

"And that means what, exactly?"

"During my summer breaks over the years, I interned, worked, and networked. I want to have ideal references. I *need* to have the best references for when I draft my application letter to Stanford. It's non-negotiable."

"I guess that one does make sense," he pondered, taking the now-empty glass out of my hand and placing it on the live edge table in front of us. "So, tell me." He rubbed his hand along my exposed thigh, prompting me to push my knees together to fight the tormenting sensation his touch sent through me. "What is the final essential rule to be Celeste Kinney?"

I tried not to get distracted by his hand against my skin as I remembered my last rule. "I think you're going to like this one. No boyfriends, no hookups, and especially no love affairs."

He let out a substantial laugh. In fact, the depth of his laughter shook the whole couch.

"Why are you laughing?" I couldn't help but join in. "What's so funny?"

"I mean..." He paused. "That explains what happened earlier, I guess."

My laugh faded as I looked away, embarrassed about my lack of experience—let alone confidence in the realm of sex and intimacy.

It wasn't like I hadn't had a boyfriend before. I had. But usually, I'd end things way before they even approached that turning point. Yet, there I was. I'd only known Zeke for a mere few hours, and I'd already gone further with him than I ever had with anyone else.

He caught me looking to the side, torturing myself with my thoughts as he gently rested a hand on my chin and turned my head towards himself. "Well then, to follow rule number three, I guess I must ask you to leave."

What?

He'd left me speechless. Completely and utterly dumbfounded. "Are you?" My voice trailed off, his stoic expression unchanging.

He was serious.

I quickly stood up and flattened out my dress. I should've known better than to get into a situation like this with someone I'd just met. Zeke was a complete stranger, despite how much I'd been trying to convince myself otherwise. I'd trusted my body over my brain—a mistake I had never made before and would never make again.

But before I could even take a step, Zeke grabbed my waist and pulled my body back down on top of his.

"But..." His mouth hovered inches away from mine. "I'll let you in on a little secret. I don't mind breaking the rules."

His green eyes seemed to relish in the fact that I'd taken everything he'd just said quite literally.

"Is that right?" I squinted at him, hoping he couldn't feel my heart pounding against my chest.

"I mean, as long as you promise not to sue me." He tilted his head forward in temptation.

"I can't make any promises," I murmured, my eyes locked on his lips as I waited for them to touch mine. Instead, he lingered before he pulled back.

"Let's go to bed." He shifted beneath me.

"What?" I frowned. "Didn't you want to...I mean, didn't you

bring me back here to hook up?"

"Not at all." He shook his head firmly.

"But I thought..."

"Celeste." He held onto my hands. "I've never brought anyone back to my place before. And before tonight, the thought hadn't so much as occurred to me. I told you; you deserve better than that. I want to give you better than that."

"But I thought you said you wanted to break rule number three," I whispered, the disappointment coloring my voice like a toddler who'd just been told "no."

"I did. But if I'm not mistaken, rule number three had three parts. No boyfriends, no hookups, and no love affairs," he repeated the rule word for word. "Right?"

I nodded reluctantly.

"And last time I checked, I'm not your boyfriend, and we haven't hooked up. At least, according to my definition of a hookup. But that leaves the last part." I fell flush in the face as his thumb brushed against my cheek. "Remember what I said at the club?" he asked.

As if I could forget. Which part was he referring to?

"If you wanted me, you should've just said."

"I want you all to myself."

"Do you like one or two, baby?"

"I intend to know everything about you, angel." He surprised me with his answer. "And I certainly can't let you walk out of that door unless you give me a chance to." His lips now hovered over my ear, "so, what do you say, Celeste Kinney? Will you give me a chance to break one of your rules?"

My mind was spinning. What in the world did a guy like Zeke want anything to do with a girl like me? We were complete paradoxes. If I was hot, he was cold. If I was the sunshine, he was the clouds. And if I was the good, he was undoubtedly the bad.

It made no sense. But there I was, craving the cold, the clouds and the bad. I craved it more than I'd ever known.

111

"Hmm?" he prompted again as I faintly nodded, a smile forming on his lips as he connected them tenderly to my cheek. "Good," he spoke. "Now that that's settled, it's time for bed."

Before I could even question where I was meant to sleep, he'd picked me up effortlessly as my legs wrapped around his waist. "You do know I know how to walk, right?" I laughed quietly as he made his way into his bedroom and placed me on his king-sized mattress.

"I know." He reached over to his drawers, handing me a simple black t-shirt. "But I'd much rather have you in my arms. You're sleeping with me tonight."

To You, Iyla

CHAPTER EIGHT

I Y L A

PRESENT DAY

Never in my life had I seen so many variations of flowers. It was like I'd died and gone to heaven. If heaven included a very cute but very congested boy constantly trailing behind you.

"Are you sure you're okay?" I asked Ambert, who'd just sneezed for the seventeenth time since we'd arrived.

"Yeah," he replied, although his watering eyes and bright red nose indicated the contrary. "I'll be...*ah-choo!*...okay."

"Alright, Rudolph," I teased, grabbing his hand and pulling him toward the main entrance. "It's time to go."

"No, really," he insisted. "I'm okay, let's stay a bit...*ah-choo!*... longer."

"I've seen so many plants today, I could become a botanist." I reached for a tissue on the way out, handing it to him. "Besides, I want to see what else you have in store for me."

"Thanks," he mumbled, taking the tissue from my hand.

"Have you always had allergies like this?" I asked as we reached his car and climbed inside.

"Pretty much." He sniffled.

"Then why did you decide to bring me here?" I laughed, beginning my award-winning performance of pretending Hallie hadn't spoiled the entire day for me beforehand.

"Hallie told me that you loved gardening and plants...you do, right?" he stammered, worry washing over his face as he looked over at me.

"I do," I reassured him with a smile, his shoulders relaxing in relief. "I had a lot of fun, Ambert. I promise."

"Good." He crumpled up the tissue and placed it inside his pocket. "So, what do you say? Off to our next spot?"

I nodded excitedly as he reversed out of the parking lot. "Where are we going?"

"There's this spot by the waterfront with some of the most delicious food. I hope you're hungry."

"Definitely," I remarked in laughter. "Looking at plants all afternoon builds up quite the appetite."

He joined in on the laughs as a ringing radiated throughout the car, and the word "Dad" appeared on his display screen.

"Oh, sorry." His face fell into an unimpressed expression as he glanced over at me, his finger hovering over the screen. "Is it okay if I take this?"

In the short time since I'd met Ambert, I could tell that he was notorious for saying the word "sorry" all the time. Like, every time he'd sneeze, move around someone, or even accidentally bump into a plant. Had he not told me he was born and raised in California, I would've assumed he was a Canadian.

"Don't be sorry," I shook my head reassuringly. "Answer it."

He nodded apologetically and tapped the "accept" button on the screen. "Hey, Dad," he spoke. "What's up?"

"Ambert." A deep voice came through the phone, evidently catching him off guard.

"Z?" he responded, confusion written across his face.

"Yeah, sorry to bug you, A, but I'm just down at the shop, and I can't seem to find my phone, so your dad gave me his instead."

"That's alright," Ambert answered. "What's up?"

"Did you happen to pick up my torque wrench from the other

night? I can't seem to find it anywhere."

He scratched his head. "Oh, I might've..." He leaned over to me. "Would you mind checking if there's a tool in the backseat?"

"Wait, are you with someone?" the voice asked as I began my search for the tool.

"Yeah..." Ambert responded, a hint of shyness coming through in his tone. "Everyone seems to have impeccable timing when I'm out."

"Is this it?" I lifted a clunky silver tool from the backseat into the air.

"That's the one!" He nodded in confirmation.

"You're on a date?" the mystery voice lifted in surprise. "God, that makes me feel old."

"Alright, when do you need the tool?" Ambert shot me an embarrassed look.

"Now. Can you swing by?"

"Fine." Ambert sighed. "You're lucky I'm heading in that direction. I'll be there in fifteen minutes."

Even through his frustration, I couldn't help but appreciate his soft features. His delicate lips. The freckles that cascaded along the bridge of his nose and across his cheeks.

"Ugh." He cut my internal admiration short as he placed his head on the steering wheel. "Next time we go out, I'm leaving my phone at home."

"It's okay..." I chuckled, reaching for his hand. "A little detour won't hurt."

He brought my hand up to his lips and planted a soft kiss on my knuckle. I couldn't help but think about how his lips had now grazed my cheek, my hand, and not the one place I wanted them to touch: my lips.

"You're the best." He held onto my hand until we pulled into his father's auto shop.

The exterior appeared recently re-finished, with a new sign, windows, and freshly painted parking lines. "Nice shop," I commented, clutching the door handle. "Let's go."

"You...you want to come in?" The hesitation in his voice stopped me, causing me to turn toward him.

"I mean, yeah," I replied. "Unless you don't want me to."

"No, no, it's not that I don't want you to. It's just...you know, my family can be a lot. They ask tons of questions, and I don't want you to feel uncomfortable."

"I get it. I'll just wait for you here." I smiled, releasing my hand from the door and settling back in my seat. Maybe Ambert was right. Perhaps the time wasn't right for him to just spring out some random new girl.

"Are you sure?" He seemed stressed. "I don't want you to feel like I don't want you around. I really like you, Iyla. Like, *really* like you."

I didn't even realize the smile that was plastered across my face as I watched him speak. Before I could stop myself I leaned over and gently planted my lips on his.

Never in my life had I instigated a first kiss. But for some reason, the timing felt right.

Ambert felt right.

Besides, seeing how his lips had been about to form the words, "I'm sorry," yet again, I couldn't help myself from cutting him off.

He embraced the kiss instantly, his hands making their way into my hair as his tongue gently caressed my lower lip. I could feel him smile against my lips, which only made me want to kiss him more. By now, I'd almost completely forgotten that we were inside his car, let alone in the parking lot of his dad's auto repair shop. It was as if time had stopped, and all that mattered at this moment was—

Thud.

Thud.

Thud.

Three loud taps on the window. I broke the kiss and ricocheted back into my seat.

"Goddammit," Ambert muttered under his breath before swiftly turning his head. He was met with a man who, by the looks of it, was thoroughly unimpressed with our antics. "I'll be right back." Ambert reached for the tool I still had in my lap.

As he stepped out of the car, I exchanged a momentary glance with the man, and immediately, I fixated on his eyes.

They were green. Incredibly green. Some of the greenest eyes I'd ever seen in my life.

But that wasn't what struck me the most. The weirdest part of it all was that this man seemed to be looking at me as intently as I looked back at him. It was almost as if we knew one another— yet his face was unfamiliar, and before I could analyze it further, Ambert stepped in front of the window and blocked us from each other's views.

I faced forward and sat back in my seat, trying not to think too much about the interaction. I mean, the guy was a stranger to me. Perhaps I just looked like someone he knew. Or maybe I reminded him of someone. Either way, a mindless stare was nothing to be concerned about.

A moment later, Ambert climbed back into the driver's seat as the man headed towards the shop.

"He seems kind of scary," I remarked, watching his long strides carry him across the parking lot.

"Z?" he questioned as he buckled his seat belt.

"Is that his name?" I wondered. "Z?"

"No, his name is Zeke," Ambert clarified. "Well, Ezekiel." He shifted the gear into drive. "But don't let him fool you. He may seem scary on the outside, but Zeke's a good guy with a good heart."

As we pulled out of the lot, Zeke and I exchanged one last stare through the window before I finally turned away.

Although I believed what Ambert had said was true, something about Zeke made my head feel flustered, and my mind flood with questions.

"How do you know him?" I let one slip past my lips.

"He's been close friends with my parents for a long time. So, growing up, he was always in my life...except for the first few years."

"What happened the first few years?" I continued to prompt him, noticing a hint of hesitation on his face before he responded.

"Some stuff happened back in the day," he paused. "It's something my family avoids discussing, so I don't know much. And if I'm being honest, I try not to ask."

He seemed flustered by the subject as he pulled up to a red light, triggering my own apologetic side.

"Oh, Ambert, I didn't mean to push or anything. I know it's not my place to be asking you these personal—"

This time, he cut me off as he re-connected his lips with mine, picking right back up where we'd been cut short moments before. Ambert's kiss was soft and tender this time—it was as if my lips had finally found the one place they were meant to be: with him. It was pure bliss until a loud honk reminded us that the light had turned green, pulling us away.

"I think I like this form of communication." He smirked.

I felt a rush of heat wash over my cheeks. "I think I do, too."

"So, how about that dinner?" He reminded me why we were driving in the first place.

But by now, the only thing I wanted to taste was his lips pressed back against mine.

� ✩ ☆

"Those seriously might've been the best French fries I've ever tasted in my life. We've got to come here again," I grinned, looking up at Ambert as we walked hand in hand along the beach, swinging our arms back and forth.

He knit his brows together in thought. "Is that an invitation for another date?"

"Maybe..." I shrugged, trying to hide my smile with a bite of my lip. "Just maybe."

"I'll take what I can get." He laughed that adorable laugh of his, pulling us down so that we both sat in the sand as he wrapped his arm around me. "I want to know so much more about you," he spoke softly after a brief moment of silence. "Tell me who Iyla Larson is."

I let out a breath of air at the weight of his question. "Oh boy, where do I even start?"

"Well, for starters, what's something that not everybody knows about you?"

Without a second passing by, I thought of the most obvious snippet of my past. "I'm adopted."

"Really?" Ambert's eyes widened in surprise as he looked at me. I confirmed with a nod. "I'm not sure about all the details, but since my birth mother passed away and my dad wasn't in the picture when I was born, I was eligible for adoption. My adoptive parents got the call, and I guess the rest is history."

"Wow. I would've never guessed." Ambert took a moment to process what I'd just said.

"Well, you also haven't seen my parents," I responded with a laugh. "We look nothing alike. They both have icy blonde hair and blue eyes and here I am, a brunette with green eyes. The genetics don't exactly line up there."

"Hey, you have something against blondes with blue eyes or something?" he pouted, making a reference to his own features.

"Not at all." I pecked his lips softly with a smile. "I think they might very well be my type," I spoke before silence settled between us for a few moments.

"Were you born in Columbus?" he finally spoke up.

"Los Angeles."

could almost see the lightbulb go off in his mind. "It's all starting to make sense now." He nodded, deep in thought.

"What are you talking about?"

"The other day, you told me that California was your dream and that being here felt like home. I guess that's because it *is* your home."

His words surprised me as he connected the dots between what I'd just said to our conversation on my birthday.

"See, you *are* intelligent." I playfully nudged him, referring to the meaning of his name, which made his eyes light up. "What?" I smiled innocently. "You're not the only person that remembers something that happened that night."

He placed a gentle hand behind my head and ran his thumb across my cheek. "You want to know another thing I remember telling you that night?"

"What?" I bit down on my lower lip as I glanced at his, my voice just quiet enough for him to hear.

"That you were beautiful in blue. But..." He glanced down at the purple top I was wearing today. "I think I like purple more."

I blushed at his words.

"Beautiful in all colors." He leaned into another kiss.

Except for this time, there was no one knocking on the window.

No traffic lights telling us we had to go.

It was just him and I by the water, in the sand and under the stars as night fell and closed out what felt like the perfect day.

To You, Iyla

The Eighth Entry
CELESTE
19 YEARS AGO

JULY 19

I woke up tangled in soft white sheets the following day as faint beams of sunlight illuminated the bedroom.

As my eyes fluttered open, so did the memories of the night before and the reality that I had Zeke's arms wrapped around my waist. I peered down at him, taking a moment to analyze his delicately refined features. To my dismay, my admiration was quickly replaced by realization and panic.

Oh my gosh.

I was in his bed. We'd slept together all night.

Not *slept*, slept, but you know what I mean.

I'd never slept in a bed with a man in my life. Hell, I'd never even had a sleepover before going to college.

Everything with Zeke felt like a first.

I sat up, moving carefully so that I wouldn't wake him. As I straightened out, an imminent headache radiated throughout my temples, reminding me that my binge of alcohol from the night before wouldn't be so easily forgotten.

I made my way back into the kitchen, reaching up on my tiptoes to explore his cupboards and hopefully find some pain relief.

121

"See what you're looking for?" Zeke's voice frightened me.

"Shit." I jumped, causing him to smirk. "I, uh...I just...I just needed something for my headache."

I wasn't sure if my anxiety resulted from being jump-scared from behind or seeing Zeke's shirtless body in front of me.

He dissected my gaze for a brief moment before placing his hand on my lower back, barely having to reach up as he grabbed the bottle I'd been searching for. "Were you looking for this?" He handed it over to me. "Or were you just being nosy?"

"A little bit of both." I couldn't help but reveal a hint of the truth as I untwisted the cap and shook two tablets into my hand, Zeke handing me a freshly poured glass of water to take with the pills.

Before we'd gone to sleep last night, I'd changed into one of his t-shirts. It almost mimicked the feeling of his hands running down my body—a feeling that I'd be lying if I said I hadn't been awake most of the night thinking about.

Not to mention what he had said to me.

"Will you give me a chance to break one of your rules?"

I shook myself out of my daydream as Zeke found his way into one of the chairs surrounding his dining table, a coffee in hand. "Come," he called out. "Have a seat."

I made my way over to the table and pulled up a seat beside him.

"How did you sleep?" he asked.

"Good," I responded, mentally kicking myself for being so awkward. "You?"

He shot me a devilish look. "Never better."

I had to gulp down the lump in my throat as he spoke up again. "Are you hungry?"

I placed my hand on my growling stomach, "starving."

"Perfect." He took a final swig of his coffee. "Because I'm taking you for breakfast. And..." He stood up, "a certain someone wants to make sure you're okay."

122

I shot my head up. "Claire?"

"Yeah, remember her?"

"Vaguely. How did she get in touch with you?"

"It was Korey who texted me. He suggested we meet up at his friend's coffee shop in an hour or so. But I think he just wanted to make sure I didn't kidnap his girl's best friend."

I raised an eyebrow. "Do you have a history of kidnapping?"

"Not that I recall," he responded. "But there's a first for everything."

I rolled my eyes at his sarcastic comment, a smirk playing on my own lips. "Can I use your shower before we go? And maybe stop back at my hotel to grab some clothes?"

"What? You don't want to wear this?" He looked my body up and down. "I quite like it."

I smacked his arm. "Just give me a towel."

Laughing, he guided me back into his bedroom and placed a fresh towel in my hands. "I'll wait for you out front." He threw on a white t-shirt from his drawers. "If you need me for anything, just give me a shout."

✕ ☆ ☆

"Zeke," I called out from the bathroom, a towel wrapped around my body. I'd been in the midst of getting dressed when I realized that I would *not* have a repeat of the night before and wear a dress on his bike. I needed some pants, at the very least.

"Zeke?" I raised my voice a bit louder.

No answer.

"Zeke," I yelled out a final time, walking out of the bathroom and back into his bedroom.

Which drawer did he grab his t-shirt from?

I let out a sigh. Zeke was nowhere to be seen, leaving me with no choice but to take matters into my own hands. I started to search through his drawers, beginning with the bottom left one.

Socks.

Wrong.

Next, the middle drawers.

T-shirts, dress shirts, sweaters.

Shit.

How about the bottom right?

I pulled it open to reveal nothing but a mixture of ties and miscellaneous items.

"Where is it?" I muttered, slamming the drawer closed and getting one of his ties stuck in the process. "Crap." I pulled it back open to push down the tie when my hand grazed a paper-like material.

Paper?

Curiosity got the better of me as I moved aside a few articles of clothing to reveal stacks upon stacks of cash. Cash that was tightly wounded and bundled together.

What is this?

Why is this here?

Why does it look like he's trying to hide it?

"Celeste?" I heard Zeke call out from the hallway. My heart skipped a beat at the sound of his footsteps approaching as I quickly shoved everything back to where it was and closed the drawer.

"Hey." He walked into the room, his eyes pausing on the towel still wrapped loosely around my body as I stood up. "Did you call me?"

"Um, yeah," I stuttered. "I was just...wondering if you had a t-shirt and shorts I could wear. You know, until we get back to the hotel? I just don't want to wear my dress on your bike again."

"No fun." He playfully winked before nodding towards the dresser. "Check in the top right drawer."

Of course, the one I didn't check.

"Thanks," I mumbled as he disappeared from the room, yet, my mind wandered back to the money I'd seen before. What was it for? And why was it there?

The looming questions kept my mind alert as I dissected the challenge that lay ahead of me—*Zeke*. But a challenge never scared me. Being challenged was what I both hated and loved the most in the world.

Why was that?

It was an oxymoron that I couldn't quite get past. With pursuing a career in law, every case would be a challenge and possess its own unique setbacks—but that was what made it so exciting.

Perhaps I hated the challenge but grew to love the rewards from it. Maybe that's what intrigued me about Zeke, that first time we met eyes. It wasn't his looks or body or how he could effortlessly protect me against anyone that stood in my way. It was the challenge that I saw within him.

A challenge that, all of a sudden, I was determined to conquer. A mystery I was sure to solve.

I quickly slipped on the first pair of shorts I could find, threw on the black shirt I'd slept in, and walked out of the room.

"Look at you," Zeke commented as he looked over at me.

"I feel ridiculous." I held my arms out to demonstrate how ridiculously oversized his clothes were on me.

"I mean, it's definitely a look. I'd let you borrow my shoes, too. But at this rate, I'll have to charge you a rental fee. Plus, I doubt they would fit you." He seemed amused by the situation. "Unless you're a men's size twelve. Which honestly would be hot." He reached out to pull me into his arms.

His sense of humor always caught me off guard. Zeke wasn't just some big, angry-looking guy all of the time. He knew how to laugh. How to joke. How to make me smile.

"You're gross and ridiculous." I reached for his door handle, desperate to get to the hotel as soon as possible. "Korey told me that you didn't speak much," I remarked as he followed me through the door and towards the elevator. "Why does that appear to be untrue?"

He smiled. "I only talk when there's someone worth talking to."

"Well, I like your voice. I want to hear you talk."

"I'll say whatever you want to hear," he responded, brushing a hand over my face.

"Oh, yeah?"

Tell me what all that money was in your dresser.

"I'm not another one of your conquests, am I?" I pressed, bypassing the burning question in my mind and instead referring to his words from last night. Would our breakfast be the final hurrah before he sent me on my way?

He appeared taken aback by my question as the elevator door re-opened. "Of course not."

"So, I'm not just some mission along the way?" I raised my eyebrows at him suspiciously.

"You, my angel," he took a step toward me so I was now looking up at him, his dark curls resting so delicately above his forehead. "Would never ever be a mission. You're a destination, and I only want a one-way ticket."

126

CHAPTER NINE

I Y L A

PRESENT DAY

"Where are they meeting us?" I asked Hallie as I brushed out my curls in the mirror.

"Just outside Dickson Court, according to Vic. It's close to the School of Law building for you and not too far away from my classes either."

The day had finally come. A big day, might I add: orientation day.

This was my chance to familiarize myself with the campus, meet some faculty and ensure I got started on the right foot. Thankfully, since Vic was a junior at UCLA, the campus environment was second nature to him.

In other words, not only would he be our personal chauffeur for the day, but he'd also be our campus tour guide—a role I'm sure he was utterly thrilled about.

On top of it being orientation day, today also marked one month since mine and Ambert's second date. Since that night, I'd seen Ambert almost every day. We'd basically turned into Vic and Hallie.

"So..." Hallie took a seat on her bed. "How are things with Ambert? Are they good?"

"They're more than good, to be honest," I responded, trying to hide my lovestruck smile. "Things are great."

"Oh..." Hallie raised an eyebrow suggestively. "I see. Lucky you."

"Hallie, no." I ran my makeup brush along my cheeks, ignoring her remark. "We haven't even gotten there yet. Things take time, and it will happen when it happens. How long did it take you and Vic to..." I tried to beat around saying the word itself. "You know..."

"Have sex?" Hallie looked at me intently as she spat the words out of her mouth.

"Yes," I mumbled under my breath, awkwardly meeting her eyes in the mirror.

"Well, it depends on the type of sex you're referring to. If we're talking about oral—"

"Hallie," I cut her off. "You know what I mean. Please, don't tell me about the other stuff you two get up to. God."

"Fine, fine," she caved. "I was trying to avoid saying this, but you've left me no choice...it was your birthday."

"What?!" I snapped in disbelief, whipping around to face her.

"I said it was your birthday," she repeated point-blank.

"You mean to tell me that you had sex with Vic for the first time on my birthday? Of all days, Hallie?" My shock was overtaken by a fit of laughter, and I wasn't sure if it was because I was uncomfortable or if I genuinely found the thought of it funny.

"It wasn't like you were having birthday sex, so I had to take one for the team."

"What a sacrifice you had to make."

"Oh, get over it," she scoffed. "If it makes you feel better, it might not have even been your birthday 'cause it was just before midnight. So, like, it could have started on and then ended after."

"I get it." I tried to stop her. "Trust me, I do."

"Do you want to have sex with Ambert?" she caught me off guard with the sheer bluntness of her question.

"I mean...of course," I replied, avoiding her very direct eye contact.

"Have you two gotten close yet?" she pried.

"A little bit," I responded briefly, giving her little to work with as I turned back to the mirror and ran an applicator over my lips.

"What the hell does 'a little bit' mean?"

"We've gotten into heated make-out sessions. But I shut it down before things escalated," I admitted, taking a seat across from her on the bed.

"How'd you shut it down?" Her brows creased in curiosity.

"I'd tell him that I wanted to take things slow. Or that where we were wasn't the right space to, you know...go there. He understood, and he never made me feel bad about anything. He just reassured me and suggested something else for us to do."

"How charming," she responded. I couldn't tell if she was impressed or being sarcastic. "Why is there hesitation on your part? It's not like it's your first time."

"I don't know." I huffed in annoyance as I brought my hands up to my forehead, trying to process all the thoughts rushing through my mind. "Maybe that's exactly why I'm nervous. I don't want to open up to someone and get hurt again."

Hallie opened her mouth.

"Don't you dare turn that last part into an innuendo."

She pouted. "You know me too well. But listen, Iyla," she began. "Don't let Dalton and his cheating ass stand in the way of you doing something you want to do with someone you care about. At the end of the day, do what's best for you. If that means waiting, then that's okay. But if that means going to the next step with Ambert, then that's okay, too."

I let out a breath, knowing damn well that everything she was saying was true. I couldn't let the past affect my future or interfere with someone I cared about.

"Wait," she added with a long pause. "Is Ambert a virgin?"

"I...uh...I don't know, actually."

"Does he give off virgin energy?"

"*Virgin energy*? What the hell is virgin energy, Hallie?" I felt so out of tune with her vocabulary. "Is that even something I should've asked him? Did you ask Vic?"

"You bet your ass I asked Vic. One, I'm nosy, and two, because I was curious."

I frowned. "Sometimes I wish I had your confidence."

"You do." She stood up from the bed and pulled me up with her. "You've just got to find it within yourself."

I pondered internally over her last sentence as we gathered some final things around the room.

"He wasn't, for the record," Hallie clarified after a moment. "Judging by the way that tongue worked, it was pretty obvious."

"Okay, enough of this sex education conversation." I headed towards the door.

"You're right." She winked. "We've got some hot guys to meet and hopefully some even hotter professors to talk to."

☆ ☆ ☆

"Fancy seeing you here!" Hallie squealed, running into Vic's arms and wrapping her legs around his waist. At the same time, I walked over to Ambert far less theatrically and embraced him in a hug.

"Hey, Iy." He pulled me in for a kiss as we interlocked our hands.

"So, Mr. Tour Guide," I looked at Vic as he let Hallie down. "Where's our first stop?"

"There are a couple of orientation events. Depends on what you three want to do first," he responded.

"Let's meet some of the faculty members first," I suggested to the group.

"Oh no, it's the fun police," Hallie teased, nudging me with her shoulder. "But she's right. We should focus on the school stuff first."

Ambert nodded in agreement, displaying another thing I'd learned about him: his carefree and go-with-the-flow nature. As much as he'd say "sorry," he'd also say, "sounds good," or "works for me," almost every time I'd suggest an idea.

"Okay, Iyla, that's the law building there." Vic pointed towards the building behind me. "Ambert, your classes are in Royce Hall, and Hal, you've got some classes in MacGowan Hall, which isn't too far away from here."

"Perfect!" Hallie clapped in excitement. "Let's meet back here in an hour."

"Works for me." Ambert smiled, causing me to chuckle to myself.

See what I mean?

As Hallie and Vic walked towards the northside of the campus, Ambert gently squeezed my hand and rested his forehead against mine, clearly sensing the anxiety that threatened to wash over my face once the laughter had passed. "Hey, are you okay?"

"Yeah," I responded, desperate to convince myself just as much as I was trying to convince him. "Just a bit nervous, that's all."

"I'm not nervous for you." He kissed my forehead. "My girlfriend is going to blow everyone away."

I still couldn't get over how the word 'girlfriend' rolled off his tongue. It had only been a few weeks, but even so, the feeling hadn't worn off. "I just want to make sure I leave a good first impression. They say first impressions are the most important, and if I mess this up, then—"

He pressed his lips against mine to cut me off; this tactic had somehow become our way of reassurance or confirmation—and I wasn't mad about it.

"Just be yourself, okay? I know you, and I know you'll do amazing."

I took a final deep breath in. "I hope so."

"No more stalling." Ambert walked me towards the front door.

"Now, it's your time to shine."

The Ninth Entry

CELESTE

19 YEARS AGO

JULY 21

As we pulled into the parking lot at Tim and Sally's, I noticed Claire sitting on the hood of a blue sedan with Korey by her side. The two seemed to be engaging in a conversation that was soon interrupted by the revving of Zeke's motorcycle as we pulled up beside them.

Claire's jaw dropped as I removed my helmet and stepped off the bike. "Celeste?" she questioned, clearly in disbelief.

"Hey, Claire." I smiled at her before her shocked gaze shifted and landed on Zeke.

"I don't know who you are, but all I can ask is, how did you manage to get her on that bike? Do you know she's always had a personal vendetta against them?"

Zeke smirked in my direction. "A vendetta?" he repeated.

"Not so much a vendetta," I argued. "But a personal distrust in the safety and level of risk associated with motorcycles."

"It's a vendetta, Celeste." Claire rolled her eyes as she walked back over to Korey. "Hey, can you feel my head? I think I might have a fever. Too much is happening this morning."

"You're fine." He laughed, pulling her to his side as they

embraced in a kiss.

Claire and Korey were an immediate match. It was as if I could see their whole future in just a few seconds as they stared at each other.

A big house, dream jobs, kids running around. That cookie-cutter life, the one Claire always wanted. The one she deserved.

"It's great to see you again, Celeste," Korey spoke up in my direction. "And Zeke," he shifted his attention. "You remembered how to get here?"

"It wouldn't be my first time," Zeke responded, prompting a momentary pause.

"Well, all right then. Let's go get some food, shall we?"

We followed Korey as we made our way inside.

"I thought you said you never break your rules," Zeke whispered into my ear as we inched towards the door.

"I don't," I hissed back, doing my best to ignore the heat that soared to my core as a result of his warm breath.

He cocked an eyebrow, amused at how every syllable that left his mouth always forced a redness to my cheeks.

"*Usually*," I muttered as the door chimed once we'd walked through the door.

"Welcome to Tim and Sally's!" a man appeared from behind the counter, pausing when he recognized Korey's face. "Korey? What are you doing here?"

"What? I can't stop by to support my best friend's business?" Korey mocked.

"Is that what you call it when you want someone to cook for you?" he shot back, brushing some flour off his hands and onto his apron.

Korey rolled his eyes as he gestured towards Claire. "Timmy, this is Claire. Claire, this is my best friend, Timmy."

"It's nice to meet you, Claire." He waved. "And don't listen to anything Ree-Ree tells you. It's Tim."

Korey's face turned red as Claire burst into laughter. "Ree-Ree?" she repeated.

"What? He hasn't told you what his mom calls him yet?" Tim's eyes sparkled with delight as he playfully teased him.

"No, but after this conversation, I know exactly what I'll call him from now on."

"Okay, okay." Korey put his hands up in mercy. "Let's continue with the introductions, please. Zeke, you've met *Tim*." He emphasized his name. "And Celeste, this is Tim. My annoying best friend, who happens to own this coffee shop with his wife, Alma."

"It's great to meet you, Tim." I reached over the counter to shake his hand. "The food smells amazing and I'm ready to eat." My stomach rumbling confirmed my words.

"Whatever you guys want, it's on the house!" Tim smiled. "Alma would kill me if I made you pay for anything."

"What would I kill you for?" A pregnant woman appeared from the back. "Oh, hi, everyone." A grin formed on her face as she examined ours. "Tim, you make sure everything is on the house for them, okay?"

"What did I tell you?" Tim shook his head and took each of our orders before we found a comfortable booth by the window.

Zeke sank down beside me, Korey and Claire sat across from us, and Alma pulled a chair from an empty table to join us.

"I'm Alma," she more formally introduced herself. "And this..." she placed her hands on her swollen belly. "Is the bun that needs to get out of the oven."

"Can I?" Claire reached to place her hand on Alma's stomach, who nodded agreeably.

"Do you like babies?" Alma asked as her eyes shifted to Korey with that "I like her already" look.

"I do," Claire responded, not catching Alma's glance at Korey. "I can't wait to have my own."

I shook my head internally, knowing just how much Claire did, in fact, love babies, kids, and any children for that matter. Claire had always talked about being a mom. She'd told me she wanted to have a baby within a year of graduation.

"Don't you want to work a little bit?" I would ask her, questioning why that was her plan after spending so much time in school.

"Being a mom *is* work," she'd scold me. "But this way, I'll be an educated mom who will begin her career after she's had all her babies."

"Alma!" Tim shouted from across the restaurant, breaking me out of my flashback. "Could you give me a hand?"

"I'll be right back." She slowly got up from her chair and waddled behind the counter.

I looked over to Zeke, who had been awfully quiet throughout the entire exchange. "You said this isn't your first time here, right?"

"Yeah, it's not. I've been here a few times before. With Korey, of course."

I gave him an affirming smile as I placed one of my hands on his leg, hopeful that he'd remember our conversation back in the elevator.

"I want to hear you talk."

"I'll say whatever you want to hear."

"So, Korey," I butt in. "How long have Tim and Alma owned this place? And how come it's called Tim and Sally's, not Tim and Alma's?"

Korey smirked at my curiosity. "Full of questions," he remarked with a cock of his eyebrow, wrapping an arm around Claire. "They've owned it for about a year. Sally is a nod to Tim's grandmother—the person who got him into cooking. Not some other lover, so don't worry." He winked.

"How old are you?" Claire asked Korey in an attempt to continue the conversation.

"Twenty-five," he responded.

"You better watch out, Claire," Zeke finally spoke up. "Korey's an old man."

"Zeke." Korey sighed, seemingly unimpressed. "I'm one month older than you."

"Still older, *Ree-Ree*." He wrapped an arm behind me as I settled in, a faint laugh escaping my lips.

"You know what?" Korey crossed his arms. "You guys are being childish. And besides, age is but a number. I'm seasoned. I'm ripe."

"That you are." Claire raised her eyebrows suggestively, prompting my cheeks to redden.

"I've got goodies!" Alma sang out, working her way back over to the table as she carried an assortment of baked goods and drinks. "Enjoy your brunch, guys. If you need anything, let us know."

"This smells amazing!" Claire reached for her croissant and what I assumed was a chai latte as I grabbed my blueberry scone and tea.

Zeke had ordered a modest black coffee and a sesame bagel. In contrast, Korey must've been ravenous, considering he ordered a donut, breakfast sandwich with a hash brown and a large orange juice.

"Zeke?" Claire peered up at him after a few bites. "Tell us more about you. How long have you worked at Club Affinity?"

"A couple of years," he answered briefly as he sipped on his drink.

"And how do you like it?"

"Yeah, it's okay." He shrugged. "Spring break tends to be a nightmare, so I take the week off."

His response made me think. "Then why were you there yesterday?"

"I got called in." He looked over at me, but my gut told me that that was far from the truth.

As if he could see my mind piecing together the follow-up questions I had already formulated, Zeke started to slide his way out of the booth.

"Where are you going?" I asked.

"Just to the bathroom." He kissed my cheek. "I'll be right back." As he fell out of earshot, I looked over to Korey. "Is he always this mysterious?"

He shrugged. "Yes and no. I told you, it really depends on the day with Zeke."

"Well, what do you know about him? He said you guys were good friends."

Korey let out a sigh. "Zeke's complicated. Let's just say that he's been through some tough shit, and I helped him for a while."

"What did you do?" My eyes carefully scanned the café for any sign of Zeke returning. Nothing yet.

"When I met Zeke years ago, he didn't have a place to stay. He'd been sleeping inside the club during the day and working all night. I mean, I felt bad." He reached for his drink, taking a momentary sip. "Anyway, I told him, 'listen, if you ever need a place to go, my door is always open.'"

"Did he stay with you?" I asked, shifting in my seat as my mind whirled in response to this new information.

"At first, no. It took him a couple of weeks before he actually took me up on the offer. Then when he did come, he ended up staying for a few months."

I was taken aback by this revelation when Claire spoke up. "Did you learn anything more about him in that time?"

"Not really," Korey shrugged. "Zeke's always been secretive. He didn't even tell me when he was leaving. One day I came back from work, and all his stuff was gone, with a thank you note and a stack of cash. *Way* more than it would've cost in rent during that time."

Stack of cash...the dresser...were these two related?

"Have you seen his place?" Korey asked me, although he knew it was a rhetorical question. Of course, I had. That's where I was all night. "I have no idea how he can afford that. He's a bouncer, for God's sake...but between us three, I've learned that sometimes it's better not to ask. Besides..." He leaned back. "Zeke's a—"

"Asshole? Idiot? Better looking person than me?" Zeke's voice caught us all off guard.

Korey scoffed; clearly a bit flustered by his sudden reappearance. "Definitely the former."

Zeke winked as he sat back down in the booth and wrapped his arm around my body. "Everything good?"

Far from it.

Why were you sleeping in the club?

Why didn't you have a place to stay?

How were you suddenly able to afford your new place?

"Everything's good," I responded with as convincing of a smile as I could muster. As everyone else jumped back into the conversation, I couldn't focus. All I could think about was the tormenting questions in my mind.

Zeke had said he intended to know everything about me, and now, I could say the same about him.

✫ ✩ ✩

"This has been fun, guys!" Korey was the first one to tap out of our conversation. "But, I promised this one that we'd go out for the day." He nodded in Claire's direction. "Let's do this again, okay?"

As we peeled ourselves one by one out of the booth, Claire reached for my arm. "Mind if I steal her for a moment?" she asked Zeke.

Zeke released me from his embrace with a smile. "We'll meet you guys at the front."

I nodded as Claire pulled me over to the side of the café. "You're not mad at me, right?" she whispered.

"No," I responded with a confused shake of my head. "Why would I be?"

"I just..." She paused momentarily, chewing on her lip hesitantly. "I feel bad. I shouldn't have left you in the dust last night. But I saw you with Zeke, and honestly, I thought if anyone could take care of you," her eyes darted in his direction, "it was him."

Him.

"You know...he seems interesting," she added, her eyes still on him as she spoke.

"That he does." I rubbed the back of my neck. Zeke was interesting, but in a way, I couldn't quite put my finger on it.

"Hey, I wouldn't worry too much about what Korey said earlier," she tried to reassure me. "You should give him a chance."

"You think?" I wondered.

She smiled. "I know."

"Claire, are you ready to go?" Korey called out.

"Coming," she called back. "I'll talk to you later, CeCe. And remember, *anything* is possible with an open mind."

I rolled my eyes.

"What?" she laughed. "I told you I could be philosophical."

"It's better than the ice cream analogy. I'll give you that."

"Hey, that analogy's proving to be true, isn't it?" she teased. "Zeke is definitely *not* strawberry. I'm guessing he's more of a rocky road guy. But you can confirm that and report back to me later." She winked, resulting in another shake of my head as we headed back to the front and said our final goodbyes to Tim and Alma.

"Wait, hang on!" I heard Claire call back out as I reached for my bike helmet.

"What?" I asked, freezing in place as she pulled her disposable camera out from her bag and snapped a picture of Zeke and I.

"Claire!" I scolded her. "What the heck?"

"Oh, hush." She stepped into the car and rolled down the window. "Now I have photographic evidence of Zeke if he doesn't come back with you."

Zeke, who had evidently started to warm up to Claire's unique sense of humor, seemed to find her statement entertaining. "See you around, Claire," he smirked.

I gave them a slight wave as they pulled out of the plaza and honked their horn as they drove down the street.

"Well, that was...fun." I looked towards Zeke, trying to find a word to best describe what had been a brunch I hadn't anticipated.

"I thought you might enjoy that." He secured my helmet on top of my head. "Ready to go?" he asked as he ignited the engine.

"That depends. Where are we going?"

"Somewhere special," he answered simply.

"Should I be worried?" I murmured, wrapping my arms around his waist.

"With me, never."

CHAPTER TEN

IYLA

PRESENT DAY

The law building was unreal with its ridiculously tall ceilings, magnificent brick walls, and grand staircases. I was in total awe.

As Ambert left to talk to his faculty, I went on the hunt for my own. So far, the two I'd spoken to—Dr. Rodrigues and Dr. Lowe—seemed friendly but firm. They'd explained that attending the pre-law program would undoubtedly take a *lot* of work but assured me that I seemed like a "smart girl" and someone who would thrive with the challenge.

My anxiety was through the roof as I tried to visualize how much work I would have to put in over the next four years. After all, I hadn't come all this way to not put every ounce of my being into this program. The reality was I had something to prove—and someone I needed to prove it too.

It gave me some confidence knowing that I'd taken the time to introduce myself to them. My hope was that they'd recognize me by the start of class or at least go a little bit easier on me.

"Who's next on your list?" Dr. Lowe asked as she peered at the list of classes and professors I'd printed out and now held tightly in my hands.

"Dr. Sanders," I responded.

"Oh, Dr. Sanders is wonderful!" she smiled warmly. "This might be one of his last years teaching with us."

"Really?" I questioned. "How come?"

"Dr. Sanders has been here a long time. Over twenty-five years, so I'm sure he's getting the itch to retire."

"I can only imagine." I laughed softly as I glanced back down at his name on my sheet. I couldn't help but wonder if Dr. Sanders had taught my birth mother—or at least heard of her. I could feel my eyes light up from just the idea that Dr. Sanders might be another piece of this pre-law program and my journey to connect with her.

"It was great meeting you, Iyla. Dr. Sanders is upstairs and to the left." Dr. Lowe gave me a gentle pat on the back as I headed towards the grand staircase and made my way toward his office.

As I moved down the hallway, I passed a row of class graduation pictures on the wall. They started in the eighties and worked their way up to the latest graduating class of last year.

Would her picture be here?

My heart skipped a beat in anticipation that I might see a picture of my birth mom for the first time in my life. By now, I was rushing through the hallway, following the years as they went by, hoping I'd see the year she graduated...the year I was born.

What would she look like?

Did I look anything like her?

Would she be proud of me right now?

I was consumed by so many thoughts as I intricately scanned the dates. When I finally reached her year, I braced myself in search of her name...

But instead of a photo, a small gap was what my gaze was met with.

"What?" I whispered to myself. I desperately turned around to head back down the hallway and double-check that I hadn't missed another board from the same year when my body collided with someone else's, causing a handful of papers to fall on the floor. "I am so sorry." I scrambled, heat rushing to my cheeks in embarrassment as I bent down to gather the papers. "I wasn't paying attention."

"It's alright," an older male voice spoke as he kneeled down to give me a hand.

"I was just looking for Dr. Sanders."

"Look no further," the man replied as he took the papers out of my hands.

I peered up as I read the "Hello, My Name is Dr. Sanders" tag on the suit of the older gentleman.

Of course.

"Dr. Sanders, I'm so sorry," I stuttered, frantically standing up and straightening my shirt before holding out my hand to shake his. "My name is Iyla Larson. I'm joining the program this year and wanted to introduce myself. This certainly wasn't the introduction I was hoping for."

"Don't worry about it." He chuckled, giving my hand a firm shake before gesturing for me to come into his office. "I'll definitely remember you now."

His office was decorated with UCLA memorabilia, photos, diplomas, and a plush chair he indicated towards. I hovered by the front door as he sat at his grand desk. "Please sit down."

I nodded, still slightly flustered and embarrassed by our interaction, as I sat across from him and analyzed our surroundings.

A moment of silence passed until I redirected my eyes back to Dr. Sanders. His brows were furrowed as he chewed on his bottom lip and stared at me watchfully, causing me to straighten my back awkwardly before he finally spoke up.

"I'm sorry, Iyla, I don't mean to stare." He shook his head and raised his hands with a laugh. "You just...you look a lot like someone I used to teach."

My stomach fell to my feet. "Really?"

"Oh, yes," he responded. "She was among the best students I've ever taught in my twenty-five years here at UCLA."

"Wow..." I could barely keep my hands from shaking as I held them in my lap, so I resorted to tucking stray strands of my hair in place. "That's a lot to live up to, I guess."

"Celeste," he spoke up. "Her name was Celeste Kinney. She was remarkable. Truly one of the most naturally gifted people I've ever met."

Did he just say Celeste Kinney?

As his words slowly started to sink in, I could feel the color draining from my face. It was like I'd been transported back to the Pacific Plummet roller coaster. The way I had to gulp down the nausea festering inside of me reminded me of it.

Did Dr. Sanders really know her?

"Iyla?" Dr. Sanders shook me out of my trance, leaning forward as he attempted to assess the shock ridden all over my face. "Are you okay?"

"No...I mean, yes...but no," I told him, barely able to answer such a simple question. I paused momentarily and took a deep breath before finally locking my gaze with his. "I'm sorry, Dr. Sanders. It's just...I really didn't expect you to say that name."

He seemed even more confused as he tilted his head to the side, prompting me to explain further.

"The student you're referring to," I began, my voice shaking. "Celeste Kinney. She's...my mom."

He narrowed his eyes slightly at my response. "Your mom?" he questioned. "Are you sure? I don't believe Celeste ever had any children. I saw her a few months before...she passed. She was pregnant? I had no idea."

I hated the fact that I couldn't clarify a single one of his questions. All I could do was confirm that Celeste did have a child, and that child sat right in front of him, just as in shock as he was.

"I'm so sorry, Dr. Sanders. I really don't know what to say. The whole thing is a long story, and I don't want to keep you." The words rushed out of me so quickly that my mind struggled to keep up.

"I've got time," he responded, his calm demeanor being undercut by the sense of urgency in his tone. "Believe me, for Celeste, I've always got time. Tell me everything, Iyla. Please tell me everything you know."

"Everything?" I gulped, internally evaluating how to best approach this. I'd only ever told select people in my life the little details I knew of my birth mother, but never anyone who'd actually known her. Would my words even do her justice?

"If I'm being honest, Dr. Sanders, everything isn't all that much."

He allowed for a long-drawn-out period of silence to fall between us before I finally gathered enough courage to get somewhere with my words.

"After Celeste gave birth to me, she passed away for reasons I only wish I had the answers to. And once she was gone, I ended up being adopted."

"Adopted?" he repeated. "What about your father?"

"He wasn't in the picture, I guess." I shrugged, dropping my gaze back to my hands in my lap. "Nor were any other immediate family members."

I could feel him assessing me as my hands now started to clam up.

"So, you grew up in California, then?"

I shook my head. "Columbus, Ohio. That's where my adoptive parents are from."

"All the way out east." He pursed his lips curiously. "Yet here you are, finding your way back west. I'm guessing you being here isn't a coincidence, is it?"

It amazed me how he intuitively dissected each of my words, reading into the real meaning that hid behind each of them.

"It's certainly not a coincidence." I sighed, meeting his soft gaze.

"Growing up, the ins and outs of my adoption remained pretty tight-lipped. All I ever really grew to know about my birth mom was her name and that she came to UCLA for school and took this program."

"That's it?" His voice was full of disbelief.

"That's it." I nodded in confirmation as the emotion built up in my eyes. "As I said, everything isn't much."

He paused, thinking over my words. "You know, my dear, everything can become something in time. In fact..." He handed me a tissue as I dabbed my tears away. "Look at what it's becoming right now."

A smile formed on my lips, his reassurance and understanding encouraging me to ask him for one of the many wishes that always consumed my thoughts. "Do you think you could tell me more about her?"

"Oh, boy." He leaned back in his chair, his eyes sparkling in memory of Celeste as he looked up at the ceiling.

I couldn't believe I was sitting with someone who had memories of my birth mother.

"Where would I even begin? Celeste was the brightest, most driven, and kindest student I had ever met. In all my years of teaching, I'd never written a reference letter for a student. Celeste was the only person I ever ended up doing it for."

My heart picked up in pace as I listened attentively to his words, clinging to each one.

"You see, Iyla." Dr. Sanders pushed his chair away from his desk and stood up. "Celeste made quite an impact on this program." He gestured to the wall on his right, where a sole class graduation photo hung. "And me."

I raced out of my chair and towards the picture Dr. Sanders was pointing at, doing my best to ignore the lump forming in my throat. "Is this...is this her—"

"Class graduation picture?" he finished my sentence. "Yes, yes, it is."

"Oh, my goodness." My hands found their way to cover my mouth in awe as I scanned through the series of faces.

"Here she is." Dr. Sanders pointed to a blonde girl in the front row, standing beside a younger, much less gray version of himself.

I was astonished. I didn't think I could ever pull my eyes away. There she finally was.

Perfectly posed with long blonde hair, hopeful blue eyes and a soft smile. Her cheeks gave her the essence that one would call a "baby face." As I looked at her, I couldn't help but feel as though I was looking right back at myself.

"I have another picture of us together." Dr. Sanders walked back over to his desk and opened his drawer.

"You do?" I achingly broke away from the photo.

"Ah, yes." He pulled the picture out of his drawer and placed it into my eager hands. "Here you are."

Dr. Sander's had his arm wrapped across her shoulder in this photo. This time, she wore a graduation cap and sash with the words "Kinney" and "honors" stitched into it.

She had her hair tucked back as the redness rose into her cheeks. Small lines formed around her eyes as she smiled, and instantly, I could feel a sense of love and joy that she radiated outwards.

"When was this taken?" I asked as my eyes darted down to her stomach.

"At her graduation, which must've been the end of May." He scratched his head. "I told you she didn't look pregnant."

He wasn't wrong. Standing in a white dress, she had no visible baby bump whatsoever. She was petite, lean, and in no way, shape or form looked as if she would give birth to me a few months later.

Had she even known she was pregnant at this point?

"You seem surprised." Dr. Sanders chuckled softly. "It's as if you've never seen a picture of her before."

I remained silent, meeting his eyes after a brief moment.

"You *have* seen a picture of her before, right?"

I shook my head. "I told you, when I was adopted...my parents didn't speak about my birth mother and life before me. The information I've shared with you has been the only information I've ever known."

"Well, then let me be the first to say this to you," he spoke softly. "You look just like her."

I felt my breath hitch in my throat at his words, completely unsuspecting of the pang they caused in my heart. "You think?" I whispered, scanning the picture even more carefully now, desperate to compare every intricate detail of myself with hers.

"You must've gotten your dad's eyes and hair, but other than that, you're all her. You remind me a lot of her, too."

"You have no idea how much this means to me." I shook my head. "The reason I wanted to come to UCLA, the reason I wanted to join this program, was to learn more about my birth mother. Even if it was just a single detail. I want to do everything in my power to retrace her footsteps. So, meeting you right now is just...unbelievable."

"Oh, Iyla..." A smile fell over his face. "This is just the beginning."

I smiled appreciatively up at him. "Would you mind if I take a picture of this?" I pulled out my phone, worried that I might never see the photo again if I didn't take the chance now.

"It's all yours." His words took me by surprise.

"Are you sure?" I asked incredulously. "I don't want to take away something that's just as important to you as it is to me."

"You deserve it a whole lot more than I do," he insisted. "And besides, what are photocopies for?"

I choked out a laugh as tears welled back in my eyes, my gaze returning to the photo of her. I couldn't look away.

"I'm going to tell you something, Iyla, and I want you to remember it now, okay?"

I nodded in response.

"When you come from greatness..." Dr. Sanders placed an arm on my shoulder. "You're destined for greatness. And you are going to do great things, dear Iyla. I know you are."

The tears that had been brewing in my eyes flowed onto my cheeks as I pulled him into a hug. It felt like only the right thing to do at that moment. "Thank you, Dr. Sanders," I whispered against his chest. "Really, thank you."

"Dr. Sanders?" A knock came through the door as a small group of students poked their heads in, causing us to pull away as I brushed away my tears.

"I'd better get going." I reached for my bag. "Thank you again. And I'm so sorry about what happened earlier."

"If I was only going to remember you because of that, I will certainly never forget you now," he responded with a grin, prompting a smile to tug on my lips as well.

As I made my way down the hallway after our goodbyes, I focused on the picture in my hand with a new sense of ignited hope.

"I'm going to make you proud, *Mom*." I smiled down at her through my tear-filled eyes. "I promise."

The Tenth Entry

CELESTE

19 YEARS AGO

JULY 30

It took us half an hour before we arrived at Surfside, a spot Zeke had mentioned wasn't as popular for the tourists and college crowd—which meant some privacy and, more importantly, an opportunity to talk. I felt like so much, yet so little had been said between us, and I was ready for that to change.

Once we'd hopped off the bike, Zeke pulled out a small blanket from below his seat.

"Do you always keep that in there?" I joked, considering the thought of this burly man carrying around a blanket in this motorcycle made me want to burst into laughter.

"For the most part. You never know when it might get cold." Zeke intertwined his large hand in mine, kissing my temple as we walked along the waterfront.

After a few minutes of walking, Zeke stopped under a small cluster of palm trees that perfectly shaded us from the sun.

"This is your spot?" I questioned.

"This is my spot," he confirmed as he threw the blanket onto the sand. "It's the spot where I can chill, breathe and escape."

We laid down on the blanket together as I glanced up at his dark green eyes, desperate to sneak a glance inside his stubborn mind.

"What are you thinking about?" he mumbled softly, tucking some hair out of my face.

"Wouldn't you like to know?" I threw back at him, trying to give him a taste of his own medicine—one that leaves you searching for answers that don't seem to exist.

"I would, actually." He flashed a grin, turning on his side and prompting me to do the same. "Tell me what you're thinking."

"Do you want me to be honest with you?" I cocked an eyebrow.

"I wouldn't expect anything less." He shrugged. "Tell me."

I sighed. "I can't stop thinking about why you were working last night. What was the real reason you were there?"

"I told you at Tim and Sally's. They asked me to come in." His response was brief and confident enough, but I could immediately sense some underlying tension in his voice.

"Why do I feel like that's a lie?" I questioned, the inner lawyer in me beginning to come out.

He paused, visibly taken back by my shift in demeanor. My persistence to get an answer that I knew he was withholding.

"Now I want to know what *you're* thinking about," I added, keeping my eyes locked on his.

"I think that I could ask you the same thing, Celeste. Why were you at the club last night?"

I shook my head, frustrated by the fact that he had chosen to deflect my question back at me instead of answering it himself. "That's not fair. I told you, Zeke. Claire wanted to come."

"Sure..." He nodded, unconvinced. "But what about the night before? You know, when you saw what happened? Did that not make you realize that the club wasn't a safe spot for you?"

"Not at all," I protested. "If anything, I was intrigued."

"Intrigued?" He seemed dumbfounded. "You watched me get into a physical altercation with a bunch of idiots. What about that was intriguing to you?"

"It wasn't what happened with those 'idiots' that intrigued me..." My voice trailed off. "It was you."

Finally, my own truth slipped out.

"Me?"

"Yes, you," I sighed. "It was weird. After I first saw you, it was as if I'd seen you in a million different lifetimes, and each time was more surprising than the other. It's like I found you...again. I don't know. It was a strange feeling. It was like..." I paused for a moment, rolling my words over on my tongue. "It was as if I wanted to know who you were this time around. And it's true. It's not just you that feels that way. I want to know *you*, Zeke...everything about you," I clarified. "And I'm sorry if that's too forward or uncomfortable. I mean, you know I don't have too much experience with other—"

"I only worked last night because I convinced myself that there was a small chance you would come to the club," he cut me off. "And if you did, I wanted to do everything I could to see you again. Hell, I would've gone in every single night this week on the slim chance that you were there. When you and Claire actually showed up last night, I couldn't believe it."

I bit down on my lip, thankful to have at least one wall knocked down. "I could tell."

"What do you mean?" He glanced at me curiously. "How?"

"Your eyes." I ran my hands through his hair. "They seem to tell me more than your words."

"Is that right?" he smirked, widening his eyes dramatically. "And what are they telling you right now?"

"Hmm..." I placed my hands on either side of his face, staring into them steadily. "They tell me that there is much more to you, Zeke, than you let on."

He paused, shifting backwards slightly as if my statement struck a chord. "I'm not that deep."

"I'd argue otherwise." I remained solid. "Why do I get the sense that you don't enjoy talking because you're afraid of bringing up some...stuff?"

"And what *stuff* would you be referring to?" he questioned. I could see a hairline crack forming in his foundation—and I was the water, ready to break through.

"You know, the stuff that makes you, *you*."

"Maybe because it's not worth knowing," he retaliated. "It's a part of my life that I don't want to speak about."

"I feel the same way about most parts of my life," I agreed. "But maybe if I tell you about my past, you could tell me a bit about yours. You know, the stuff worth knowing."

He didn't seem convinced by my proposition. "I don't know, Celeste. I wouldn't even know what to say."

"Well, then." I fell back onto my spine. "Just let me do the talking. I seem to be the better one at it, anyway."

He smirked yet seemingly agreed as he allowed me to begin.

Re-hashing my past had always been easy. I'd learned to disassociate myself from it. It was almost as if I'd written a script and rehearsed it in my mind, waiting for its grand delivery. But the reality about my story was that so much good, change and clarity had happened since all of the bad. Therefore, rather than solely focusing on the hiccups of my life, I tried to emphasize all the positives. How hard I'd worked to get into UCLA. How much family law meant to me. How I discovered a family for myself along the way.

Silence fell between us as Zeke attempted to process everything I'd shared, visibly having difficulty overlooking my attempt at sugar-coating the past. "I'm sorry," he murmured as his hand lingered over top of the scar from the wine glass that remained all these years.

"It's okay." I pulled his hand away and planted a few soft kisses on his palm. "I'm okay, and it's all in the past now. I don't even know who that girl is anymore. All I've done since then is work to build a better life for myself. A life that you know about now."

"But your parents," he questioned. "Where are they now?"

"I couldn't tell you. I cut them off years ago. I'm assuming they're still in Oregon, but I have no interest in speaking to them ever again."

He looked down at me somberly, kissing me softly as if he wanted to take my hurt away. A part of me wished he could.

"Thank you for telling me." He turned onto his stomach and adopted a frown. "I guess now it's my turn."

I tried to reassure him. "I don't expect you to have to bare your whole soul to me. I just want to get to know you better."

He shook his head and jumped straight into his story without wasting a breath.

"I'm not from California either. I'm from New York, just outside of Queens, in an area called Murray Hill. My dad had been a firefighter my whole life, and after my parents divorced, I spent most of my time with him. We did everything together. He was my best friend." He forced a pained smile. "Growing up, I wanted to be exactly like him—so much so that I was in the works of finishing up my time at the fire academy.

It was just like any other day when he got called in for a house fire. Once they got to the scene, he and his colleagues went inside to rescue the family that was stuck on the second floor. Thankfully, they were able to get them out safely, but my dad realized that his colleague was still inside. When he rushed back in, he found him trapped by some debris."

He paused for a second, swallowing the emotions that threatened to break through his voice.

"He was trying to help him break free when part of the house collapsed. Neither of them made it out. I was almost twenty-one when it happened." His voice was barely above a whisper now.

"Oh, Zeke," I began, unsure what to say as the unmistakable sadness stained his face.

"After he passed away, things changed, and my life took a completely different turn." He let out a breath as I leaned over to rub his back. "I dropped out of the academy and fell into a depression. My relationship with my mom completely fizzled out. My dad had been the only thing that held us together. Then, in the weeks after his funeral, I found myself trying to get out of New York. Everything became a constant reminder of him and that he was gone. The first place I thought of going to was California. My dad had always told me that it was the city of angels. And with the demons I was dealing with, a city full of angels sounded like the perfect spot for me. And so, I packed up my life in New York and took the first flight out to Los Angeles with absolutely no plan whatsoever. I inherited a good amount of cash after my dad passed, but that dwindled in food and shitty accommodations. Soon enough, I realized that Los Angeles was just a hotter New York and that moving states wouldn't magically solve the issues I was dealing with."

I nodded, trying to piece together his story as he shared it with me. "So, how did you end up working at the club?"

"I was dealing with a lot of frustration and anger, and I joined a fighting club. It was a way to make quick cash and unleash my pent-up emotions. But I started to have trouble separating those emotions when it came to life outside of the ring. Because of that, a buddy of mine suggested that I come down to Long Beach. He said it would be a nice escape from the downtown core, but the second I got here, I got into a little bit of a fight on the boardwalk."

"A fight?" I repeated. "A fight over what?"

"I have no idea," he scoffed at the memory. "I blacked out. I don't even know why I reacted the way I did. But I lashed out and managed to fracture the guy's skull."

"Zeke..." I shuddered in disbelief as my hand covered my mouth. "Why would you do that? Oh, my gosh...was he okay? Did you call an ambulance?"

"I should stop." He pulled my hand away. "This wasn't a good idea. I don't want you to look at me differently."

"I'm sorry," I apologized. "It's just a lot to take in. Please don't stop. I want to know what happened after."

"Celeste..." He paused again, running his hand along his forehead.

"Please," I urged him, kissing his cheek softly. "Tell me what happened next."

He let out another breath before diving into the story once more. "Well, since this happened on the boardwalk, the owner of Club Affinity had seen the fight. He pulled me out of the situation and offered me a bouncer job right on the spot. He said that he'd never seen anyone take down someone so effortlessly. At the time, I was hesitant. I didn't think a club would be the right fit for me. Hell, nothing in California seemed to be. I still had it in my heart that I wanted to get back into firefighting and do it for my dad."

"Why did you go for it then?"

"By the time the owner found me, the cops were already on their way." He shifted. "So, in a panic, he told me he'd deal with everything and make sure I didn't get in trouble. Desperate not to get charged and finally have a better source of income that didn't come with getting punched in the face every few nights, I took him up on the offer. Let's just say that I didn't expect to still be working here after all these years. Things have gotten out of my hands now."

He looked at me with a sense of sadness and grief behind his eyes. By now, the water had more than crept into the foundation. We were swimming in this mess together.

"That's my story." He let out a sigh, falling onto his back as he looked up at the sky. "And you're right. I choose not to speak much because talking means remembering. Remembering means feeling, and feeling is something I haven't done in a very long time."

I kept my gaze on him for a moment, a look he misinterpreted as that of judgment rather than the genuine relief I felt to have finally broken through his hard exterior.

"I knew you would look at me differently. I shouldn't have said anything."

"Of course, I'm going to look at you differently, Zeke." I stopped him this time. "How could I not?"

His face turned weary, but I kept going.

"You're resilient and strong, and you've made the best out of your situation. And I'm sorry for everything you went through. I only wish I could have known you then. We weren't far from each other," I frowned.

Zeke and I were tethered to one another—whether we knew it or not. Our pasts intertwined more than I'd ever thought to be possible. It's a funny thing, isn't it? A sadistic humor that the one person who you'd need more than anything, and do more than everything for, can be so close yet feel so far away.

If only the two of us had such a hope that the best was yet to come...a reminder that something greater was in store.

"But you're here now." His lips connected briefly with mine, taking the thoughts right from my mind. "And I never want to let you go."

We held onto each other until he spoke back up. "You know, my dad was right about California being the city of angels."

"Why's that?" I asked.

"Because when I'm with you, I feel like I'm in heaven."

To You, Iyla

CHAPTER ELEVEN

I Y L A

PRESENT DAY

"What a long day," Hallie groaned as the four of us made our way back to Hedrick Hall. "I'm totally exhausted."

"You're exhausted?" Vic scoffed as he carried Hallie on his back. "How do you think I feel?"

"Are you saying I'm heavy?" she leaned down to look at his face.

"Uh, oh, stop talking right now, Vic," Ambert butt in, making me erupt into laughter.

"No, you're not heavy at all," Vic changed his tone. "Is that a feather on my back? I can barely feel a thing."

"Nice save." Hallie rolled her eyes before jumping down and sticking her tongue out at him.

I shook my head, a grin on my lips as I watched their playful interactions. I couldn't help but feel thankful. Thankful that I was in Los Angeles with my best friend in the world and grateful that I had a boy by my side who, so far, had exceeded any expectations of the person I envisioned myself with. Ambert was kind, funny, caring, and, most of all, possessed a soulfulness that made me feel as if I'd known him my whole life.

But above all else, I saw my mom. Today I walked in her shoes and fulfilled a piece of why UCLA was my dream. Part of me wanted to shout from the rooftops. The other part wanted the moment to be mine and only mine. And maybe someday, when I felt ready, I could share everything with my parents, Hallie, or even Ambert.

But for now, this victory was mine to keep.

We walked for another couple of minutes as we approached Hedrick Hall. "Thanks for the tour, Mr. Guide," I joked to Vic.

"My pleasure." He smiled. "I'll send you all the bills shortly."

"Wait!" Ambert jumped in, shifting from one leg to another. "Vic and I forgot to mention something."

"Oh, shit, yeah." Vic seemed to recall what Ambert was saying. "Our parents want to meet you guys," he said casually, his cool demeanor the polar opposite of Ambert's.

"They do?" Hallie's eyes lit up in excitement as she grabbed Vic's arm.

My reaction was far less enthusiastic. "Together?" I questioned. "Are they friends or something?"

"Best friends." Vic looked over at Ambert with a smile. "Since before we were even born. They want to know if you guys would like to come for dinner this weekend at Ambert's. I promise they aren't too bad. Well, my parents aren't, at least," he teased.

Hallie's bright eyes searched out my approval.

"Saturday?" I paused, lips pressed together.

"Saturday," Ambert confirmed. "Around five o'clock, if that works for you two."

Their hopeful glances in my direction pushed me past my hesitation as I nodded, agreeing to the idea. It wasn't that I didn't want to go. It was that Ambert and I had only just put a label on what we were—and by the end of this week, I would be meeting his whole family?

"Well, that settles that!" Hallie clapped her hands happily. "We'll be there."

"Perfect." Vic looked back over to Hallie. "Do you want to go on a drive?" He proposed. "I think I owe you an apology." He shot her a look I knew meant much more than "drive" and a simple "I'm sorry."

Without hesitation, she reached for his hand. "Catch you guys later."

"Have fun, you too," Ambert shouted as they walked off. "They're a good match, eh?" He looked over at me.

"Yeah, the kind that lights on fire, that's for sure," I agreed with a giggle.

"Burning love." He played along with a laugh. "But I'm happy to see Vic with someone like Hallie. He's had some girlfriends in the past that I don't think we're all that good for him."

Hallie's voice instantly consumed my mind telling me to ask Ambert about Vic's exes.

Instead, I pushed away her demanding voice and decided that now was a better time to lean into Ambert's former love life instead.

"There aren't a lot of girls out there like Hallie," I agreed. "But what about you? Any ex-partners I should be worried about?"

He wrapped his hands around my waist. "Like...two in high school that are hardly worth mentioning. What about you?" he threw my question back to me. "Any ex-boyfriends I should be worried about?"

For a moment, I contemplated if I wanted to get into the details of my former relationships but decided that a synopsis wouldn't hurt.

"I guess I'm quite like you. I dated some people in high school, but things didn't work out. My last relationship was a bit tougher of a breakup, if I'm being honest. He cheated on me, so that kind of sucked."

Ambert shook his head in dismay. "What a dumbass."

I laughed, thinking back to Hallie's reference to Dalton's Abrams initials. "I think Hallie would agree with you on that one."

"Hey, you know what?" He planted a soft kiss on my forehead.

"His loss is my gain."

By now, the sun had set entirely, and the only light came from the stars and streetlights above us.

"Do you want to come upstairs?" I asked, gesturing towards the residence building we'd been standing in front of this entire time.

"I think I'd like that."

The
Eleventh Entry
CELESTE
19 YEARS AGO

AUGUST 7

We must've fallen asleep on the beach sometime in the late afternoon. I woke up first and brushed my hand through Zeke's hair as I peered up at him in adoration.

How quickly can you fall in love with someone?

But also, how do you differentiate love from any other feeling? I mean, what does love actually feel like? To me, love felt a whole lot like fear. A feeling that I'd grown comfortable with my entire life.

Fear of rejection. Fear of failure. Fear of not being enough.

Yet, from the moment I first saw Zeke, I knew that this fear was one that I'd never experienced before. The fear stemmed not from what I am but from what I am not without him, and that scared me. It scared me more than anything else.

The sky grew dark as thunder echoed over the water, prompting Zeke to stir awake.

"We need to go." I sat up as a few rain droplets quickly turned into a full-on downpour.

"Shit." He stood up, grabbing the blanket and reaching for my legs before effortlessly slinging me over his shoulder.

"Zeke!" I screamed through my laughter, my body shaking with each step he took. "Put me down! Slow down!"

I could feel his own body shake with laughter as he ran to an empty bus shelter by the pier, placing my now-soaking wet body off his shoulder and onto the ground. The giggles continued to escape me as I leaned against the glass as the rain continued to pound down above us, falling so hard that I could hardly see across the street.

Instead, I could only see Zeke's white shirt turning translucent, the wet material clinging to his firm chest and abdomen.

My cheeks flashed to a bright shade of red, matching my bra that was now just as visible through my equally sheer blouse.

"Zeke, this is crazy," I shouted, trying to ignore every single nerve ending in my body that told me to get closer to him rather than standing on the other side of the bus shelter.

As if he read my mind, Zeke strode over to me, pushing the wet hair out of my face and firmly pinning my body against the glass. "God, you're a dream," he whispered against my lips, gently brushing a water droplet off of my lips before crashing his into them. I immediately melted into the kiss, letting him take control as his hands ran down the sides of my body. His mouth stayed with mine before he gently worked towards my neck and down my chest. My mind became wholly consumed by the sound of the rainfall and his soft moans against me. Nothing quite compared to how his voice sounded as he repeated my name.

"Celeste."

How he told me how beautiful I was.

"You're the most perfect woman in the world."

How he reminded me just how much he wanted me.

"Fuck, I could take you right here."

Until I could handle no more.

"Let's go back to your place." My words surprised me as much as they seemed to surprise him.

"What?" he mumbled against my lips. "Are you sure?"

"Yes," I whispered, hardly able to pull back from his touch. "Take me back to your place."

"Now?"

"Now," I demanded, as the desire burned me from the inside out.

He wasted no time lifting me into his arms as he carried me across the parking lot and placed me down and onto his bike. "This is going to be the longest ride of my life." He grinned softly as the water droplets formed at the tip of his hair and dropped onto my face.

I pulled back yet again, biting down on my swollen lips as I tried to calm my sense of urgency.

It was as if my metaphor from earlier in the day had come to fruition. The second Zeke allowed himself to open up, all the water came crashing in. It was as if his life was beginning, just like it did for me when I met Sharlene.

Yet, unlike my child-like state, Zeke wouldn't be alone. I knew being there with him, I could never leave.

He was mine.

I was his.

And there was no way I would let him drown.

As Zeke jumped onto the bike and pulled out of the parking lot, I barely had a chance to strap in my helmet.

The logical part of my brain told me we shouldn't have been speeding the way we were, especially considering how slick the roads were. But the adrenaline that pumped through my veins told me otherwise. It said the aching feeling of being closer to him was more important than anything else.

Once we pulled into the parking garage, we rushed towards the elevator, our lips reconnecting during the short ride up.

Zeke fumbled with his keys as my body pressed against his door. As soon as he could finally open the lock, he kicked the door in, causing me to fall back, but he caught me before I could touch the floor and carried me to his bedroom, slamming the door shut.

"You have no idea how much I want you." He pulled off his wet t-shirt and placed me on his bed.

My shaky hands searched for his belt, but Zeke removed it himself in one swift motion, unzipping his jeans and pulling them down.

With his now half-naked body in front of me, I attempted to tug away at my blouse. Zeke ultimately had to help me to get it over my head as the material clung to my skin.

"Fuck," he whispered as his body hovered over mine. "Can I see all of you, angel?" His hands worked their way over to the button of my jean shorts.

I nodded, despite the pounding in my chest. I'd never felt so scared but so alive, so safe at the same time.

"Talk to me." He toyed with the fabric. "You've been so quiet. Do you want this?"

I reached for the back of his neck. "Yes," I murmured into his ear. "I want you to see all of me, Zeke. God, I want only you to."

He smirked as he undid my jeans, effortlessly slid them down my thighs and tossed them away.

"God, you're the most beautiful woman I have ever seen." He kissed above my panty line tenderly before his lips trailed up to my cleavage. "My Celeste," he murmured, the slight rasp in his low voice sending my body into a complete and total frenzy.

I couldn't get over how my name rolled off of his tongue.

I was certain that it existed just so I could hear his voice say it.

"Are you sure you want to do this?" He whispered, pulling away slightly as he met his eyes with mine.

I'd always heard the phrase, "giving yourself to someone". And at that moment, I knew that there wasn't a single part of me that I didn't want to be his. And no part of him that I wouldn't claim as my own. His touch was electric, his body magnetic, and I was utterly drawn to him.

"I'm certain." I breathed out shakily. "I've never been so certain. I want to experience this with you and only you."

His hands found their way underneath my bra as he engulfed the entirety of my chest and kissed me slowly.

I felt like I was in heaven.

"Zeke," I moaned against his lips, the reality of what I'd just agreed to slowly sinking in.

He hummed in response.

"This is my...my first time doing anything. So, I don't really know what to expect."

"I'll take care of you, angel," he whispered. "We'll go slow, I promise, okay?"

"Okay," I responded softly.

"Do you trust me?" His voice was so delicate, I wished I could've wrapped myself in it.

"I do." I'd never been so sure about anything.

"Then let me give you exactly what you want." He reached over to his bedside table and into his drawer. "Fuck..." His body sunk down in defeat.

"What is it?" I questioned, my heart beginning to race.

"God dammit." He ran his hand through his damp hair. "I don't keep condoms here. I've never been...with anyone in my apartment before."

"Oh." I felt flustered, unsure what I was meant to say or do in this situation.

"I think I might have one in my jacket, but I'll have to go and—"

"I'm on the pill," I blurted out hastily.

"You're *what*?"

"I'm on the pill," I repeated nervously.

"But you said you've never had sex."

"I haven't. I'm on it to regulate my period. It's not just for contraception. You know that, right?"

"So, what are you saying? You want to have sex with no condom?"

I supposed that was exactly what I was saying.

"I mean, yeah." I gulped. "Unless you don't want to."

"Don't say that." He leaned his forehead against mine. "I want to. I want to so fucking badly. But I just want to make sure that you know exactly what you're agreeing to. What *we're* agreeing to. I mean, I promise I don't have anything—"

"Do you want me?" I asked him, wondering how he'd suddenly become the responsible one of the two.

"More than anything," he mumbled.

"Then show me," I whispered, demanding his touch. "Learn everything about me."

Without another ounce of hesitation, he pressed his lips against mine once again, the two of us desperately tugging at each other for more. It was a feeling I'd never felt before—this angst, this pure desire for nothing else but him. His hands found their way toward the back of my spine, unclipping my red bra and discarding it to the side.

His eyes darkened as he scanned my body, stopping above my panty line. "Now, as much as I love these..." His fingers ran along the seam. "They need to go."

I went to release the fabric from my hips when he replaced my touch with his mouth, planting soft kisses along my inner thighs as he used his teeth to tug away at the material. "God." He stared down at me, his hands resting on my thighs. "You're a fucking masterpiece." He swiftly spread my legs apart before kissing along my inner thigh, closer and closer before finally connecting his mouth with my heat.

I breathed in sharply at the pure bliss his touch sent through me in waves. "Zeke..." I fell victim to his touch, his tongue, his hands. "More...I want more," I whispered, my hand shakily reaching down to get tangled in his hair.

"Patience." His voice vibrated against my skin. "I'm only just getting started." His fingers found their way toward my entrance.

"Now, now. Let's answer that long-awaited question, shall we?" He gently slipped one finger inside me, pulsing back and forth as my head was forced back into the pillow.

"Zeke," I whispered breathlessly at his movements until he pulled out and slowly placed his index finger into his mouth, leaving me to gape at him as he locked his eyes onto mine.

This was sick. And I couldn't look away.

"Let's see how you like two." He toyed with me slowly before re-entering with two fingers at a much slower pace.

A soft moan immediately escaped my lips as my head fell back once more, my entire body tingling with a desire for more...and more.

"I guess the answer is two, my angel." A sly smirk formed on Zeke's face as louder moan escaped my mouth, this time prompting my hands to fly up to my face.

"Don't." Zeke pulled them back with his other hand, resting them above my head. "Don't ever hold back. I want to hear you moan for me, and only me."

"I just..." I swallowed, my breathing unruly under his touch. "I just don't want to be too loud."

"I want the whole goddamn floor to hear the way you're moaning for me." He kissed along my neck, quickening his pace with his fingers. "You're mine, angel. Remember that."

I felt a surge of sensation and pleasure built up in my lower body as my toes started to curl. "Zeke...I think I'm...I'm..."

"Come for me, angel." His words tipped me over the edge as my body climaxed, a sense of euphoria releasing against his touch. "That's it." Zeke encouraged as I carried out my orgasm. "So fucking good for me."

As my body slowly came down from its high, Zeke's touch gently pulled away before he leaned down and left a few more kisses on my skin, trailing up my body to my lips.

"Zeke that was...that was...I...I don't even know what to say," I whispered, closing my eyes.

"Baby," he murmured against my lips. "We're only just getting started."

My wandering hands found their way over the top of his boxers as I palmed his firm erection. "Let me touch you."

"Uh-uh." He grabbed both of my wrists and placed my arms above my head once again. "You're going to be a good girl," he teased as one of his hands moved to pull away his boxers. "Tonight is all about you."

I caught a glimpse of his size as he lined himself up to meet my entrance. "Maybe we should have tried three," I raised my eyebrows at him.

He smirked. "You can take it." He placed his free hand on my cheek. "But you tell me if anything is too much. You hear me? You've got to tell me."

"Yes." I trembled in anticipation. "I'll tell you. I promise."

"Good girl." He kissed me softly, lined himself up, and eased his way inside me. "God, I've been waiting for this. Craving this. Dreaming of this." His voice was raspy, filled with desire as he thrust deeper with each word. "You're all I can think about. All I'll ever think about for the rest of my life."

The feeling of our bodies connecting as one was unlike anything else. I knew in my mind that I wanted to trust him. He was the only person I'd ever want to share this with. I just had to convince my still-nervous physical being the same.

"It's okay." He finally released my hands from above my head. "You've got to relax, angel. I promise I'll go slow." He pecked my lips as he looked down at me in adoration. "Just relax," he repeated as I closed my eyes and inhaled a deep breath in and a slow breath out.

"Mhm, yes, angel." My frame eased as he continued to pick up speed. "I'm almost fully in."

"Zeke..." I breathed out shakily as our hips connected and he reached his maximum inside me. It took a moment for the slight pain to dissipate into pleasure. A pleasure that radiated throughout my lower body and reflected onto my face.

"Are you okay, baby?" he looked down at me.

"Keep going." I tried to take in every sensation as my hands danced along his back. "Please keep going."

His movements were slow but fast enough to build up a sense of rhythm. "God, Celeste." He picked up his pace as I tugged at his roots.

"Ezekiel," I whimpered as I called him by his full name for the first time.

"What did you say?" he said breathlessly.

I breathed in sharply as his lips brushed against my skin as he spoke. "Don't stop, Ezekiel," I repeated, burying my face in his neck as I planted kisses along him, my fingernails digging into his skin.

He let out an exasperated moan. "Fuck, angel. Call me by my name again," he demanded as I sensed his body clench below, his movements quickening.

"God, Ezekiel...I'm yours," I murmured out slowly. "Show me I'm yours."

"I'm going to finish, baby." He broke his mouth away from mine and connected it back to my neck as he came inside me. "Fuck." His moans echoed throughout my ear as his damp hair connected with my chest.

"Zeke," I choked out as he lifted his head, pulled out and fell beside me.

It's a strange thing, really, the idea that society calls such a quick formidable action "losing your virginity." In reality, I gained something that night with Zeke—a trust that I never thought could be possible and a bond that I recognized would never be broken.

So, sure, I lost a figurative part of myself, but in turn, I was granted something much greater—an insurmountable feeling that I'd found the one to who my soul belonged to. And I knew that that kind of feeling would only come once in a lifetime.

"Are you okay?" He scanned my face. "I didn't hurt you, right?"

"I'm more than okay." I let out a breath as I shifted my body to lie on top of his chest.

I could sense the smile on his face. "I told you, you could take it." He kissed my forehead as my mind continually replayed the absolute bliss of what had just happened.

"You know, you said you didn't have a preference," I said out loud, peering up at him amid the comfortable silence.

"What?" He seemed confused. "What are you talking about?"

"When we first met, I asked you which name you preferred. Zeke, Z, or Ezekiel. You said it didn't matter." The memory seemed to replay in his mind. "I guess that wasn't true, *Ezekiel*." I grinned, kissing his neck as I rested a hand on the other side of it.

"That's because, before you, nothing mattered." He pulled me on top of him, studying my face with a look of adoration.

"What?" I couldn't help but laugh. "Why are you looking at me like that?"

"I just want to know where you've been my whole life." He shook his head. "Where have you been, huh?"

"Waiting." I rested my forehead against his. "Waiting for *you*."

He tucked some hair behind my ear. "Celeste...you're my best friend."

His words caught me off guard.

"What?" I asked, wondering if this was just the post-sex brain talking. "Is that even possible? I mean, can you become best friends with someone this fast?"

"I'd say so," he debated. "Considering I fell in love with you the moment I first saw you."

My world stopped.

He loved me.

No one had ever told me they loved me before. In fact, I'd always believed that "love" was a pitying word—an easy escape for those who were too afraid to showcase the vulnerabilities it implored.

For it's much easier to speak a false truth than live it, day in and day out.

I'd thought that love was this fictitious view of the world that I'd never grow to experience, just as much as I'd never come to know.

Perhaps I'd been wrong.

Sure, the world is a dark, cruel and unsuspecting place. It can throw you left, right and center, and everywhere in between. It can shatter you to your core, build you back up and do it all over again without remorse.

But amidst the suffering and the pain, lies the one thing that can't be taken from us—*love*. And now I knew. I knew that love had to be real. As I heard the word escape his lips for the first time in my life, I believed it. I felt it. I saw it reflected back at me in his eyes, and I knew that a part of me loved him, too.

But with love came the fear of something new...something foreign...something I wouldn't allow myself to say or even think for a second longer. Instead, I obscurely changed the subject. "I need to ask you a quick question, okay? And you need to be honest with me."

His body tensed slightly under me. "Okay, what is it?"

"What's your favorite flavor of ice cream?"

"What?" He was evidently puzzled by the random question I'd been dying to know the answer to since I had that conversation with Claire at Tim and Sally's. "Are you being serious?"

"When have I not been?" I responded, completely straight-faced.

"Hm..." He looked up in thought, trying to hold in some laughter. "I'd probably have to say rocky road—"

"Nope, nope." I stood up from under the sheets and marched my way over to the bathroom. Of course, he said rocky road. And, of course, Claire was right. Maybe I was only meant to try one sample of a different flavour: Zeke.

"What?" he chuckled as he got up from the bed and followed behind me. "Is that bad?"

"If Claire ever asks you that question, you say strawberry or vanilla. Do you hear me?"

"Yes, angel," he responded through his laughter as he wrapped me in his arms and guided me toward the shower. "Now, where were we?"

CHAPTER TWELVE

I Y L A

PRESENT DAY

"Do you regret not living on residence?" I asked Ambert as I sat cross-legged on my bed and reached towards the French fries we'd grabbed from the dining hall.

"Partly." He leaned his head back against the wall, his long legs dangling over the side of the bed. "But it makes more sense to live at home, especially when home is only fifteen minutes away. Although, some time away from my family can be nice."

"I agree with that." I chuckled, picking up another fry and placing it into my mouth. I loved my parents—deeply, for that matter. However, some separation had been refreshing, especially now that I could develop my relationship with Ambert without being bombarded by my parent's natural interests.

"Are you okay?" I noticed a shift in Ambert's expression as his forehead creased in concern.

"Yeah. It's just..." His voice possessed a sense of anxiety. "I hope you don't feel I'm jumping the gun on introducing you to my family. I told my mom and dad that it might be too early, but you know what parents can be like."

"I mean, I'm a bit nervous." I vocalized my concerns. "I want to meet your parents, I do. I just hope they like me."

"Iyla." He shot me a frustrated look. "What isn't there to like?"

"I don't know." I shrugged. "I just get in my head about things sometimes. Like, what do they even know about me, for starters?" He paused momentarily, scratching the back of his neck in thought. "I haven't told them anything, really. My parents don't even know your name."

This time, I shot him a slightly frustrated look. What was the secrecy about? I hadn't told my family about him either, but he wasn't meeting them in a matter of days.

"Why wouldn't you even tell them my name?" I probed.

He sighed. "I told my mom that you went to UCLA, but I was worried she'd look you up or something. I just told them that you're someone who's really special to me."

My annoyance melted away instantly at his words. "I'm special to you?"

"Iyla." He pulled his legs up from over the bed. "I've never met anyone quite like you." His voice was gentle, reassuring, warm... honest. "That day when we met at Tim and Sally's, I was just trying to be friendly. But boy, my world stopped when I saw you behind that wheel."

"You didn't seem nervous," I noted, moving the fries off the bed and onto the floor as I scooted closer to him.

"Are you kidding?" He ran his hands through my hair. "I felt like I was so awkward."

"Hey, I was the one stuttering like an idiot. Not to mention that my car died the second I tried to start it. How embarrassing was that?"

"It was fate," he responded without an ounce of hesitation.

I couldn't help but roll my eyes with a laugh. "You believe in that?" I challenged, although truthfully, I was unsure where I held my own beliefs on the subject matter.

I could say meeting Dr. Sanders was fate, but was it? Had I made my own fate by deciding to come to UCLA? I chose to follow in my mother's footsteps. Is it really fate if you meet it in the middle?

"I'm not too sure what I believe," Ambert retorted. "But I do know that people come into your life for a reason, whether we know those reasons or not. And Iyla Larson," he leaned in to graze his lips against mine. "You're meant to be in my life."

I placed a hand on the back of his neck and pulled him closer, our lips slowly starting to move in sync as he gently pushed my body down and onto the bed. My curious hands found their way under his shirt, which he removed in one quick motion.

I paused, my eyes grazing down his body as I admired his tan skin and muscular torso until his lips cascaded along the nape of my neck, prompting a whimper to escape from my lips.

Chills radiated throughout my spine as we switched positions so I was straddling his waist, pulling off my tank top and revealing my less-than-impressive white bra.

Insecurities threatened to flood my mind until Ambert's electrified gaze washed them away. In a moment, he took me from being scared and unsure to feeling as though I was the most beautiful girl in the world.

His hands delicately caressed the outline of my cups until I reached behind my body, unclipped the strap and tossed it away, leaving his hands to massage my breasts gently.

His touch prompted me to grind my lower body against his, feeling him stiffen beneath me. As my lips connected with his neck, I palmed him through his joggers.

A faint moan fell out of his mouth as I worked my way to the other side, ensuring that no piece of skin was left untouched.

"Iy..." He let out the first word since our simple kiss had escalated.

"Mhm," I murmured into his ear without stopping my movements.

"Iyla," he spoke louder this time, prompting me to break away my lips and lift my head to face his.

His face was ridden with anxiety, and it didn't take me long to realize that *shit*. I'd taken things too far.

"I'm sorry." I immediately pulled back, reaching for my tank top. "That was too much, too fast...I'm sorry, Ambert."

"No." Ambert reached for my wrist to stop me. "That's not it at all. I just want to be honest with you before things get any more... heated." He shifted awkwardly.

My mind began to race. What could he possibly want to be honest with me about right now?

Unless...

"I've never..." He confirmed my thoughts. "I've never actually had—"

"It's okay," I stopped him before he needed to explain himself any further. "Ambert, I should've asked," I shook my head, backing away. "I shouldn't have assumed. I was wrong to jump into things without talking about it first."

"I want to, though," he whispered as he pulled my body back on top of his. "With you."

"Ambert, we don't have to."

"Please." His mouth kissed along my chest. "I want this. I want you." He continued his movements, eliciting a breath to release out of my mouth. "And I know you want me, too."

I caved, allowing him to flip us back around as his lips pressed against mine once more.

"Ambert," I mumbled into the kiss. "Do you...do you have a condom?" It was the first rational thought that came to mind.

"Shit." He dropped his forehead to my chest. "I don't."

I almost felt bad for asking, given that I knew what his answer would be. Still, it was a question that needed to be asked before anything escalated further.

"Wait," I said out loud as a thought came to my mind. "Hallie."

"Hallie?" Ambert lifted his head in confusion.

"Yes, Hallie. Hallie should have some in her drawer." I pointed to her bedside table, thinking back to the chaotic emergency packing she did before she spent the night with Vic.

He instantly reached over to the drawer I had pointed out, and sure enough, there lay a small box with at least a dozen condoms inside. "What did I tell you?"

"Thank God." He laughed, reaching for a gold foil and placing it on the bedside table.

Without missing a beat, we jumped right back into things as I pulled down Ambert's joggers to reveal his sizable bulge beneath a blue pair of boxers.

"Looks like blue is your color, too." I smirked.

He seemed amused at my ability to recall the first compliment he ever gave to me.

He went to respond, but I didn't let him, pulling him back into the kiss as a surge of adrenaline washed over me.

We're actually going to do this.

Holy shit.

It's happening.

I was desperate for more. More of him and more of his touch, but not where he'd kept it the whole time...above my waist.

"Can you touch me?" I asked breathlessly, reaching for his hand and guiding him to the edge of my shorts.

His blue eyes met mine, seeking a sense of approval.

I nodded, prompting him to undo the button and pull down on the zipper until he pulled them away from my hips and down my legs.

Now, only a few pieces of material separated the two of us from being completely bare in front of one another.

"Can you show me what to do?" He whispered, his hand hovering above me.

I slowly placed his hand between my thighs, guiding him with my own.

"Is this good?" he murmured softly as he continued, no longer needing my direction.

My quiet moan gave him the answer he was looking for as he

kept his rhythm, sending surges of pleasure through my body. "Ambert," I whimpered. "I want more."

He wasted no time as he pulled his hand back towards the foil, placing it between his teeth to rip it open before sliding it down his length.

I tossed my panties aside as he set his body between my legs. "Go slow, okay?" I told him as the nerves transferred from his face to mine.

"Okay." He faintly nodded, guiding himself in.

"Just like that," I whispered as he started slow but went the slightest bit further with each thrust until he reached his maximum inside of me.

"God, you're perfect." He kissed me before he picked up his movements, a grunt escaping his mouth. "This is incredible," he murmured, his pace much more natural and rhythmic.

I moaned in response, watching as his eyes shut firmly as he reached the top of his climax, his pulsating body radiating through me as his head fell forward and his hair dangled in front of my eyes.

He stayed put for a moment before he pulled out and laid down on his back beside me.

"Was that okay?" I turned onto my side to face him, worried that this silence between us meant bad news.

He shot me a look. "Was that *okay*?" he repeated back to me. "Iyla, that was amazing." His hand brushed across my cheek. "I just...wish I could've lasted longer."

I couldn't help but giggle as his face flushed red, that apologetic nature coming through once again. "Well, good thing Hallie has a whole box full of second chances." I playfully smirked.

"What? Are you serious?" He pulled back in surprise, analyzing my expression to see if I was joking.

"Practice makes perfect." I smirked with a shrug.

His lips pressed back into mine before I could continue speaking until I heard a rustling outside the door.

"Holy shit!" I pulled away. "Move over, get under the covers!"

Miraculously, as the door swung open and Hallie stepped inside, Ambert and I managed to tuck our bodies securely underneath the sheets.

"Hey!" Ambert snapped as I pulled the covers over his face.

"Shh!" I quieted him, meeting Hallie's wide eyes.

"Oh, wow. This is awkward." I could see her bite down on her lip in an attempt to hold back a laugh as she turned her body sideways, avoiding direct eye contact.

"Well, I'm going to go." She gestured back towards the door. "How do thirty minutes sound 'til I come back?" She took a few steps backwards. "Or how about forty-five minutes? An hour?" she remarked, almost out the door. "Two hours? Or is that too—"

"Hallie, leave!" I shouted as she closed the door behind her.

"Two hours it is, then!" she called back, disappearing behind the now-closed door as Ambert re-emerged from underneath the covers, laughing.

"Do you think she'll notice the missing condom?"

The Twelfth Entry
CELESTE
19 YEARS AGO

AUGUST 14

Ecstasy.

Despite all of the dangers and warnings, it was a substance that had always fascinated me growing up. I think for a while, it was because I wanted to escape from the reality of my life and transport myself into a world where things were different. Where suffering was a feeling of the past, and the pain could no longer break through.

Yet, I knew I'd never do it. For the one thing stronger than any addiction was my desire to follow the rules.

Oh, my rules. Before spring break, nothing could've come in between myself and them. But now, as the days began to fade into one another, I was struck with a harsh reality that reminded me that I was no longer falling in love with Zeke. I was long past that. By now, I was addicted.

Addicted to him.

Addicted to his love.

Addicted to the way he made me feel.

Nothing could surpass it. No ecstasy. No fictional world. Just reality. For the first time in my life, my reality was better than any dream I could ever think of, and I never wanted it to end. Never.

⭐ ⭐ ⭐

"What's your hidden talent?" I asked Zeke, snuggled into his side as we lay on the couch.

"Hmm..." He looked up in thought as if he knew what he wanted to say but was going to make me work to get it out of him.

"What?" An eagerness grew in my voice. "What are you hiding?"

"It's embarrassing," he scoffed. "You'll make fun of me."

"No, I won't." I sat upright. "You've got to tell me. Please, Zeke, please, please, please," I pestered his face with kisses.

"Fine, fine!" he laughed, closing his eyes as I kissed his face. "But I don't even know if this counts as a talent."

I raised my eyebrow, prompting him to go on.

"I can write poems."

"Poems?" I questioned.

"Yes, poems." He crossed his arms across his chest defensively. "And why do you look so surprised?"

"I do not look surprised," I argued, although the surprise was evident all over my face. How had I not known this? We'd hardly left his apartment, bed, shower, or done anything other than talk to each other the past few days, and never once had a poem spewed out of his mouth. "Well, let's hear one then," I requested.

"Nope." He shook his head. "Not happening."

"Zeke," I groaned, leaning into him as my lips grazed his cheek in an attempt to win him over.

"You realize I like this, right? There's no incentive to tell you when all you do is kiss me if I don't."

I pulled back. "Fine then." I folded my arms across my chest defiantly. "No kisses until you read me a poem."

He smirked. "You're stubborn. You know that?"

"I'm not the one being stubborn here. Why are you so embarrassed? Have you written a poem about me or something?"

His eyes diverted away from mine, causing my teasing smile to falter. He'd just told me everything I needed to know.

"Wait...there is."

"No, Celeste." He let out an exasperated sigh, standing up from the couch and walking over to the kitchen.

"Oh, there totally is!" I jumped up after him. "Now, you've *got* to tell me, Zeke."

"No chance." He reached for the fridge, but I closed it shut.

"You're telling me."

"No, I'm not." He began heading to the bedroom door, but I beat him to it.

"Yes, you are!" I laughed as I blocked his way in.

"You realize I'm almost a foot taller than you, Celeste? I can easily get by."

"No, you can't. My feet are firmly planted on the floor, and no one is getting into this room until—"

He whisked me into the air and opened the door as we fell back onto the bed in a fit of laughter. "That's not fair." I pouted.

"Sometimes life's not fair," he mocked.

"Is it bad?" My face fell flat. "Is that why you won't tell me?"

"Bad?" He pulled back. "Celeste, I could never say anything bad about you. Why would you even think that?"

"I don't know." I sat up. "I'm just overthinking it. You're right. You don't have to tell me. Besides, it's getting late. We should go to bed."

He planted a kiss on my shoulder. "I'm going in the shower first. Join me?"

"I'll be there soon."

"Okay." He smiled as he made his way into the bathroom, closed the door and turned on the shower.

I laid back in his bed for a moment, staring up at the ceiling— reminiscing on just how special the past few days with Zeke had been. I'd never felt so secure so quickly. I wondered if it was Zeke's home, or if it was Zeke who made me feel at home. It didn't matter. All that mattered was that I never wanted this feeling to end.

"You coming?" Zeke broke me free from the thought. I hadn't realized it had already been a few minutes.

"Coming!" I sat up from the bed, stretching my arms wide as I made my way into the bathroom, which was now filled with thick steam.

"Can you grab a fresh bar of soap? It's by the sink, under the mirror," Zeke called out as I began undressing.

I turned around, and that's when I saw it. Written out in the condensation of the mirror was the poem.

There they were, together in peace, lying in harmony.

Yet, when morning came, he stayed the same, and she knew it was too good to be true.

She belonged to so much more that spread beyond his wings, so when morning came, things weren't the same, for she could only ever be a dream.

I was speechless. I was overwhelmed by his words. I knew Zeke was more than capable of taking my breath away—and he had, countless times over the past few days, but I hadn't expected anything like this.

I'd never considered myself a muse—that had always been Claire. She was the inspiration. The girl that they'd tell stories about for years to come...not me. I'd always been simplistic and ordinary. But with Zeke, it was as if, for once, I was capable of being something much more significant. It was as if now I wasn't just a part of someone's story...I *was* someone's story.

"Zeke." I faced him, the genuine awe apparent on my face. "Did you actually write that?"

"Why?" he joked as he rinsed off his body. "Did you think it was good?"

I re-read it over and over, each time trying to understand what

185

exactly he meant by his words.

Did he think I was going to leave? And if he did, why did it seem as though he already had a reason for it? What was I missing?

"I'm taking your silence as I should never write anything again," he retorted.

"No." I shook my head with a shaky laugh, trying to break free from my thoughts. "That's not it at all. It's beautiful, Zeke. Really, it is."

"You mean that?" he asked as I joined him in the shower.

"I do." I leaned up and kissed his lips. "You have a gift."

He smiled softly as he leaned down and kissed me again, my hands moving to rest on the sides of his torso. Kissing Zeke had become so natural—so addictive.

"But I will say this," I added, pulling away slightly as the water from the showerhead dripped between us. "It certainly was morbid. Why did you write it as if I'm going to leave you? Is that what you think?"

He sighed, pausing in thought before responding. "They do say all good things must come to an end at some point."

I indignantly shook my head. This couldn't end. I wouldn't let it. I leaned up onto the tips of my toes so that our noses touched. "Not this," I whispered. "Not us. Not ever."

✩ ✰ ✩

"There they were, together in peace, lying in harmony."

Bang.

Bang.

Bang.

A loud pounding echoed throughout the apartment, startling me awake. I peered over at the clock, seeking out the time—it was just after four o'clock in the morning.

186

"Zeke?" my body jumped when another three bangs shook the room. "What's that sound?!" Panic began to seep into my voice as I turned to face him, his hands immediately tensing around my waist.

"Yet, when morning came, he stayed the same, and she knew it was too good to be true."

"Fuck," Zeke grumbled as he got out of bed, rushed over to his dresser and threw on a pair of shorts as quickly as possible. "You stay here, okay? Don't leave the bed."

"She belonged to so much more that spread beyond his wings."

The second he escaped the room, I instantly left the bed, ignoring his demand as I pressed my ear against the door. I know I said I tended to be a rule follower, and I am. But I couldn't help myself; I had to know what was happening.

"What the fuck are you doing here?" I heard Zeke hiss angrily.

"I'm here to pick up the shit," a deep voice responded.

"At four in the morning?!" Zeke yelled back, his voice raising slightly.

"Listen, man. You know what it's like. I had to come after work. All I need is last week's profits, then I'll be gone. Alright?"

"I told you not to come here. You know this isn't a good time."

"You want me to tell Chaz that?" The voice now matched Zeke's irate tone.

Chaz.

His name pierced my mind the second I heard it again, mentally sending me back to that night at Club Affinity—remembering his cold and unwanted touch, his sinister expression, and the way I'd never felt more terrified in my life.

Who was the guy out front?

What was he "picking up"?

And what did Chaz have to do with it?

"Wait here," Zeke instructed as his footsteps headed towards the bedroom, causing me to hurl my body back onto the bed. I closed my eyes, pretending to have fallen asleep as the door opened.

I heard Zeke shuffling around for a moment before he found what he was looking for and headed back out, closing the bedroom door behind him.

Little to my surprise, as I re-opened my eyes and sat up, I noticed that a familiar dresser drawer hadn't been closed entirely.

The money was gone.

"So when morning came, things weren't the same."

"Who was that?" I could hardly relax my body as Zeke walked back into the room.

"Just a neighbor," he responded nonchalantly, trying to downplay the situation.

"At four in the morning?" I repeated his words from earlier, unable to conceal my suspicion as he sank back into the bed.

Surely, he must've known how ridiculous he sounded. What kind of neighbor comes around at four am?

He was lying. I knew he was, but I wasn't sure why.

"They just needed something. Don't worry. They're gone now."

His blunt responses did nothing but encourage my spiraling thoughts. "I don't understand what could've been *so* important that someone would need to come at this time."

"Cel." He kissed my forehead and prompted me to lie back down. "Let's go back to sleep," he murmured gently, wrapping his arms around me and nestling his head into the crook of my neck.

"Zeke—"

"Shh." He kissed my lips gently to stop me from speaking. "Everything's okay, angel, I promise."

"For she could only ever be a dream."

Within a few minutes, his faint snores echoed throughout the room. Yet, even as the early morning light came flooding into the room, I lay wide awake. It was as if I could feel things changing—an unsettling feeling as we approached that final night of spring break.

CHAPTER THIRTEEN

I Y L A

PRESENT DAY

Hallie and I hit another red light on our way to Ambert's. "This must be the third light we've hit!" I let out an audible huff as I wiped my sweaty palms against my skirt.

"Can you relax?" Hallie looked over at me. "Everything's going to be fine. They're going to love us, and we're going to have a nice evening."

The light turned green again as she drove through the intersection. I wasn't sure why I felt so nervous about meeting Ambert's family. I suppose I attributed my nerves to my reserved and quiet nature, one of the many factors that had led to Hallie becoming my best friend. Hallie embodied everything I lacked when it came to social interaction. I would listen, she would talk, and that's how things worked.

"Just take deep breaths, smile, and if there's an awkward gap in the conversation, just know I'll cover you," she said reassuringly.

I tried to distract my mind by focusing on her words, often the only thing that could calm me down.

But lately, I'd found solace in something else, too. I opened my bag and peered inside to see the small but faint image of my mother from Dr. Sanders' office, placed right at the top.

I smiled, seeing so many pieces of myself now in her. Like Dr.

Sanders had said, my brown hair and green eyes were the only difference.

"How do I look?" Hallie asked as she pulled into the driveway, pulling out her phone camera to fix her hair and prompting me to hastily push the picture back down into my bag.

"You always look amazing," I told her with a smile, pulling down my visor and catching a glimpse of myself. Internally, I criticized everything I possibly could. My hair, my skin, my makeup—

"Stop doing that," Hallie snapped, pushing my visor back up.

"Stop doing what?" I questioned.

"Overthinking," she responded, seamlessly reading my mind. "You look perfect. Like you always do."

"Thanks to you." I brushed my hands over my ruffled skirt and matching short-sleeve top. It was, of course, an outfit that Hallie had chosen for me to wear.

She smiled, raising her eyebrows excitedly. "Ready?"

I nodded in spite of my unwavering nerves. "Let's go."

As I opened the car door and climbed out of the seat, I paused to take in Ambert's family home for the first time. It was big, with a white front-facing exterior and intricate Spanish-style roofing.

I could see why he didn't mind not living on residence. If I lived in a house like this, a 200 sq ft dorm room would also sound like a nightmare.

"Hurry up, slowpoke!" Hallie shouted, already heading up the cobblestone path to the front door.

"Wait," I called out, reaching her at the door. "You forgot to strap your shoe in."

I had just bent down to strap her heels up for her when she whirled around to face me, her purse smacking me in the face and causing me to fall straight onto my butt.

"Hallie," I groaned, instantly getting up and brushing myself off.

"Oh, Iy, I'm sorry." She started to laugh. "Are you okay?"

"I'm fine." I huffed, now fussing over straightening out my own skirt.

"Did you at least fix my shoe?" she smirked.

I shot her a glare. "You're brutal."

"Shush, you love me."

"Love is a strong word."

"They sure know how to make an introduction," Vic's voice chimed in from directly in front of us.

"They certainly do." Ambert appeared behind Vic in the doorway, looking down at me with his cheeky expression. "Klutz," he teased, kissing my cheek.

"How much of that did you see, exactly?" I cringed, causing him to laugh.

"Enough," he grinned, pulling me through the front door with an affirming hand resting on my back.

Ambert looked fresh. His hair was tame and out of his face. He'd replaced his joggers with a nice pair of jeans and a white button-down dress shirt, making me question my own outfit. "Am I under-dressed?"

"Not at all." Ambert took my bag off my shoulder and placed it on the entryway table alongside Hallie's things. "You look amazing. Everybody's out back."

"Well then, what are we doing here?" Hallie beamed. "Let's go!"

Ambert interlocked his hand with mine, giving me a reassuring squeeze as he guided me out back. His garden was wide, with a pool on the right and a kids' jungle gym on the left. The patio was decorated with string lights and a long table covered in drinks, fruits, and bite-sized hors d'oeuvres.

"Tag, you're it!" I heard a child's voice yell out as some kids played off in the distance.

"Is that your sister?" I asked Ambert, nodding in the direction of a little girl who resembled him.

He nodded. "That's her. And those are Vic's younger brothers," he added, gesturing to the two boys chasing her around.

"You never told me her name," I responded. "Is it as unique as yours?"

"Kind of..." he shrugged. "Her name is CeCe. My parents named her after their old family friend."

Her name sent an odd wave of sadness through my chest, though I chose to ignore it as four adults, each with a drink in their hand, made their way over to us after conversing with Hallie and Vic.

"Ambert!" A voice called out. "Introduce us!"

"Everyone..." Ambert jumped straight into it, a genuine smile lighting up his face. "This is my girlfriend, Iyla. Iyla." He gestured in the direction of the four adults. "This is Tim and Alma, Vic's parents."

I sent them both a faint wave before Ambert proceeded to work through the group. "And Iyla, this is my dad, Korey, and my mom, Claire."

I half-smiled, meeting eyes with each of them. "Nice to meet you all," I spoke, trying to take note of all of their names in my mind.

Tim, Alma, Korey, and Claire.

The group was analyzing me in return, although it was a much less welcoming expression than the one Hallie had received, judging by the bright grin on her face.

Ambert cleared his throat, which prompted his dad's watchful gaze to soften. "We're thrilled to meet you, Iyla." He smiled, placing a hand on Claire's back. "Aren't we, honey?"

Claire's face was strangely flushed as she gripped her wine glass, almost as if she couldn't believe her eyes.

"Claire?" Korey prompted her again, gently tapping her back.

She shook her head, letting out a breath.

"Yes...Iyla. It's so nice to finally meet you." She looked as if she was debating what exactly she wanted to say to me as an awkward silence fell over the group.

"How about we all sit down?" Alma suggested as she guided us towards the table.

"Good idea." Claire nodded, gulping down her drink. "Let's sit. Sitting down sounds like a perfect idea right about now."

I couldn't ignore her frantic movements as she rushed over to the table and grabbed a seat, putting her now-empty wine glass down on the table.

"Is everything alright?" I whispered to Ambert as we followed her over.

"They're probably just nervous," he responded quietly, although the expression on his face told me that he was just as confused as I was.

They're the nervous ones?

How do they think I feel?

"Yeah, you're probably right," I mumbled, keeping my thoughts to myself as Ambert pulled out one of the patio chairs and urged me to sit.

"Lemonade?" Vic asked as he held up a pitcher, gesturing to the empty cups in front of Hallie and me.

"Yum! Yes, please," Hallie answered for the two of us as she grabbed hold of our glasses.

"Iyla." Claire made sure to sit directly across from me. "We didn't catch your last name. What is it?"

"Larson." I took a sip of the sweet lemonade, maneuvering the glass to conveniently block my face from everyone's overly-concentrated stares.

"Larson," Tim chimed in. "Hmm. That's Nordic, isn't it?"

"Yeah," I agreed. "My dad's family is from Northern Europe, but both my parents were born and raised in the states." I could hardly suppress the nerves causing my voice to waver. "That doesn't really matter, though. I'm adopted..."

"You're adopted?!" Vic whipped his head over to me in surprise as I caught a glimpse of Alma leaning over to whisper something into Tim's ear.

"Yep." I took a massive gulp of my drink this time, deciding that drowning myself was a much more appealing option than having to utter another word.

"Wait, so were you born in Columbus?" Vic continued to pry as Hallie shot him a disapproving glare.

"I, uh...no. I was born here, in California."

"Let's talk about something else," Ambert announced loudly, evidently attempting to change the subject and save me from this ambush of questions.

"Good idea." Korey nodded in agreement. "So, Iyla, what will you be studying at UCLA?" Much to my dismay, the question trail continued as the topic of Iyla Larson suddenly became everyone's personal interest.

"Pre-law," I responded, a smile appearing on my lips as Ambert rubbed my thigh in a soothing motion, prompting me to continue. "My goal is to eventually go to Stanford—"

Claire choked on her freshly re-poured drink mid-sip, coughing as if the liquid had gone down the wrong pipe. "I'm sorry," she croaked, hastily standing up from the table and heading in the direction of the house. "I'll be right back."

"Excuse us." Korey followed closely behind her.

I looked over at Ambert, who seemed less than amused by his parents' behavior. "I don't know what's up with them today," he said softly. "They're acting weird...everyone is."

"It's okay," I responded, although it was far from it. I couldn't help but notice Tim and Alma's gaze occasionally falling onto me, despite the two of them being mid-conversation with Hallie. "Ambert, I think I need to use the bathroom. I'm feeling a little lightheaded. It must be the heat. Where is it?"

"By the front door," he explained as he stood up. "I'll come with you."

"Hey, A, how have your first few days of class been?" Tim called out in Ambert's direction, causing him to pause.

"I'll be okay," I mouthed over to him, slightly relieved at the distraction. I desperately needed some time alone.

Hesitantly, he sat back down. "It was great," he began. "My professors seem really nice."

The sound of his voice trailed off as I moved away from the table and headed inside, walking through the hallway that led to the front door and into the bathroom.

My anxiety immediately consumed me as I closed the door, letting out a breath I'd seemingly held inside of me that whole time.

This is going to be a long night.

The Thirteenth Entry

CELESTE

19 YEARS AGO

AUGUST 19

"CeCe!" Claire raced towards me as Zeke and I arrived at a pool bar for one final night on the town. "I missed you so much." She whined as she engulfed me in a hug.

Korey let out a scoff from over by the pool table. "It's only been a few days."

"So?" Claire released me from her embrace. "That's a long time for us."

I shot a pleased look over at Korey. "It's true."

He shook his head in disapproval, laughing as Claire reached for her purse. "Alright, everyone, let's kick this night off, shall we? Drinks, anyone?" she proposed. "Korey? Do you want a beer?"

"Yes, babe," he called out, lining up his pool stick in front of the cue ball and concentrating on his shot.

"And Zeke?" Claire eagerly turned towards him. "Do you want sex on the beach, or did you and Celeste have that already?"

"Claire!" I placed a hand over her mouth, completely mortified by her words. "Stop!"

Despite my embarrassment, Zeke, as per usual, found the statement amusing as he jokingly rolled his eyes. "A gentleman doesn't kiss and tell." He responded, joining Korey for a game of pool. "But get me a Gin and Tonic," he shouted as I pulled Claire as far away from the table as possible.

"Claire," I spoke, my voice full of frustration. "That was so embarrassing. What the heck?!"

"Oh, he didn't mind." She waved her hand in my direction with a laugh, leaning into the bartender to order everyone's drinks.

"How did you know we had sex?" I crossed my arms in a huff, lowering my voice when she pulled back.

She shot me a stare before reaching for a menu and ignoring my words.

"What are you looking for, anyway?" I demanded, the annoyance still tainting my voice. "You just ordered."

Her devious eyes peered up at me, chewing on her bottom lip. "Oh, just a dose of whatever post-sex glow you've got going on."

"Claire," I groaned, throwing my head back as she burst into giggles, clearly amused by her endless stash of innuendos.

I glanced back over to the pool table where Zeke and Korey, caught up in the game, were shouting at each other for what I could gather was a "cheap shot." Yet, it was Zeke who I couldn't peel my eyes away from—eyes narrowed as he carefully lined up his next shot, running a confident hand through his hair when it effortlessly sunk into the hole.

"Is it really that obvious?" I finally built the courage to look back over at an overtly amused Claire.

"For anyone else, no. For *me*..." She leaned against the barstool, arms folded across her chest. "Yes. And given how you're practically undressing him with your eyes, something's definitely happened."

She was right. So much had happened. It had only been a week, but I'd felt like I'd lived an entire lifetime throughout this spring break. Where could I even begin? With Zeke, so much good had happened.

"I wouldn't have let anything happen to you."

"I intend to know everything about you, angel."

"Because when I'm with you, I feel like I'm in heaven."

"Do you trust me?"
"I do."

"I just want to know where you've been my whole life."
"Waiting. Waiting for you".

"Celeste...you're my best friend."
"Can you become best friends with someone this fast?"
"I'd say so. Considering I fell in love with you the moment I first saw you."

"They do say all good things must come to an end at some point."
"Not this. Not us. Not ever."

Yet, with all the good that transpired over the last week came the bad.

The questions.

The doubt.

The sheer confusion haunted me more than I'd let on.

"Remember all that I've done for you. You're on thin ice now, pal. I'd hate to see you fall through."

"Zeke's always been secretive."
"Have you seen his place? I have no idea how he can afford that. He's a bouncer, for God's sake."

To You, Iyla

"I told you not to come here. You know this isn't a good time."
"You want me to tell Chaz that?"

"Who was that?"
"Just a neighbor."

"CeCe!" Claire impatiently snapped her fingers in front of my face. "Are you okay?" I noticed a hint of concern behind her eyes. "You totally zoned out for a second."

I shook my head and plastered a smile on my face in a weak attempt to do some damage control. "I'm fine," I reassured her. "Just tired, that's all."

She wasn't buying it. "Why did you look so sad? Is everything alright?"

I opted to withhold the real reasoning behind my troubled state, trying to suppress all the thoughts consuming my mind and offer the easier and safer response instead. "I think I'm just sad that we're leaving tomorrow, that's all."

Claire released a breath, the relief in her eyes telling me she'd just bought my fib. "All the more reason to enjoy tonight, then, am I right?"

✰ ✰ ✰

"Okay, I'm done with this." Claire sighed, placing her pool stick back onto the rack after Zeke and I had beat the two of them for the fifth time in a row. "Let's do something else," she proposed. "I saw a photo booth at the back of the bar. How about we all take some pictures together?"

"Please, no!" I sighed as Claire dragged us over to a photo booth, pushing us in one by one. "There's no room," I complained as I hardly managed to shove my body inside.

"We'll make room." Zeke pulled me on top of his lap and

planted a kiss on my lips, immediately pulling me out of my mood. "Claire!" Korey cringed at our PDA. "Get in here. Save me from this."

"I'm coming, I'm coming!" she squealed, running in and jumping onto his lap as the countdown began.

Despite my initial objections, we all smiled, laughed, and planted kisses on our respective partners' faces as the camera flashed a few times.

It was a moment I knew would forever be ingrained into my memory—a feeling of pure fulfillment that I still hold on to.

"Come on out, babe." Claire tugged on Korey's arm. "Let Zeke and Celeste take some pictures alone."

I immediately tried to protest, ready to get out of that booth myself, before Claire swiftly closed the curtains and the next countdown began.

"Don't be shy." Zeke brushed some hair out of my face. "No one is more beautiful than you," he whispered against my lips as the first flash came through.

"Don't lie," I told him, shying away from his compliment.

"I'd never lie to you." He pecked me again as another flash illuminated the small space.

I had to fight to ignore the way his words felt like a jab to the stomach.

"Now..." He pulled away as the final countdown began. "Let's actually take a nice picture."

"Fine." I caved, wrapping my arms around his neck and smiling as bright as ever at the final flash.

"You know, I didn't take you as the picture type," I teased once we'd climbed out of the booth, placing the freshly printed image into my bag as Zeke stuck a copy inside his wallet.

He smirked before leaning down to peck my lips. "I'm a lot of things I never thought I could be when I'm with you. Want to go on a walk?"

I nodded in agreement, allowing him to wrap me underneath is arm before we found Korey and Claire on the dance floor.

"We'll be back," Zeke informed them as we made our way into the brisk outdoors and he removed his black leather jacket, wrapping it around my body. "Put this on."

"No." I shrugged it off despite my trembling state. "You'll get cold."

"I promise you, I won't," he insisted once more. "Here, take it."

I sighed, placing my short arms inside the jacket's long sleeves, a sense of warmth instantly engulfing my cool skin. "Thank you." I smiled up at him gratefully, the two of us walking hand in hand down the boardwalk.

"So..." He prompted my attention. "Are you going to tell me what's been bothering you, angel?"

"What's been bothering me?" I repeated, playing dumb despite the heat that rushed to my cheeks. "What do you mean?

He looked at me as if to say *do you really expect me to believe you?* "You just seem to be in your head, that's all."

I sighed in resignation, hopeful that the fib I'd now come to accept as my truth would do the trick yet again. "I'm just going to miss this week," I confessed. I couldn't deny that a part of that was true. "I'm sad it's almost over."

Zeke paused and pulled me in close to him, tilting my chin up. "Just because you're leaving tomorrow doesn't mean we can't still have times like this," he spoke inches from my face. "This..." He gestured between the two of us. "This is only the start. Remember?"

I assessed his words carefully. "And what exactly is 'this'?"

"What do you want it to be?" He threw the question back at me. "It seems like people think you're my girlfriend or something." He raised his eyebrows, a look of feigned shock on his face.

"Uh oh." I played along. "Wouldn't want to completely dismantle all of my rules now, would we?"

He paused. "Rules are made to be broken."

"You don't say." I pulled back, leaning against his shoulder as we continued down the path.

"So, what do you say?" he continued. "You think you can leave Long Beach as my *girlfriend*?" he emphasized the word in such a manner it almost sounded ridiculous. Of course, we were together. Of course, I was his girlfriend. But even so, it still didn't feel like enough.

I nudged him with a laugh. "I was going to, even if we didn't have this conversation."

He joined in with that laugh of his own, the one that made me feel like everything in the world was healing just by the sound of it. "Let's sit down," he suggested after a moment, gesturing towards a quiet spot along the beachfront.

I nodded, planting myself in between his legs as we fell into the sand and stared up at the night sky.

"You know," he whispered into my ear, his breath so close that it sent tingles down my spine. "Your whole destiny is mapped out in the stars."

"Really?" I wondered out loud. "You think?"

"That's what my dad told me when I was younger. He said that in the stars, you'll find your fate. So, I guess the universe knew we were meant to find one another."

There was that universe talk again. The one that Claire had mentioned on our way down to Long Beach. It was a concept I hadn't ever had much faith in until I heard Zeke speak of it.

"I've always loved the stars," I admitted. "When I was a little girl, I begged my dad to put those little peel-and-stick stars everywhere in the house. That way, when night came, the ceilings in our house would illuminate."

Zeke smiled softly down at me, cascading his hand along my cheek as I continued. "The night that the incident happened with my parents, the only thing I could really focus on were those stars.

And since then, any time I've ever experienced some turmoil in my life, I've always looked up at the sky—trying to capture an image and seek clarity." I let out a small breath, looking up at him. "So, when you tell me that our fate is written in the stars...I believe that."

Zeke nestled his head on my shoulder, wrapping me in his arms as we lay still for a moment.

Staring, admiring, and thinking as night fell.

"What do you see for yourself in five years?" The thought came to my mind suddenly. "Do you always want to work at Club Affinity?"

"Definitely not," he answered with assurance. "I'd love to try and get back into the fire academy to finish up or even re-start my training altogether. Following my dad's footsteps would mean everything to me, Celeste."

"Back home in New York?" I asked.

He scoffed. "Home isn't New York." His voice lingered at the end of his statement. "Home is more about the people I'm with than where I live. Home is wherever *you* are."

His words brought an overwhelming sense of peace to my heart as I leaned back into his chest, tilting my chin upwards and resting our foreheads as one. "You mean that?" I whispered.

"More than anything."

I stayed put momentarily, absorbing each second as if it were my last. What would a future with Zeke look like? "Do you want to know what I see for you in five years?"

"Oh, boy." He broke into a playful smile. "I guess."

"Well, here it is," I lifted my head from his shoulders and raised my hands into the air. "In five years, Ezekiel Reeves will be thirty years old...an old man." I pretended to gag at the thought.

"All right, all right," he hushed my laughter, nudging my shoulder. "Anything else besides old?"

I suppressed the playfulness in my voice, meeting his eyes this time as I spoke the truth. "I'm certain that he'll be an amazing firefighter—making his dad proud. He'll be happy, content and at peace. But most of all..." I placed my hands on either side of his cheeks, swallowing softly as our eyes met. "He'll still be loved by that same girl from spring break."

Loved.

His face froze in surprise as if he was trying to process what I'd admitted equally as much as I was. I'd just confessed that I loved him too.

I'd known those words to be true for a long time before I'd verbalized them, yet it still felt strange—scary, even.

Still, it was, without a doubt, the most fulfilling truth I'd ever confessed to.

I loved him. I did.

His taken-aback expression hadn't faded in the slightest. "You love me?"

I brushed my hand through his hair. "From the moment I laid eyes on you, I knew. I knew you were the one. I love you, Zeke... all of you."

His face was flooded with an emotion that was pure joy mixed with relief as he pulled me into his embrace, solidifying my words with a kiss that I never wanted to end. This was heaven. This was joy. This was the start of saying those three words to one another for the rest of our lives.

"Do you mean that?" He sought reassurance in my eyes. "You think that I'm worth loving?"

Despite the sliver of questions that propelled my mind, nothing made more sense than him. Zeke was more than just "worth loving." He made loving worth it—and despite my reservations, I knew this was right.

In the span of a week, Zeke had made me laugh, smile, and *feel* more than I had my entire life. But most of all, he taught me how to love. Not just him but a new version of myself that I'd never known could exist. One that I'd hold onto from that day forward.

"More than anything," I whispered against his lips, closing my eyes shut. "I. Love. You."

I'm certain the stars started to shine brighter at that moment as if they were listening to every truth.

"Now, it's my turn to tell you who I think Celeste Kinney will be in five years."

I bit down on my bottom lip. "Go easy on me."

We rocked together as one while he spoke. "In five years, Celeste Kinney will be a lawyer. Graduating at the top of her class from Stanford. In fact, when she does, employers will be on their knees begging for her to join their law firm." He squeezed me tight as I blushed. "By then, she'll be..." He appeared to be doing the math in his head. "Twenty-seven. Getting old just like someone else she knows," he teased. "But she'll be just as beautiful, if not more beautiful than ever. Not to mention..." He leaned in closer. "She'll be irrevocably loved back by that same boy from spring break."

I leaned over to plant my lips on his. His words always left me in a daze.

"Did that sound right?" he whispered against my ear.

"It sounded..." I pulled his arms back around me. "Perfect." I smiled. "Absolutely perfect."

"Good." It's as if I could feel his own smile without needing to look. "Because I wasn't sure if you wanted to have kids immediately after graduation like Claire."

I rolled my eyes without him seeing. Kids weren't a thought that occurred to me often. My life had always revolved around school and work. Before I'd met Zeke, it was not like I'd been with anyone else long enough to even think about the next stage...nor did I need to worry much about an "accident."

"I mean, I want to have a family." I paused. "But I'm not sure when. Do you want kids in five years?"

"I might." He shrugged. "Considering I'll be getting up there, of course."

I chuckled at his joke. "How many kids do you want?"

"I'm not sure," he responded. "I'll start with one and go from there. Pretty standard."

"You're an only child, right?" I probed.

"Just like you," he hummed, kissing my cheek.

I looked back up at the stars when a simple sentence escaped my lips. "I'd love to have a daughter," I admitted. "And if I ever did, I wonder what she'd be like."

He looked down at me with those breathtaking green eyes. "What would you name her?" he questioned.

I paused, assessing the question with every ounce of my being. "I have no idea. I've never really thought about it."

The statement was a total lie. I'd always known that there was a special name in my heart—a name that one day, if I was lucky enough, I'd use.

"Any type of name you like?" he pried further, more interested in this conversation than I'd expected him to be.

"I like something unique but not too unusual. Something short, but not too short. A name that has meaning, and a name that—"

"It sounds like you've thought about it." He cut me off with a laugh.

"*Iyla*," I spoke, my mouth moving ahead of my mind. "I like that name."

The air settled around us. I'd only ever spoken the name to Claire once, many years ago. But now, saying it with Zeke, seeing how his eyes softened with each syllable...I knew it was perfect.

"And why's that?"

"It means a shining or bright light," I told him. "I've always liked it because of the connection to the stars. And now, it seems fitting given the circumstances." I peered up at him adoringly. "I think there would be nothing more special than our daughter to be named Iyla."

"*Our?*" he interrupted my thought, causing me to pause in place

"I mean..." I opened my mouth to speak, closing it a few seconds later and repeating it a few times before finally responding. "I'd hope so. I'm sorry if that came across weird."

He kissed me. He kissed me in a way that was so reassured, so confident, so full of *love* that it washed away any reluctance. "Iyla, it is then," he spoke against my lips. "That's her name. That's what we'll name our daughter."

Our daughter.

A life with Zeke.

A family, a future I never thought was possible. Zeke as a firefighter, me as a lawyer, and a perfect little girl by our side. We'd live somewhere in California. We'd have a simple life. A happy life. A life where we'd be nothing more than a family. A real family. Something that I'd subliminally dreamed of but never knew could be possible.

"One day." I kissed his lips once more, pushing the sentimental yet premature thoughts to the back of my mind. "We've got time."

"That we do," he agreed. "But speaking of time, we should probably get going. Claire and Korey might be wondering where we are."

I nodded as he helped me stand up from his lap, intertwining our hands as we headed back to the boardwalk.

"I love you, Zeke," I said one final time, resting my head against his shoulder as we walked.

"I love you, Celeste. I love y—"

"Hey, Z!" An unsettling voice called out from behind us. "We've been looking for you."

CHAPTER FOURTEEN

I Y L A

PRESENT DAY

I splashed the cool water from the sink into my hands before placing them behind my neck.

What is going on?

Why is everyone acting so strange?

Calm down, Iyla.

You're just overthinking it. Everything's fine.

I took a second to analyze my appearance in the mirror. Maybe I just had something in my teeth, and they didn't want to say anything.

I forced a smile. *Nothing.*

I released a tense sigh, staying put in the bathroom for a few long minutes before mustering up enough courage to open the door and work my way back to the patio.

"Korey," Claire's fraught voice echoed down the hallway from the kitchen. "What in the world is going on?"

"Just take a breath." I heard Korey instruct her in a gentle, calming tone. "You need to relax."

I halted in place, my body tense as I tucked myself behind a wall in the living room.

"Relax?" she repeated, her tone almost condescending. "How am I supposed to relax? You need to call Zeke right now," she demanded. "Tell him not to come."

"You're assuming!" Korey fired back, his own voice rising. "This all could just be a coincidence."

Zeke?

That scary guy from the auto shop?

"*Assuming*? *Coincidence*? You heard what she said, Korey." Claire sounded borderline erratic. "It's her! I know it's her. I know by just looking at her!"

I nervously peered around the wall, watching Claire place her wine glass onto the counter and run her shaking hands through her hair.

"Regardless," Korey lowered his voice once more before taking a patient step toward her. "You need to calm down. The poor girl must think she's done something terribly wrong. I'll call Zeke, but you need to go back out there and make this right. We might not get another chance."

"What are the odds, Korey?" She sounded nearly breathless as she shook her head in visible disbelief, ignoring his request as she continued to ramble. "After all these years. All that searching, she's here...in our home, dating our son."

All that searching?

I furrowed my eyebrows in confusion. Had they been searching for me?

"Claire." Korey placed his hands on both her shoulders, physically grounding her. "Go back outside, okay? We'll discuss this later."

"I just need a few minutes." She shook her head and placed a hand over her forehead, stepping away from him. "I'm going to the bathroom. Call Zeke *now*!"

As she began walking in my direction, I quickly tucked myself back against the wall, praying she wouldn't look up and spot me.

My prayers were answered when she walked past me without so much as a glance. I kept a watchful gaze on her as she headed into the bathroom, her eyes barely pulling away from the ground.

This was my moment to escape the room. I couldn't have anyone knowing I'd overheard their conversation, much less found a hiding spot to spy on them.

Yet I couldn't pull my eyes away from the fireplace mantle across the room.

As my legs carried me over by their own command, I noticed an array of photos on the mantle. The first was a family portrait of Claire, Korey, Ambert and his sister.

"Her name is CeCe. My parents named her after their old family friend."

Gulping despite my dry throat, I continued onwards. The following few photos on the mantle were an assortment of baby pictures of Ambert and CeCe and a wedding photo of Claire and Korey.

Lastly, standing out from the rest was an older photo in a baby blue frame. It was a photo of two young women along the rails of the beach. Without a doubt, I could tell that the girl on the right was a younger version of Claire, her arm wrapped around an innocent-looking blonde—with an unmistakable face.

"Mom." The word instinctively fell from my mouth, my breath catching in my throat.

This was her—the face I'd spent the last few days studying harder than anything else in my life clicked in my mind.

My heart rate skipped a beat as I grabbed the frame and held it in my clammed-up hands, carefully scanning each of her features. Her round cheeks, pink lips, and kind yet straight smile.

"There's no way," I whispered shakily, bringing the photo closer to my eyes to examine it. As I pulled the photo back, I revealed a series of pictures.

It was my mom again, but this time, she stood beside a motorcycle with another familiar face by her side. One with the greenest eyes that resembled mine.

Zeke.

As I reached for the next photo and turned it around, my face dropped in disbelief as I assessed what appeared to be a photo booth strip—and not just any photo booth strip. The strip contained four pictures of Claire, Korey, Zeke and my mom.

They were laughing, smiling, and kissing their respective partners.

Claire kissing Korey.

My mom kissing...Zeke.

I nearly dropped the photos as a hand flew to my mouth, and reality started to crash down on me. This couldn't be true.

Claire knew my mother.

"No," I spoke, much louder than I had expected, as I ran a flustered hand along my damp forehead. "This can't be happening. There's no way."

Did everyone outside know my mother? Tim? Alma? Was that why they had been looking at me? Whispering? Is it because I look like her? Was that what Zeke had thought when he saw me at the auto shop?

Zeke.

I had never felt my heart thudding as fast as it was at this moment.

If Zeke was the one kissing my mother in those photos...

"No." I dropped the picture, taking a reluctant step back as the glass shattered across the floor. I could barely process any of it.

"Iyla?" Claire's voice stopped me in my tracks as she stood in the doorway, her gaze narrowed on the picture lying on the ground before she looked back up into my eyes.

"You...you knew my mom?" I trembled, the lump in my throat returning as I held her gaze. I wasn't wasting any time. I'd waited enough. Now, I needed answers.

"I..." She managed, just as unnerved as I was. "Iyla...your mom... she was my best friend, my family," she whispered, tears brimming her eyes as she held her hands close to her chest and took a hesitant step forward. "I've spent a long time searching for you. Did you get my letter? My package?"

"Searching for me?" I shook my head. "Letter...package?" my voice faded into silence.

Nothing was making sense. Nothing at all.

"You're her." She finally reached me, the recognition in her eyes overbearing her other emotions. "You're literally her." Her eyes scanned my face and down my body, hands reaching towards my face. "But even then so, I can see so many pieces of Z—"

I stepped back before she could touch me, cutting her sentence short.

It was as if everything that I'd been searching for my entire life was suddenly hitting me at once. It was as if I now held all the answers to my questions in the palm of my hand.

Only to realize that I was nowhere near strong enough to carry the weight of them.

I've made a mistake.

"Zeke's not answering." Korey walked down the hallway, his face buried into the phone. "He must still be at the shop. I'll try calling again, but..." His words trailed off as he looked up, eyes widening as he took in both mine and Claire's shaken demeanor.

"I...I need to go." I pushed myself past the two of them and toward the entryway, hastily grabbing my bag along with Hallie's car keys.

"Iyla, wait!" Claire called out after me, but I ignored her and let her voice fade away as I flung open the front door and raced towards Hallie's car.

"Claire, don't!" I turned my head to see Korey attempt to reach for her arm, to no avail—she followed me outside and onto the driveway.

"Iyla," she pleaded, just steps behind me. "Please, don't go. You deserve to know about the past. I want you to know. Let me tell you everything."

"All I need to know is one thing." I breathed heavily as I whirled back around to face her, completely overwhelmed with emotion.

She halted in place, a blank yet hesitant look in her eyes.

I built up the confidence to get the following words out of my mouth. "Is...is Zeke my dad?"

She looked away, answering my question without even having to speak. "Iyla," she whispered, a pained expression covering her face.

"Is Zeke my dad?" I repeated again, this time with determination and infliction. "Tell me," I demanded. "Tell me, Claire! Is he, or is he not my dad?"

A long, painful, drawn-out silence fell between us—surmounted by four words that stung like nothing else ever could.

"He's your dad, Iyla," Claire admitted apprehensively, her voice quiet.

I swallowed hard. How do you process the answer to a question that you've asked your whole life? Truth can be so simple but feel so complex at the same time. I'm relieved...I'm scared...I'm so confused.

She spoke up before I even had a chance to breathe. I hadn't realized I'd stopped. "Iyla, you need to let me explain." She took a step forward, treading carefully with her hands raised. "Please, there is so much to tell you. So much you need to know—"

"What is it that I need to know?" I snapped in response, my impatience boiling before my attention was diverted to Ambert, who rushed through the front door and over to me.

"Iyla, what's wrong?" he asked, his familiar eyes clouded with worry as he reached a hand out to rest it on my arm. "Where are you going?"

"I'm sorry," I told him as tears brimmed my eyes. I couldn't stand here any longer. I turned on my heel and continued making my way down the driveway.

"No!" He stopped me, placing his hands on either side of my face before looking back at Claire in confusion. "What's going on?"

"Let her go, Ambert." Korey instructions were cut short by the sound of a motorcycle echoing down the street.

I truly felt as though I was about to have a heart attack.

Get into the car.

I willed my legs to carry me down the driveway as Ambert rushed his way ahead of me. "Iyla..." He sought any sense of clarity in my distressed face. "Talk to me. Tell me what's going on."

"I...I really can't be here anymore." I clutched onto the door handle. "I just can't, Ambert."

"But why?" he intensely scanned my face. "Did I do something wrong? I'm sorry if I did, Iyla."

Nothing ached quite like seeing his expression turn weary and stressed at the thought that this was in any way his fault.

"It's not you, Ambert, it's—"

A motorcycle pulled into the driveway, my legs going limp as I became certain that I would collapse from total disarray at any moment.

"Is everything alright?" an unfamiliar voice triumphed over the chaos.

"Zeke..." Korey spoke, causing me to whirl my head over to the man who had just arrived.

Dad.

The shock of seeing Zeke again was far greater than I'd imagined. A few minutes ago, Zeke was nothing but a stranger, but now, that stranger meant so much more—he *was* so much more.

I was frozen in place.

"What the hell is going on?" Zeke raised his voice with a look of concern.

Korey positioned a hand on his shoulder, one that Zeke immediately brushed off as his eyes fell on me, staring with a look of sheer absolution. I'm confident we were both thinking the same thing at that moment—*is it really you?*

We both stood still in disbelief. It was as if the world had stopped and time was standing still. I would've believed it if the tears weren't streaming down my cheeks.

"I'm sorry," I choked out, stepping back into the car as Zeke inched his way forward. "I need to go...I can't do this anymore."

My weak hands attempted to reach for the door handle, but Ambert beat me to it. "Let me go with you, Iyla. Let's talk this out."

"No!" I shouted, my anxiety and confusion finally expressing themselves as frustration. Everyone turned silent for a second—halted in place as they stared at me, whereas I'd shifted into full-blown hysterics. "Did you know?!" I turned around, meeting Ambert's eyes. "Have you known this whole time? Was this all a part of your search?!"

Ambert was perplexed as I threw Claire's words back to him. "Search?" he repeated as if it was a foreign language. "Iyla...I don't know what you're talking about." He looked back at his parents and Zeke, who clearly did.

I couldn't carry on like this. "I'm leaving," I announced. I'd had enough. I needed time. I needed to process this.

"Iyla." Zeke stepped towards me, causing me to cower inwards...I didn't know how to react to hearing my name come out of his mouth. It was a name that he seemed to know all too well.

"I don't want to see you again," I said with assurance, cutting off whatever he was about to say. It didn't matter anymore. Nothing did. "Any of you."

"Stop," Ambert pleaded, tears swimming in his eyes, the eyes I had come to know and love. "We can talk about this...whatever *this* is."

"*This*," I met his eyes before swinging open the door. "This was a mistake."

The Fourteenth Entry

CELESTE

19 YEARS AGO

AUGUST 23

"Go back to the bar," Zeke demanded, his voice stricken with panic.

"What? Now?" I asked in confusion as I looked up at him.

"Yes, now!" The look of concern behind his eyes betrayed his attempt to keep his voice steady. "Go!"

I attempted to step backwards, my mind whirling in confusion until my body collided with another, causing me to spin around and see who it was.

It was a face I couldn't imagine ever forgetting.

Chaz.

"Hello, beautiful." He smirked, firmly grabbing hold of my arm. "Long time no see. Has Zeke been hiding you from us? We never did get a chance to finish up our dance."

"Get the fuck off her, Chaz," Zeke snarled, charging his way over. "You and I can talk. She doesn't need to get involved."

"I beg to differ," Chaz retorted, pulling me back into him and placing a hand on both of my cheeks. "She does need to be involved. Perhaps it will give you some incentive to answer me."

Frozen.

216

There I was, yet again, frozen in fear. My stomach dropped to my feet—a deep-rooted sense of anxiety rattling my core.

Danger. You're in so much danger.

"Where's the money, Zeke?" Chaz spat out, the impatience in his voice jarring.

"Get off of her, then I'll speak to you." Zeke's aggression grew, along with my fear.

"Wrong answer." Chaz clutched my face much firmer as a result, forcing a whimper to fall out of my mouth. "Oh, you are a beauty." He peered into my eyes, the malicious look in his own causing me to cower away in fear. "Now, ask your little boyfriend here where my money is."

I didn't even get a chance to process his request before Zeke lunged at him, forcing a scream to escape my mouth as he sunk his fist into Chaz's face. Two of Chaz's posse instantly appeared from the shadows, almost as if they'd been waiting there for ages, grabbing Zeke's arms and dragging him back.

They each wore a leather jacket embellished with their initials and a skull in the corner. In my frenzied state, I found my eyes locking onto their jackets. They seemed familiar, and as I looked down at my frame, I realized they were. I was wearing the same one with a matching skull and the initials "E.R."

Ezekiel Reeves.

"Oh, son..." Chaz messily wiped some blood from his nose. "You've got some explaining to do." He aggressively grabbed my arm, his fingers pressing into my skin with such an intense force that I let out a cry, already feeling a bruise forming. "Now I'll ask you again," he demanded, his voice growing more impatient by the second. "Where. Is. My. Money?"

"I gave it to Blake," Zeke spat out as he struggled to break free from the other guy's grasp. "I gave it to Blake a few days ago. He told me he would give it to you."

"Hmm..." Chaz shifted his glare onto me, his tongue sliding

along his teeth. "Blake, huh? Did Blake come by a few days ago, beautiful?"

My mouth was parched as I hesitantly opened it to respond. "Blake?" I countered stupidly—my mind was in disarray, tears prickling my eyes and blurring my vision. "I have no idea what you're talking about."

Chaz's eyes lit up with delight. "Well, well, well." He coyly looked over to Zeke. "She doesn't know, does she?"

"Chaz," Zeke pleaded. "Don't get her involved."

"Zeke...what is he talking about?" I stood still in fear but somehow managed to mutter out that question. "What don't I know?"

"My love." Chaz tucked me into his side—as if his comfort would ease this situation rather than send a shiver down my spine. "Z is my right-hand man. One of my best employees...as much as I hate to say it. You see, I've saved his ass time and time again. Quite a temper on this one." He shook his head in disdain.

I glanced over at Zeke, whose face was pained as he realized I was slowly piecing the details together.

Chaz was the owner of Club Affinity. Which meant that Chaz was the person who found Zeke after that fight on the boardwalk. Chaz was the person who gave him the job.

But that still left one unresolved question: why was Chaz asking him for money?

"Tell me, darling, do you know what Z does for a living?" Chaz questioned, running his hand along my cheek.

"He works at Club Affinity," I weakly responded, my stomach churning from his cold and daunting touch.

"Ding, ding, ding!" he answered theatrically. "But..." He lifted his finger into the air. "You're forgetting one key piece of information. Dig into that little *lawyer* brain of yours and figure it out."

How the hell did he know what I was studying? How did he know anything about me, for that matter?

"I don't know…" I felt the tears threaten to spill down my cheeks as I shook my head, desperate to get out of there. "I don't know."

"Let me save you the suspense." He released me from his grasp as he strode towards Zeke, placing a hand on his shoulder. "Z-man here handles underground financial affairs…and dare I say, he's pretty fucking good at it."

I stared momentarily at the two of them, unwilling to believe that any of this was happening. "What does that mean?" I finally dared to ask, my voice just barely above a whisper.

"Well, doll face," he spoke condescendingly. "Zeke ensures that I get my money…in whatever way necessary."

"What money?" My gaze shifted from Chaz's devious grin to Zeke, who refused to meet my eyes and instead kept his own trained on the ground.

Chaz nodded with sickening amusement on his lips. "Lots of questions. There's that lawyer brain. I can see why you like her." Chaz shot a suggestive glare at Zeke. "Is she this vocal in the bedroom too?"

"Chaz, I swear to fucking God!" Zeke attempted to push his way forward but was held back once more by the two men holding onto him.

Chaz smiled wickedly before turning back to me. "Club Affinity is what's on the surface, my dear. That's what pretty little people like you see when they come down here for spring break. But we run a much grander scale operation that you wouldn't have seen." He reached into his pocket, pulling out a small bag of white powder.

I squinted at the bag before looking back at Zeke. His eyes were visibly full of despair.

"Let's just say all of us, Zeke included, like to *blow* our guests away." He confirmed my assumption that the crushed-up powder was, in fact, cocaine. "But sometimes, people don't like to pay up. So that's when my friend Zeke here gets involved. Without him, we wouldn't be able to run this whole thing."

I refused to believe any of this. "No." I shook my head. "Zeke wouldn't be a pusher. That's not who he is!"

"That's not who he is?" Chaz mimicked me, letting out a maniacal laugh. "Guys..." He turned back towards his posse. "That's not who he is," he repeated, prompting the group to join in on the laughter.

"Oh, my dear..." He stopped inches away from my face. "If that's not who Zeke is, then how do you think he can afford the bike he drives? The place he lives in? The bed he *fucks* you in?" he snarled, pulling back with a smug look on his face. "I thought you were a smart girl. I guess not."

"Celeste," Zeke desperately spoke back up. "It's not what you think. Let me explain, please...let me tell you everything."

"I'll report you to the police," I snapped, disregarding his pitiful attempt at an explanation and simultaneously halting Chaz in place.

He turned around with a blank stare on his face as I carried on. "I'm not kidding!" I held my ground—finding a brief stint of confidence. "Do you think you can get away with something like this? This is wrong. This is illegal."

An eerie silence fell between the group until it faltered by Chaz's hysterical laugh. "Aw..." He wiped the moisture out of his eyes. "Guys, princess over here is going to report us to the police." He turned towards his buddies, who joined in on the laughter once again.

I was still frozen in fear when Chaz's demeanor changed in a split second, his menacing smile dropping from his face as he charged his way toward me, wrapping his hand around my throat. I instantly gasped for air, desperately trying to grab his wrists and pull them back—but it was useless. His hands were strong, determined, and commanding. He wasn't going to let me go.

"You listen to me, *Celeste*," he hissed my name, his hot breath singeing against my skin and making me feel sick to my stomach. "You don't think we already know enough about you? I can make your life a living hell. Do you realize what reporting us will do? It'll do nothing but land *you* and your little boyfriend in a lot of trouble. So, if you tell a single fucking soul, let alone a police officer, about what's going on, just know this." He rested his face against mine, causing me to force mine away in disgust. "I. Will. End. You."

And just like that, there I was.

That helpless little girl watching in fear as my father's hands clasped around my mother's throat. But this time, my mind replaced my mother's face with mine and my father's with Chaz's.

Life was playing a trick on me.

Was nine-year-old me going down the stairs that night the same as 22-year-old me going to Long Beach this year? A cruel and unforgiving metaphor?

I didn't know. All I knew was that as the oxygen heading to my brain dwindled, and black spots started crowding my vision, I had to force myself back into reality.

I was seconds away from collapsing to the ground when the tension was suddenly released from around my neck. I immediately fell onto my knees, my heart thudding against my chest as I blinked rapidly to get the black spots out of my vision.

"Blake better have my money, Z." I heard Chaz snarl, listening as his footsteps slowly inched away from me. "Let's go."

The guys followed Chaz's demand and released Zeke from their grasp. Without wasting a second, he raced to my side and knelt beside me, wrapping his secure arms around my disoriented frame. "Angel, I'm so sorry. I'll explain everything to you, I promise. I'm so sorry, Celeste."

"Let go of me," I whispered shakily, pulling back from his embrace and slowly getting up on my feet. "I don't have anything to say to you right now."

"Celeste," he pleaded. "I promise, I've been trying to stop, but it's much harder than it sounds."

"You told me I didn't need to worry when I was with you," I spat out. The tears I had been holding in this entire time finally started to flow down my cheeks as I pathetically gasped for air between each word. "You lied to me, Zeke."

"Cel, I—"

"Tell me the truth right now!" I cut him off, angrily brushing my hands along my inflamed neck. "That day when we went to Tim and Sally's, Korey mentioned that you were living with him at one point. It's true, isn't it?"

He nodded his head reluctantly, swallowing deeply. "It's true."

"Then, out of the blue, you just up and left. Somehow managed to buy your place. Korey thought it was weird that you could afford it. I guess I know the reason now."

He released a breath, closing his eyes for a moment. He looked tired, overwhelmed, but most of all, unfamiliar. "Celeste," he whispered. "I didn't have a choice. When I started working for the club, I had no idea what I was really signing myself up for."

I couldn't believe this was happening. How had I been stuck in the dark this whole time?

"So, let me get this straight. You've had me staying at your place, which you only own because of your drug money. You let me sleep in your bedroom where you keep stashes of hidden cash. That's why those sketchy people were pounding on your door in the middle of the night!" My voice inflated with each word. I'd never screamed at someone before.

But I'd never felt so betrayed by someone before, either.

"The money?" My words took him by surprise. "How did you know about the money?"

"I found it, Zeke!" I cried, physically feeling the pain of each teardrop as it fell from my eyes. "I found it earlier this week. But I thought I knew you enough...hell, I thought I trusted you enough not to question it. I guess I was wrong."

"Celeste, this isn't what I wanted." He took an urgent step forward, holding a hand out for me. "I don't give a shit about Chaz's money," he insisted. "I swear to you!"

"Yet, here you are, still working for him years later. Taking advantage of others, using his money to funnel your life, and most of all...lying to me."

He gently placed his hand on my arm as I watched the panic swimming in his green eyes. "Please, Celeste," he begged. "You have to understand that there was no real reason for me to change before I met you. What the fuck did I have in my life?"

His statement answered everything that I needed to know.

"Then you didn't really want to stop, did you?" My voice broke in realization as I looked up at him. "If you only wanted to stop because of me, then that's not good enough of a reason."

"Celeste," he pleaded. "You're the only reason I would want to do anything good in my life. You're the only good thing that has ever happened to me."

I shook my head, pulling away from his touch—a touch that was now foreign to me. I didn't know this man. This wasn't my Zeke. "I don't want to see you again." The harsh words left my mouth. "Ever."

"Celeste," he repeated my name again, desperate to hold my attention. "What about everything we just spoke about, huh? Did that mean nothing to you? You told me that you loved me!"

"I told the person I thought you were that I loved them!" I shouted back at him. "I don't love this person."

"Please...stop. You know the real me." He lowered his voice shakily. "The man you fell in love with, that's me. I'm not this other person. This is only what my life is right now."

"If this is the life you want to live, then I don't want any part of it." I turned away from him, my voice resolved.

"I want a life with you!" His voice was shaking as he pulled me back into his embrace, burying his head into my shoulder before turning me around to face him and gently lifting my chin up. "I'll change. I'll get myself out of this mess. I'll do anything, Celeste..." Tears threatened to fall down his cheeks. "Because I love you."

Finally, I met his gaze—looking into the eyes that I had gotten to know so well this week.

I thought I'd fallen in love with this man, when in reality, maybe I'd fallen in love with an idea. An idea that he would save me.

Zeke was a false sense of promise. A trick. There was no fate between us, just an inherently wrongful disposition—one that had haunted me my whole life. I was foolish to think this would be anything different...and I was smart enough to know better. Nothing good has ever happened to me naturally.

Celeste Kinney makes her own luck. She writes her own story.

"I need to go," I muttered, looking away from his eyes and onto the ground. I couldn't say anything else. "This is over, Zeke."

"No," he protested, the desperation evident in his voice as he tightened his hold on me, unwilling to let me go. "Please, let's try and talk this through."

"There's nothing left to say." My voice turned weak as I pulled away once more, Zeke giving up as he let me go. I was tired...so tired. "This was a mistake. You were a mistake," I whispered.

When he didn't respond, I finally looked up at him. I had to because the second I turned away, I knew I could never look back.

CHAPTER FIFTEEN

IYLA

PRESENT DAY

There comes a time in your life when everything changes. In a moment, everything you once knew falls to your feet, leaving you to pick up all the pieces. And there I was, trying to piece back together a part of myself I hadn't known was broken until now.

As soon as I arrived back at the campus, I fell onto my bed and closed my eyes.

"People come into your life for a reason, whether we know those reasons or not. And Iyla Larson. You're meant to be in my life."

Ambert's words plagued my mind as they repeated on a loop.

Was the universe trying to play some sick joke on me? Was my mockery towards the idea of fate coming back to bite me once and for all?

How could this have happened? And why did it feel so wrong?

Hadn't I wanted this all along? A chance to re-trace my mother's footsteps—an opportunity to learn who she was. Yet, the moment I could taste it...I fled.

Tears streamed down my cheeks at the thought of Ambert's hurt and confused expression in my mind. I felt terrible leaving him the way I did. I hadn't meant what I'd said. I was just overwhelmed, desperate, and looking for an easy way out.

Ambert didn't deserve that, though. It had only been a short period of time, but Ambert had become someone who I could envision a life with.

Had he been more to my story than that all along?

Had Ambert been a vessel? A calculated attempt to get me closer to connecting with my mom...with Claire...with my dad?

Dad.

The answer I'd always been curious to uncover was now crystal clear.

Zeke was my dad.

My brain pounded in my head as I attempted to recall everything I knew about him.

"He's been close friends with my parents for a long time. So, growing up, he was always in my life...except for the first few years."

"What happened the first few years?"

"Some stuff happened back in the day. It's something my family avoids discussing, so I don't know much. And if I'm being honest, I try not to ask."

What had my parents told me about my father?

"He wasn't around."

"You wouldn't want to know him anyway. He was a deadbeat."

A rush of adrenaline made its way through me as I shot up from my bed, pacing the room. "Think, Iyla," I whispered, wringing my hands together anxiously before raising them to my temples and massaging either side of my head. "What else do you remember?"

But there was nothing. Absolutely nothing.

I hung my head in defeat, doing everything possible to calm my breathing when the most important words somehow managed to rush through my mind.

"We'll always be a phone call away. If you need us, we'll get on the first flight out."

I stumbled over myself as I reached for my phone to dial my mom's number. Each pained and prolonged ring stung worse than the last as I anxiously awaited her voice.

"Hey, Iyla bear, how is everything?" She picked up on the third ring.

"Mom..." I paused, my mouth open for a moment before I closed it. I didn't know where to start. I thought hearing her voice would have calmed me, but instead, it filled me with an unexpected anger and sense of betrayal that left me physically shaking.

"Iyla." I could hear the sudden concern in her voice as she picked up on my perplexed state. "Honey, what's wrong? Are you okay?"

"What haven't you told me?" I cried, wiping away a few tears that pricked at my eyes. "How could you and Dad let me come here being so naïve? How could you?"

"Iyla," she paused, seemingly assessing my words before I heard sounds of her shuffling through the house. The infliction in her tone was evident. "Your dad and I are getting on the next plane there."

"No, tell me now!" I demanded. "You've already made me wait my entire life. Tell me about my real mom...my real dad... everyone."

"Iyla..." I could hear her voice start to break. I'm sorry...I'm so sorry. Your dad and I will be there as soon as we can. In the meantime, don't do anything irrational. Please wait for us," she begged. "We'll tell you everything. I will bring you the package...the letter. I promise. Just wait for us."

I was reluctant to agree, attempting to understand how it all came down to this. The answers to my questions had been with them all along, yet there I'd been, struggling my whole life to fight for the truth.

I wanted to hang up. I wanted to pretend that I'd never even picked up the phone and called them to begin with.

As I stared down at the ground, the picture from Dr. Sanders had fallen out of my bag, and there she was, smiling up at me and reminding me *why*.

Why all of this had to happen. Why I was even in California, to begin with.

It was for her.

Everything had been for her.

"Iyla?" my mom spoke once more. "Are you there? Please, Iyla, are you listening?"

"Okay," I muttered out the agreement. That one syllable broke me as much as I knew it would fix me. I had just hung up the phone when Hallie rushed through the door.

"Iyla." She embraced me in a hug, her voice full of relief once she'd wrapped her arms around me.

I hugged her back, feeling the guilt from my actions wash over my body. I'd abandoned her at Ambert's with no warning or explanation whatsoever.

"I'm so sorry," I said shakily. "I shouldn't have taken your car. I just couldn't be...*there*...I needed to leave...I've made a mistake, Hal—"

"Take a breath," she instructed me, rubbing my back. "I'm not upset with you, Iyla. I was just worried about you, that's all."

"I'm sorry," I whispered, burying my head into her shoulder as I sobbed out loud, no longer fighting to hold the pain back. "I'm sorry."

"Shh..." She soothed me. "Everything is going to be okay."

I pulled back from her embrace, assessing her face through my blurred vision. "What happened after I left? What did they tell you?"

"Korey came back out into the garden," she explained calmly. "He said that you'd left and taken my car and that I should probably make sure you were okay. Vic dropped me off. I didn't even see Claire or Ambert on my way out."

I wiped the tears from my face, nodding in understanding.

"Iyla, what happened to you?" she asked gently. "Did you and Ambert have a fight?"

"No," I choked out. "Hallie, it was him. It was my dad."

"What?" She furrowed her brows. "Lance?"

"No." I rapidly shook my head. "Not Lance, my real dad...Zeke."

"Zeke?" The name left her even more dumbfounded.

"Zeke...he was in the picture with her...we have the same eyes... hair...then Claire said something about a package, and now my parents are coming here, and I don't..." My words trailed off as I pinched the bridge of my nose and closed my eyes, shaking my head. Nothing made sense anymore.

"Slow down," she instructed me. "Iyla, you need to start from the beginning. You need to tell me exactly what happened."

I let out a slow and controlled breath, brushing back some tears. "Oh, Hallie...where do I even begin?"

The *Fifteenth Entry*

CELESTE

19 YEARS AGO

AUGUST 28

I stumbled over my shaky feet, finally reaching my dorm room after fleeing Long Beach and slamming the door shut behind me.

"Twelve."

"One."

"Thirty."

"Fifteen."

My erratic counting wasn't working. Nothing was. My mind, the room, my whole world, it was spinning. Spinning faster than I could physically keep up with.

"Forty."

"Eight."

"Two."

"Six."

Work. Please work.

I raised my arm towards my forehead, my skin making contact with a cool unfamiliar material.

Zeke's jacket.

I was still wearing his jacket. The jacket that confirmed his loyalty to Chaz—the jacket that was only a piece of the many lies he'd kept from me.

"Get off...get off...get off!" I whipped it off my body and flung it across the room, expecting to feel some sort of sick satisfaction from it.

But it wasn't enough.

With my anger boiling over, I snatched it from the ground and marched to the tiny trash bin in the corner of the room.

"I hate you!" I screamed through my uncontrollable tears, shoving the jacket inside the bin as far as possible. "I hate you...I hate you...I hate you!"

I needed to get rid of him, and if the task proved to be impossible in my mind, then that meant that no physical trace of him could stay.

Rushing towards my purse, I reached for the photo of the two of us from the photo booth. In shame, I caught myself as I momentarily paused to stare down at it.

"No!" I tore my eyes away. "No, no, no, no, no!" I ripped the photos apart with each syllable and threw them into the trash alongside the jacket.

I needed to start over. I knew how to do that. I'd done it before, so who was to say I couldn't do it again?

The only solution was to go back to the life that existed before there was *him*.

A simple life.

A predictable life.

A life that made sense.

As the hours achingly passed, I fell onto my bed, the tears faded, and my body exhausted itself second by second.

This dream had become a nightmare.

"Celeste, wake up!" A familiar voice shook my body awake. "CeCe!" The voice repeated, rocking me back and forth.

I squinted as the air made contact with my tired eyes. "Claire?" I looked up to face her worried expression.

"Celeste." She pulled me into her tight embrace.

Still dazed, I took a moment to assess my surroundings. Where was I? And most importantly, why was I there?

As I lifted my head from my pillow, it all came flooding back to me.

I'm at the campus.

Claire called me after I raced into a taxi, pleading for me to tell her where I was.

Then, it all went dark.

Claire sighed in relief, running her hand over the back of my head. "Thank goodness you're okay. You scared me." Her expression went from one of joy to concern. "What were you thinking?!"

"Sorry..." I shook my head, unsure what else to say.

She looked at me with a frown. "What happened, CeCe? Zeke came rushing back to the bar. He said you were gone, that you'd disappeared. We didn't know where you were."

"He's not here, is he?" my breathing intensified, and suddenly it felt like I couldn't breathe in enough. "Please tell me he's not here."

"No." She shook her head. "He's with Korey. He doesn't know where I am. I promise."

I reluctantly took her words for truth, despite the lingering panic I felt at the thought that he could appear at any moment.

"What happened?" Claire ran her fingertips along my freshly bruised neck, eyes widening in shock. "Did Zeke do this to you?"

"No," I told her. "It was Chaz. Chaz did this."

"Chaz?" she repeated, her face full of questions. "Who's Chaz?"

"Claire..." I started to sob into my hands. "There is so much I need to tell you."

"Oh, CeCe." She pulled me back in as I continued to cry. "You can tell me." She soothed me. "You can tell me everything." She prompted me to lie back down, and slowly but surely, I explained everything to her.

That first night on the boardwalk.

Dancing with Chaz at the club.

Uncovering the money that haunted Zeke's drawers.

The truth surrounding Zeke and every finite detail that led up to the moment before I ran away.

I'd never seen Claire this way. So hurt...so afraid...so desperate to take my suffering away. I wished it could have vanished so easily.

For hours, she cried with me, became angry with me, and consoled me. And most importantly, she listened to me when I told her that I wanted everything that happened on spring break to be a distant memory.

CHAPTER SIXTEEN

I Y L A

PRESENT DAY

A faint knock came from the door almost exactly 24 hours later.

They were here.

My parents.

They'd finally arrived.

"Iyla." They engulfed me in a hug as soon as I opened the door—
one that I made little attempt to reciprocate.

Pulling back from our one-sided embrace, they looked at me as
if waiting to hear me talk, yet I remained silent. I had nothing to
say. They were the ones who needed to do the explaining.

My dad cleared his throat as he pulled in their luggage, followed
by an envelope and a box he firmly tucked beneath his arm.

I sought refuge back in my bed. It's where I'd been glued from
the moment I got off the phone with them. It was the only place
I felt safe. I'd learned that the world beyond the four walls of my
dorm room contained too many truths, and they were ones that I
no longer had the strength to chase.

"Iyla, I think the best thing is to jump right into it," my mom
spoke softly as she and my dad planted themselves onto Hallie's
bed.

"I think so, too," I murmured, pulling a pillow into my chest.

My dad let out a breath. "Let's start from the beginning. Earlier this year, we received this package along with a letter." He gestured toward the items he'd now placed in his lap. "Although these were intended for you, they came into our possession first. Both the letter and the package were signed by a name that your mother and I recognized. It's a name that I'm guessing you now know, too— Claire Wells, who at the time was Claire O'Donnell."

"Claire was best friends with your birth mother, Celeste." Mom picked up where he'd left off. "We had the opportunity to get to know Claire for the final few weeks you were in the hospital. She visited you almost every single day for the months you were admitted. Claire made sure that you were loved and well taken care of." Her voice trailed off as I could see the guilt kick in.

I swallowed hard at that revelation. *Claire did that...for me? But why?*

"There were pieces surrounding Celeste's death and the circumstances of your father that we wanted to keep shied away from you, Iyla," she continued, cutting my thoughts short. "Not because we were jealous...but because we wanted to keep you safe. When we adopted you, we decided it would be best to close off all contact with Claire. She was a vessel into that world. We never realized the hurt and suffering we would've caused by doing that, not only to her and her family but to *you*."

As my dad spoke, I shook my head, trying to wrap my mind around their words.

"You can imagine our worries when you told us that you wanted to come to UCLA and back to California. This is where the answers to all your questions lay, and we knew without a doubt that you'd search for them."

Had I gone searching, or had everything managed to find its way to me?

My mom placed a hand on my dad's leg. "Iyla, here's what we're trying to say. We were wrong to keep things from you all this time. You deserve to know what happened. You deserve to know the truth, and you deserve to have a chance to learn about your real mom and dad."

The latter part of her statement sent chills down my spine as my dad handed me a visibly opened letter, yet a perfectly sealed box.

"We read the letter Iyla, and for that...we're so sorry. It was never meant for us, and after we read it, we couldn't hardly look at ourselves in the mirror, let alone at it. We pushed everything into the back of our closet. We knew we were wrong, and we couldn't face it," my dad admitted, the shame and regret written all over his face.

"But with that said, we want you to take the time to read the letter and process everything that could be inside that box," my mom added, a hint of hope in her eyes as she locked them on mine. "And if there are still questions by the end of it, we can promise you, Iyla, that we'll tell you everything we know."

As they both stood up from the bed, I brushed away some tears. I was too weak to join them.

"We're staying in a hotel tonight, but we're going to fly back home tomorrow evening. Please just remember that we love you... and we hope that you can find it in your heart to forgive us."

With a final glance in my direction, the two of them worked their way toward the door, leaving behind the answers I'd been looking for...and a letter that was about to reveal everything.

With shaking hands, I pulled it out of the envelope and unfolded it.

Dear Iyla,

When you've had just over 18 years to think of exactly what you want to say to someone, you'd think it would be easy to write a letter.

But here I am, staring at this blank sheet of paper for the past two hours, just like I have been all these years.

My hands shake as I try to think of everything I want to tell you, how badly I want to see you and how much I've thought about you all these years.

But this letter isn't about me. This letter is about you, and boy, oh boy, where do I begin?

I guess an introduction is a good enough place to start. My name is Claire Wells, formerly O'Donnell, and I knew your mother, Celeste. I don't know how much you know about your mother. But I'm going to assume it's not much going into this letter, so let me tell you everything I can in the simplest way possible.

Your mother was tenacious, strong, kind, and my best friend in the entire world. We met in our first semester of college when we got paired as roommates. It was a match made in heaven.

The two of us were inseparable—we did almost everything together. And after no time at all, your mother became a part of my family. A piece of me I didn't know I needed so badly until she was gone.

Initially, I intended to send this letter to you on your eighteenth birthday. But I couldn't bring myself to do it when the time came. I had yet to learn where you were.

Our family has spent many years searching for you, only to be unsuccessful with each attempt.

It wasn't until about two months ago that the universe gave me a sign in the form of an application. It came across my desk with the words "Iyla Larson—pre-law" written on it.

Let me tell you, nothing took my breath away quite like seeing your name...and I knew in my heart that it had to be you.

It didn't surprise me one bit to see that a few months later, you'd been granted an offer of admission. Not to mention the irony of your residence application...Hedrick Hall. The same building both your mother and I stayed in.

History was now repeating itself, and granting me, after almost two decades, the perfect opportunity to reach out to you.

So, here it is.

Along with this letter, I've sent you a package that contains a small collection of your mother's things. Most importantly, you'll find a *journal. A journal that was written by your mother in the months before you were born.*

Iyla, this journal is a crucial part of her story. It was a story that she never got a chance to finish and a piece of her life that is important for you to know about.

You might wonder why I'm so adamant that you read this letter, have this box, and know her story. It's been so long. What's the point anymore?

There is a point...and it's this.

Years ago, I made you a promise. One that you likely won't remember, but I've never forgotten. It was a promise that when you were old enough, I'd give you a chance to know what I know. A chance to learn about the life before you and an opportunity to begin a new chapter in the journal.

I understand if this is all too much—and if this isn't what you want, please know that I completely respect your decision.

But, if by the end of this, you feel the desire to know more, I can promise you that I'll spend the rest of my life telling you anything you'd want to hear.

I'll leave you with this, Iyla.

A chapter left untold will become a book well-written.

-Claire

I could hardly keep the letter still—my body was shaking erratically, trying to sort through all the thoughts racing through my mind before I finally honed in on one single task.

The journal. I need to read the journal.

Scrambling across my room, I searched for a pair of scissors, tearing apart my desk drawer until I found them and wasted no time slicing them into the package.

I tore through the box until I found a purple journal with *Celeste Kinney* written in cursive on the front.

I ran my hand along her name carefully and calmly, breathing in softly. My mother had touched this journal. She'd written her story in this with her own hands. Finally, I would get to hear from her and not from someone else on her behalf.

I delicately opened the journal to the first page, where beautiful handwriting lay on top of worn-out white pages.

I slowly released my breath as the first few words came into view, and I started to read.

"The First Entry."

The *Sixteenth Entry*

C E L E S T E

19 YEARS AGO

AUGUST 31

Twenty-six.

That's precisely how many ceiling tiles Claire and I had in our dorm room. I knew this because the only thing I did in the weeks after our return from Long Beach was stare up at the ceiling and count.

As I lay there, day after day, I quickly realized that time is the enemy, and in moments where you want it to move faster than ever, it slows down. It achingly slows down, especially when all you can think about is the one thing you know you shouldn't.

I was consumed by the hurt, the sadness, and the desire for things to have turned out differently. But things weren't different, and there I was, reminding myself that as quickly as Zeke's presence had entered my life, it had also disappeared.

"They do say all good things must come to an end at some point."

When Zeke had said that to me, I'd taken it lightheartedly. Little did I know that it would come to fruition just a few short days later.

I wanted to hate him, and hell, I'd said I hated him so many times out loud that it almost felt real.

I thought the path forward was supposed to be simple. I was supposed to move on, forget that this measly week of my life had ever happened and continue on my path to greatness. I now knew that that was easier said than done. I could hardly move, think, eat, or sleep. I was barely in a position to leave our room, let alone attend any of my classes.

Nothing seemed to matter anymore. All I wanted to do was hold onto the pain because the pain was the only emotion that reminded me that Zeke was, in fact, real. What we had was real, and as much as I hated to admit it, if I could go back and relive it all over again, even despite knowing the outcome, I would. Just to feel him one more time...kiss him one more time...allow myself to love him again.

I didn't hear from Zeke after I left Long Beach, and at first, I wasn't sure how I felt about it. I'd told him that he was a mistake and that I never wanted to see him again, so could I even fault him for not reaching out to me? Honestly, a part of me feared that if I so much as heard his voice on the other end of the phone, I'd forgive him. Because running from the one thing you want more than anything isn't a sprint; it's a marathon for life.

Claire knew that that was also the reality. She'd been trying her best to sneak around with Korey without my knowledge. It wasn't like she was ashamed to be with him—in fact, the two of them were getting quite serious as time passed. No, the real reason for her newfound selectiveness was an effort to uphold her promise to me. Korey reminded me of that week, that world, that life I'd claimed I no longer wanted anything to do with.

I often wondered if Korey and Claire still spoke to Zeke, and if they did, did they talk about me?

I wanted to ask Korey the odd time I would see him, yet every time we were face to face, I could never bring myself to mutter the simple question.

All I could do was make pathetic small talk that resulted in straightforward answers on his part and nothing to dissect on my own besides my ever-present thoughts.

Had I made the right choice leaving Zeke?

Should I have tried to make things work?

Should I not have given up so easily?

I never found the answers to those questions. I just tried to keep moving.

And slowly, oh so slowly, I was reminded of something that I'd known to be true. That as much as time can be the enemy, with time comes healing.

So, as March went by in a daze, I started to re-attend my final classes by early April. Somehow, I managed to get back on track with my work and prep for final exams.

As May came to a close, so did mine and Claire's time at UCLA. Our graduation was a well-attended ceremony by Claire's family, Korey, Dr. Sanders, and even Sharlene, who'd flown in from Oregon to surprise me at the commencement.

After graduation, Claire and I moved out of our small dorm room and into a two-bedroom apartment in downtown Los Angeles.

At first, we worried about how we'd afford rent, but within the first few weeks of moving in, Claire got a job as an administrative coordinator at UCLA. I cashed in on my savings as I studied tirelessly for the LSAT.

It was May 28th when my test results finally slid through our door slot. I ran over, picked up the envelope from the ground, and ripped it open. Uninterested in reading the templated words on the letter, I focused on finding my score.

174.

I scored 174 out of a possible 180.

I was floored.

I fell to my knees the second I digested the number. The thud of my body echoed throughout the apartment, causing Claire to rush out of her bedroom.

"CeCe? What is it? Are you okay?" she asked, dramatically falling to my side.

I held up the letter. "My results," I whispered. "They came in."

Claire snatched the letter from my hands and scanned her eyes across the words. "Oh my gosh, my best friend is a genius!" She screamed, pulling me onto my feet and into a hug. "You'd better start writing that application now!" she grinned widely as she handed me the paperback. "'Cause you're going to Stanford."

Like Claire had insisted, I wrote up and submitted my application to Stanford that night.

But there it was again, coming back to bite me.

Time.

With the submission of my application came the long and excruciating wait. By now, it was June, three months since I'd left Long Beach and 92 days since I'd last seen Zeke. Each day became more challenging than the last. The hurt never subsided. As much as I tried to mask it, it was always there, slowly becoming a part of me.

A lingering thought that can pull you back as much as it can propel you forward. But as life started to move like it used to for the first time in what felt like a lifetime, all at once, everything changed.

✫ ✩ ✬

"It's okay." Claire soothed me as I woke up for the fifth night in a row, vomiting my insides out. "Let it out."

"I'm so sorry," I groaned, leaning over the toilet. "You shouldn't have to see me like this."

"Nonsense." Claire rolled her eyes, soothingly rubbing my back. "But you need to go to the doctor. Stop putting it off."

I fell back from the toilet, sighing in frustration. Claire was right, I needed to go, but I hated the fact that I'd gotten to the point with this sickness that I had no other choice.

"It's probably just a virus or something." She tucked some hair behind my ear. "Just go tomorrow and get it checked out, okay?"

At Claire's request, I bit the bullet the next morning and mustered up enough energy to see the doctor.

I'd never been a fan of hospitals. Frankly, since the incident with my parents, the only times I'd been to a hospital was when I broke my ankle in high school and had my tonsils out a couple years back.

Hospitals reminded me of the past. And as much as they brought me so much good, healing, and life, they reminded me of a turning point in my life. As much as I'd tried to run from those memories, they always managed to catch up with me.

"Celeste Kinney?"

I stood up at the sound of my name as I was guided into a private room and greeted by my doctor.

"Celeste, I haven't seen you in ages." Dr. Lang had always been one to skip the formalities of a hello. "Something must be seriously wrong for me to see you here."

"Yes." I faintly nodded, explaining my nausea and other hell-like symptoms to her.

With a swipe along her notepad, Dr. Lang stood up from her chair, took some bloodwork, instructed me to take a urine sample, and asked me to lie down on the examination table until she got back with the results.

I waited patiently, hoping my problems would be easily resolved with an antibiotic and some words of encouragement.

That wasn't the case at all.

When Dr. Lang walked back into the room, the two words that fell out of her mouth changed my life forever.

"You're pregnant."

"Pregnant?" I basically had to choke the word out. I was overwhelmed by sheer confusion, skepticism, and disillusionment. There were hardly enough adjectives in the English language to describe the terrified buzz inside of me at that moment.

"Yes," she confirmed with absolution. "You're pregnant, Celeste. The results of your urine sample were clear as day. We're still waiting on the blood work to confirm, but I can do you one better. I have an ultrasound technician on site today. Let me see if she can run a quick scan, okay?"

I can't recall if I even answered Dr. Lang's questions, for I only remember being paralyzed in fear. The color had entirely drained from my face as I stared at her as if she would hold all the answers to my questions.

Pregnant?

How?

Well, I guess I knew how. But how hadn't I sensed it earlier? "But I don't feel pregnant," I blurted out before Dr. Lang stepped out of the room.

"My dear." Her face softened. "All of the symptoms you're feeling right now are signs of pregnancy."

"But..." My voice turned stressed. "I haven't had sex with anyone in over three months. How could I not have known?"

"You'll be surprised just how many women don't realize they're pregnant, Celeste." She placed a reassuring hand on my shoulder. "Take a deep breath. I'll go get the ultrasound technician, and we'll confirm."

A few minutes later, another female doctor saved me from my distress as she joined Dr. Lang back in the room.

"Hi, Miss. Kinney." Her voice was tender as she set up the machine in the corner. "Dr. Lang here wants me to run a quick ultrasound on you. Is that alright?"

Hesitantly, I nodded, lying back down and letting her run the doppler over my lower abdomen.

"Let's see what we've got here." She spoke under her breath, my eyes darting over to the screen.

"Well...there's definitely a baby," she confirmed, pointing out a little head, nose, mouth and faint arms illuminating the screen. "You didn't know, Miss Kinney?"

My chest was rising and falling quicker than ever as I shook my head. "No," my voice was just that of a whisper. "I had no idea."

"Were you taking any precautions?" Dr. Lang chimed in.

"The pill," I responded bluntly.

"The pill isn't always effective," she explained. "Especially when it's not taken properly, and if I look at your file, Celeste, you haven't gotten a repeat since the end of March."

Reality hit me like a truck. Dr. Lang was right. More than right. Since Long Beach, I hadn't taken my pills. I quit cold turkey without even knowing why.

My head fell back in disbelief.

"From what I can see, it looks like you're just over fourteen weeks," she announced. "Congratulations."

"Fourteen weeks?" my voice grew shakier by the second.

She nodded her head. "Give or take."

I felt like all the air had been sucked out of the room. "Oh my gosh. Is the baby okay?" The panic started to kick in as I realized how *real* this was. I had a baby growing inside of me, and all this time, I'd had no idea.

"The baby looks perfectly healthy, Miss Kinney." She attempted to ease my worries. "But we'll just need to run a few more tests to confirm."

Her words only partially eased my worries. Now my fear wasn't that of a lack of knowledge. It was the fact that all of my plans were about to change, and holy shit. I was beyond terrified.

"Aha!" The ultrasound tech pressed the doppler a bit more firmly into my stomach, prompting my eyes to shift back over to the screen. I hadn't realized I even had them closed shut. "I can see the sex," she announced. "Do you want to know?"

"I...I don't know." I could hardly process a simple thought. "I can't believe this is happening. This...doesn't feel real."

She gave me an understanding look. "Maybe finding out the sex will do the trick?" she suggested.

I swallowed the lump in my throat. "Okay." I nodded my head, my voice scraping the inside of my dry throat.

The seconds felt like minutes as the tech looked back at the screen, examining.

"It's a girl."

"Iyla," I spoke, my mouth moving ahead of my mind. "I like that name."

The air settled around us. I'd only ever spoken the name to Claire once, many years ago. But now, saying it with Zeke, seeing how his eyes softened with each syllable...I knew it was perfect.

"And why's that?"

"It means a shining or bright light," I told him. "I've always liked it because of the connection to the stars. And now, it seems fitting given the circumstances." I peered up at him adoringly. "I think there would be nothing more special than our daughter to be named Iyla."

"Our?" he interrupted my thought, causing me to pause in place

"I mean..." I opened my mouth to speak, closing it a few seconds later and repeating it a few times before finally responding. "I'd hope so. I'm sorry if that came across weird."

He kissed me. He kissed me in a way that was so reassured, so confident, so full of love that it washed away any reluctance. "Iyla, it is then," he spoke against my lips. "That's her name. That's what we'll name our daughter."

The memories with Zeke under the stars that night came flooding back to me.

"A girl?" I repeated. "Are you sure?"

"I'm positive." She nodded. "It's a little girl."

Before I knew it, a single tear fell down my cheek as I envisioned Zeke by my side.

"You're okay, angel. We'll get through this together...you and me."

247

I pictured him soothingly rubbing my hand with his thumb, planting gentle kisses along my stomach, and cheering me on as our baby, our daughter, *Iyla*, made her grand entrance into the world.

"*She's perfect,*" he'd say. "*She looks just like you.*"

I'd argue otherwise. She'd be so much like him. She was a part of him. A part of our story together. Perhaps the only logical reason why we'd gone through hell and back...was for *her*.

"Celeste?" I glanced over at the ultrasound tech, who was handing me a tissue with a pitying look in her eyes.

"Sorry." My voice came out so quietly that she had to lean in to hear me. I accepted the tissue from her hands and dabbed away some tears, trying to accept the harsh reality that Zeke wasn't there and push out my lingering question: would he ever be?

"We're all done now." She removed the doppler, cleaning it off.

"Wait...that's it?" I sat up, suddenly feeling terrified at the thought of walking out of this hospital with this news on my shoulders. "What now?"

Dr. Lang handed me a paper towel to wipe down my stomach before placing a printed sonogram image in my hand. "I guess that choice is yours."

☆ ☆ ☆

"Hey, you're back late." I was greeted by an eager Claire as soon as I made my way through the door. "How'd it go?"

I held back my emotions. Frankly, I didn't know if I had any left. I'd cried in my car for hours in the parking lot of Dr. Lang's office, wrestling with my thoughts.

"It *was* some type of stomach virus, right?" she pried, studying my face.

I remained virtually silent and opted to nod my head as I kicked off my shoes. I hated lying to Claire, but at the same time, how could I tell her the truth when I hadn't come to terms with it yet myself?

"Good." She sighed in relief loudly before walking over to me. "Well, not good, 'cause you're sick. But I'm glad you're just a few antibiotics away from getting better."

"Right," I murmured in agreement, making my way toward my bedroom door before she stopped me.

"Hey." She placed a hand on my arm. "Do you need me to stay in? I had plans to go out with Korey tonight, but if you need me, I can reschedule."

"No, go," I told her, my short response causing her to narrow her eyes.

"Are you sure? I'm happy to stay—"

"You've taken care of me for days, Claire," I reminded her. "So go. Besides, I don't want to get you sick."

As if pregnancy is contagious.

"Okay..." She settled for my response, shooting me a smile before pulling me in for a hug. "Now go to bed, rest, and get better, okay?"

I forcefully smiled as she pulled back, throwing on her jean jacket and shoes before making her way to the front door.

When the door slammed shut, I rushed into my room and fell onto my bed. My tear-filled eyes soaked through my pillow within seconds, worsening my already erratic breathing. Each breath felt like a piercing ache, an ache that hadn't left since...that night.

My bones felt like they were going to break.

My soul felt empty.

My body felt weak.

My mind wouldn't stop racing.

The tears continued to fall.

And I became angry.

Angry at him.

Angry at everything.

Angry at myself.

In one swift motion, I removed the pillow that I'd been clinging against my chest and threw it across the room, forcing a few items to be knocked off my bookshelf in the process.

"Shit." I released an exasperated sigh as I pushed myself up from the bed and bent down to pick up the fallen items.

Amidst the chaos, the glint of a purple notebook caught my eye and forced repressed memories to swarm back in.

"This is for you." Sharlene handed me a small item wrapped in her signature vintage paper, one I'm sure she'd had since the eighties. I took it from her grasp, peeling back the taped sides. "Sharlene..." I laughed softly, taking in her kind yet unnecessary gesture. It was a journal. "You really didn't have to get me anything. You know that, right?"

She hushed me, brushing her slender hand along my face and through my hair. "I know, dear, but I wanted to."

My eyes scan over the simplistic yet personalized star details Sharlene had added to the purple cover.

"I need to tell you one thing before you go," she commanded my attention with her deep eyes as the two of us stood at the airport terminal. "And you can't forget this, okay?"

A faint nod from me prompted her to continue. "No one will ever be able to tell your story quite like you. And sometimes, Celeste, in order to move forward, we need to re-discover the past."

Before I had the chance to respond, she pulled me into a hug, one that was tender and short but full of love. Love—a feeling I'd been a stranger to my whole life.

As my response to her statement loomed on my lips, her presence was gone without a single ounce of clarity to follow.

The tears that had momentarily paused began falling back down my cheeks as I reminisced on the words she had once spoken to me. Words that, at the time, felt foreign, unheard, uncanny. I was leaving Oregon and everything that came with it to escape from my story, not rewrite it.

I needed to start fresh. A new city, a new life, a new Celeste, a new book entirely.

Besides, why would anyone want to hear my story when the author herself didn't want to share it?

Still, I couldn't shake the words away.

"In order to move forward, we need to re-discover the past."

"Goddammit." I sunk my head down, feeling completely drained as a few tears fell onto the empty pages in front of me.

No more running. No more hiding away. No more pretending like Zeke never happened. "You've got to try and move forward." I sniffled. "Re-trace your footsteps. Try to make sense of *him*. Make sense of...*you*." I placed my hand on my stomach, pausing when the idea came to mind.

With the blank notebook in my other hand, I made my way over to my desk and flicked on my lamp, connecting my pen with the paper and starting at the place where this journal began.

The First Entry.

June 21.

At the time, I could've never imagined how impactful writing in this journal would become. Nor did I think it would take me three consecutive months of writing to finally get to the point where I could say, "we're all caught up."

But that's the truth, and that's where we're at.

It's now the end of August. August 31st, to be exact, and at this moment, I'm glued to the same spot where this story began.

But now, there's a big difference. I'm 26 weeks pregnant and using my room as a safe haven, considering I still haven't told Claire the truth about my hospital visit.

At first, it was easy, and my attempts at wearing flowing tops and covering my relatively small bump were working. But as time continued to pass, my bump continued to grow, as did the reality that I couldn't keep this up for much longer.

I want to tell Claire. I want to tell her so badly. I do. And I'm not *not* telling her because I'm scared to. I just know that in my heart, there's only one person I need to speak to right now. One person who needs to know first.

And so, here's the reality of it all. The grand revelation that these 16 entries have guided me towards. A truth that I'm confident I've known all along.

I need to go back to Long Beach.

I need to see Zeke.

Not for me.

Not for him.

But for *you*. The one person who's been with me this entire time.

The heartache, the pain, the tears, the joy, the laughter, the love, the confusion. It's all been for something because it all led me to *you*, Iyla.

My girl.

My shining light.

My star.

My daughter.

I never imagined this would be the case—at 22, I'd be a few months shy of being a mom. But as I stare down at your sonogram picture and place my hand on my growing stomach, I know I wouldn't change anything.

When I go to sleep at night, it's as if I can see exactly who you are...who you will be without having to wonder.

Iyla, you're the vulnerability and strength of your father.

You're passionate and hopeful, just like Claire.

You've got a sense of compassion and kindness, like Sharlene.

You possess the intuitiveness and knowledge of Dr. Sanders.

But most of all, you're resilient...like me.

I couldn't be prouder of you.

I want you to know that despite all the trials and tribulations, I'd do it all again for the chance to be your mom.

Remember that it's okay to laugh, cry, and not know why life throws things in your way, but understand that you'll get through it no matter what.

Life is going to be full of love and loss, Iyla, but it's what you choose to do with those emotions that'll make you who you are.

And so, what is there left to say but this?

At the start of these entries, I wrote, "bravery is a virtue possessed by all, but only used by some." And that's what I wanted to be with him.

Braver.

But now, brave is what I want to be for you, Iyla. It's all I'll ever be for you. I promise.

Although I may not know the day we'll meet, I know that when that time comes, I'll be waiting for you.

I'm being brave now, Iyla. You remember to always do the same, too.

Until this story continues.

I love you.

Mom.

CHAPTER SEVENTEEN

IYLA

PRESENT DAY

I was numb.

Utterly and completely numb.

How had I gone from knowing nothing to knowing everything in a matter of hours?

Everything that I'd read had been written for me. It had always been for me. Although, I can't imagine my mom intended for me to receive it this way.

"God." I placed my head into my hands and let out a few long breaths, unsure of how much more I could handle but certain that if there was one thing I needed to do right now, it was to keep reading.

There was no other choice.

The journal still had a few pages left to go, and with the way the last entry concluded, I still had so many remaining questions. Most importantly: what had happened? With these questions came fear—the fear that these final pages could very well tell me just that.

As I flipped the journal back open, something felt off. Even through wet eyes, I could tell that the handwriting was now someone else's.

"What?" I whispered out loud, my heart sinking as I read the name on the page.

Claire.

"Claire?" I brushed away some tears before scanning the words written below.

Iyla,

You might be wondering why I'm writing in this journal...trust me, I'm asking myself the same thing.

It feels wrong.

Invasive.

But how could I read that last entry knowing there is still so much more to your mom's story that you need to know?

So, just like this journal intended, these few entries are to you, Iyla. They will always be to you.

The Seventeenth Entry

CLAIRE

18 YEARS AGO

FEBRUARY 10

"You've reached the voicemail of Celeste Kinney. Please leave a message after the tone."

"Celeste!" My distraught voice began. "Where are you? Zeke came back into the bar and said you disappeared...ran off? I don't know what happened, but CeCe, we're all worried sick about you. Where are you? Call me, text me, just...let me know you're okay. Okay?"

I tucked my phone into my pocket and walked back over to Korey, who was doing his best to calm Zeke down as he paced back and forth—mumbling bits of nonsense about how he was "stupid" and a "terrible person."

"Just relax." Korey placed his hand on Zeke's shoulder. "I bet she's just gone back to the hotel. Let's stop standing around here and go there, alright? Let's go check."

Zeke seemed to like the sound of Korey's plan as he nodded in agreement. "Okay," he breathlessly spoke. "Let's go...let's go now." He rushed toward the door as I followed quickly behind him.

"Did she answer?" Korey whispered, pulling me back from going any further.

"No." I pulled my phone out of my pocket, ready to type another message. "But you might be right. Maybe she's just back at the hotel. So, we'll all go and make sure that she's okay."

"No." Korey looked down at me, releasing my arm. "You need to stay here."

"What?" I retaliated. "What do you mean? I want to come with you guys. I need to make sure she's okay, Korey. She's my best friend!"

"I understand." He was visibly attempting to stay calm throughout the entire situation. "Trust me, I do. But what if she comes back here and we're all gone? Then what?"

He made a good point.

"Just stay. It won't take us too long to get to the hotel. I'll call you."

I placed my hands over my face as the overwhelming stress bristled over my skin. "What do you think happened, Korey? Do you think she's okay?"

"It sounds like they just got into a fight." He rubbed my back soothingly. "I'm sure she's okay. She's probably just upset. Wait here, and everything will work out."

"Korey!" Zeke shouted by the front door as he urged him to follow. "Let's go!"

"I'll see you soon, alright?" Korey placed a kiss on my forehead before running over to the door and disappearing onto the boardwalk behind Zeke.

I stayed put momentarily, staring at the door before pulling up a seat and sending yet another message.

My fingers were numb from the continued slamming on the keyboard in an effort to type as fast as possible.

As the agonizing minutes passed, I decided it was no use. Maybe her phone had died, or perhaps she'd left it somewhere. But when a buzz finally came through to my phone, I realized that that wasn't the case.

"I'm okay."

A message from Celeste read, prompting me to immediately dial her number. "C'mon, CeCe, answer," I whispered desperately as my hands anxiously tapped against the counter. Another ring passed until, finally, it stopped. "Hello?" I spoke eagerly. "Celeste, are you there? Where are you?"

"I'm at...I'm going to the dorm," she barely croaked out. "I'm on my way there."

"Stay there, okay?" I sprinted outside the bar and down the street as I called for a taxi.

"No, it's fine," she protested. "I'm fine."

I dismissed every single one of her objections. "I'm on my way," I announced as a taxi pulled up, and I hopped inside, instructing them on where to go.

"Please don't bring Zeke...don't tell him where I..." Her voice hiccupped through her uncontrollable tears. "Don't bring...don't bring Zeke."

"I won't, CeCe," I tried to reassure her, her incoherence a tell-tale sign that she wasn't doing okay. "I promise you. I will be there as soon as I can."

The line went dead, leaving me in a speeding taxi as I questioned what the hell to do next.

I needed to tell Korey where I was going so we didn't have two hysterical messes on our hands. Still, I also needed to respect Celeste's wishes. Zeke couldn't know.

"Call me when you're alone."

I typed out to Korey as I rested my head against the seat, waiting for his agonizing call.

It arrived just a few seconds later.

"Claire? What's going on? I'm away from Zeke, so if you don't want him to see me on the phone, you need to talk quickly," he demanded.

"She's okay," I informed him. "She called me...she's on her way back to the campus."

"Okay." He let out a sigh of relief. "Thank God I'll get Zeke, we'll pick you up, and we'll head over."

"No!" I promptly shut him down. "She doesn't want to see him. Besides, I'm already in a cab and on my way there."

"What? But Zeke is freaking out, Claire! He's worried something happened to her. You can't just expect him to drop it."

"Tell him she's okay, and that's all I told you. Nothing else, Korey. I mean it."

"Claire," he whispered through the phone as I sucked deeply.

"Korey," I pleaded. "Please. You need to do this for me. I care about you, okay? But Celeste...Celeste is everything. Just tell Zeke that she's okay. I'll talk to her. I'll figure this out," I rambled, nervously waiting for his agreement as the line went silent.

"Okay," he finally spoke. "Okay, I will."

Relief washed over my body.

"Thank you." I felt the tears well up in my eyes before I ended the call, unwilling to utter as much as another syllable. Now, my mind was focused on one thing: getting back to the campus and being with Celeste.

☆ ☆ ☆

Iyla, in your mother's entries, she described her suffering, pain, and grief after she left Zeke. But no words could ever adequately describe the sight that was her when I arrived back on the campus.

The room was in shambles. And shoved into the garbage bin were ripped-up photos that she and Zeke had taken earlier in the night along with Zeke's leather jacket.

I paused and debated what to do. My brain told me to leave it, don't touch it. If she threw it in there, she must've thrown it in there for a reason.

But I couldn't listen to my brain. Piece by piece, I pulled the shredded photos and the jacket out and safely hid them in one of my drawers. I couldn't explain why I did it, but I knew in my heart that those items couldn't be gone forever. They just couldn't.

After I closed my drawer, I walked over to her bed and placed a gentle hand on her back to stir her awake.

It didn't take long for her to explain everything that had happened to me. As she spoke, my heart broke alongside hers.

A part of me felt an immense amount of guilt in those moments, knowing that my constant prompting and begging were the real reason why she'd gone to Long Beach in the first place. It's something that, even to this day, I blame myself for.

However, I knew that the words of hatred she expressed towards Zeke were the words of her hurt and not her heart. You didn't even need to open your eyes to see how in love Celeste was with Zeke and vice versa. It was written all over her face that night at Club Affinity when I'd encouraged her to go and speak to him.

Your mother had said I had my tells when it came to talking to guys, but she also had hers.

Celeste was very to the point, factual, and one to ensure that she had all the details. I guess that's why she loved law so much. But one thing about your mother was that if she wasn't interested, she wouldn't ask. So, the way she'd prompted Korey with questions that night at Club Affinity was a clear giveaway that she wanted to know more about Zeke.

But despite what I'd seen, what I knew about the fire and ice that were your mother and father, there was only one thing I could do: respect your mother's wishes, and respect that if she wanted Long Beach and everything in it to be a thing of the past, I would never, ever mention it again.

✰ ✰ ✰

The next morning, I left a note on her bedside table, informing her that I was going back to Long Beach to grab our things and that I'd be home as soon as possible.

I hoped I'd be back before she even woke, but within the first 20 minutes of arriving at the hotel, I was startled by someone loudly knocking on the door.

I swung the door open to reveal a distraught Zeke. He had dark bags under his eyes and messy hair. His arms stayed firm on either side of the door frame as his head sank in exhaustion.

"Claire?" He seemed surprised to see me. "Where is she?" he pushed his way into the room, attempting to search for her.

"She's not here." I tried to calm him down. "How'd you know I was here?"

"I didn't." He laid down on the bed, running his hands over his face in defeat. "I just thought I'd give it another try."

"Zeke." I sighed, sitting down beside him. "She's okay...she's just upset."

"She's not going to forgive me." He shook his head. "I'm a terrible person. I put her at risk, I...I love her, Claire, and I ruined everything."

"She loves you too," I reminded him softly. "But you can't expect her to just forgive you. She feels betrayed. Trust and honesty are everything to her. You should've known that, considering everything she told you."

He met my eyes. "What exactly did she tell you?" he probed.

"Everything." I shook my head, looking ahead. "She told me everything."

He frowned; pain and regret washed over his skin. "What do I do, Claire?"

"You need to wait until the universe is ready to give you two another chance." I hugged his large build, attempting to soothe him with any hope that remained. "And in the meantime, you need to get yourself out of your situation." I pulled back and sternly looked him directly in his eyes. "You hear me? You need to do that. Not because I'm telling you, not because of Celeste, but because you are capable of so much more than just moping around."

I allowed him a moment to process my words as he ran his hand over his mouth in thought. "Okay," he muttered bluntly, standing up from the bed and heading towards the door. "Just please make sure she knows how sorry I am, Claire. I will change...I promise you, I will change."

"I know you will." I nodded in reassurance.

The image of his disheartened face would haunt my mind for the next six months—the amount of time it would take to see him happy one last time on a night that I will never forget.

To You, Iyla

CLAIRE

18 YEARS AGO

FEBRUARY 18

"We haven't been out in months," I reminded Celeste as she lay on the couch, feet up, face glued into the same purple journal she'd become consumed by lately. I had no idea in the moment just how special that journal was. "I know you're still waiting for your acceptance to come in, but let's be realistic. You're a shoo-in." I assured her. "Let me take you out. Your choice. Me and you, just like old times. What do you think?"

She continued to write for another moment before finally closing the journal and resting it on top of her stomach. "Fine." She sat up from the couch. "We'll go."

"What? Really?" I laughed, surprised by her sudden willingness to agree when I'd been begging her for weeks. Hell, I'd been begging her for *months* to do anything other than stay within the four walls we called "home."

"You're right. I deserve to enjoy myself and spend a night out," she responded, but her brief responses weren't convincing. She had an ulterior motive—I just didn't know what it was quite yet. "How about we go to Casa Riel?" she proposed.

I recognized the name. Casa Riel was a nice restaurant we spotted on our way to a certain somewhere. "But that's...that's right along the boardwalk in Long Beach—"

"I know," she cut me off, nodding confidently. "I want to go there, so let's go," she shot me a look as if to *drop any further questions.*

"Alright." I did just that as she disappeared into her bedroom, and I pulled my phone out to call Korey.

He picked up after the second ring. "Hey. What's up?"

"Where's Zeke tonight?" I skipped any small talk.

"He had to work at the club," he responded with a hint of confusion and fear. "Why?"

I let out a deep sigh, frustrated that, of course, *that* was where he was.

Little to your mother's knowledge, although I'm sure she had a hunch—Korey and I continued to see Zeke. I needed to make sure that he was getting on the right track, which was something that proved to be much more complex than we'd anticipated.

It turned out that Chaz had grown a keen liking to Zeke and that he was one of his key sources of revenue.

It was no secret that Zeke wanted out. In fact, he was doing everything in his power to cut ties with Chaz.

He managed to get rid of his condo and move back in with Korey. He took small steps away from the club and even began working part-time with Korey at the auto shop. But despite all of the changes consuming his life, he never stopped asking about Celeste. *Is she doing okay?*

Should I reach out?

Should I see if she'll forgive me?

Korey and I would always respond to him with the same thing. "She's fine. Are you happy with where you are in life? And would you feel safe having her around?"

Our straightforward questions would always sway the trajectory of his actions. I felt awful. I knew the silent suffering that your mother was experiencing, but she'd said she wanted to start fresh.

She tried to keep busy, but the sadness never faded, as much as she tried to pretend like it had.

"Why do you ask if he's working tonight?" Korey asked suspiciously.

I walked into my bedroom. "Because..." I sucked in a deep breath. "Guess who wants to come down to Long Beach for a nice dinner out?"

"You're kidding." I pictured the surprised look that washed over his face.

"Yes. So, if Zeke's working tonight, don't tell him we're going to literally be up the boardwalk."

"I won't," Korey responded. "I swear. Just try and have a nice evening, okay? Maybe this is a good sign."

"I don't know," I told him. "Maybe this is a bad one."

"Ready to go?" Celeste asked as she entered my room, wearing a beautiful flowing white dress with her hair tucked up and out of her face, like usual. She looked...*normal*. Familiar. I hadn't seen her like this in what felt like forever.

I quickly ended the call before Korey could respond, worried about how much of our conversation she'd already overheard.

"Korey?" she assumed, nodding towards the phone in my hand.

"Yeah..." I tucked my hair behind my ear, trying to put on a nonchalant front. "He was just telling me how busy it is at the shop."

"Good for business, I guess." She shrugged. "Are we leaving or what?"

I looked down at my simple yet passable outfit and reached for my jacket. "Sure. Let's go."

As we hopped into the car, she reached towards the dashboard and grabbed her sunglasses, reminding me of the day we first drove to Long Beach together—a simpler and happier time.

We turned up the radio and listened in silence for the entire car ride before eventually pulling up to the restaurant. I couldn't help but notice her eyes darting to the very visible Club Affinity sign just up ahead on the boardwalk.

I pulled her attention away, prompting her to follow me inside the restaurant as I requested that we'd be sat at a table towards the back—far enough away from the window that if Zeke were to pass by, he certainly wouldn't be able to see us.

At first, we laughed and joked around, and for a moment, there she was again. Celeste, my best friend, my sister, the person who she was before that spring break.

"I've missed you." I couldn't help but blurt out. Sure, we'd been around each other non-stop, but I'd never felt farther away from her than I had those last few months,

She frowned, placing her fork to the side. "I'm sorry, Claire," she admitted, meeting my eyes with sincere sadness reflected in her own. "I've been so distant from you."

"You don't need to apologize," I stopped her. "Really, you don't."

"But I do," she insisted. "I've been so consumed with everything that happened, and I haven't been a good friend to you. You were there before anyone else ever was. I can't thank you enough for everything you've done for me...not only these past few months but for the past four years. You know how much I love you, right?"

My eyes watered as she reached for my hand, and I let her take it. "I love you, too. And I mean that with all of my heart."

She smiled at me and squeezed my hand, prompting a smile back from me. "Okay, enough of this emotional stuff." I laughed softly, re-lifting my fork and taking another bite of food before I burst into tears. "Tell me, when should you hear back from Stanford?"

"The sooner, the better," she responded, sneaking a quick glance down at her phone as if she was checking the time. "But it might take a couple more months."

"I'm so proud of you," I told her, smiling. "You've worked so hard, and I know how incredible you're going to be at Stanford."

She flashed a weak smile back. "Thanks, Claire. I guess we'll see what the future holds. You never know." She looked down at her food, playing with it with her fork as if she was questioning things.

"Yeah, I guess..." I took another bite of my pasta. "But your future is Stanford Law School. It always has been. That's all you've ever wanted."

She seemed uncomfortable with my statement, shifting in place as she took another sip of her water. She'd insisted on not wanting to drink tonight.

"Either way." I tried to do some damage control. "I will always be there for you, and you will always be my best friend. Nothing will change that. Stanford or no Stanford."

"I know." She nodded, silence falling over the table as she looked down at her phone once again.

"Everything okay?" I questioned, curious as to what she seemed to be waiting for.

She looked up. "Yeah. I just need to use the bathroom...I think I ate too fast." She stood up, placing a hand on her stomach and grabbing her purse.

"Okay," I said, a slight sense of suspicion creeping over me. "I think it's down the hallway."

She shot me a final half-smile before tucking in her chair and disappearing out of sight.

I continued to eat, peering down at the time occasionally while I waited for Celeste to return to the table.

Yet, as I continued to sit and wait, she didn't return.

Five minutes.

Ten minutes.

Where was she?

I got up from my chair and worked my way over to the wash-room, calling out her name as I stepped inside. "CeCe?" I shouted. "Are you okay?"

No answer.

I walked over to each stall and pushed them open one by one, quickly realizing that the bathroom was completely empty.

"Oh no..." I whispered, immediately understanding exactly where she was.

I ran out of the bathroom and flagged down our waiter, pulling a hundred-dollar bill out of my purse and handing it over to him. Enough to cover both of our meals and a sizable tip.

I sprinted out of the restaurant and towards Club Affinity, pushing past everyone in the line as I made my way straight to the front.

"There's a line!" The bouncer looked down at me with annoyance.

"I'm with Zeke," I argued, out of breath.

He gulped, moving to the side and letting me through without hesitation.

The club was busier, louder and darker than I remembered. I could hardly see anyone's face, let alone make out Celeste's small frame.

I urgently shoved my way over to the bartender, one whom I recognized from doubling the ounces of liquor in our drinks the last time we were here.

"Where's Zeke?" I demanded. His eyes darted straight for my chest before he even looked at my face.

"I was wondering if I'd ever see you again." He smirked, pouring me a shot and sliding it in my direction.

"I'm flattered," I lied. "But I really need to find Zeke. So, if you know where he is, please—"

"I just saw him disappear out back with some blonde." He gestured towards the back doors. "They just left, so you can probably still catch them—"

I refused to entertain another word of his as I pushed past the crowded bodies in the club and out the back door.

As soon as I exited the club, I saw them. Celeste and Zeke about ten yards away from me.

They hadn't heard the door, so I decided to hide behind one of the massive garbage containers that lingered out back, ready to jump in at the first sign of trouble.

"What are you doing here?" Zeke's eyes widened as he pulled her in for a hug, holding onto her tightly.

"I needed to see you," she responded, her voice faint but just loud enough for me to make out what she was saying. "I needed to talk to you."

"I..." he stuttered before pausing, seemingly gathering his thoughts mentally. "Let me speak first," he said, looking down at her and prompting her to meet his gaze. "Not being honest with you was the worst mistake of my life, Celeste. A day hasn't passed by where I haven't beaten myself up over what happened. Over these past few months, I've been trying to get better, and things *have* gotten better." He ran his hands through his hair. "I got rid of my place. It's gone. Fuck, it never should've been mine to begin with. I've been working with Korey at the shop part-time. It's been harder to cut ties with Chaz all at once, but I'm trying. I promise you, I'm trying."

She stared up at him, visibly weighing up his words before she spoke, her voice filled with pain. "Why haven't you reached out to me? Called me? Found me? Didn't you care too?"

He placed his hands on either side of her face. "Of course, I cared! But how could I reach out to you knowing what I did to you? How could I be a part of your life when I knew I couldn't give you everything?"

A silence fell between them. "You *were* everything, Zeke," she said, her lip quivering as her eyes welled up with tears, causing his face to drop as he pulled her into his embrace once more.

"Do you think these past few months have been easy for me?" I heard her muffled voice, her face buried into his chest. "Do you know how hard it's been to wake up every day, trying to pretend that I'm okay? I haven't been okay since the night I left." Her voice turned into a whisper.

Zeke kissed her forehead, trying to soothe her as she shook with her weeps. "I'm so sorry," he kept repeating. "I love you so much. I am going to get out of this mess, fuck Chaz and this club. I'll leave right now. Nothing matters to me more than you."

Celeste pulled away from his grasp. "I love you too, Zeke. I never stopped." She shook her head, the emotion overwhelming her face as she placed a kiss on his lips.

And there it was.

The first smile in months washed over Zeke's face. I'd forgotten what he'd looked like when he was happy.

"But I'm still so upset with you," she murmured against his lips. "You let me down, Zeke. You really did."

Zeke ran his fingers through her hair. "I know, angel...I know. And I'm so sorry."

"But I want to work through this, Zeke," she spoke confidently, stopping him before he could continue apologizing. "We need to work through this because..." she paused, biting her lip nervously before dropping her gaze to her stomach, placing a trembling hand on it. "Because I'm—"

"Well, isn't this beautiful?" A man exited from the other side of the club, taking slow steps towards the two of them. "A reunion like no other."

I didn't need to have seen him before to recognize exactly who this man was. How the color completely left Celeste's face, and the panic crept into her eyes told me everything.

It was *Chaz*.

"My, my, it's been some time, Celeste. How are you? How have you been?" He pretended to display any sense of interest in her life. "You look ravishing, as always."

"I'm going to kill you!" Zeke attempted to lunge forward in a fit of anger.

"Not so fast." Chaz reached into the back of his pants, pulled out a small handgun and held it directly in front of Zeke, stopping him in place.

Celeste froze. I froze. We were both shaking in fear as the air escaped my lungs—the realization of just how dangerous this situation was made my legs go limp.

"Like I told you, Celeste." Chaz kissed his teeth, shaking his head. "Quite a temper on this one." He waved the gun around in the air as if it was nothing. "So..." He took a step towards the two of them. "What's this about 'fuck Chaz' and you're 'going to leave here right now'? I thought we were closer than that, Zeke," he placed a hand on his heart, pretending to be offended. It was like watching a theatre with the sickest, twisted main character. "You, young man, you're stuck with me. Do you hear that? You aren't going anywhere." He cocked the gun and pointed it directly at Zeke's chest. "Let alone off into the sunset with this stupid fucking woman—"

Zeke charged forward, tackling Chaz to the ground as the gun fell out of his hands and onto the floor.

"Zeke!" Celeste screamed, rushing over to him. "Zeke, stop!" she cried as he continued to pound relentless punches into Chaz's face. "Stop!" I'd never heard her voice so petrified in my life.

I'd never felt more helpless than I did at that moment. I wanted to run over and help—yet, when I attempted to break free from hiding, I was reminded of what Celeste had told me about Chaz. He was dangerous and irrational, and I feared what greater danger I'd put us all in if I showed up unannounced.

"You're going to kill him... Zeke, you're going to *kill* him!"

Zeke pulled back only when Celeste grabbed hold of his arm and

KATE LAUREN

dragged him off, urging him to calm down. "Zeke," she pleaded. "Stop. He's not worth it. Let's just go, okay? Let's just go before you get into any more trouble."

His eyes softened as he looked up at her, taking in her words.

"Please!" she begged. "It's you and me. There's no one else. It's only us, remember?"

Zeke fell back into her arms as she steadied him. "It's only us," he mumbled. "It's only us."

"That's right," she agreed. "You're okay...we're okay. I love you, alright? We're going to go, and we're never going to come back here again. You and me," she gestured between the two of them. "We're going to be a family...we're going to have a—"

Bang.

In his limp state, Chaz had mustered up enough strength, reached towards the gun on his left, picked it up, and loosely fired it.

"No!" I shrieked, the ringing of the gunshot penetrating my eardrums as I watched the bullet graze past Zeke and firmly land in the side of Celeste's collarbone.

You know that cliche, "the world seemed to move in slow motion"? I never understood how that was possible until I experienced what happened next. I had to watch as Celeste stumbled back, her small frame collapsing to the ground.

"Celeste!" Zeke cried out, catching her at the last second.

Suddenly, my trembling legs and numb hands didn't matter. Without wasting a second, I broke free from behind the garbage container. It felt like it took me ages to finally reach her side as I pulled off my jacket and placed it on top of her wound.

"Claire?" Zeke looked at me in shock as I met his fearful eyes.

"Apply pressure!" I sputtered, my breaths short. "Don't let go! Keep holding on firmly!"

He quickly nodded, although I could tell he was questioning where I'd come from and what in the world to do.

272

Celeste was shaking uncontrollably. She was coughing, wheezing, crying—but doing everything in her power to keep breathing.

"Talk to her," I demanded frantically, fumbling for my phone to dial 9-1-1. "Talk to her, Zeke!"

Between the operator and Zeke whispering to Celeste in desperation, I heard Chaz rustling movements as he slowly stood up from the ground.

His face was in shambles as he hobbled out of sight, wincing with every step. A part of me wanted to go after him, but I knew he wouldn't get far. He was hurt, bleeding everywhere, and besides, the only person I needed to dedicate my attention to was Celeste.

I placed my phone to the side as the operator stayed on the line and informed me that the ambulance was coming.

"Celeste!" I brushed away some tears from her cheek. "Hey, it's me. It's Claire. Help is on the way, okay? You just need to hold on..." My voice started to break as I looked into her eyes, which were more pained than I'd ever seen. "You've just got to hold on, Celeste. Please."

She continued to wheeze out as the tears fell down my cheeks.

"How bad is it?" I asked Zeke, keeping my eyes on CeCe.

He pulled his hands back ever so slightly. Her once-white dress was now soaked with blood.

"This isn't working!" The distraught was evident in Zeke's voice as he removed the jacket and applied direct pressure with his hands. "You'll be okay, angel," he continued to reassure her. "Just keep breathing."

Yet with each passing second, her eyes became more dazed, preoccupied, and distant. She was falling in and out of consciousness.

"Celeste!" I screamed as I shook her face, my voice shaking through my tears. "Listen to me right now," I demanded. "You're a fighter. You've always been a fighter. Don't you dare give up on us, do you hear me? Don't you dare give up!"

Her eyes slightly re-opened at the sound of my cries. "Keep

talking to her, Zeke!" I shouted.

It felt like it was taking ages for the ambulance to arrive.

"Just keep her awake...make sure she stays awake!"

Zeke pulled one hand away from her chest and tilted her face up. "Celeste, can you hear me?" he placed his head against her forehead. "I love you. I love you so much," he whispered through tears. "But you have to stay awake, okay? It's just like you said. We're going to get out of this. You're going to be okay."

"I..." she began to choke out. "Iy..."

"That's it," he encouraged her. "Talk to me, angel."

"*Iyla*," she mumbled, her eyes closing yet again.

"No!" Zeke's movements became panicked as he shook her awake. "What do you mean, *Iyla*? What are you trying to tell me?"

Bright lights and sirens approached us as Celeste weakly lifted her hand and placed it over her stomach, an action she'd repeatedly done that night. She was too weak now to even keep her eyes open.

"Stay awake!" Zeke held her onto her face, unnoticing her movement as the paramedics jumped out of the ambulance and rushed to her side.

"Get the stretcher now!" one paramedic shouted, replacing Zeke's hands with his own.

"You're going to be okay..." Zeke seemed in a daze as he stumbled back and let the paramedics take over, the distance between the two of them growing, his eyes brimming with tears. "I love you, Celeste."

The paramedics worked quickly as Celeste was strapped into a gurney and lifted into the ambulance.

"You need to wait here." An officer placed a hand on Zeke's chest as he attempted to step in behind her.

"What? No," he argued as I watched in fear behind him. "Please, let me go with her!"

"You." The officer pointed over to me. "You can go."

"Me?" I placed a hand on my chest. "No, I'll be the one to stay. I'll tell you everything that happened. He needs to be with her."

"Go!" Zeke looked at me, causing me to pause in fear. "Now!" he demanded, and just like that, I shook myself out of it and hurried towards the ambulance.

As soon as I hopped in, the doors closed behind me. The sirens turned on as we pulled away, leaving me with nothing more than a final glance out the back window.

There was Zeke, hands cuffed behind his back as he was guided into a cop car.

The Nineteenth Entry

CLAIRE

18 YEARS AGO

FEBRUARY 22

"Stay with us, Celeste!" The paramedics instructed as her eyes weakly opened and closed, over and over.

"We're almost at the hospital. We're almost there!" I clung to her hand, praying with each breath that she'd hold on and continue to fight.

I couldn't shake her voice out of my mind.

"Iyla."

"What do you mean, Iyla?"

Zeke had looked over at me momentarily as if I had known what she was talking about. When I'd stayed silent, he continued to prompt her instead.

"What are you trying to tell me?"

What was she trying to tell him? Tell *us*? And why did that name sound so familiar to me?

"Don't you think I'll look amazing when I'm pregnant?" I stretched my gut out as far as possible in the mirror.

"Are you kidding me right now?" Celeste rolled her eyes. *"You just turned eighteen!"*

"Yeah, so?" I argued. *"A girl can dream, right?"*

"*Why don't you focus on studying?*" Celeste shook her head in disapproval.

"*What do you think of the name Ambert?*" I asked, completely disregarding her mom-like response.

"*Ambert?*" she furrowed her brows. "*I've never heard of it.*"

"*It's interesting, isn't it? I like it. It's unique, fun, different.*"

"*All words that describe you,*" she joked. "*But yeah, I like it. I bet he'll be a real lover-boy with a mama like you.*"

"*Oh, hush.*" I started laughing, planting myself beside her. "*Don't act like you've never thought about baby names for your future kids.*"

"*I haven't,*" she protested. "*Unlike you, I have other priorities at the minute.*" She pointed toward her textbook.

"*I feel like you'd like names like Jamie, Jennie, Julia, oh, maybe Justine?*" I continued to egg her on.

"*Why do they all start with a 'J'?*" she cocked an eyebrow. "*And for the record, I don't like any of those names.*"

"*So, you do like a name?*" I pestered with a grin. "*Is it Erin? Ruby? Christina? Stacy? Jill—*"

"*Oh my gosh, if I tell you one name, will you leave me alone?*"

"*Yes!*" I sat up straight, extending my pinky finger. "*I promise.*"

"*Fine.*" She sighed, closing her textbook and interlocking her pinky finger with mine. "*It's Iyla. It's always been Iyla.*"

All of a sudden, everything started to make sense.

Her sudden desire to go to Long Beach.

Her unwillingness to drink.

Her words to Zeke.

Her hand gestures towards her stomach.

And most importantly, the name.

Your name.

Iyla.

"Pregnant," I mustered out to the paramedics. "She's pregnant."

As I announced it, I felt her hand, still clasped in mine, twitch.

"Celeste?" I had to push aside my emotions as I brushed my hand through her hair to calm her. "It's okay. We know now. You and the baby...you're both going to be okay. Okay?"

A tear fell down her cheek as we approached the hospital. "Make...make sure," she weakly spoke, wincing with each word. "Make sure...that she's okay...take care of her." Her body began to shake with sobs once again, my heart clenching at the sight. "Promise me, Claire." Her pinky finger stirred shakily in my hand. "*Promise me.*"

"I won't have to, Celeste." I tried to fight the tears, the fear, and the sense of doom and mortality that flooded our conversation. "You're going to be okay. You're going to make it through this. You're going to live. We're going to drive back to campus, listening to our music and singing and laughing. It's going to be okay."

Despite her shaking frame, she almost seemed at peace as she interlocked our pinkies as one. "Take care of her." Her voice fell into a whisper with each syllable.

"Alright, watch out!" The paramedics instructed, opening up the back doors and carefully unloading the stretcher as they wheeled her down the corridor.

"Take her straight into operating room three. They're waiting for her there," they instructed a few nurses.

"Celeste!" I continued to run alongside them, the gap between us widening more and more by the second. "I will always take care of her!" I shouted as she rushed through the doors of the ICU. "I promise, Celeste. I promise."

"Ma'am." A nurse placed a hand on my shoulder. "You need to stay here, okay?"

"No," I argued. Trying to force my way through the doors as Celeste fell out of sight. "I need to be with her. I need to make sure she's okay."

The nurse kept me still in place until I collapsed into her arms and began to sob uncontrollably.

"C'mon..." The nurse guided me into the waiting room. "You'll be alright, c'mon."

Seconds turned into minutes. Minutes turned into hours. And hours felt like days as I waited for any updates. But it wasn't until four hours passed that I finally heard my name called out.

"Miss O'Donnell? Claire O'Donnell?"

I stood up in a rush. "That's me," I responded. "That's me. Is everything okay? Is Celeste, okay?"

"Miss O'Donnell." The nurse slowed me down. "I can see that you're indicated as an emergency contact on Miss Kinney's file."

"Yes." I nodded my head. "That's true."

A few years prior, Celeste had had her tonsils removed and needed to provide a name should anything have gone wrong. My guess was that she'd never removed me.

"Is everything okay?" The words felt tangled in my mouth, like they didn't belong there. "What's going on?"

"Follow me, Miss O'Donnell. The doctor is waiting for you."

Her lack of a response made my heart sink into my stomach, but I attempted to gulp down the lump forming in my·throat as she guided me through the stark white hallways and into a private room.

"Miss O'Donnell," a doctor greeted me somberly.

"It's Claire," I told him as I sat down. "It's just Claire. Can you tell me if Celeste is okay? When can I see her?"

"Claire..." His voice dropped an octave as he leaned forward in his chair, placing his arms on his knees. "I'm afraid I have some bad news."

That was it.

"No, no!" I immediately began to sob, shaking my head frantically. "She's okay!" I insisted through my tears. "Tell me she's okay!"

"Claire..." He sat up, a pained expression on his face as I got up and started to pace the room. I couldn't sit still. "She lost a lot of blood. By the time she got to the operating table, she was already undergoing hemorrhagic shock."

I froze in place, my only movement being my erratic breathing. I felt like I couldn't breathe, yet simultaneously, I wanted to scream and sob at the top of my lungs. I felt trapped. Physically trapped. What would life be without Celeste? Where would I go without her by my side? Nothing in the world made sense anymore as I listened to the doctor explained it was too late. That she was gone.

"This can't be possible." I continued shaking my head, sobbing loudly between my words. "She's a fighter. She's always been a fighter!"

"And she *was*." The doctor placed a hand on my shoulder, his use of the past tense breaking my heart more than he already had. "She fought until the very last second so that we could safely deliver the baby."

My hands went numb, partly from the crying and partly from the shock of his words. "The baby?" My voice was hoarse, barely audible. "*Iyla*. She's okay? Iyla's okay?"

"She will be," he confirmed. "Thanks to you."

"Thanks to me?"

He guided me to sit down once again, my entire body shaking so hard that there was no way I would've been able to stay standing. "Without you informing the paramedics that Celeste was pregnant, we wouldn't have been able to prepare for the emergency delivery."

"Emergency delivery? How far along was she?" I asked, forcing my shaking hands to rest in my lap as I hiccupped through my tears. "Celeste doesn't...*didn't* even look pregnant."

"Well, she certainly was."

I couldn't fathom that she was truly gone. That we'd never speak to one another again. Now, every moment with her would be a memory of her legacy—who she *was* and not who she is.

I felt sick to my stomach.

"Just about twenty-six weeks. The date of conception must've been sometime in March."

Twenty-six weeks.

March.

Spring break.

I fell even more into shock.

"But you said she will be okay? Iyla...the baby...she's okay?"

"She's in the NICU right now," the doctor explained. "We're doing everything we possibly can to ensure she'll be alright."

"Can I...can I see her?" I asked shakily. I fell victim to the combination of grief as the result of death, followed by hope as the result of life.

"Follow me." The doctor stood up, guiding me down the hallway and into a small room. "Before you go in, you'll need to thoroughly wash your hands and put these on." He handed me a mask and a gown.

I did as he instructed, patiently waiting to be let in by the door. "Ready?" he asked.

I nodded.

"She's just over here." The doctor led the way to an incubator at the side of the room.

And there you were.

The smallest thing I'd ever seen in my life, entangled in wires and a breathing tube. Ten perfect fingers. Ten perfect toes. And the sweetest little face, eyes closed. Just the sight of you made me break into an aching smile. I knew Celeste would have adored you.

"She's going to be here with us for quite a while," the doctor explained. "Until she's strong enough to be discharged."

As he continued, my hands hovered over the incubator that separated you from my touch.

"Do you know where the baby's father is?" he asked. "Would we be able to get in contact with him?"

I remembered my last visual of Zeke getting into a police car as we drove away.

I gulped.

"I know who the baby's father is," I confessed. "I can contact him."

He nodded as my eyes diverted back down to your frail, tiny body.

"Claire, unfortunately, we're not allowed overnight visitors here. But, if you'd like, you are welcome to come back tomorrow, okay?"

I faintly nodded, taking one final tearful glance at you before leaving the room. I didn't spend much longer in the hospital at all. I headed straight outside, desperate for some fresh air.

As I stepped outside into the cold breeze, I pulled my phone out of my bag, noticing that I had eight missed calls from Korey.

I hit re-dial and moved the phone up to my ear, taking short breaths as I tried to bring a stop or even a pause to my tears.

"Claire?" He answered after the first ring. "Why haven't you been answering? I've been calling non-stop. I got a call from the police station about Zeke. Is everything okay? Is Celeste okay?"

The mention of her name was enough to cause me to burst into tears, my legs giving way as I fell onto the pavement in front of the hospital and buried my face in my hands.

"Claire," he spoke, his voice full of panic. "Tell me she's okay!"

"She's gone, Korey," I choked out. "She's gone," I repeated, still trying to come to that realization myself.

"Claire..." The line went quiet. "Claire, I'm so...I...I don't even know what to say right now."

"Where's Zeke?" I sniffed and tried to calm my breathing, hoping to redirect my focus to the fact that you lay in that hospital, waiting for him. "He needs to come down here now. Celeste was pregnant, Korey. She was pregnant, and...and they were able to save the baby."

"Wait..." Korey hesitated. "Celeste was pregnant?"

282

"Yes," I responded, not waiting for any follow-up questions. "Zeke needs to come down here now and—"

"He can't, Claire," Korey cut me off.

"What do you mean 'he can't'?"

"He's at the station," he explained. "He's been taken into custody."

"What?! Why is he being taken into custody?" I stood up, my head dizzying at the sudden movement. "Zeke didn't do anything wrong. It was Chaz!"

"I know." Korey let out a breath. "They found Chaz shortly after and arrested him. But it turned out that the police department was already aware of what had been happening at Club Affinity, and they saw now as their perfect opportunity to act."

"No..." I squatted down, hovering over the ground, willing the shaking in my body to subside.

"Stay where you are, okay? I'm coming down to get you."

I ended the call, falling back onto the concrete with my head in my hands as I tried to remotely process everything that had just happened. The loss of your mother, my best friend, my family, my everything.

"Promise me, Claire." It was as if I could still hear her voice. *"Take care of her."*

I choked back some tears, sniffing as I looked up to the sky. "I promise Celeste," I whispered, a feeling of desire overwhelming my tired body. From that day onwards, that same feeling would remind me that I'd devote the rest of my life to you...and never break that promise.

The Final Entry

CLAIRE

18 YEARS AGO

FEBRUARY 28

"Why can't I see him?" I demanded. "I need to talk to him, please!"

"Ma'am, I'm sorry, but you need to calm down," the officer instructed me calmly, just like he had been doing all week long. "Mr. Reeves is still not allowed any visitors at this time."

I released an angry huff, marching away from the desk and towards the exit. "You know what? No, this is bullshit!" I spun on my heel and stormed right back over to the front, pushing whoever was necessary out of my way. "I'm sorry, but it's been days. *Days*! I need to speak to him. This isn't right. I told you and your buddies everything that happened that night, absolutely fucking everything, and you can't even let me have five minutes?!"

The officer released a breath, shocked by my sudden outburst, as he pulled back from the desk and whispered something into the walkie-talkie on his chest.

Zeke had been arrested on account of drug trafficking. We hoped that as a first-time offender, the sentence would come with a maximum sentence of ten years.

I couldn't help but hiss at that timeline. Given that, I knew it meant that his presence throughout your youth would be virtually non-existent—if he was charged, that was.

"Miss O'Donnell." The police officer re-emerged at the desk. "You can go in."

"I can?" I said in disbelief, wondering what caused his change of heart. "Really?"

"Follow the officer to your right." He dismissed me. "You'll be able to see Mr. Reeves shortly."

I nodded. I couldn't believe they were actually letting me through. I'd been kicking up a fuss for days with no leniency. Maybe they'd just had enough of me by now.

I waited in the visitor's booth for over an hour before Zeke came into view, his hands shackled together until the guard took off the handcuffs and gestured to where I was sitting.

"Zeke?" I reached for the phone on the wall. The only way he'd be able to hear me through the thick glass that separated the two of us.

"Claire," he spoke desperately as soon as the phone was held to his ear. "They haven't told me anything. Where's Celeste? Is she okay?"

My heart sank to my feet.

"Zeke..." I tried to speak but closed my mouth immediately. I could already feel the tears forming in my eyes, and if I spoke, I wouldn't be able to stop them.

"Where is she?" he exclaimed, his face growing anguished as my eyes broke contact with his, and I blinked rapidly. "God dammit, Claire!" He was near hysterics. "Tell me she's okay! She's okay, right?"

"I'm so sorry..." I whispered into the phone, completely paralyzed as the memories of that night replayed in my mind.

The screams, the blood, her final words to me. They'd consumed all of my thoughts, day in, day out, and there I was, having to re-live and re-tell it all over again. This time, to the one person I knew it would break the most.

"No..." The realization washed over Zeke's face as he leaned back slightly. "You're fucking lying to me."

"I'm not, Zeke," I responded quietly, my own voice shaking with each word. "She didn't make it."

"No...no...no!" He slammed down the phone repeatedly. I could feel the glass shaking between the two of us.

"Hey!" The guards rushed over. "You need to calm down right now!" They ordered, walking over to him. "You hear me? Calm down, or this conversation is done!"

I noticed Zeke's broad shoulders shaking as he put his head down momentarily, clearly trying to gather himself but feeling just as sick with sadness as I was. I sat in silence, allowing him to let it out before he weakly reached towards the phone and lifted it back up to his ear.

"I'm so sorry," I spoke once again. "They tried, Zeke. They really did. But she was too weak, and it was too late." I brushed away another tear as it rolled down my cheek.

Zeke shook his head—visibly shutting down. His eyes were distant, cold. "She's gone," he repeated. "She's gone. Everything's gone."

I placed my hand on the glass, wishful that I could soothe him somehow. "Not everything is gone, Zeke, okay? Not everything."

He barely looked up. "What are you talking about, Claire? I have nothing without her. There's no point in life if she's not in it!"

He was sick with sadness. I could tell because I'd looked the exact same way since that night at the hospital. My heart broke for him.

I allowed for a moment of silence, debating how to tell him the next thing. He was hurting, and he was going to be hurting for a long time—but if there was one thing that would ease that pain in the slightest, it was you. "But what if your daughter was?"

He snapped his head up at me in disbelief, dried tears staining his cheeks. "What did you just say?"

"You have a daughter, Zeke," I revealed to him, my voice gentle.

"A baby girl."

He just stared at me for a long, hard moment before taking in a breath. "A daughter? A baby? What...what are you even saying, Claire? You're making no sense."

"I know it's hard to believe, Zeke. I still can't believe it myself. Celeste was over twenty-six weeks pregnant. That's what she was trying to tell you...what she was trying to tell us."

The news was all-consuming. It was as if, in one single moment, right in front of my eyes, Zeke had gone from wanting to die to wanting nothing more than to live.

"Pregnant?" he said yet again. "Did you...did you know?"

"No." I shook my head. "I had no idea. She kept it a secret, but that's why she came down to Long Beach. She wanted to tell you, Zeke. She was trying to tell you."

"Oh, my God." He ran his hand along his face, beads of sweat forming on his forehead. "And the baby...she's alright?"

Finally, some good news.

"She's one of the youngest preemies the doctors have seen at their hospital," I told him with a faint smile as the image of you popped into my head. "She's hooked up to so many wires and machines, lying in this little incubator. But she's strong. So strong, Zeke. And already she's making so much progress."

"You've seen her?" His eyes widened, the tears reappearing. "You've met her?"

I nodded, reaching for my bag and pulling out a photo that I'd taken of you on my camera. "Look." I held the picture up against the glass, Zeke immediately leaning forward so that he could see. "There she is."

He dragged his hand along the glass, pausing for a moment. "Our daughter," he whispered. "*Iyla*."

The pure emotion, the *love* in his eyes, was enough to re-trigger that familiar lump in my throat. "That's what you want to name her, right?" I asked quietly.

He didn't peel his eyes away from the photo. "That's what Celeste wanted." His voice trailed off. "What we'd talked about. God, it's all making sense. I just can't believe it."

"Neither can I." I looked at him. "But she's here now, and it's all the more reason for you to fight these charges against you. This is your daughter. You're a father now, Zeke, and you owe it to her to be that."

"Claire," he stuttered, fear entering his eyes briefly as he looked at me. "What's going to happen if I don't get out of here? Who's going to take care of her? Where will she go?"

"We'll figure that out," I tried to reassure him, even though I didn't have a single answer to any of his questions. "I'm certain your charges will be dropped, and I'm certain that by Christmas, you'll be home."

He nodded his head at my naïve comment. For when December came, things were nowhere near what we'd hoped.

✩ ✬ ✩

"He pleaded guilty?!" I shouted in disbelief. "What do you mean?"

"He didn't have a choice, Claire. His lawyer said it was the only way to possibly receive a reduced sentence."

"Of five years without the possibility of parole?" I placed my head into my hand. "Do you realize what this means, Korey?"

"Of course, I know what this means," he argued back, just as exasperated by this situation as I was. "But this is the reality, Claire. Five years is better than ten, and when he's out, then he can be involved in Iyla's life."

I shook my head. "It'll be too late."

"It won't be!" He placed his hands on my arm. "Did you talk to the social worker? Did you tell them that we want to take custody of her?"

Of course I did!" I shook him off, standing up and pacing across the room. "But do you really think they're going to let us? I'm twenty-three, I have no job security, we're barely making enough for rent, and I'm eight weeks pregnant!" My voice rose hysterically as the panic and realization started to set in.

"Claire..." He pulled me into his warm embrace. Korey always had a way of being the calm in the storm. "Relax, okay? You need to breathe. It's not good for the baby to get upset like this."

I did as he instructed, but I knew the reality. I knew the social worker had already begun talks with a family in Columbus, Ohio, who had been waiting for a chance to adopt for years. Now was their opportunity, and I knew they wouldn't let it go.

To no one's surprise, within a day of Zeke's trial, the adoptive family had flown across the country to be by your side. Amanda and Lance Larson.

They fell in love with you the minute they saw you. It was one of the most bittersweet moments of my life. I was happy knowing you'd be loved, adored and, most importantly, taken care of, fulfilling your mother's wish. But on the other hand, I was deeply saddened, as with each passing day, I knew we were approaching our last.

I waited until only a week before you left for Ohio before breaking the news to Zeke. I hated that I had waited so long, but I also hated that I had to be the one to tell him the truth.

The defeat and heartbreak that washed over his face was unlike anything I'd ever seen. We'd already decided that if I took custody of you, I could bring you to see him weekly. That way, you'd get a chance to know your dad, even if it was through a glass.

"Will they at least give us updates?" Zeke asked in concern. "Maybe allow you and Korey to see her?"

I nodded my head. At the time, Amanda and Lance seemed okay with the idea of an open adoption. That way, we'd still be able to communicate and potentially visit you from time to time—something we all found comfort in.

But in the days that led up to your departure, things changed. Boy, did they drastically change.

In conversations with the social worker, Amanda and Lance became aware of the circumstances surrounding your mother's death, the charges against Zeke, and my continued involvement with him.

And so, after they officially took legal guardianship over you, they cut ties with me altogether. No details, no visits, no interactions, nothing.

I waited every day in the lobby with the hope that they'd let me inside, that they'd change their mind. But it wasn't until the night before your discharge that they had one final change of heart.

"Claire?" I lifted my head in surprise as Amanda and Lance stood before me in the same spot I'd haunted for days. "We want to give you a chance to say goodbye."

"Really?" my eyes widened in disbelief. They nodded. "A *final* goodbye, though," they clarified, causing my growing smile to disappear. "After today, we want things to be different. We want *Iyla* to have a fresh start."

"Iyla?" I said doubtfully, hearing them confirm your name for the first time.

"The social worker told us that you've been calling her that all this time. Plus, it was the name Celeste had chosen for her." Lance looked down at Amanda. "Nothing fits her better."

I brushed away a tear that had rolled down my cheek as I looked over at the clock to see that I only had ten minutes left before the visiting hours came to a close.

"Thank you." I smiled up at them gratefully. "You don't know how much this means to me."

I raced towards your room, seeing your body swaddled in a soft blanket and hat. Over the past few weeks, you'd really come into your appearance.

You looked just like your mom but had bright green eyes identical to your father, something that I once loved taking pictures of to show him—proving that you were just as much his as Celeste's.

I cried, holding you in my arms as I looked down at your little face, wondering when I'd get another chance to see you again. But I knew this moment couldn't just be about that, so I whispered my promise to you.

"One day, Iyla, I will tell you everything. But right now, you need to live the most amazing life possible." The tears continued to flow. "That's all we want for you. Your mom. Your dad. " I kissed your cheek softly and placed you back in the hospital crib. "I promise," I whispered one final time, taking a moment to just watch you. You were so small and peaceful, and I wished I could keep you by my side forever. It took everything in me to walk out of that room, past Amanda and Lance and towards my car. I felt like I was leaving a piece of myself behind with me.

In the following months, I continued to see Zeke as often as I could, updating him on life beyond his four walls. All he really wanted to know was about you, something that I no longer had the privilege of sharing with him. Instead, our conversations were filled with empty words or reflections of the past. It was the only way the two of us could cope.

Zeke will always be a part of my life. We've been through too much together for him not to be. When he gets out of prison, I'll do everything in my power to ensure he's taken care of, supported, and has a place to stay.

But his sentence has only just begun, which means that all that's left to do is wait.

It's now February of the following year. I've decided to break the one-year lease on the apartment that your mother and I shared, forfeiting any losses and moving in with Korey as we prepare for our baby to arrive in the late summer.

A baby boy.

Breaking the lease was the only logical choice, considering I hadn't spent a single night in the apartment since your mother passed away.

When the time came to clean everything out, I avoided your mother's room until the last possible second. When I eventually got around to it, I discovered something I hadn't been expecting.

This journal.

I flipped through it, skimming the words that lay inside and seeing the story unfold page by page, only to see that it was unfinished.

For days after my discovery, I contemplated what to do. Should I make copies? Give one to Zeke, keeping one for myself? Track down Amanda and Lance and give it to them?

But those thoughts quickly passed. Deep down, I knew that only one person in this world deserved the journal—*you*.

So, here we are, Iyla. I've filled in the rest of the story for you. A story that I hope, one of these days, you can continue yourself. A story filled with pain, hope, heartache, and, most importantly, *love*.

A love that I desire for you. A love that you deserve.

So, I guess now, I'll wait. Wait for the day the universe gives me a sign, and I can fulfill my promise.

We'll always love you.

Claire.

CHAPTER EIGHTEEN

I Y L A

PRESENT DAY

I'd wondered for so long why I couldn't write the next chapter, only to learn that it was because I hadn't read the book.

But now I had, and I was heartbroken.

Everything about what had happened hurt me.

The tragedy that surrounded my mother's death.

The real reason why Zeke wasn't around.

The realities of my parent's choices.

How could I read my mother's words, and learn about her aspirations, dreams, and hopes, only for it to all come crashing down and move on?

I'd felt so compelled to know my birth mom my whole life, but deep down, a part of me always did. It was as if she'd guided me the entire time and led me down a path she didn't get a chance to finish. She allowed me to right her wrongs and give everyone, Zeke included, an opportunity for closure as my life began.

For hours, I'd been lying in bed, clinging to the journal tighter than anything I'd ever held. It was a part of me now, a crucial limb that could never be detached.

I flipped back through the words, reading them repeatedly, almost hopeful that the outcome would change in the end. But it couldn't, and it wouldn't. That was the reality.

This was the life I was desperate to know about, and these were the consequences that followed.

The band-aid had been ripped off, and now all I was left with was the stinging sensation that I didn't think would ever pass.

I brushed my hand along my tear-stained cheeks as I sat up from my bed, my foot making contact with the box I'd left on the floor and causing a series of items to fall out. Without wasting a second, I fell to the floor and began sorting through them. Before I'd read the journal, the box seemed as though it was filled with miscellaneous items that held no meaning. But now, as I looked down at those not-so-simple items in front of me, I knew they meant so much more than I could've imagined.

The first item I lifted was the same series of pictures placed on Claire's fireplace mantle.

The one that was taken by the pier at Long Beach. The one by the motorcycle outside of Tim and Sally's. And not one, but two photobooth strips. The first was a replica of what I'd seen at Claire's, and the other was a version of my mom and Zeke, taped up after it had been visibly ripped apart.

She kept it. My heart skipped a beat. But if Claire had saved the picture, then that meant...

"The jacket," I mumbled as I dug through the box and pulled out a smooth leather jacket with a skull and the initials "E.R." embellished on it, just as my mother had described.

Seeing my dad's jacket filled me with a mixture of emotions. I was happy that Claire had kept it, knowing that my mother never really wanted it gone. But at the same time, what the jacket represented made me angry. I was so mad that I wanted to throw it away, just like my mom had, but I knew I couldn't do that.

I knew that at that moment, I needed to make things right. So, I stood up from the floor, reached for my phone and called Hallie.

"Hey." She picked up after a few rings, likely anticipating my call. "Did everything go okay with your parents? What happened?"

"Mind if I borrow your car?" I ignored her questions, her keys already in my hand.

"Of course," she responded. "But where are you going?"

I released a shaky sigh. "To see my dad."

✫ ✫ ✫

Korey's auto shop had proved much more challenging than I'd anticipated finding, especially when you type in "auto repair" online, and 15 different locations appear. Yet, as I pulled into the third shop that evening and saw a motorcycle parked out front, I knew I was in the right place.

I took a deep breath inside the car before mustering up enough courage to get out and walk toward the entrance. I pushed open the front door as the chimes echoed throughout the empty storefront, the clock reading just after five o'clock.

There were a few workstations, most of them vacant except for one with a light still on. I carefully stepped in, noticing a bulletin board filled with family photos on the wall.

There was one of Korey and Claire.

A younger photo of Ambert holding his little sister.

A few miscellaneous images from what appeared to be other co-workers, and then a photobooth strip.

Zeke and my mom.

My mom had said in her entries that Zeke had put his own copy in his wallet. My heart softened seeing the picture, knowing that Zeke had kept it all this time.

But the image that struck me the most was one I recognized. One that I'd seen all my life. A picture of me, a few weeks shy of my hospital discharge, with my eyes wide open. It was a photo my parents had put into one of my childhood albums and one that I'd always assumed they had taken, but I was wrong. It was Claire. Claire must've taken this photo.

"We're closed," a voice shouted from inside, causing my heart to skip a beat as I pulled away from the board and continued to make my way in.

"I said we're closed—" Zeke froze in place as he looked up and saw me. A moment of complete silence passed between us as he met me with an intent gaze. It was a look I'd grown familiar with...a look I finally understood.

In her entries, my mom said she wasn't paralyzed with fear the first time she locked eyes with Zeke the way she'd expected to be. Instead, she was intrigued. Yet, there I was, standing in front of the person I'd just come to realize as my dad and my body was scared, still and uncertain.

What do you say to someone you feel so close to yet so distant from? I knew nothing about the man that stood in front of me. Hell, nothing that wasn't a reflection of someone else's perception of him. Who was he? And more importantly, who was he going to be for me?

"Ambert's not here." He looked away awkwardly, breaking eye contact.

I released a breath. "I'm not looking for Ambert," I shakily spoke. "I was looking for you."

He peered back up at me, his narrow eyes honed in on mine as he clearly attempted to process this interaction. The last time we'd seen each other, I'd told him I never wanted to see him again. Now, 48 hours later, I was standing in front of him.

"I guess I should properly introduce myself, considering I didn't get a chance to the other day." I tried to laugh, but it came out as more of a cough, causing me to awkwardly fidget in place. "I'm Iyla...your daughter."

He looked at me, and with the way he stared, I knew that he knew. He'd always known.

These were the eyes that my mom had fallen in love with. I swallowed deeply to hold back the tears that formed in my eyes, the two of us standing in complete silence.

"I want to hear you talk," I repeated the exact words that my mom had once said to him.

He took small steps towards me, inch by inch, making his way over before he stopped, assessing my frame, mentally taking in that I was real. We stood there for a few moments before he pulled me into his warm embrace, wrapping his arms around me tightly— almost as if he was afraid of letting go. "Iyla," he whispered into my hair, repeating my name as if he was still trying to accept that I was there, talking to him and now hugging him back. "I want to talk, but fuck." He ran his hand through my hair. "What do I even say?"

"Anything," I whispered. "Just say anything."

Tears flooded his eyes as he gently placed his hands on either side of my face. "You're everything I thought you would be." He brushed away the tears that now fell down my cheeks. "Don't cry, Iyla." He grabbed a tissue for me. "Please don't cry."

I took the tissue from his hands to dab my eyes, trying to calm my nerves before I reached for my bag. "I have something for you," I said quietly, grabbing his leather jacket and placing it in his hands.

His eyes widened as he looked down at the worn leather material, running his fingertips over it. "How did you get this?"

I toyed with the hair tie on my wrist. "I suppose I have a story to tell you. Do you think we could go somewhere to talk?"

Without wasting a minute, he closed the hood of one of the cars he'd been working on, nodding as he anxiously encouraged me to follow him to the parking lot.

"Do you need my help?" I asked hesitantly as he tried to lock up the storefront, his hands shaking so badly that he could barely get the key in.

"I got it." He finally managed to get it inside, twist it shut and double-check for security. "I...uh." He seemed just as uneasy as I felt. "Where do you want to go to talk?"

"Long Beach," I responded without a second thought. "I want you to take me there."

"Long Beach?" he seemed taken back. "No, Iyla, that's not a good idea—"

"Please." I looked up at him, clenching my bag on my hip. "It's the only place I want to go."

He sighed, meeting his green eyes with mine. "Okay," he caved, walking over to his motorcycle. "Hop on."

"Wait..." my voice trailed off as I watched him step onto his bike. "Is this the same bike that you took my mom on?"

He seemed to question how I knew so much but carried on anyway. "No," he responded. "I try not to ride that anymore. It brings back too many memories, so I only ride it one day a year."

"What day is that?" I wondered.

He looked away solemnly. "The best and worst day of my life," he answered. "August 31."

A family friend and my dad's co-worker decided that it would be a smart idea to go out on his old motorcycle. The thing is over twenty years old. Needless to say, it didn't end well, and my dad insisted that I go in to learn how to fix it.

That's why Ambert had to leave on my birthday.

He was helping Zeke fix the bike.

My birthday is the best yet worst day of his life.

The birth of me and the death of my mother.

"You know what? Never mind." He stepped off the bike, shaking his head. "Listen, I'll just borrow one of the other cars. We can talk on the way there."

"I'll go on your bike," I responded confidently before I could sike myself out of it. "I will."

"Really?" he asked.

I nodded. "But on one condition."

"Anything." A faint smile appeared on his lips as he looked at me, his eyes thoughtful.

To You, Jyla

"Only if you have a spare helmet."

CHAPTER NINETEEN

IYLA

PRESENT DAY

My mom was right. There's nothing quite like sitting on the back of a motorcycle, feeling the air cascade over your body and sensing the thrill of the world around you.

Zeke and I pulled off the freeway after about 45 minutes of riding. We parked alongside the road." Are you okay?" he helped me to remove my helmet, slightly alarmed by my pale expression.

"Just a bit of motion sickness," I explained. "I'll be okay, though, don't worry. That was insane...absolutely insane."

He smiled, reaching under his seat and pulling out a blanket. I held in a giggle, thinking of the irony that he still had a blanket in there after all this time.

"Where exactly are we?" I questioned as he urged me to follow him as we walked in stride alongside the beach.

"Somewhere I want to tell you about...or maybe you already know about it." He stopped under a spot that seemed familiar to him, laid out a blanket and encouraged me to sit down.

I sat cross-legged next to him, looking out at the water that expanded ahead of us before turning my head to him. I wasn't too surprised when I noticed he'd already had his eyes on me. "You have no idea how long I've waited to meet you, Iyla."

"That makes two of us." I felt entirely overwhelmed by the fact that the man in front of me was my dad. My real dad.

"How did you find us? And a better question, how did you know it was me?"

I let out a breath. "I only came to Los Angeles, desperate to retrace Mom's footsteps. I wanted to know everything about the past. Everything that I felt had been hidden from me all this time. I never really knew exactly what I was looking for at all. But then, all of a sudden, things started to fall into place. I was finding details that individually made no sense at all, but put together, they unraveled the truth."

"The truth?" he repeated back to me.

I nodded, explaining to him everything that had happened since the day I arrived. From first meeting Ambert, then Dr. Sanders, seeing the pictures at Claire's, my parents withholding the letter, and finally reading the journal—the most crucial component of all.

"This is how I know so much." I pulled the journal out of my bag and placed it into his hands. "I want you to read it. I want you to read what she wrote about you."

He hovered his hand over my mother's name, his eyes glazing over as he seemingly froze at the sight of it. It took him a moment to finally open it up and flip to the first page. "Iyla, I...I can't." He handed it back over to me. "I'm sorry."

"What?" I voiced. "Why not?"

He ran his hand behind his neck. "It's not for me to read, Iyla. The journal was meant for you."

"But don't you want to know what she said? How she felt about you?" I questioned. I could hardly believe he was turning this opportunity down.

"I don't need the journal to know how she felt about me. I already know." He placed a hand over his heart sincerely. "I've always known because I feel it every day. I'll always feel it."

I nodded, peering back down at the journal before placing it off to the side. Zeke continued to look at me as if he never wanted to look away.

"Did you always know it was me?" I wondered, changing the subject as I referred to the day he saw Ambert and me kissing in the car.

He nodded his head. "Without a doubt."

"Then why didn't you say anything?" I questioned.

"Like?"

"Like hey, you look just like..." I trailed off. "I think you might be..."

He let out a faint laugh. "Not that easy, huh?"

I chuckled softly and shook my head. "But how did you know it was me?"

"Well..." He placed a hand back on the journal. "If these entries have anything to do with the time your mother and I spent together, then I imagine she would've written a thing or two about fate." He reached to graze my cheek. "I always knew that you'd find your way back to us one day. And look, after all this time...you did."

"It's been nineteen years, though. Didn't you want to try and find me first?"

"Of course I did," he responded without hesitation. "The day I got released from prison, I was desperate to find you, but the task proved harder than it sounds. Claire and I searched for years, but all I could think about was what was best for you. Was some newly released guy from prison really the right fit for you in your life?"

"But you weren't just some 'guy,'" I argued. "You're my dad."

He shook his head in disagreement. "I lost that privilege the second I made the choices that I did." The defeat was evident in his voice, and it broke my heart. "There were people out there willing to take on a role that I couldn't. How could I come in the way of that?"

I looked away, hurt but doing my best to understand his perspective. "What about when I turned eighteen? Even then?" I asked, picking at a loose thread in the blanket.

"A part of me worried that maybe it was too late," he confessed.

"It was never going to be too late." I shook my head. "I want more than anything to have a relationship with you. I've always wanted that."

"Iyla..." He sighed, pulling me in for a hug. "You don't know how much I want that. Fuck, you don't know how much I've wanted that all these years. All I did was exist for you, for the slim chance that you'd come back to us."

The tears reformed in my eyes as I felt, for the first time, the love that Zeke had always had for me, whether I knew it or not.

"You know why I brought you to this spot specifically?" He wiped away my tears once more.

I shook my head.

"This is where your mother and I were the night before she left me. This is where we spoke about fate, the stars and most importantly, *you*."

I looked up at the sky, remembering the conversation from the entries. Who would've thought that nearly two decades later, I'd be here with him.

I sniffled back some tears and rested my head on his shoulder. "I wish she was here," I admitted. "I wish I could've met her."

"She's always here." He looked up, the stars shining bright above us. "Believe that, Iyla. Always."

We sat silently, staring up at the sky until I lifted my head off his shoulder in thought. "So, the other day at Claire and Korey's. You had a feeling it was me, yet, decided to come anyway?"

"Of course," he responded without a doubt. "Why wouldn't I have?"

"But you didn't think to tell Claire and Korey about seeing me with Ambert?"

"Nope," he simply responded.

"But why not?" I was confused at his response.

"Iyla, I couldn't even wrap my own mind around it. I thought I was delusional or hallucinating. When the opportunity came to see you again, I couldn't turn it down. I needed to confirm it was you."

I swallowed, nervously asking another question that popped into my mind. "What did you think when you first saw me?"

A smile played on his lips. "Do you really want to know?"

"Of course." I nodded. "Tell me."

He briefly fumbled in his back pocket before pulling out a folded paper. "I hadn't written anything in years... I think after everything transpired, nothing inspired me to. After I saw you, it all came to me. I felt compelled."

"You wrote something for me?" I was awestruck as he unfolded the paper and smoothed it out.

He reluctantly nodded, handing it over. "Here. You can read it."

"Can you read it to me?" I encouraged him. "Please?"

He let out a breath and gave me a knowing look, making me smile back at him before he diverted his gaze to the page and started to read.

"There she was, in front of his eyes, yet he didn't know a single thing about her. Who was the girl that stood in front of him? Was she kind? Was she sweet? With gentle eyes and curiosity that lay beneath? He didn't know, for as much as he wanted to believe she was his, all she reminded him of was what he'd lost and who he'd been.

How could someone be yours if they don't even know you exist?

And so, he lived his life, paying the price, though he could never be fulfilled by any sort of money, for she was invaluable.

He knew that he'd awoken long ago from his slumber but never knew the reason. Yet, as he watched her drive away, he finally understood the pain. For all along, *she* was the reason for the dream."

The sound of the waves crashing along the beach was the only thing that followed his words—I didn't know what to say. I didn't know how to feel. "You...you wrote that for me?" I asked once more in disbelief.

He toyed with the edge of the paper, which I assumed was a nervous tell of his. "I guess your mom wasn't the only one who vented through words." He delicately placed it in my hands. "But I imagine she was much better at writing than me."

I looked down at the handwritten note, seeing his penmanship, rereading his words, and brushing away a tear before I tucked it inside the journal. Their words belonged together, and now they forever would be.

"Thank you," I whispered. "It was beautiful."

"You don't have to say that," he protested.

"I'm not." I shook my head. "I love it with all my heart. I mean that." I brought my hands towards my chest. "I do."

"Then why are you crying, angel?"

Angel.

My breath hitched in my throat as I heard him call me by my mom's nickname for the first time.

"I..." I paused, taking a moment to try and calm my suddenly heavy heart. "I just don't know what to do. Everything feels like a mess. I haven't spoken to my parents. I haven't even told them I'm here with you."

"Wait." Zeke stopped me. "They don't know? But you said they gave you the letter and the package."

"They did," I confirmed. "But then they left and went back to their hotel. I haven't spoken to them since. You were the first person I wanted to see."

"Oh, Iyla..." He trailed off in thought, running a hand along his stubbled face.

"I want them to meet you. I want them to know that you, the Wells family, Am—" I stopped. The name of the person I kept pushing to the back of my mind nearly found a way to slip out of my mouth.

"Ambert?" Zeke finished my sentence for me.

I looked away.

"I want to hear you talk." He returned the statement from earlier back to me as he tilted my chin in his direction.

"I messed things up," I confided to him. "I told Ambert I didn't want to see him again. I told him that he was a mistake."

Sorrow filled his eyes. "Hearing those words leave your mouth completely pierced me."

It all started to sink in. "My mom," I whispered. "Oh my God... she...she said those same words to you." I held my head, groaning in regret. "I really messed up. I didn't mean it, just like she hadn't meant it. I was upset. I was overwhelmed. I was saying anything to get out of there."

"I know, angel." He soothed me, gently rubbing my back. "I know, and Ambert knows that you didn't mean it. He knows everything now."

"What?" I looked up at him, surprised by his statement. "What do you mean *everything*?"

"Claire and I finally explained it all to him after all this time. We told him to give you some space...to give you a chance to process it all."

"He never knew?"

"He never knew much," he answered.

"Not even about you and my mom?"

"He knew bits and pieces but never knew I had a daughter. That, we'd always kept to ourselves."

I closed my eyes shut as I tried to come to terms with all of the emotions buzzing through me—with the fact that I was dating the son of a family who now hit so close to home.

"What do I do?" I asked Zeke for his first piece of parental advice. "How do I make this right?"

He wrapped his arm across my shoulder. "All I know, Iyla, is that

I lost my one chance at love, and I don't want the same for you. When you find your soulmate, you hold onto them, bare your soul to them, and you fight for what's yours."

The weight of everything fell back onto my shoulders at his advice. "I love him," I admitted. "I really do."

"I know." He placed a hand on my cheek. "So, let's make a plan. Whenever you're ready, we can go and talk to your parents. After that, I'll go with you to talk to the Wells family...and Ambert, okay? We'll make everything right, my girl. I promise you."

Hearing him call me *his girl* warmed every inch of me as I leaned back against his shoulder, continuing to look up at the sky. "Are you proud of me?" I asked.

He paused. "Proud of you? How could I not be? We've only just met, and I'm already completely marveled by you. I want to spend every day for the rest of my life catching up on what I've missed. I want to know everything about you."

"I'll say whatever you want to hear."

CHAPTER TWENTY

I Y L A

PRESENT DAY

"Don't be nervous," I instructed Zeke as he meticulously adjusted his buttoned-down top. It was the next morning, and the two of us were waiting outside my parents' hotel room.

"How can I not be nervous? I'm meeting my daughter's parents." He frantically shifted in place. "Fuck...never thought I'd actually say that."

I half smiled. "They're definitely going to be shocked," I told him as I knocked on the door. "But we're doing this together."

"Iyla." My mom appeared at the doorway with a familiar smile, her eyes shifting from me to the tall frame on my left. "Lance!" she called out behind her shoulder as my dad quickly approached the door.

"Mom...Dad." I hardly gave them a second to process what was happening. "This is—"

"Ezekiel Reeves." My mom finished my sentence as the pair stood paralyzed in shock as if measuring exactly what to do.

"Can we come in?" I asked, taking a step forward.

"Of course." My mom nervously opened the door for us.

"Actually..." My dad stopped us with a hand. "How about we go get something to eat?" he proposed, looking over to my mom for approval.

"Yes, food sounds great right about now," she agreed. The two of them were tenser than I'd ever seen, completely caught off guard by Zeke's presence.

"How about Tim and Sally's?" I suggested. "I mean...it only seems fitting."

They seemed receptive to the idea, nodding their heads.

"We'll meet you there, then." I shot them a small smile as they closed the door. I could only imagine what kind of conversation they were having.

My brows furrowed as I looked up at Zeke. "Why didn't you say anything?" I questioned as we walked back over to the elevator.

"I'm sorry." He followed behind me like a sad puppy that had just been scolded. "I got nervous. I'll talk when we get there. I promise."

"You'd better." I raised my eyebrows as the elevator doors closed. "God, you're just like her."

☆ ☆ ☆

It was incredibly awkward watching Zeke dance around my parents, clearly unsure whether or not to go in for a handshake, a hug or go running for the hills as they approached the booth. Instead, he stepped back, opting for none of the above. "How about I get everyone something to eat? Something to drink? Coffee, tea sound okay?"

"I'll take a coffee. Two creams, one sugar," my dad requested.

"Tea for me, please," my mom added.

Zeke looked down at me.

"I'll have an iced coffee." I tried to keep it simple, considering I could tell that Zeke was already overwhelmed by our orders.

"Got it!" I could tell he was lying. "I'll get some food, too," he added before walking towards the counter and leaving me as the nervous one, sitting alone with my parents for the first time since learning everything they'd kept from me all these years.

"Iyla?" My mom caught my attention. "We just want to say we're happy we're doing this. It's important that we support you in your decisions, and if you want to have a relationship with Zeke and the Wells family, we want that for you, too."

My eyes flooded with relief. "You mean that?" I asked incredulously.

"Yes." My dad nodded firmly. "We were wrong for keeping you in the dark all these years. It's time to do what's right—something we thought we'd been doing all along."

"Thank you." I smiled as my shoulders relaxed. I was so grateful that my parents were on my side with this. I don't know what I would've done had they not been. "That means everything."

"We love you, Iyla. We always have, and we always will."

"I love you, too." I reached across the table to pull them both into a hug. "But while we're also being honest..." I released them from my embrace and leaned back. "I have something else to tell you both."

They looked at me in confusion. "Oh? What is it."

"Uh...well, I have a boyfriend."

"A boyfriend?" my mom seemed just as overly excited as I'd anticipated.

"Well, sorta..." I raised my hands in defense. "Things are a *little* complicated right now."

"What's his name? Where did you meet? How long have you been dating?"

Zeke walked back over to the table with an assortment of items in his hands—saving me from my mom's endless list of questions.

"I got some muffins, donuts and cookies." He awkwardly sat down beside me. "I wasn't sure what everyone liked."

"This is great, thank you." My mom reached for her drink and a chocolate chip muffin as my dad continued to look between Zeke and me in fascination.

"Well, I'll be damned." He rubbed his hand below his chin.

"What?" I asked in curiosity.

"Look at their eyes, Mands." He pointed between the two of us before glancing back at my mom, whose awestruck eyes mirrored his. "We always wondered where those green eyes came from. Guess the apple doesn't fall too far from the tree." He sipped his coffee.

"I guess not," I agreed, gently nudging Zeke before my mom jumped in.

"I suppose we have a lot to learn about you, Zeke."

Zeke released a breath. "Mr. & Mrs. Larson," he began. "I don't even know where to begin. What you've done for me, Celeste, and Iyla, how can I ever repay you for being her parents?"

"Hush." My dad waved his hand at him. "No need to go soppy on us, son. This young lady is the brightest light in our lives. Now, she'll be your light, too. And by the way, call us Amanda and Lance," he clarified with a wink.

A genuine smile came across Zeke's lips, and we sat together for hours on end, my parents reminiscing on all of my baby, child and teen years. They showed hundreds of photos of me growing up, Zeke's eyes sparkling with delight as he studied each one and asked for all the stories. The memories and happy times in my childhood that I only wished Zeke could've been a part of.

"Okay, okay. That's enough," I scolded them, pushing their phones back as they showed Zeke a photo of me going through my dorky 12-year-old phase.

"Oh, stop, you were adorable," my mom hushed me as Zeke laughed. "But you're right. That's probably enough for one day." She tucked her phone into her pocket as the laughter slowly faded.

"So, Zeke..." My dad cleared his throat. "I think I owe you an apology."

Zeke seemed just as confused and taken aback by the statement as I was. "For what?" he asked.

"All these years, I'd thought you were some sort of deadbeat," he paused awkwardly. "I was wrong. You're far from it. The man sitting in front of us today seems to have turned his life around." He smiled. "And there is no one else I would rather be another dad to my daughter than you."

"Mr. Lar...*Lance*." He corrected himself. "That means more than anything to me. I promise I'll do whatever it takes to continue to be a part of Iyla's life." He peered down at me. "If she allows it, of course."

I gave him an affirming nod and a reassuring smile which he mirrored back to me, making me feel completely loved and safe.

"So, what time are you flying out tonight?" I asked my parents as Zeke gathered the mess on the table to toss it away.

"Not till nine," my mom responded as we all stood up from the booth. "Your dad and I have got to get back to work."

"Did you want to come back to the campus with me?" I questioned, realizing I only had a few hours before they left. "Maybe I can show you around, and we can—"

"It's okay," my dad chimed in. "We will come back another time. We want you to spend some time with Zeke. Get to know him, and most importantly, go make things right with Ambert."

"Make things right with Ambert?" I was taken aback at the last part of his sentence, considering I'd never told them his name.

"When you went to the bathroom earlier," my mom leaned in to whisper. "Zeke told us about him, about everything that happened."

"Zeke told you?" my voice raised in disbelief.

"Parent talk, dear." My mom smirked as she threw her purse over her shoulder.

"I can't believe he told you that," I huffed, crossing my arms.

"Iyla, don't be upset." My dad placed a hand on my shoulder. "We can tell that he loves you and wants what's best for you. He's earned the ultimate parent cliche."

My mom pulled me in for a hug. "Now, go say your peace. You have with us. You know who you need to see next."

"I guess now you know why I've been saying, 'a chapter left untold will become a book well-written.'" My dad smiled warmly as he joined the hug and planted a soft kiss on my head. "Now, it's time for your story to begin."

CHAPTER TWENTY-ONE

I Y L A

PRESENT DAY

"Everything will be okay," Zeke reassured me as we waited by Ambert's front door. "Just relax."

"Relax?" I scoffed. "Hallie told me the same thing last time I was here. Look how that turned out."

"You'll be fine." He attempted once more as a couple more seconds passed, and no one answered the front door.

"It seems like no one's home. Maybe we should just come back another time." I couldn't hide my relief as I began walking back over to Zeke's bike.

"Iyla!" he called out. "They're home. Just give it another minute."

"Zeke?" I heard Claire exclaim from the front door, stopping me in place. "Iyla?" her voice went up another octave.

"Hey, can we come in?" Zeke asked as I turned back around and slowly walked up the front steps with a shy smile on my lips.

"Of course." She nodded intently, completely overwhelmed by the sight of the two of us. I knew this because it was the same look she'd given me the day we met.

"Is Ambert here?" Zeke lowered his voice to a whisper, yet I still caught wind of everything he'd said.

"He's gone out for a bit with Korey, but he'll be back soon." She did an equally terrible job of keeping her voice down.

"Good." He gestured for me to follow him.

"Let's go out back," Claire instructed as she guided us through the hallways I'd walked down just a few days ago.

Once we reached the back garden, I sat beside Zeke. My dad. I still wasn't sure exactly what to call him.

"I'm going to come right out and say it." Claire looked directly at me as she took a seat. "I didn't think I would see you here again for a while, Iyla. Let alone see you sitting here beside *you know who*."

I looked down at my hands nervously. "Claire, I owe you an apology. I didn't hear you out when I left. I was just really taken back by everything."

"Iyla, honey, you never need to apologize to me. You did nothing wrong."

"But I do," I explained, meeting her eyes. "After all you did for me after I was born—"

"What?" she didn't allow me to finish. "You...you got the letter? The package?"

"She just got it," Zeke clarified, explaining how I'd finally received the parcel and everything that had happened since I'd arrived in Los Angeles.

"Oh, Iyla..." Claire sighed. "Well, I'm thankful you finally got it, even though it was long overdue."

"Better late than never, right?" I tried to find some humor in the situation with a faint smile.

"Right." She smiled softly, her gaze lingering on me for a second before she turned back to Zeke. "She's just like Celeste, eh?"

Zeke chuckled under his breath. "Oh, you have no idea."

"Oh, yes, I do!" She sat up straighter with her crossed arms, the Claire I'd read about in those journals making herself known in her actions. "I lived with her for four years. Trust me, I know."

"In what way am I 'just like her'?" I asked with a laugh, curious to know more.

Claire's eyes softened when she looked at me, and as she reached out to place a hand on my cheek, I could tell she was fighting her emotions. "In every spectacular way possible." She smiled. "I just wish she could see you. Be here with you. I'd give up anything for that."

I frowned, feeling a sense of grief build in my chest as a result of a relationship that I was cheated out on. A life that was taken from me.

Zeke shifted in place as he rubbed his hands back and forth. I could sense that he, too, was feeling emotional after what Claire had just said.

"I'll be right back," he spoke quietly, standing up and heading back inside.

"Shoot!" Claire sighed as he closed the door behind him. "I should go talk to him. That was the wrong thing for me to say."

"No, I'll go." I got up from my chair. "Maybe I can try and talk to him."

She seemed to agree with the plan as I reached the door. "But wait, Iyla," she called out, prompting me to turn around.

"If you read the journal, then I know that you could tell just how much your mother loved Zeke. But believe me when I say this—no one has ever loved anyone quite how Zeke loved her. It's been almost two decades, and I know how much that situation eats away at him every single day. I know how he still feels responsible for everything that happened."

"He can't keep destroying himself over this, though. I want him to be happy, and I know my mom would want that too."

She released a breath. "You're right. She would. And Iyla?" She met me by the door. "Maybe this is the start. I'm certain you're his second chance at love. I hope you'll allow him to do right by you—because I know he can."

Before I could stop myself, I pulled her in for a hug, closing my eyes as I buried my face in her shoulder. "I promise I will," I spoke softly. "But Claire?" I paused. "I need to tell you something."

She pulled back slightly to look into my eyes. "What is it?"

"Thank you," I whispered, although I wish I could've shouted it from the mountain tops. She deserved that and more. "Thank you for everything....I hope you know that you more than followed through on your promise to my mom...and to me. How can I ever make it up to you?"

"Iyla..." She laughed softly, a sense of sadness in her eyes as she brushed away her own tears. "Seeing you with your dad just did." She smiled lovingly, kissing my cheek before releasing me from her embrace.

I made my way through the house and into the living room, where I found Zeke. He stood in front of the fireplace mantle as he stared over the images I'd found the other day. The photos that had changed everything.

"She was special." I found myself beside him as I glanced at the pictures.

"One of the most special girls in the world," he responded, a slight frown on his face.

I looked up at him. "Why are you still beating yourself up for what happened?" I asked gently.

He sighed. "None of this would have happened had I just been honest with her from the start."

"No," I disagreed with a firm shake of my head. "Don't try to tell me that what happened was your fault, and don't tell me that you don't deserve happiness in your life because of it."

"I fucked up, Iyla. I constantly fuck up. It's all I know how to do." His vulnerable side started to come out. "Everything I did was a mistake. I don't know how to do anything right, it seems."

I looked away, feeling a pang in my heart due to his poor choice of words. "Surely, not *everything* was a mistake."

"Iyla." I could hear the remorse in how he said my name, yet I ignored him as I looked away. "Iyla," he repeated, gently placing his hands on either side of my face as he turned me to face him. "Listen to me. I don't believe for one second that *you* were a mistake. If anything, you seem to be the only damn good thing I've ever done. And even then, I wasn't a father to you. While you were taking your first steps, learning to talk, riding a bike, hell, singing in some God-damn school play, I was in fucking prison, making up for the stupid choices I made." He released his touch, anger mixing with sadness apparent on his face.

I let out a huff. "Don't stand there and villainize every single thing about what happened. It's done, it's gone, it happened, but I'm here now. I'm standing in front of you. Can't you see?"

"I know you are." He shook his head. "But no matter how much I'll appreciate your parents for what they did, how they took care of you, gave you a life I wasn't capable of...I will never, ever forgive myself for not being around. I just can't."

"You didn't have a choice." I placed my hand on his arm.

"I chose my actions, Iyla, and I knew the consequences of them. I still did things despite the risk."

Silence now flooded through the room filled moments ago with his saddened voice.

"You made a mistake, yes. I won't stand here and tell you that you did everything right because I can't. You did mess up, Zeke. You made some bad choices!" I was honest with him, realizing quickly that the only way our conversation would go anywhere was for some accountability to come into play.

"I know, I'm a mess, I'm an idiot, I'm a piece of shit—"

"But does that mean that you can't be better now?" I challenged, wishing that my words would just translate for him. "God, don't you think my mom wants that for you? Mom loved you. She believed in you. She believed you could do so much more in your life."

"In five years, she said I'd be at peace, happy, firefighting, in love…" His voice fell off. "Instead, I was angry, depressed, in prison, and heartbroken."

"Screw five years," I raised my voice in desperation, my heart breaking at his words and his willingness to put himself down. "What about nineteen years? What about the man you are today? Not the man you were then!"

He placed his head into his hands. "I loved her. I still love her. I want to do right by her. I just don't know how."

I pulled him into a hug. "It starts with forgiving yourself."

My short arms barely wrapped around his body as his head rested on top of mine, holding onto me like he never wanted to let go. "Do you think you can do that for me, *Dad*?"

I paused immediately after speaking, feeling Zeke suck in a breath. That was the first time I'd called him that out loud.

His eyes glazed over as he looked down at me and searched my face.

"You hear that?" I repeated with a soft laugh. "Do it for me, Dad."

"Iyla…" He pulled me in again, holding me closer to him than ever. "You have no idea what hearing you call me that means to me. You have no idea what *you* mean to me. I can't promise that I'm going to magically forgive myself. A part of me will always live with this guilt. But I promise that I'll do everything I can to be better for you."

"That's all I want," I whispered, speaking from the bottom of my heart.

"I love you, Iyla," he confessed once more, gently rubbing my arms. "I always have."

We stayed together until footsteps entered the room, followed by a familiar voice.

"Iyla?"

Ambert.

"Now, it's time for you to forgive yourself." Zeke kissed my forehead, gently patting me on the back before exiting the room.

As I turned around, I was met with those blue eyes and the smile I knew from day one would be in my life for a long time. I gave Ambert a nervous nod as he walked over to me.

"Iyla, what are you doing here?" he seemed confused, yet a slight flutter of happiness flushed through his eyes once he'd reached me.

"Ambert, I..." I was unsure where to begin. "Ambert, I'm so sorry. What I said to you...the way I left...I was wrong. I didn't mean to hurt you." A single tear fell down my cheek as I quickly brushed it away.

"Hey, it's okay!" He went to pull me in for a hug, which I denied, despite how badly I wanted to be in his arms.

"No, let me finish," I instructed softly as he stepped back. "These past few weeks have been the most chaotic in my life. Coming to Los Angeles, meeting you, and discovering all these things about my past. It's all just been a total rollercoaster."

"You don't have to explain yourself. I understand now—"

"But meeting you has been one of the best things that has ever happened to me," I continued, determined to get my feelings across once and for all. "You told me that people come into your life for a reason, whether we know those reasons or not. At first, I didn't know what you meant. How could the universe know to send us someone exactly when we needed them?" I stepped towards him and gently ran my hand through his hair. "But now I know that fate is real, and I know, Ambert Wells, that you belong in my life. You're the vessel that has allowed my life to start. You're the person I was meant to be with."

His eyes were full of love as he pressed his lips against mine and kissed me softly, wrapping his arms around my waist and pulling me closer to him.

"I wasn't done," I mumbled against his lips.

"I don't care." I could feel him smiling. "We were made for each other, Iyla," his words struck me to my core as it all started to come together.

The journey. The rollercoaster. Every single piece of it. It was all worth it in the end because, despite everything, I was granted the most powerful gift of all...*love*.

"I love you, Ambert," I whispered.

"I've always loved you, Iyla Larson. Whether I knew it or not."

I was engulfed in his touch and taste and how his hands effort-lessly caressed my hair and sent shivers down my spine. The world stopped, time paused, and no one else existed except Ambert and me.

"Let's go upstairs..." He reluctantly pulled away from the kiss and pulled on my wrist. "I never did get a chance to give you a full tour."

"And that's where you want to start?" I giggled.

"That's where I want to start, where I want to end, where I want to stay with you for—"

"Ahem!" A loud voice startled the two of us.

Zeke.

Dad.

"Really, Zeke?" Ambert playfully scoffed. "Didn't you already interrupt us once before?"

"That's Mr. Reeves, now that you're dating my daughter, A." He grinned, wrapping an arm around my shoulder, which prompted Ambert to roll his eyes jokingly.

"I'm trying to get the hang of this whole dad thing." He nudged me slightly. "Plus, Lance gave me strict instructions. He said no kissing longer than fifteen seconds and under no circumstances, any hanky panky—"

"You're so embarrassing!" I escaped from my dad's embrace, reaching for Ambert's hand and pulling him out of the room.

"Well then, I must be doing something right for once."

EPILOGUE

I Y L A

FOUR YEARS LATER

"Iyla?" Ambert's voice called out as I rushed into our home, a letter in my hand and a heart that wouldn't stop racing. "Are you here?"

"I'm here." I smiled as he leaned in to plant a kiss against my lips.

"Come out back," he instructed excitedly. "Everyone's waiting."

"Everyone?" I questioned. "Who's everyone?"

"My parents, your parents, Hallie, Vic, Tim, Alma—"

"Wow, so quite literally, everyone."

"No one wanted to miss out on this." He laughed, reaching for my hand. "C'mon, let's go."

"She's here!" Hallie jumped away from Vic's embrace and raced to my side as we entered the backyard, making me smile widely as I hugged her.

"It arrived?" my mom asked as she turned away from a conversation with Claire.

I nodded my head enthusiastically.

"Dad!" I called out, causing both Lance and Zeke to turn away from the BBQ simultaneously. That never seemed to get old. "I got my results!" I lifted the letter into the air and waved it in their direction. "Come over here!"

"We're coming!" They smiled at one another as they made their way over.

"Open it," Ambert encouraged me. "Don't leave us all in this suspense."

I let out a deep breath, saying an internal prayer before lifting my shaky hands and gliding my fingers over the top of the sealed envelope. It was an envelope that contained the result of all my hard work these past four years. My eyes rushed over the page as I started to read out loud.

"Dear, Iyla Larson-*Reeves*," I spoke with a smile. I hyphenated my name a few years back, including both sides of my blended family.

"Well?" Hallie urged me as her eyes attempted to catch a glimpse of what was on the page. "What does it say?"

"Congratulations, you have been accepted into Stanford's law program starting this fall!"

Hallie let out a massive scream, jumping into the air enthusiastically. "I knew you would do it!" She beat everyone else in, wrapping me into an enormous hug. "She did it, she did it, she did it!" She cheered, making me jump up and down with her in a circle.

"I can't believe it." My hand fell over my mouth in shock as Hallie released me.

"We can." My parents pulled me in for a group hug. "We're so proud of you, Iyla. So proud," my mom spoke.

"Zeke!" my dad shouted. "Get over here. This is a family hug, after all."

Zeke smiled as he walked over to us, his eyes on me the entire time. "I love you, Iyla. I'm so proud of you." He planted a kiss on my forehead, his embrace triumphing over my parents as his arm span practically engulfed us all. "And I know *Mom* is, too."

I smiled up at him. "I love you, too."

"Congratulations, Iyla!" Tim and Alma cheered as Vic gave me an affirming nod, clapping his hands together.

"I guess being the teacher's pet paid off after all." I smirked, earning a playful eye roll in response.

"You deserve it!" Korey proudly patted my shoulder as Claire pulled me into her arms and whispered her congratulations into my hair.

I was in total shock. I knew I scored fairly well on the LSAT, but truthfully, I think there was one key thing that gave my Stanford application that extra edge—a reference letter from Dr. Sanders, who, once I graduated a few months ago, decided that only then was it the right time for him to retire.

"The first lawyer of the family." Ambert proudly looked down at me, wrapping an arm around my waist and gently squeezing me. "I told you I'd hold you to it," he whispered in my ear before leaning down and kissing me on the lips.

Four years together, and he still managed to make me blush as I kissed him back.

"Wait, there's one more thing!" Claire interrupted our PDA session as she reached into her bag and pulled out what appeared to be another envelope. "This is for you." She handed it over to me.

"For me?" I asked. "What is it?"

"Let's just say it's something that's long overdue."

My eyes scanned the envelope in front of me, the paper wrinkled, and the ink faded, a dead giveaway to just how old it must have been.

"Miss. Celeste Kinney..." I read aloud, seeing her name alongside the Stanford logo plastered on the front. "Wait..." I peeled my eyes back. "Is this my mom's acceptance letter?"

She nodded with a smile. "It came while I was cleaning out our apartment. I wanted to put it in your box, but I thought I should wait until the timing was right."

My eyes searched for Zeke's, seeking his comfort as my hands shook slightly. "You...you open it," I instructed him nervously.

"No, Iyla." He pushed it back into my hands. "That letter is meant for you to open."

A sigh left my body as my fingers carefully opened the letter, much more delicately than I'd opened my own.

"Dear Celeste," I whispered as I scanned over the page with blurry eyes until the reality of the words hit home.

"Iyla..." Ambert pulled me in for a hug as the emotion washed over me.

"Read it." I handed it over to Zeke, clutching onto Ambert tightly. "Please."

"Dear Celeste." He paused. "We are pleased to offer you an early offer of admission into Stanford's Law Program. With your exceptional academic achievement along with your distinguishable references, you are one of a few candidates that have been granted this—"

"She did it," I said as the tears now poured from my eyes.

"You both did." Zeke joined me in Ambert's embrace, everyone else following suit.

"Good timing, Claire." Korey winked, planting a kiss on her cheek. "Good timing."

After a moment, I broke away. "I'll be right back." I wiped away some tears. "I just need a few minutes."

"Do you want me to come with you?" Ambert asked.

"No," I told him with assurance. "I have to go do something really quick."

"Don't be long," Vic, who had taken over the BBQ, called out. "The food is almost ready."

"Yeah, and we've got a lot to celebrate!" Hallie clapped her hands excitedly before getting distracted by the engagement ring on her finger, the one that Vic had proposed to her with only a few short weeks after graduation.

"I'll be quick, I promise."

I rushed inside, passing through the hallway and over to my office desk, where I pulled a familiar journal out from inside of my drawer.

A journal that has remained glued to my side for the past four years and one that I hadn't felt ready to begin a new chapter in until that moment.

Brushing away the happy tears in my eyes, I lifted my pen and finally connected it to the paper, starting the beginning of my own story.

Chapter One.

Iyla.

You see, my mom and I had always been more similar than I'd ever imagined. Just like her, once I started to write, I couldn't stop. The words in this journal needed to be perfect. After all, not only was I continuing our story, but I was writing it so that one day I could read them to *you,* just like I am right now...

That's right. You didn't think I'd not fill you in on what you've missed, did you, *Mom?*

I've made it a routine to sit by your gravesite these past few months, reading these chapters to you.

Sometimes as I read, I try to envision that you're here with me, sitting across from me, looking into my eyes. But deep down, I know I don't have to because even though you're not physically here with me, Mom, you've managed to find a way to be a part of every single component of my life.

You've made me find *strength* and *vulnerability* like my dad.

You've shown me how to be *passionate* and *hopeful* like Claire.

You've given me the *compassion* and *kindness* of Sharlene.

You've guided me into being *intuitive* and *knowledgeable* like Dr. Sanders.

But most of all, throughout this whole journey, I've learned a small portion of your *resiliency.* Your *strength* and your *bravery.* Those are traits that I will hold with me for the rest of my life.

So, as I go to close out these final words to you, I want you to know one last thing. That although your entries may have been for me, and my chapters may have been for you, together, this journal is for *us*.

I may not know when we'll meet, but I do know this. When that time does come, you'll be waiting for me, and without a single ounce of hesitation, I'll run to you with open arms.

I'm being brave now, Mom. I always will be.

I love you.

Iyla.

ACKNOWLEDGMENTS

To the book that consumed my life for the past two years, and to you who's taken the time to read it—*thank you*. I can't wait to see what we accomplish together.

Writing my debut novel has taught me so much about who I am and helped me re-discover my passion for storytelling. My only hope is that this story inspires you to seek out a far greater love than just a fairytale ending. Love can exist in so many parts of our lives if we just open our hearts to find it.

There is one person without whom the culmination of this book would not have been possible. They know exactly who they are— and *to you*, I'll forever be grateful.

What's left for there to say, besides a chapter left untold, became a book well-written...(hopefully).

To You, Jyla

ABOUT THE AUTHOR

Kate Lauren is a "certified fangirl" whose passions include writing contemporary romance novels, using suggestive innuendos any chance she can, and subliminally tying Taylor Swift song titles into her books.

Based out of Toronto, Canada, when Kate's not daydreaming about which fictional character she'll create next, you'll find her with her friends, family and husband—or nose-deep in her next novel.

Printed in Great Britain
by Amazon

35971797R00183